THE

FRANK BELKNAP LONG

SCIENCE FICTION MEGAPACK®

THE
FRANK BELKNAP LONG

SCIENCE FICTION MEGAPACK®

FRANK BELKNAP LONG

WILDSIDE PRESS

CONTENTS

ACKNOWLEDGMENTS

Published with the kind permission and assistance of Lily Doty, Mansfield M. Doty, and the family of Frank Belknap Long.

AN AUTOBIOGRAPHICAL MEMOIR

INTRODUCTION

It is often taken for granted—I've always felt quite unjustifiably—that a fiction writer's characters are thinly disguised aspects of himself wearing multiple-personality type costumes.

If that were true the writing of an autobiographical memoir would be the height of folly, because whatever he may have been somewhat reticent about in his stories would be more fully revealed to the least friendly of his critics. With all his defenses demolished he would become a stripped-to-the-bone kind of figure, haunting cemetery shadows until he could find an ope grave to his liking (ope is an archaic but "just right" term for a certain kind of grave, since it conjures up, for me at least, a vision of a yawning pit surrounded by heaped-up mounds of freshly turned earth, and containing no trace of its previous occupants).

There are risks, however, that must be taken when circumstances of an unusual nature make the avoidance of a risk factor seem—well, at the very least, unworthy. Besides—and I must stress this again—I've always refused to believe that imaginative fiction writers have to project some aspect of themselves into every character they create. Even naturalistic fiction, at its most candid, seems at times to be peopled by at least a few characters so alien to the writer that they could hardly have been based on more than careful, extremely objective observation. How much more true ("true" can hardly be a comparative adjective, but let it stand) would that be of science fiction and fantasy writers, particularly of supernatural horror story writers, when at every "turn of the screw" in some dark, high house in the mist in the small hours, or while standing with a quickly assembling crowd at the site of you-know-what kind of landing, they encounter something or someone so unlike themselves that the character trait identification factor would become a mockery.

The unusual circumstances that made the writing of this memoir almost mandatory can be set forth quite simply, in no more than a paragraph or two, and without the intrusion of anything controversial. The closely related genres of science fiction and fantasy writing have far more than simply "come of age". A decade ago that statement, which quite often appeared on book jackets and in review columns in the 1950s, had become "outdated" and clearly needed to be rephrased. Today it would be ridiculous to refer to the growth and present standing of both genres as a surprise development of comparatively recent origin, when for a full generation now the maturity, scholarship, and depth and brilliance of characterization that has been achieved in both realms on their highest levels has not been surpassed by the great majority of mainstream novelists. An exaggeration, a wish-fulfillment fantasy? I think not. My point is strengthened here by the simple fact that no less than five widely acclaimed mainstream authors have written novels in either the science fiction or dark fantasy categories in the past few years, in an apparent effort to stand shoulder to shoulder with a round dozen battle-scarred veterans on that no longer side street platform as the bands go by. How well they have succeeded can be safely left to the future to decide.

When a new century draws near there is no laborer in the vineyards of the old whose personal recollections may not be of some value in years to come, even if only stumbled on by accident in, let us say, 2025. And that imposes an obligation which I cannot in good conscience evade, and is the chief *raison d'être* for the pages which follow. One further word—in Chapter One I have dwelt at considerable length on my childhood. Although it may seem to strain credulity, the ancient but never really trite assumption that the child is father to the man was largely absent from my thoughts when I was writing it. I was thinking instead—and I stressed this in a recent interview—that there are imaginative worlds of strangeness and wonder which can never be re-entered in adult years, or that the memories of adults can never hope to recapture in more than a transitory, infinitely incomplete way. It is in those worlds that the wisdom of children seems often to transcend every sophisticated insight acquired by adults through their vastly greater experience and orientation to what is commonly thought of as reality in the course of the years.

CHAPTER 1

The imagery to which very young children are most sensitive creates for many of them a world so different from the rule-obeying, outwardly sane and ordered world of adults that it can be said that it bears a collision-course potential that is more remote from immediate, everyday reality than most people suspect. More often than not, however, an actual shattering does not occur and that secret world becomes a refuge that changes very little as the years pass. All it actually does is drift away to regions apart, where it still remains accessible, along mountain pathways, and across shining valleys, to the imaginatively defiant and the bold.

Though city-born—incredible as it may seem to some—that world has always contained dark and mysterious woodland vistas for me, perilous crags, haunted marshes, goblin-infested caves and crows on the wing. Great beauty as well, shapes of light and loveliness, and one image that has always symbolized for me exactly the opposite, horror in an extreme form—a great, white-maned horse, trapped in quicksand and sinking slowly down until its struggles cease and only its rump remains visible.

It was not from books that such images came, for my parents never read to me by gaslight in a house where the scampering of mice was never absent, despite the setting of many traps. (If you were not born before the early years of the century you will find it hard to imagine how it would be possible to live in a spacious but wholly non-electrified house!)

But I'm distorting the facts just a little here, because my particular world of early childhood was far from entirely urban, and I spent two and a half months of every year in a summer wonderland with some backwoods aspects. As not a few professional men did at the time, my father spent July, August and sometimes most of September as a vacationist; fishing and hunting were very important to him, and enabled him to feel that the practice of dentistry could be mixed with such outdoor interests with no detriment to either.

His location of choice was the Thousand Islands on the Canadian shore, about seven miles from the then small village of *Cananoque.* Through one of his patients he had heard of a successful but not too prosperous Canadian farmer who owned a large tract of land which was only partly cultivated—a youngish married man who took in summer boarders to supplement the family income.

I have no recollection at all of the first summer I spent there, since I was exactly six months old. But my mother informed me—much later, of course—that I was placed in a bureau drawer in an upstairs bedroom, because there was no cot available. (The farmer's two sons were six and eight, and their cots had long since been used for firewood.) Some slight deception may have been practiced by a false assurance, by letter perhaps, that a cot would be available. I never asked my mother about this, because the entire matter distressed me and I had no desire to talk about it. A future supernatural horror story writer could well have developed an infantile coffin complex through such an episode!

Another distressing event occurred during my third year at the farm, and I may as well dispose of it here. I developed pneumonia (I had recklessly fallen into the river at the end of a long pier the day previously). My father leapt into a motorboat in the middle of the night and went to *Cananoque* for a doctor. He returned with a Chinese physician who later became quite renowned as one of Canada's most distinguished research physicians, and at that time was the only physician for miles around.

My entire chest was plastered with almost boiling hot compresses, and my mother was left with instructions to complete the emergency measure every two hours. Or perhaps it was every half-hour. All I can remember is the almost unbearable horror and pain that accompanied the descent of those plasters, again and again and again, from throat to navel.

In fact—and I'm quite serious about this, as I was not, of course, about my totally unremembered, hastily-improvised crib experience earlier, trying as it must have been to my mother—it was the only memory from that period that I can recall today as truly frightening. My actual fall from the pier I do not remember at all, and it was told to me for the first time several years later.

That memories of infancy sometimes go back to the birth trauma itself I have never doubted, for it bears a striking resemblance to the accounts of what happens when people who have been pronounced dead by an attending physician are later restored to consciousness, and may well be a repetition of that experience and far from proof of after-death survival.

Like almost everyone else I would much prefer to believe otherwise, for there is nothing quite so appalling as the thought of total, after-death extinction. HPL, of course, preferred to believe it was the opposite of appalling, and said to me, more than once, "What difference does it really make, Belknapius, if we become again what we once were—a totally at peace aspect of nothingness?"

We remained on the farm during the summer months until I was eight or nine years old, and my father found new lodgings where the fishing and hunting was even better at another point on the Canadian shore—it was truly a wilderness in those early years—where the St. Lawrence widened out a little, and there were more of its many islands. It was an inn that at one time had been a boys' school and the library was still overflowing with instructional volumes, including a huge one dealing with beetle and butterfly collecting, which could hardly have failed to stimulate my already growing interest in natural history.

We moved to still another location several years later and I remained a summer vacationist in the Thousand Islands until I was seventeen. If I attempted to dwell at length on those long, unforgettable summers there would be little space left in this memoir for my New York childhood, which, of course, was of just as great a formative importance, although it did not always seem so. But here are a scattered few of the highlights, as I remember them:

Visiting *Cananoque* perhaps fifty times in the family launch, which my father had named *The Rover* and ascending from the wharf at the base of the village over a road that was darkened a little by belching smokestacks to its long main street and adjacent dwellings. In the earliest days it had been little more than a small village, but it soon became a medium-sized town of growing industrial importance.

Seeing, as a child with even the possibility of World War I almost totally absent from my thoughts, that long peaceful street suddenly fill with men in uniform, with wagons lumbering past overladen with military equipment, and even cannons on wheels and officers with shoulder straps shouting orders... This has remained so visibly recapturable a memory for me across the years that I can still bring it sharply into focus just as it was, with no need to embellish a single one of the details.

It was only later on, when a dreadful word was whispered and the lengthy casualty lists began appearing in the Canadian newspapers, that I could have wished for a memory recall that would, in the years to come, fail me utterly. That word was *Verdun,* and its aftermath could hardly have been more in tragic evidence in a French or English village than on that long street in *Cananoque.* At one time wounded soldiers seemed almost to outnumber civilians, and there were more amputees than accounts of that period ordinarily record. If some one thing were needed to bring home to a child the horror and fiendish irrationality of war—all wars everywhere—that was it.

It is perhaps better to begin rather than to end with a tragic memory if only because, while nothing can diminish the tragedy in any way, it is more sanity-preserving to follow it with some happier ones.

I was never entirely sure whether it was hunting or fishing that had the most appeal for my father, for he liked both enormously. He was the kindest of men, and I'm quite sure that if he had met someone with the views so prevalent today as to the cruelty involved in shooting birds and small mammals with a rifle—instead of with a camera—he would have stared at them in totally honest incomprehension. It was simply something that was done, by the overwhelming majority of sportsmen, and is, of course, still very widely a popular sport today, as a brief glance at a current outdoorsman-type magazine will confirm. There are severe penalties attached today to the shooting of native songbirds—and other native birds as well, the laws varying in different states—but otherwise duck shooting is as popular as ever, and if you shoot a deer in open season you can still join a wildlife preservation club.

My father never shot a robin, thrush or woodpecker—not to mention the more snowy-crested birds—but he did seem to have a fondness for bringing down chicken hawks, buzzards and great, rather resplendent-looking birds in the predatory hawk range.

I can remember accompanying him back through the woods to the inn three or four times, with at least ten such birds dangling from his shoulder on a string, all dead, and encrimsoned masses a few of them were. I was a little squeamish about it, but it never occurred to me to wish that he had used a camera instead. Bird watching with the aid of a camera was, of course, an extreme rarity in those days.

In the St. Lawrence small-mouth black bass—the most likely of all freshwater fish to give a sportsman a real run for his money—were twenty times as common as the large-mouth variety and my father must have caught an astronomical number of them at various favored fishing spots on the Canadian shore, along, of course, with perch and pike. The perch he usually unhooked and threw back, although they are highly prized by sportsmen in other regions, particularly Lake George, where they grow to impressive size.

In two or three of those summers I became an up-and-coming young entrepreneur to an extent that I have never been since, collecting minnows to serve as bait and selling them to other guests at the inn.

CHAPTER 2

In earlier years, at any given period, the image I usually had of myself was slightly futuristic in nature. I achieved this through a process of thought projection. I imagined myself to be three or four years older than I actually was at the time, with a state of mind and some achievements to my credit that had not as yet materialized. It was unquestionably a foolishness. But it harmed no one but myself, and I never felt the slightest twinge of guilt about it.

Hence it was that when HPL returned to New York after his brief, earlier visit and settled down as a married man at Parkside Avenue in picturesque Flatbush, I considered myself not just a young student at New York University, but a very serious young writer with certain literary standards I had no intention of relinquishing, and a background which enabled me to mingle with other writers in the Village and elsewhere without an awkward lack of self-confidence.

It didn't matter that I had not as yet sold a single story—my first sale to *Weird Tales* was still a few months in the future—or that I had not acquired anything like the intellectual maturity of HPL's other voluminous young correspondent, Alfred Galpin. It was the kind of person I felt myself to be, and I refused to let anyone talk me out of it.

In the weeks that followed the first Parkside Avenue apartment-warming reception—I seem to recall that it was on a Sunday—I met and talked at length with perhaps a dozen of HPL's early New York correspondents and of Sonia's Brooklyn friends.

It was an enlivening period indeed. HPL's initial enchantment with New York had not even begun to wear off, and none of those early visitors had reason to believe that it might. I was present at three or four of the gatherings, but must have missed many more.

In *The Conservative* and not a few other amateur journalism publications HPL had been at sword's point with perhaps half of the members of the Brooklyn-based *Blue Pencil Club,* castigating them in no uncertain terms for what he regarded, at the time, as political and social views of a sadly misguided nature. But despite the fact that his own ultra-conservative views had far from vanished in the early nineteen twenties, he greeted those enemies on paper with a total lack of rancor, and a friendliness so unmistakable that its sincerity could not be doubted.

Charles D. Isaacson and James F. Morton were the two most prominent members of the *Blue Pencil Club* and with both he was in strenuous disagreement in several areas. By that time, however, Morton had become one of his four or five closest and most highly valued friends—and of mine as well—as I've set forth at considerable length in *Howard Phillips Lovecraft: Dreamer on the Nightside.*

Isaacson, prominent both as a musical critic and a political analyst, with a column in a New York newspaper, was the kind of persuasive talker who could demolish many opponents with a few carefully chosen words. But with HPL he did not score a point in a two-hour discussion of views which were certainly sounder than a round dozen advanced by HPL. I was present at that discussion, and it lingers in my mind ineffaceably across five intervening decades.

The Kalem Club, as has often been mentioned in discussions of the Lovecraft Circle, in its early stage consisted of members whose last names began with K, L, or M. It was Samuel Loveman who hit on this nomenclature, and it was Loveman who became a slightly more frequent host to the group than I did on our monthly gatherings during HPL's stay in New York.

He resided in Brooklyn Heights just one flight above Hart Crane, with a splendid view of New York harbor, and, of course, the Bridge.

I will not attempt to include in this or later chapters the material concerning Loveman that will be found in *The Dreamer* for the simple reason that if I added all of that to what I am about to relate here my attempt to keep the entire volume in balance would go by the board. A brief recapitulation, however, is in order and, I fear, necessary.

Sam, at the time, was thirty-five. He had visited New York briefly two years before HPL's marriage and, with Howard, had been a guest at Sonia's Parkside Avenue home. He then returned to New York and became a permanent resident, and held various positions in the rare book field for a great many years.

He was born in Cleveland and had been a boyhood friend of the Cranes, and when Crane's mother died he officiated, as her will stipulated, in the disposal of her ashes over the waters of the harbor from Brooklyn Bridge.

He was a very fine poet. But during his lifetime recognition was confined to only one slim volume, published by the Caxton Press, and his early correspondence with Bierce (Twenty-one *Letters of Ambrose Bierce*) whom he met in person just before Bierce vanished in Mexico. Bierce greatly admired his early poems and so did George Sterling, Clark Ashton Smith, Edwin Markham and, of course, HPL. His position as a minor poet with certain rare and unusual qualities which made him in some respects an unique voice will, I think, undergo no diminishment in the years ahead, in the eyes of historically-minded poetry lovers. Like Smith, he became entrapped, to some extent at least, by a poetic tradition that has become almost totally replaced today by a different kind of poetry except, perhaps, here and there, on the popular magazine verse level, and Sam's poetry had even less in common with that kind of sentimental rubbish. His poems dwell on the splendors of the ancient world and there is a certain despairing bitterness, combined with a great sympathy for the outcast and the afflicted that is all too often absent from poems in that particular vein. For anyone fortunate enough to have the Caxton volume my suggestion is: Take it down from the top shelf and re-read it at least three times a year. His translations from Baudelaire, Rimbaud, and Verlaine are among the finest I have ever seen. (They are not in this volume, unhappily.)

Here is another in a somewhat different vein:

> *Li Ho Chin, in the sunset's gleam,*
> *Murmurs "Life is an opium dream,*
> *Drugged or drunk were the gods that blew*
> *This world on their opiate pipes of dew,*
> *That wrought in the poppy's emerald deep*
> *Laughter and love and an endless sleep."*
> *Li Ho Chin descries from afar*
> *The yellow moon and the evening star.*

Both in my Doubleday volume, *The Early Long*, and in my contribution to *Marginalia* (an Arkham House volume many years out-of-print)

I have described HPL's early meeting in the Village with Hart Crane and how it coincided with a copy of *The Bridge* in manuscript which Sam had shown me earlier on the same day. I did not know until quite recently, when I had occasion to consult some biographical material dating back to that period, that HPL had met and talked with Crane again, two or three times during his New York period. The error was understandable, for those meetings were apparently quite brief, and in all his conversations with me HPL never discussed Crane to any extent. Both HPL and Alfred Galpin had been guests at Crane's home during an early, quite brief Cleveland visit but his only reference to Crane had been in relation to what Loveman had told him—that he had an ungovernable temper when intoxicated and had, at one time, hurled a typewriter through a window.

But two incidents concerning Crane come to mind which I have not previously related, the second a quite spectacular one, told to me by Loveman, which, as far as I know, has received no biographical mention.

At a Kalem Club gathering in Brooklyn Heights, a short while before HPL's return to Providence, we passed the door of Crane's apartment on descending to the street from Loveman's apartment on the floor above. (I can't recall with absolute certainty whether or not HPL was present at that gathering.) The door of Crane's apartment was about one-third open and from it there came a continuous hum of voices.

When we reached the street Sam told me, "Frank, *everyone* is there. Tate, Waldo Frank, e e cummings…a dozen others just as important. He urged me to join them, and I promised to drop in later. It's *The Bridge*, of course. He keeps telling me the poem's 'just rhetoric' but they don't think so. And I don't think he does either. If you like, we can go back and I'll introduce you."

It was a tempting offer, but I decided to depart with the other Kalem members—about seven in all. I felt I'd be just a little ill at ease in such a prestigious gathering. If HPL had been present that evening—and, as I've said, I'm far from sure he was—he probably slipped quietly away as he sometimes did at the end of a talkative evening. I don't remember accompanying him to the subway, and discussing that other gathering.

The second incident, the spectacular one—though it would not have seemed so to Sam if Crane had ended up dead—began with the feeling that Sam had when they were both standing on the roof staring out over the harbor. He had never, Sam told me, seen Hart in so black a mood. He had been drinking heavily for two or three days and somehow to Sam the roof seemed the wrong place for him to be at that particular time. That feeling was confirmed when he made a despairing gesture, rushed to the parapet and started to ascend it. There was never any doubt in Sam's mind that if he had not rushed forward, grabbed him by the legs and pulled him back to safety, he would have hurled himself over.

During that early New York period there were three writers whom I met and talked with frequently who remain, across the years, as firmly entrenched in my memory store of important friendships as they did, I'm sure, in the treasure house of HPL's memories until the time of his death.

My close friendship with Donald Wandrei and, later, with his brother Howard dates from after HPL's return to Providence and will be discussed in another chapter. So did my first meeting with Wilfred Talman and Vrest Orton.

The three writers were Samuel Loveman, H. Warner Munn, and James F. Morton. Morton was, of course, far less of a writer in a strict sense than the other two, for his main activities at the time were of a social, educational and political nature. He lectured frequently for the New York Board of Education, attended political rallies, and was one of the earliest of Black Rights crusaders. He was, for a number of years, and before he became curator of the Paterson (New Jersey) Museum, a quite prominent New Yorker whose name appeared often in the newspapers.

He was so well-known, in fact, and so assured when he spoke in public that one of my father's patients recognized his voice in the living room when he accompanied HPL on his first visit to our home on West End Avenue. "Goodness, Dr. Long," she said in the dental chair, "that must be James Morton. We've moved in much the same circles and there are some voices you can't be mistaken about."

Despite his strenuous round of activities Morton managed to write a number of urbane and scholarly essays, ranging in theme from nineteenth-century English literature in general (Browning, whose optimism he shared, was the poet he most often quoted) to social and political matters a little remote from the ones of more immediate concern to him.

He always thought of himself as something of a radical and, as I mentioned in *The Dreamer*, knew Jack London in his youth, and continued to embrace, at least in theory, the semi-socialism of the long outdated single tax. He continued to believe in "free love", as it was then called—an odd-sounding term indeed today! It's hard to imagine what he would have thought of X-rated films.

Today his views in general would still make him seem just a trifle to the left of center, perhaps, but even of that it is impossible to be sure. In many respects he was the exact opposite of HPL—of sturdy physique, florid complexion, reddish hair (a little faded at the age of fifty), he was a perfect example of a Lovecraftian contending image. But the two still got along famously.

As I also mentioned in *The Dreamer*, he took great pride in his Harvard M.A. (which carried more prestige in the 'twenties than a Ph.D does today) and had managed to get himself in *Who's Who in America* at the age of forty, no mean feat at any period, however you slice it.

H. Warner Munn was thirty years younger than Morton—exactly my age, in fact, give or take a few months—and he arrived in New York on his first visit at the time of HPL's marriage. That visit stands out very pronouncedly in my memory because we traveled about the city so extensively in the course of not more than two or three weeks.

We visited the Metropolitan Museum of Art twice (he was particularly interested, as was HPL, in the Egyptian exhibits), the Central Park Zoo, and the marine, three-masted schooner survivals just north of Battery Park. At that time old three-and four-masteds still plied the seas to an extent undreamed of today. Oh, yes—the old Battery Park aquarium—superior in many respects, I've always felt, to the one at Coney Island today, despite its Melville-marvelous "white" whales and dolphins.

We took Harold in the family car to Woodlawn Cemetery, where there is a Long burial plot topped by a pyramid-type monument and until a few years ago—it was lost through a storage mishap—I possessed a snapshot of the Werewolf of Ponkert and Chaugnar Faugn in their terrestrial incarnations standing at the foot of the grave I shall probably eventually occupy.

On Harold's second, somewhat later visit to New York—and I may as well dwell on that here—an event took place of tremendous importance to a man who may conceivably be still alive today because of an exceptional act of heroism.

Harold arrived at the beginning of summer, in search of some measure of economic security that would enable him to remain in the city until September. At that time he seemed new-adventure disposed, in robust health and in search of some job that would not involve any kind of business office confinement. The mother made a suggestion that I would not have thought of. Why not try to secure a job as a crewman on one of the once-famous Iron Steamships that made two or three trips daily between Battery Park and Coney Island? She had read somewhere that the company that operated the boats had difficulty in securing deck hands.

Harold immediately acted on the tip and secured the job without difficulty. I can't recall exactly how long it lasted—perhaps three weeks, perhaps for the major part of the summer. But it lasted long enough to enable him, at the risk of his life, to leap from the rail during an unusually rough-weather passage and rescue a passenger who had fallen overboard. It was on the front page of the *New York Times* the following morning. Not in headlines exactly, but in at least a lengthy column.

Until I met Harold it would have been hard for me to believe that so young a writer could have possessed so brilliant and spontaneous a tale-spinning ability. Elaborate and intricate plots—not just ideas for stories—seemed to leap fully developed into his mind, and in the course of a long subway ride or even a thirty-or forty-block walk he could make you feel that the narrative he was reciting with hardly a pause was something he must have memorized from a book.

There were times when just the spell cast by the narrative itself obsessed him to the exclusion of almost everything else. It had never been quite that way with me. Until I actually sat down to write a story there were a hundred other matters that concerned me more—life's uncertainties, its tragedies and moments of joy, the strangeness of something I'd just seen, how promising had been the look of the girl I'd dined with the previous night and what would happen if I were a little more audacious the next time, and how I could get out of working long hours over some task that bored me to death and gave me no pleasure at any point.

I don't mean to imply by that that writing wasn't as important to me as it was to Harold. It was always one of the two or three things at the very center of my life. But the simple telling of some marvelous tale and then another and another, like some medieval balladeer or village-roaming Homeric-age bard, too absorbed in a continuous procession of wonders to give heed to anything else, is the mark of a storyteller apart. I had to wait for inspiration to strike, and just the right circumstance to arise, or series of circumstances. I had to have seclusion, as a rule, a chance to shut myself away from the distractions of the moment for a reasonable period of time.

To Harold, in those far-off days at least, what happened to Alerac the Dragon Slayer in the Misty Isles or some member of the Werewolf Clan became, when the tale-spinning demon took possession of him, the sole source of his concern.

Life can be strange indeed in the way some early friendships go into eclipse for no reason that can be rationally explained. Harold returned to New England and did not visit New York again for a long period of time, and so many events took place in my life that even keeping in touch with him by letter—well, it simply didn't happen. (Much the same thing happened after my quite voluminous early correspondence with Clark Ashton Smith.)

I had no idea that he had married and was the father of grown children, or even that he had just recently lost his wife and was a West Coast resident, still actively engaged in writing, until I met him again in Providence at the First World Fantasy Convention in 1975!

CHAPTER 3

A complaint that is often voiced today by writers of science fiction, supernatural horror, and heroic fantasy has as its target the so-called literary establishment and is of so confused and contradictory a nature that it is greatly in need of clarification. It seeks persuasiveness by resting its claims on the assumption that there is no more than one literary establishment, if one must use that term, and that the three genres in question are separated, not only from one another—and there is a *little* truth in that—but from the far more important and enduring "main stream."

What I shall try to do here, in a humble way, may provoke so much disagreement that it will please no one. But when one's concern is deep and genuine there are risks that must be taken, even if it means watching one's head being served up on a platter (an occurrence by no means impossible to imagine in some fourth-dimensional milieu!). The best way of tackling it is to break it down into categories, which I've numbered accordingly.

1. The literary establishment. There are, in America alone, at least six such establishments. What one thinks of first, perhaps, is the somewhat elitish, highly sophisticated one that brings to mind, almost immediately, the *New York Review of Books.* A total failure to be even so much as mentioned in that one can cause a few writers, even in our three genres, to lie awake nights. Actually, however, it is considerably less of a literary establishment than the slightly academic one (in recent years, at least, in its roping in of distinguished literary figures who are full professors) best represented by the *New York Times Book Review.* There follows in rapid sequence the Midwestern establishment and the West Coast establishment, almost as prestigious—perhaps even more so in a few respects—which is often at complete variance with Eastern seaboard criteria concerning books of enduring literary worth. Oh, yes—the Southern one as well, and to downgrade its literary standards in recent years would be a major critical mistake.

Last of all—but probably far from the least—there is the college-university establishment, with its hundreds of classrooms, presided over by brilliant young Ph.D.s or "stodgy" elderly professors too secure in their tenures to worry much about anything except reaching the enforced retirement age and preserving their health. (It is interesting to note in passing here that our three genres are still sometimes judged in this particular milieu, incredible as it may seem, by literary standards at least a century old—standards which even quite a few eminent Victorian and American writers of the same period would have regarded as a trifle old-fashioned.)

A résumé as brief as this must, of necessity, be somewhat simplistic, and I have failed to include establishment factors of considerable importance apart from the ones I've mentioned, such as many of the small literary reviews, and magazines such as *Harper's, The Atlantic Monthly, The New Republic,* et cetera. But, as the walrus said when gobbling up the most appetizing parts of a spiny sea urchin, "One can't include everything."

2. The supernatural horror story. I've decided to let the other two genres go for a moment and concentrate on this one, if only because its popular aspects and the serious literary recognition it has been accorded by the literary establishments are in sharper contrast.

That supernatural horror—in folk tales, and in fiction—has exercised a very great influence on the American imagination over the past four centuries seems to me beyond dispute, with Cotton Mather's *Magnalia* setting the original pace. In popular fiction its role has never been a minor one and that is just as true of so-called elitist or high-culture fiction.

To what extent then—and that is our central problem here—have the literary establishments I've listed failed to accord it the due its importance deserves? That all of them, except perhaps the first, have accorded it some due also seems to me beyond dispute.

But not anything like enough? The answer, I think, would have to be in the affirmative. Not nearly enough and it is very difficult to understand why. About all I can do is advance a few suggestions, in highly idiosyncratic, pinwheeling fashion, as a possible explanation of this cultural lag.

Establishments have a tendency to draw a distinction *between* genres that ignores the way they often merge and blend. The horror story, standing alone, is just one ripple, albeit an impressive one, on an infinitely broader fictional stream which embraces every kind of writing. There are numerous examples of so-called mainstream writing, for instance, that contain as much, or almost as much, of the horror or occult element as individual works by, let us say, Poe or Hawthorne (and even *The House of the Seven Gables* is far from completely dominated by that element alone) or HPL or, to cite a current example, Stephen King in *The Shining.* In sober fact there is a very strong horror or terror tale element—while not of a supernatural nature—in Faulkner. In the Dashiell Hammett anthology *Creeps by Night* there is a horror story, "A Rose for Emily," far more chilling than mine in the same volume, or one by John Collier which has also become a classic of its kind. And in Faulkner's novels, particularly the early ones, the horror element is very strong.

No question can arise at all as to the ghostly story's *popular* recognition, in a general readership sense, both today and in the past. In America, from the days of Washington Irving onward—and even earlier—written and oral accounts, very frequently in fictional form, of haunted mansions, vanishing stage coaches, night-riding demons, flesh-eating ghouls and a wide variety of other ghostly presences have gripped and held the American imagination. And no sooner had the English eighteenth-century Gothic novel made its influence felt on this side of the Atlantic than a host of new story tellers arose, minor figures for the most part and almost totally forgotten today. But they were widely read and popular enough in their time. Far from forgotten today is Charles Brockden Brown, the first major American novelist in the genre.

Then came Poe, and Hawthorne, who were certainly the opposite of minor in that particular realm and spread out across the rest of the century. Fitz-James O'Brien, Ambrose Bierce, F. Marion Crawford, Mary Wilkins Freeman, Charlotte Perkins Gilman of "Yellow Wall Paper" fame, Lafcadio Hearn (his Japanese ghost stories were close to major literary contributions to the genre, even though he wrote them after he arrived in Japan) and two or three other writers, often one-or two-story figures, which space limitations prevent me from dwelling on here.

Then the twentieth century dawned, and the supernatural horror story really began to gather momentum, in both a popular and a literary sense. I would have to write a thousand-page essay to go into all of that here. The best I can do is place on the turntable names, associations, publications et cetera known to all, as the phrase goes. I have set the record to revolving more or less at random here, with jerks, stops and a backward shifting of the needle here and there. What we get—and it must be remembered I am covering only *American* contributions—would sound something like this. Algernon Blackwood and *The Wave*, "The Willows," "The Wendigo"—raise no eyebrows, please: read *Episodes before Thirty* and you'll realize how much he identified with American writers in the genre during his stay here, and how extensively his books bore American publisher imprints later on—Irvin S. Cobb, a magnificent horror writer as well as a famed humorist whose contributions in the horror realm were unique of their kind—HPL—*Weird Tales*, the most legendary of horror genre pulps, with at least five early contributors who were later to establish major reputations in the field including Robert Bloch and Ray Bradbury—the early movies, the Boris Karloff sort of thing, some going back to silent film days, with vampires, werewolves and Frankenstein-created monsters competing for the allegiance of the young on the widest possible graveyard scale. (And not just one age group, for the general popularity of such films contributed, to some extent at least, to the importance of the genre on a far more serious and indisputably literary plane, just as even so space-opera-ish a film as Star Wars has done the opposite of harm in paving the way for a more mature and sophisticated understanding of science fiction on an Isaac Asimov, Robert Heinlein, Arthur Clarke or Frank Herbert plane.)

Then—the tremendous upsurgence—it could almost be thought of as an explosion—which has taken place in the supernatural horror story genre in the past six or seven years. I am spared the necessity of going into that here by the simple fact that Stephen King has covered it from all angles—recent, historical, hardcover, paperback and films—in a splendidly comprehensive way in *Danse Macabre.*

What establishment critics in general perhaps most wish to avoid is being thought of as *genre* critics, and the horror story, standing alone, presents an unusual pitfall in that respect. Its roots go so deep and it involves so much that is universal in its strangeness and hold on the human imagination that to accord it a very high place as an important branch of literature could make such a critic conspicuous as an "odd man out" amongst his peers, an esoteric defender of writing that should be approached with a greater degree of caution and balance.

What further complicates all this is the simple fact that in no other genre is it so hard to place an evaluation on writing that covers so wide a range in both its popular and serious literary appeal—from very badly, even atrociously written novels like *Dracula* (and a stylist on any level Bram Stoker was not) to such pocket masterpieces of great literary distinction as the ghost stories of M. R. James, or Henry James' *Turn of the Screw.*

I am far from a pessimist, however, concerning the eventual acceptance of the supernatural horror story by all the literary establishments in America—and overseas as well, of course—as an important branch of literature, and, at its best, very much a part of the main stream. Like almost everything else in our "future shock" era, literary evaluations seem at times to be changing almost overnight.

3. Science fiction and fantasy in general. This appraisal would run to an inordinate length indeed if I attempted to cover more than two rather vital points. In so far as the three genres overlap in many ways, the feelings I've always had about supernatural horror in literature would be equally applicable here, with a few qualifications; in several areas of discussion I shall have to put these feelings aside until I start my dark-side-of-the-moon Ph.D thesis on 2020.

What seems most important to me, with such limitations in mind, is the extent to which science fiction today—the best of SF in a literary sense—is still thought to be ghettoized. I refuse to believe that it is. A few years ago perhaps, but not in 1985. In this I find myself in disagreement with three or four of the foremost practitioners, Robert Silverberg for one and particularly Harlan Ellison. For my chips they are both magnificent writers indeed, and have achieved so great a measure of professional success that their opinions have to be accorded weight. But so much can be placed on the other side of the scales to refute such a belief that I can't see how it can be any longer maintained.

A few examples should suffice. At least a dozen establishment critics of major stature—as such criteria go—have ceased to draw any distinction between the best of science fiction in a literary sense and novels in other categories. A few of them have gone so far as to hail it as quite possibly the most important literature of tomorrow. I shall mention no names here. There is no need for me to do so. Just open the *New York Times Book Review* on any rainy Sunday—if it is not raining it might be wiser to follow Walt Whitman's suggestion: "I listened to the learned astronomer and then went out and looked up at the stars."

But at any rate, with the *New York Times Book Review* opened, glance at some of the recent full-page ads. The ads themselves mean very little in a purely literary sense. If a publisher feels like purchasing one, that is entirely—or almost entirely—irrelevant. But just glance at the quoted "rave notices" and some of the names attached to them.

How many of those names would it have been possible to assemble even a decade ago—academic, literary, prestigious or otherwise? Write off all log-rolling, all friendship ties, and you'd still have something to marvel at on the "establishment-accepted" side of the scales.

The second point of rather vital importance which I feel should be mentioned here is a quite simple one—nothing I have said regarding the entire fantasy field should be accorded more importance than any other portion of this "fireside chat" memoir. I may well be mistaken in as many ways as a hedgehog who meets himself coming back out of a cavern which he had gnawed in space-time and can't quite decide whether he is one hedgehog or two or some creature of a different breed entirely.

CHAPTER 4

I've sometimes wondered what I might achieve in the realm of self-discovery if I could see and talk again to everyone I've ever known from the ages of two until the present time. To carry it back to the day of my birth might well involve a whole new ballgame of vast, mysterious forces too consciously ill-defined to be important to me in quite the same way, although it is interesting to note in this connection that Ray Bradbury has stated he can remember with considerable clarity the day of his birth.

Just suppose that, by some miracle of astral communication, with an instrument outwardly resembling nothing more complex than the easily attachable desk telephones one can now buy at bargain prices in department store sales, I could dial any one of the aforementioned individuals and find them at home and they could, in turn, dial me. Suppose, further, that few would refuse an invitation to visit me in person, if only because an invitation so unusual, in circumstances so extraordinary, would be difficult to brush aside.

Almost immediately, unfortunately, other problems would arise. With so many individuals to talk to—multitudes, in fact—I could allot no more than a few seconds for a visit from each, even in so narrowed down a list that it would make the New York telephone directory seem, by comparison, a volume no more than a few millimeters thick. I could, of course, make a few exceptions, and allow an occasional visit to last for a minute or two. But even then—

All at once, a solution occurred to me.

Aside from my childhood, with its family ties, and my marriage, and the writing of books, nothing has played a more important role in my life than friendships I could only hope to renew through the kind of astral plane communication I've been dwelling on here. Not only were the majority of such friends fellow writers, the three or four I remained in communication with the most, over the longest periods of time, were writers in the closely related genres of science fiction and fantasy (with the latter's several subdivisions). My other friends of a great many years, who outnumber them still, I have dwelt on elsewhere. But they hardly provide a solution to the problem I've just been discussing. Only this one does. If I confine the visits from each to no one else, the time available for a quite long visit ceases to present a problem. So—

I step to my desk, and pick up the astral phone communicator. I dial a number I've memorized by ESP perceptivity, the one that comes instantly to mind as the most important of several. You've guessed it—it is that of HPL. Where is he residing now? What will he have to tell me?

Bear in mind that the instrument is new to me. Its availability has dome as a revelation. Imagine my startlement then when my "hello" is answered in a matter-of-fact tone of voice, and before I can even ask "May I speak to—?", by several quick reproaches: "Did you have to call me at so early an hour, Belknapius? I've been sleeping for not more than two hours. A terrible revision job. I was hoping I wouldn't have to think about it again until noon, after I've had breakfast, and at least two cups of coffee."

"Why don't you drink them black, for once, without sugar?" I heard myself saying, before it came to me that I was taking for granted an impossible kind of occurrence. How could he possibly be talking still about revising stories on a plane where even the drinking of coffee would have been the wildest kind of absurdity?

Let it go for the moment, I told myself. This is the first testing out of a new, incredible kind of communicator. There could be some kind of time distortion involved, a blending of the past and the present that would be no more them momentary. With a little patience I might still receive an astral realm visit from HPL that would be entirely in conformity with what I could visualize as a 1985 look, with an astral-plane spectral aspect, of course, that would seem in accord with almost any year of the past half-century, since details of attire et cetera would be replaced by a kind of luminous nebulosity. Not necessarily, of course, but specters in general, as often as not, failed to wear the costumes of some particular historical period. In HPL's case, of course, it might even have been that of the eighteenth century.

He had fallen silent for a moment, but when he spoke again it was almost as if he'd anticipated what I'd "phoned" to suggest. "If you won't be going out this afternoon," he said, "I'll drop in for a short while. I'll be taking the IRT to Manhattan in any case. There are some Pope and Dryden manuscripts, letters for the most part, on exhibition at the 42nd Street Library. You may have read about it in the papers. It goes off in a few days."

I decided then to accept the possibility that he might at any moment begin to recede and vanish into the past to find out exactly how he would feel if he knew about the recognition that would follow his vanishment into the astral realm in 1937, particularly after the publication of *The Outsider and Others* by Arkham House in 1939.

"I've always felt," I said, "that your best stories should be preserved in hardcover before *just* the readers of *Weird Tales* think they're great and all that, but forget why you don't send a collection to Putnam's or Scribner's to preserve them. It's so easy to do, and if they come back—well, what have you lost, really?"

"I could lose more than you think if I make a fool of myself, Belknapius. I wouldn't care to submit stories to one of the major publishers unless I could be sure they conformed to the critical standards I've always set for myself. And in many ways I've failed dismally—"

"That's simply not true," I said. "'The Dunwich Horror,' 'The Colour out of Space,' 'The Shunned House,' 'The Music of Erich Zann,' even 'The Rats in the Walls'—although I've never cared for that one quite as much—are tremendous things. In fact—"

"Things?" he interrupted me with one of his customary reproving denials. "Despite your usual youthful over-exuberance you've chosen a very good word there. That's precisely what they are—things altogether too mechanical and contrived, largely because I made the mistake of letting myself think—to some slight extent at least—of Wright and the readers of *Weird Tales* when I wrote them. I should never have allowed for a moment such a thought to intrude. But that's only one small part of it.

When I wrote those stories what I most sought to do was to capture the feeling of alienage, of utter strangeness, I felt would be present in the minds of anyone exposed to some ghastly reversal of ordinary, usually taken-for-granted rules of Nature, either in some quite familiar New England setting or in some vortex of dissolving energy and matter that would make such an entrapped individual a hostage to terror. I always know what I *wanted* to achieve in those stories, but knowing and succeeding do not automatically coincide. Never has a single one of my stories completely satisfied me."

"I've often wondered," I said, "precisely how you would feel if you discovered, at some time in the future, that you were totally mistaken concerning that failure, and if acclaim as one of the truly great writers in the genre, perhaps comparable only to Poe, would set you a little apart from even such masters as Machen and Blackwood."

"How would I feel? Very much the same way as anyone lost to all sanity would probably feel if you succeeded in making him believe he had much in common with Leonardo on the strength of a not wholly bad water-color he'd produced while riding in the subway from Red Hook to Manhattan."

"I'm quite sure you do not feel that way about your best stories," I told him.

"But I do," he assured me. "They seem to me to fall short, in one way or another, of what I hoped I might succeed in achieving when I sat down to write them. Something is *simply not there*. A feeling of terrifying lack of purposefulness in the entire physical universe. If my stories seem to you successful it is only because I've succeeded in accomplishing that to some very slight extent on rare occasions."

For the first time since we had been talking the look of strain that arose from obligations and duties postponed returned to his features, making me realize that even on the astral plane there could be no escape from household worries.

"Sonia will be expecting me back by seven and—Good grief, it could almost be that now."

He removed from his vest the heavy, conspicuously ornate gold watch that was still attached to an equally massive, many-years-out-of-date chain that he'd often told me was a "Grandfather Phillips legacy," and glanced at it in consternation. A kind of subdued, spectral radiance streamed from the dial across his fingers.

"Six fifteen," he murmured. "At this hour the subway crush will for the most part be over, but I'm afraid it will be well past eight when I get to Clinton Street."

"You mean—Sonia is back from her last trip? You never told me."

"She'll be here very briefly this time," he said. "Well, I'll have to be going. There's something else I forgot to tell you. Wright thought your last story was utterly splendid. Even better than 'The Hounds of Tindalos.' What was the title? I seem to have—"

"'The Space-Eaters,'" I said. "You are the central character. I thought of course you'd received my letter."

"Mrs. Gamwell"—he always spoke of his aunts in formal fashion—"has not been too well the past fortnight. That accounts for her delay in forwarding it. It is probably now in my mailbox."

He nodded and, quite suddenly, ceased to be standing before me. I had expected that there would be a gradual fading, and the abruptness of his departure was extremely startling.

I crossed to the window, sat down, and devoted a full hour to reflection.

In recent years I've come more and more to realize that while the world may undergo profound changes—often in a comparatively short period of time—basic human relationships remain startlingly the same. This can make us feel, at times, that the past is simply repeating itself, over and over, and that hardly anything changes. Paradoxically, that assumption is both true and false, because, to a very large extent, much depends on the position in which we find ourselves in a kind of traveling observatory that is constantly in motion, and the way we feel, both outwardly and inwardly—subjectively, if one prefers that term—about everything that is observed.

Why then should all this not be equally true on an *astral* plane? I felt I now knew pretty much what to expect in relation to the age and appearance of my spectral visitors when I dialed the communicating instrument. It could well vary with every such materialization and depend to a large extent on what was most in conformity with our *shared* memories and emotions at some one particular observation post as the great time clock swung back and forth in constantly changing orbits.

HPL had been in my presence again at a particular post which the communicating instrument had made very real on the astral plane, or I had been in his presence. But that did not mean that the next time I made use of the communicating instrument I would encounter the spectral presence of the HPL I knew in his New York days and not find instead that he was greeting me from Providence with some much later memories to share, in the Poe-haunted shadows of the Ancient Hill.

HPL had a rare capacity for analyzing with total honesty and without so much as the blinking of an eyelash—I'm speaking figuratively here, of course—the changes in his thinking that time and circumstances had made inevitable across the years. Much of that stemmed, I've always believed, paradoxical as it may seem, from the great kindliness and generosity of spirit that no one who met and talked at length with him could have failed to sense. He wished to spare others from blaming themselves too harshly for errors in judgment and personal shortcomings—intellectual, aesthetic, emotional—which he had, at various times in the past, possessed. No one, he was very careful to make plain, could ever hope completely to outgrow his or her shortcomings, even with an extended life span of a hundred and six, but trying was of tremendous importance and should never be abandoned. Even if the entire cosmos reeled with an ultimate kind of absurdity, there was nothing quite as valuable as preserving one's inner integrity in that respect. Although I did not always see eye to eye with Howard about not a few areas of human thought and experience, with that one I could not have been more in agreement, except that if I had ever been called upon to exercise such total candor I fear that the kindliness I've mentioned would have been less in evidence, swallowed up by an egotistical kind of self-preoccupation.

Since the space limitations imposed by this memoir prevent me from dwelling more than very briefly on areas in which our views did *not* coincide—and they are of far less importance than what he achieved in realms of dark splendors—I've chosen one that sheds some light as well, if only by a kind of indirection, on several of the others.

In his last lengthy letter to me, which I received late in 1936, he made it unmistakably plain that he had not modified even slightly the way he felt about American poetry after it began to depart from traditional patterns with Whitman far back in the Pleistocene, and, much later, of course, with Pound and T. S. Eliot and Hart Crane. *The Waste Land* became for him a kind of paragon or symbol of a new kind of nonsense verse, which he parodied hilariously soon after it appeared in *The Dial* in 1922. In the ensuing fifteen years his view of that poem remained unchanged. I also read it for the first time in *The Dial,* and thought it an extraordinary poem.

To me there has always been something irresistibly challenging about the *avant-garde.* It can perpetuate both a wide variety of horrors or shining achievements which the years will vindicate as having been certain to endure. Perhaps the way I've always felt about it is a little crazy, in a way. But so is the way Howard always felt about Pope, and *"His Britannic Majesty"* and the eighteenth century in general. If we cannot all be a little crazy in our various ways, the world would be a very dull place indeed.

I waited more than a week before I turned to the astral phone communicating instrument again, not wishing to greet another spectral presence before a completely serene mood had come upon me.

I've never known any member of the writing profession who was more genuinely well-liked as Otis Adelbert Kline. In the course of a long friendship I met and talked with many of both his close personal friends and his business associates, and dissenting voices in that area were conspicuous by their rarity. He was a man of firm convictions, and always resolute in his defense of them. But it was never to the point of belligerent contentiousness. Life, he seemed to feel, was much too short and peace of mind too important to go into a rage over anything that was no more than an opinion. (There are some opinions I've experienced difficulty in exercising quite the same kind of restraint about, but I've never been entirely sure as to whether that was wise or foolish.) I doubt if Otis would have felt exactly as Will Rogers did when he said he had never met a man or woman he did not like. But he never seemed to feel a need to take off the gloves and sail into an opponent on the argumentative level in bare-knuckled fashion. By the same token the ironic, black humor way of demolishing an opponent he seemed content to leave to others who could forge anger into a kind of aesthetic weapon, and derive great pleasure from doing so.

Despite the infinitely greater maturity of the science fiction and general fantasy genres today, in at least their literary level, close to mainstream importance, three early travelers—Burroughs, Merritt and Kline—were as influential as Gernsback, I've always felt, making it possible for journeys to other planets and into other dimensions of space and time to become a widely acclaimed, widely popular newsstand phenomenon of those times. (The Buck Rogers cartoons accomplished much the same thing, but on, I've always felt, the even more often naive, far from sophisticated, entertainment plane to which writers of serious literature were very careful not to descend. Just a little *too* careful, perhaps, for when there were certain untrodden wastes to cross the early far Western pioneers welcomed into their companionship men of exceptional gifts whose story-writing capabilities created legends of enduring worth.)

Before uncradling the astral communicator I went over, in retrospect, the periods—many long, but others no more than a few days in duration—in which I had talked at great length with Otis concerning my own stories and how he felt they shaped up professionally, since, as my literary agent, he had to consider whether or not they were likely to please at least two or three out of—at that time—about twenty magazine editors in the science fiction and fantasy genres. Important as most of those discussions were they now seemed to dwindle in significance when I remembered how much greater had been my enjoyment when, in the few years preceding his passing, we had traveled in a rowboat a mile or so beyond where wheeling gulls arose in flight from barnacle-encrusted rocks and dropped anchor where the fishing never failed to be rewarding.

How could I ever forget summers spent at *The Midge,* and the "fish-roasts" that were enhanced by the fragrance of the surrounding woodland and the presence of his wife and charming daughter, on whom had been bestowed at birth the miraculous name of "Orafay"? What made all this seem just as miraculous was the simple and incredible fact (the synchronicity factor almost had to be present here) that as a very young child—not more than six at the most—I had walked on a Short Beach strand not very different from the one that I had found at *The Madge* on my first visit to that New Haven shore point. When Otis had moved there with his family I had never once told him that he would find the name of the Mansfields, my maternal ancestors, on a small village-green monument a short distance away!

With all that in mind I couldn't help wondering what period-aura, what memory-shared moment in time would accompany his spectral presence when my "phone call" was followed by a visit in the small hours. (It was long after midnight when I uncradled the communicator with, suddenly, slightly unsteady hands.)

He spoke quite briefly on the phone, and, as had happened with HPL, nothing about his voice seemed changed. "Frank? Ellen told me you'd probably phone to find out if I'd be coming over tomorrow to have another tooth extracted. The one your father took care of yesterday. Had been giving me the most trouble, but there are two others that have been acting up. You told her you wanted to be at home if I decided to get the whole damned mess taken care of in one more session. I suppose I might as well. I've some bad news, but it will keep until I get there."

HPL's visit had seemed a kind of ghostly repetition of a dimly remembered occurrence that had actually taken place at some time in the past. But a phantom with a toothache? I had a very dim recollection of one such visit, but two? Yet it must have taken place, and what he had to tell me came as so great a shock that my every doubt was dispelled when it came in a slightly shaken voice. "Bob Howard is dead. He killed himself. And he sent me a new story less than five weeks ago."

If a spectral shape can have a toothache, a sudden change of mind concerning anything as trivial as a dental appointment under stress of strong emotion is understandable enough, and it did not surprise me in the least when his faintly luminous form quivered, and was gone.

However you may choose to define genius—even keeping in mind the simplistic claim that it stems largely from a capacity for hard work and the taking of pains—I have never doubted that John W. Campbell, Jr., had considerably more than a touch of it. Both as an editor and as a writer it gave him pleasure—and this, too, I have never doubted—to discuss with conviction one or two aspects of an important subject as if there was little likelihood that future developments might not bear him out. As often as not they did, but it could lead as well to some wrong guesses that he knew would be forgiven by the indisputable fact that it is human to err.

The one that I look back upon with close to incredulous awe—so monumental was it in relation to what the swiftly passing years have revealed—appeared in an editorial column when TV was still in its infancy. The new visual medium, he assured the readers of *Analog,* would never be a major one in the entertainment realm because—hold your breath!—the limits it imposed on the viewer were far too much on the busy housewife, kitchen activity side! At most TV could serve as a momentary daytime distraction between the almost constant need of answering the phone or doorbell amidst the clatter of dishes or to check on the washing machine, and the impatience of waiting for the infinitely greater pleasure of entertaining guests or dining out and watching the movies, in the company of many others, on the wide screen.

Whether or not something close to such a view was held by many others at the time, the *tremendous* growth of TV could hardly have been foreseen in the sober actuality realm. J.W.C. still has to be faulted here, I've always felt, for so complete a failure to realize that a medium that could bring so much of the outside world into millions of homes on the visual plane would usher in the kind of change in human communication that the computer is now carrying forward in another Gargantuan leap. Entertainment, of course, is just one aspect of the change, but in dealing with that factor as he did he bad-guessed a great deal more. It is difficult to imagine a housewife today who would not rush from the kitchen into the living room to watch the emergency recovery of a satellite in space, or a mountainside view of a wrecked plane with a helicopter hovering overhead on a quite large screen. And on returning to the kitchen she might well be upset to discover she had missed both *General Hospital* and *All Our Children* on an only slightly smaller screen.

But—there were right guesses, too, often tremendously insightful ones, and it was to J.W.C.'s everlasting credit that he always spoke his mind, and never soft-pedaled what he honestly believed. There was no evasiveness or self-aggrandizing pretense in him at all.

He excelled as an editor in his almost instant appreciation of new and exceptionally original ideas, and encouraged writers to enlarge on what they had written by freely offering ideas of his own for improving a story if he felt it needed strengthening at one or more vital points.

He was the last writer I spoke to before the astral communicator broke down. Just how or why it happened I simply do not know, even to this particular day and hour in 1985. It happened last October and could well become a subject of interest to the soon forthcoming World Fantasy Convention in the Southwest, and the eerie All-Hallows Eve spirits which stalk the shadows at that particular time of the year.

CHAPTER 5

I have never actually seen a ghost or had what is commonly referred to as an "occult experience." Whenever I mention this to one of my friends who are firmly convinced they have had such an experience they shake their heads in disappointment or stare at me reproachfully, as if such an admission on the part of a supernatural horror writer verges on the unforgivable.

HPL, of course, was a total disbeliever in the supernatural as a realistic possibility, but the cosmic vistas in his stories create so overwhelming an impression in the opposite direction that a great many readers prefer to go on thinking of him as possessing a key that could unlock undreamed-of portals in every direction and that he is inwardly smiling still, in some other segment of space-time, at the tremendous deception he preferred to indulge in for some whimsical reason known to himself alone.

I am quite sure that nothing could be further from the truth. I am equally sure that in the entire course of my life I have practiced no such deception, even on a self-deceiving plane. I possess no keys whatever beyond a very speculative small one that might conceivably have dropped out of a small rusty lock that would turn more than it has if I worked over it painstakingly enough, with just the right kind of oiling.

I am thinking here of what Jung calls synchronicity and what surrealists prefer to think of as "objective chance." The occurrence, in close association, of two or more events with striking features in common, can, in many instances, be accepted without puzzlement as no more than *normally* coincidental. But when the similarities are *very* striking, and the coincidental factor does violence to the law of averages or seems to involve an ESP factor as well, the aforementioned lock becomes less resistant to my turning effort.

What it suggests, to me at least, is that in some strange, incredible way everything in the universe may be mysteriously linked to everything else; and if you pluck a beetle from a planet in a summer garden, the better to examine it, another beetle, in some other segment of space-time, perhaps an anti-matter beetle, will be stirred to much the same kind of resentful activity. If you wish to think of this as an occult event or manifestation of the ghostly, I am prepared to go along with it.

There are events of this nature that are simply prophetic in some unusual way, and the unusualness does not become apparent until years later. To group them all under one heading or label—Jungian synchronistic or whatever—would be a mistake in logic. But I am less concerned with logic here than with the simple fact that they have served, more than anything else in the realm of the inexplicable, to keep me from becoming the kind of dogmatic scientific materialist that turns thumbs down, as did HPL, on the possible intrusion of something very close to the supernatural into our everyday lives.

I have discussed in *The Dreamer* four or five such occurrences which seemed to bear a close relationship to the many talks I had with HPL in the ten years following the first time I met him in person—talks and walks that took place in regions as scattered as Brooklyn, Providence, Newburyport and the tip of Cape Cod. A Hudson River Valley occurrence of much the same general nature I described several years ago in *Whispers* magazine, "A Day in the Life of H. P. Lovecraft."

What is perhaps most curious in that respect is the HPL-Providence associational nature of the next to last one, for it took place during— rather, immediately following—the First World Fantasy Convention at which the assembled guests included Robert Bloch, H. Warner Munn, Fritz Leiber, Jr., and Willis Conover. Perhaps there is something about the invocation of the Mythos that can hardly fail to take place when inner-circle Lovecraftians assemble on such an occasion that breaks down all barriers between the known and the unknown and permits synchronicity to come fully into its own.

The incident I have in mind was, in a sense, a thing apart, and bears no direct relationship to the Convention. But it did take place in Providence and would not have taken place if I hadn't decided to go roaming about the city for the first time in years after the Convention broke up.

I was curious concerning its possible bookstore "finds," particularly several out-of-print volumes I had been unable to secure in New York. As I approached a very modern, well-stocked bookstore not far from the Ancient Hill, *I went over in my mind a brief article I was writing about HPL.* In it I had dwelt on some length on Henry James and H. Rider Haggard. It would not, I felt, be possible to imagine two widely read novelists more unlike, Henry James was a major literary figure, and Haggard, despite the fame which *She, King Solomon's Mines* and a host of other books had brought him in a popular readership sense, was in a different category entirely.

The instant I stepped into the bookshop I saw that it presented a browsing temptation of a superficial sort, for there was a gigantic rack of recent paperbacks close to the door. I stopped for a moment to look over the titles and a recent reprint of an H. Rider Haggard novel caught my eye. On the cover there was a ten-or twelve-line blurb, praising the book in the highest terms, and the author of that turn-of-the-century blurb had been—you've guessed it—Henry James!

This occurrence was not exactly of a spectacular nature and if it rips the law of averages to shreds it does so in a rather quiet, unobtrusive way. But for some reason, perhaps because of that very unobtrusiveness, it made a deeper impression on me than most of the others in recent years.

There was one so extraordinary in a threefold way that I must, however, relate it here, and then I am through. (To the profound skeptic who regards synchronicity as a delusion and a snare that "through" could take on another, unintended meaning and provoke a chuckle! But I shall go on undaunted notwithstanding.)

This one has nothing whatever to do with HPL, the Mythos or Providence. Six or seven years ago my wife and I were invited to a party in the Village, and were so late we feared the Martinis would have to be put back in the refrigerator. So we hailed a taxi at random in the neighborhood, even though the distance still to be covered was short, and settled back with sighs of relief. The driver almost immediately began to talk and he was good at it.

He was, it seems, an artist of considerable talent—he had even been on TV several times, once on prime time—and he specialized in the drawing of hands, chiefly of theatrical celebrities. He passed a sketch book back to my wife, because her interest had been aroused in an easily understandable way. She was for a number of years in the theatrical promotion field—and still is, but in combination with other involvements—and had only the week before been in the office of one of the celebrities whose hands were in the sketch book. She had also talked with at least a dozen of the others.

We were both impressed by the coincidence but I didn't think too much about it, because occurrences of that nature happen more often than is commonly supposed, and are not synchronistic to a very pronounced extent. Besides, I can be a little impatient at times with extraordinary things which happen at the wrong time, when one's mind is on something else and I was still concerned with being late for the party.

My wife took down the artist's address, but later lost it, and when we arrived at our destination and I paid the cab fare he drove off, and we never saw him again. The party, despite our late arrival, was wholly a success and we did not depart until the small hours. On descending the stairs—it was on the third floor—we encountered on the second floor landing a huge painting, just a little on the crude side, of two hands, interlocked!

There were several artists in the huge brownstone and I was sure then—and I'm still convinced—it was put out into the hallway by its unsatisfied creator to be carted off by a garbage disposal truck later in the morning. I should, of course, have checked on this, but I never did.

THE LAST MEN

Maljoc had come of age. On a bright, cold evening in the fall of the year, fifty million years after the last perishing remnant of his race had surrendered its sovereignty to the swarming masters, he awoke proud and happy and not ashamed of his heritage. He knew, and the masters knew, that his kind had once held undisputed sway over the planet. Down through dim aeons the tradition—it was more than a legend—had persisted, and not all the humiliations of the intervening millenniums could erase its splendor.

Maljoc awoke and gazed up at the great moon. It shone down resplendently through the health-prism at the summit of the homorium. Its rays, passing through the prism, strengthened his muscles, his internal organs, and the soft parts of his body.

Arising from his bed, he stood proudly erect in the silver light and beat a rhythmic tattoo with his fists on his naked chest. He was of age, and among the clustering homoriums of the females of his race which hung suspended in the maturing nurseries of Agrahan was a woman who would share his pride of race and rejoice with him under the moon.

As the massive metallic portals of the homorium swung inward, a great happiness came upon him. The swarming masters had instructed him wisely as he lay maturing under the modified lunar rays in the nursery homorium.

He knew that he was a man and that the swarming masters were the descendants of the chitin-armored, segmented creatures called insects, which his ancestors had once ruthlessly despised and trampled under foot. At the front of his mind was this primary awareness of origins; at the back a storehouse of geologic data.

He knew when and why his race had succumbed to the swarming masters. In imagination he had frequently returned across the wide wastes of the years, visualizing with scientific accuracy the post-Pleistocene glacial inundations as they streamed equatorward from the poles.

He knew that four of the earth's remaining continents had once lain beneath ice sheets a half mile thick, and that the last pitiful and cold-weakened remnants of his race had succumbed to the superior sense-endowments of the swarming masters in the central core of a great land mass called Africa, now submerged beneath the waters of the southern ocean.

The swarming masters were almost godlike in their endowments. With their complex and prodigious brains, which seemed to Maljoc as all-embracing as the unfathomable forces which governed the constellations, they instructed their servitors in the rudiments of earth history.

In hanging nursery homoriums thousands of men and women were yearly grown and instructed. The process of growth was unbelievably rapid. The growth-span of the human race had once embraced a number of years, but the swarming masters could transform a tiny infant into a gangling youth in six months, and into a bearded adult, strong-limbed and robust, in twelve or fourteen. Gland injections and prism-ray baths were the chief causal agents of this extraordinary metamorphosis, but the growth process was further speeded up by the judicious administration of a carefully selected diet.

The swarming masters were both benevolent and merciless. They despised men, but they wished them to be reasonably happy. With a kind of grim, sardonic toleration they even allowed them to choose their own mates, and it was the novelty and splendor of that great privilege which caused Maljoc's little body to vibrate with intense happiness.

The great metallic portal swung open, and Maljoc emerged into the starlight and looked up at the swinging constellations. Five hundred feet below, the massive domed dwellings of Agrahan glistened resplendently in the silvery radiance, but only the white, glittering immensity of the Milky Way was in harmony with his mood.

A droning assailed his ears as he walked along the narrow metal terrace toward the swinging nurseries of the women of his race. Several of the swarming masters were hovering in the air above him, but he smiled up at them without fear, for his heart was warm with the splendor of his mission.

The homoriums, sky promenades, and air terraces were suspended above the dwellings of Agrahan by great swinging cables attached to gas-inflated, billowing air floats perpetually at anchor. As Maljoc trod the terrace, one of the swarming masters flew swiftly between the cables and swooped down upon him.

Maljoc recoiled in terror. The swarming masters obeyed a strange, inhuman ethic. They reared their servitors with care, but they believed also that the life of a servitor was simply a little puff of useful energy. Sometime when in sportive mood, they crushed the little puffs out between their claws.

A chitin-clad extremity gripped Maljoc about his middle and lifted him into the air. Calmly then, and without reversing its direction, the swarming master flew with him toward the clouds.

Up and up they went, till the air grew rarefied. Then the swarming master laid the cool tips of its antennae on Maljoc's forehead and conversed with him in a friendly tone.

"Your nuptial night, my little friend?" it asked.

"Yes," replied Maljoc. "Yes—yes—it is."

He was so relieved that he stammered. The master was pleased. The warmth of its pleasure communicated itself to Maljoc through the vibrations of its antennae.

"It is well," it said. "Even you little ones are born to be happy. Only a cruel and thoughtless insect would crush a man under its claw in wanton pleasure."

Maljoc knew, then, that he was to be spared. He smiled up into the great luminous compound-eyes of his benefactor.

"It amused me to lift you into the air," conveyed the master. "I could see that you wanted to soar above the earth; that your little wingless body was vibrant with happiness and desire for expansion."

"That is true," said Maljoc.

He was grateful and—awed. He had never before been carried so high Almost the immense soaring wings of the master brushed the stratosphere.

For a moment the benevolent creature winged its way above the clouds, in rhythmic glee. Then, slowly, its body tilted, and it swept downward in a slow curve toward the sky terrace.

"You must not pick a too-beautiful mate," cautioned the master. "You know what happens sometimes to the too beautiful."

Maljoc knew. He knew that his own ancestors had once pierced the ancestors of the swarming masters with cruel blades of steel and had set them in decorative rows in square boxes because they were too beautiful. His instructors had not neglected to dwell with fervor on the grim expiation which the swarming masters were in the habit of exacting. He knew that certain men and women who were too beautiful were frequently lifted from the little slave world of routine duties in the dwellings of the masters and anaesthetized, embalmed, and preserved under glass in the museum mausoleums of Agrahan.

The master set Maljoc gently down on the edge of the sky terrace and patted him benevolently on the shoulder with the tip of its hindermost leg. Then it soared swiftly upward and vanished from sight.

Maljoc began to chant again. The Galaxy glimmered majestically in the heavens above him, and as he progressed along the sky promenade he feasted his gaze on the glowing misty fringes of stupendous island universes lying far beyond the milky nebulae to which his little race and the swarming master belonged.

Nearer at hand, as though loosely enmeshed in the supporting cables, the pole star winked and glittered ruddily, while Sirius vied with Betelgeuse in outshining the giant, cloud-obscured Antares, and the wheeling fire chariot of the planet Mars.

Above him great wings droned, and careening shapes usurped his vision. He quickened his stride and drew nearer, and ever nearer, to the object of his desire.

The nursery homorium of the women of his race was a towering vault of copper on the edge of the cable-suspended walk. As he came abreast of it he began to tremble, and the color ebbed from his face. The women of his race were unfathomable, dark enigmas to him—bewildering shapes of loveliness that utterly eluded his comprehension.

He had glimpsed them evanescently in pictures—the swarming masters had shown him animated pictures in colors—but why the pictures enraptured and disturbed him so he did not know.

For a moment he stood gazing fearfully up at the massive metal portal of the homorium. Awe and a kind of panicky terror contended with exultation in his bosom. Then, resolutely, he threw out his chest and began to sing.

The door of the homorium swung slowly open, and a dim blue light engirded him as he stood limned in the aperture. The illumination came from deep within the homorium. Maljoc did not hesitate. Shouting and singing exultantly, he passed quickly through the luminous portal, down a long, dim corridor, and into a vast, rectangular chamber.

The women of his race were standing about in little groups. Having reached maturity, they were discussing such grave and solemn topics as the past history of their kind and their future duties as obedient servants of the swarming master. Without hesitation, Maljoc moved into the center of the chamber.

The women uttered little gasping cries of delight when they beheld him. Clustering boldly about him, they ran their slim white hands over his glistening tunic and caressed with fervor his beard and hair. They even gazed exultantly into his boyish gray eyes, and when he flushed they tittered.

Maljoc was disturbed and frightened. Ceasing to sing, he backed away precipitously toward the rear of the chamber.

"Do not be afraid," said a tall, flaxen-haired virago at his elbow. "We will not harm you."

Maljoc looked at her. She was attractive in a bold, flamboyant way, but he did not like her. He tried to move away from her, but she linked her arm in his and pulled him back toward the center of the chamber.

He cried out in protest. "I do not like you!" he exclaimed. "You are not the kind of woman—"

The Amazon's lips set in hard lines. "You are far too young to know your own mind," she said. "I will be a good wife to you."

As she spoke, she thrust out a powerful right arm and sent three of her rivals sprawling.

Maljoc was panic-stricken. He pleaded and struggled. The woman was pulling him toward the center of the chamber, and two of the other women were contending with her.

The struggle terminated suddenly. Maljoc reeled, lost his balance, and went down with a thud on the hard metallic floor. The metal bruised his skull, stunning him.

For several seconds a wavering twilight engulfed Maljoc's faculties. Needles pierced his temples, and the relentless eyes of the Amazon burned into his brain. Then, slowly and painfully, his senses cleared, and his eyelids flickered open in confused bewilderment.

Two compassionate blue eyes were gazing steadily down at him. Dazedly, Maljoc became aware of a lithely slim form, and a clear, lovely face. As he stared up in wonderment, the apparition moved closer and spoke in accents of assurance.

"I will not let them harm you," she said.

Maljoc groaned, and his hand went out in helpless appeal. Slim, firm fingers encircled his palm, and a gentle caress eased the pain in his forehead.

Gently he drew his comforter close and whispered: "Let us escape from these devils."

The woman beside him hesitated. She seemed both frightened and eager. "I am only eight months old," she told him in a furtive whisper. "I am really too young to go forth. They say, too, that it would be dangerous, for I am—"

A blush suffused her cheeks.

"She is dangerously beautiful," said a harsh voice behind her. "The instructors here are indifferent to beauty, but when she goes forth she will be seized and impaled. You had better take me."

Maljoc raised himself defiantly on his elbow. "It is my privilege to choose," he said. "And I take this woman. Will you go forth with me, my little one?"

The woman's eyes opened widely. She looked slowly up at the Amazon, who was standing in the shadows behind her, and said in a voice which did not tremble: "I will take this man. I will go forth with him."

The Amazon's features were convulsed with wrath. But she was powerless to intervene. Maljoc was privileged to choose, and the woman was privileged to accept. With an infuriated shrug she retreated farther into the shadows.

Maljoc arose from the floor and gazed rapturously at his chosen mate. She did not evade his scrutiny. As Maljoc continued to stare at her, the strained look vanished from his face and mighty energies were released within him.

He stepped to her and lifted her with impassioned chantings into the air. Her long hair descended and enmeshed his shoulders, and as he pressed her to his heart her arms tightened clingingly about him.

The other women clustered quickly about the exultant couple. Laughing and nudging one another, they examined the strong biceps of the bridegroom and ran their fingers enviously through the woman's dark hair.

Maljoc ignored them. Holding his precious burden very firmly in his muscular arms, he walked across the chamber, down the long outer corridor, and out through the massive door. Above him in another moment the Cyclopean luminous cables loomed beneath far-glimmering stars. He walked joyfully along the sky promenade, chanting, singing, unquenchably happy in his little hour of triumph and rapture.

The woman in his arms was unbelievably beautiful. She lay limply and calmly in his embrace, her eyes luminous with tenderness. Orion gleamed more brightly now, and the great horned moon was a silver fire weaving fantastically in and out of the nebulae-laced firmament.

As Maljoc sang and chanted, the enormous droning shapes above him seemed mere alien intruders in a world of imperishable loveliness. He thought of himself now as lord of the earth and the sky, and the burden in his arms was more important in his sight than his destiny as a servitor and the benefits which the swarming masters had promised to bestow upon him if he served them diligently and well.

He no longer coveted slave joys and gratifications. He wished to be forever his own master under the stars. It was a daring and impious wish, and as if aware of his insurgent yearnings a great form came sweeping down upon him out of the sky. For an instant it hovered with sonorously vibrating wings in the air above him. But Maljoc was so obsessed with joy that he ignored the chill menace of its presence. He walked on, and the woman in his arms shared his momentary forgetfulness.

The end of their pathetic and insane dream came with a sickening abruptness. A great claw descended and gripped the woman's slim body, tearing her with brutal violence from Maljoc's clasp.

The woman screamed twice shrilly. With a harsh cry, Maljoc leaped back. As he shook with horror, a quivering feeler brushed his forehead and spoke to him in accents of contempt:

"She is too beautiful for you, little one. Return to the homorium and choose another mate."

Fear and awe of the swarming masters were instinctive in all men, but as the words vibrated through Maljoc's brain he experienced a blind agony which transcended instinct. With a scream he leaped into the air and entwined his little hands about the enormous bulbous hairs on the master's abdomen.

The master made no attempt to brush him off. It spread its gigantic lacy wings and soared swiftly into the sky. Maljoc tore and pulled at the hairs in a fury of defiance. The swiftness of the flight choked the breath in his lungs, and his eyes were blinded by swirling motes of dust. But though his vision was obscured, he could still glimpse dimly the figure of the woman as she swung limply in the clasp of the great claw a few yards above him.

Grimly, he pulled himself along the master's abdomen toward the claw. He pulled himself forward by transferring his fingers from hair to hair. The master's flat, broad stinger swung slowly toward him in a menacing arc, but he was sustained in his struggle by a sacrificial courage which transcended fear.

Yet the stinger moved so swiftly that it thwarted his daring purpose. In a fraction of time his brain grew poignantly aware that the stinger would sear his flesh before he could get to his dear one, and the realization was like a knife in his vitals. In despair and rage, he thrust out his puny jaw and sank his teeth deep into the soft flesh beneath him. The flesh quivered.

At the same instant the master swooped and turned over. Maljoc bit again. It screeched with pain and turned over and over, and suddenly, as it careened in pain, a white shape fell from its claw.

Maljoc caught the shape as it fell. With one hand clinging to the hair of the master's palpitating abdomen, and the other supporting the woman of his choice, he gazed downward into the abyss.

A mile below him the unfriendly earth loomed obscurely through riven tiers of cirrus clouds. But Maljoc did not hesitate. With a proud, exultant cry he tightened his hold on the woman and released his fingers from the hair.

The two lovers fell swiftly to the earth. But in that moment of swooning flight that could end only in destruction, Maljoc knew that he was mightier than the masters, and having recaptured for an imperishable instant the lost glory of his race, he went without fear into darkness.

GREEN GLORY

As the tiny human shapes poured alertly through the subterranean artery, sharp clicks emanated from the magnetic audition disk in the roof of the passage. The clicks announced that the bee swarms were preparing to wage gruesome and relentless war.

To the ant people and their tiny human servitors the bee army's dissolving-fungus tissue was a menace that obscured the splendor of the sun and stars and the joys of shared labor in the sweet-smelling earth. In grim procession the midget shapes moved forward, and Atasmas sang and chanted as he led them. He sang of war and glory and sacrificial death. A huge yellow aphid sat perched on his gauze-clad shoulders and fed him as he advanced.

In his inmost heart Atasmas despised the little stupid insect with its cumbersome-clawed tarsi. He knew that wingless aphids had once served the ant hordes with complaisant humility far back in the dim legendary ages when his own race was the opposite of complaisant. The aphids were mere contented cattle, mere unthinking milk producers for the omniscient ant people.

Atasmas knew that he was nearly as insignificant as the aphids in the ant people's sight, but he knew also that his own little race had once wielded immense power on earth, holding all other animal forms in abject thralldom. The aphids had never enslaved the hostile forces of nature, and had no idea of the majesty of the far-flung constellations and the vague, tender glory of the night shapes which visited men in dreams.

Deep in the earth, in luminous damp tunnels Atasmas' kind had labored, dreamed, and died for millions of years, enduring their little Mayfly span of life with ardent heroism, and remaining unflaggingly devoted to the ants' exalted creeds, their world-subduing techniques.

The ants were great. Even strong-willed men like Atasmas conceded it and were proud to serve as nurses for the large-brained grubs, as removers of excrement in the dark pits, and as relayers of such scented delicacies as the embalmed bodies of small spiders, roaches, and still smaller mammals. Along the damp, glowing tunnel Atasmas marched, the triumphant head of the tiny human procession that had formed by itself in response to the sharp clicks in the circular magnetic disk in the roof of the tunnel.

"War formation—war formation—war formation," announced the revolving disk, and Atasmas had marshaled the others into a smoothly progressing service line, thirty abreast.

"A man should die gladly when the disks move," he chanted. "With singing and rejoicing he should merge his little worthless personality in the great dream. When men die in defense of the great dream, the eggs in the abdomen of the queen mother are preserved for a destiny so great that—"

The words froze suddenly on his lips. A circle of light appeared in the roof of the tunnel and a long, attenuated feeler fastened on his shoulder. The aphid hopped to the ground with a frightened screech. Atasmas groaned and his little body stiffened. He knew that incompetent men were lifted at frequent intervals from the tunnel by the small workers and carried up through long arteries and vertical chambers to the directing queen mothers in their luminous cells.

At the thought of losing his comparative supremacy as a leader of his kind, Atasmas' brain grew numb. He had thought himself secure, for he had served always with alertness and efficiency. But many were the sins of omission which a man could commit almost unconsciously, and Atasmas was sick with the thought that he had perhaps violated some minor but important taboo.

The feeler laid him gently in repose in the center of an immense, chitin-armored back. Then the small worker began its slow ascent to the cells of the directing queens. From his vantage point on the insect's back, Atasmas was privileged to survey with swift wonder the war preparations in a hundred intervening cells.

He saw enormous, green-bellied grubs resting with a kind of repressed fervor in long earthen trenches filled with fungus-dissolving ichors. Their soft, flabby bodies absorbed the ichors with a spongelike greediness, and Atasmas knew that when the bee swarms dropped their deadly fungal tissues the grubs would be impregnable. Though the fungus poison filtered down through the damp earth to the lowest of the nursery cells, the dissolving ichors would protect the young maggots.

* * * *

Up through many cells Atasmas was carried. He saw enfeebled drones submitting with patient resignation to impregnation with the needle death. He knew that the drones would be spewed forth to mingle with the bee swarms and sow piercing agony in their midst. The needle death was a microscopic animalcule that propagated with unbelievable rapidity and feasted on insect viscera. Atasmas observed also huge, glistening black workers preening themselves for combat, and soldier ants with flattened heads a hundred feet in diameter which would be thrust into the enormous entrance vents above to serve as stopgaps against the downsweeping swarms of envenomed bees. He knew that the heads would be battered into loathsome pulps, and that the thin, flabby bodies beneath would writhe in unspeakable agony as the bees pierced them with their long stingers; but to the ant people death was a kind of rapturous dedication when it served a socially useful purpose. Something of this same sacrificial zeal flamed in the midget breast of the little creature on the insect's back. He, too, was part of the enormous dream, and he would have died to save the maggots intrusted to his care as selflessly as the ants who owned him.

There was an ominous vibratory stirring throughout the great central artery adjoining the cells of the directing queen mothers. Down it Atasmas was swiftly carried, his bearer moving with a sure-footed celerity uncommon in a small worker.

For several minutes dark dripping surfaces swept past his upturned gaze, and a peculiarly fragrant odor assailed his nostrils. Then the glow deepened about him, and the small worker came to an abrupt halt before a towering barrier of wax. The barrier was fifty feet in height, and it shone with a radiance as of burnished metal. Without hesitation the insect raised its elbowed feeler and tapped lightly upon it. For an instant there was no response. Then the luminous partition bulged slowly outward, and the glistening globular head of a queen-preening ant emerged through it. Instantly the head withdrew, and through the rent thus produced the small worker moved with reverence into the cell of the directing queen.

* * * *

The queen cell was aglow with a soft blue radiance. As the little creature on the small worker's back looked upward at the enormous swollen bulk of the single occupant of the cell, a great wonder came upon him. The eight slender scarlet rings encircling the majestic insect's abdomen, and the green dots on her thoracic segments revealed that she was the supreme ruler of the colony, the great founder queen whose wisdom and power had filtered down as a legendary fable to the little human servitors in the depths.

The small worker turned slowly on its side, and Atasmas slid from its back onto the soft, moist loam which covered the floor of the cell. Quickly he struggled to arise, to stand with dignity before this great being, whose power was so immense, and whose attributes were so godlike and omniscient. But his foot slipped as he rose from his knees, and he toppled over backward on the soft loam. He was rescued by the queen herself. Leaning slightly forward, she stretched forth a curving flagellum and set him gently on his feet. And then, as he stood staring reverently up at her, she laid the flagellum on his forehead and spoke to him in speech that surged in cool vibrations through his tiny human brain.

"You are wiser than all the others, little one. The others think first of themselves, but you think only of us. In your humble way you have the sublime, selfless mind of an insect." In awed silence Atasmas continued to stare up into the great complex eyes, bulbous head, and swiftly pulsating thorax. A hundred feet above him she towered, and her immense, hairy abdomen bulged with its momentous burden of a hundred million eggs. Not even the planets in their courses were so awe-provoking in Atasmas' sight.

"Even the very humble can sometimes be of service," said the queen mother. Still looking up, Atasmas gestured with his hands. He made a sign speech which conveyed that he had no mind apart from her mind; that her willing was the light of his little human life. The queen mother said: "Little one, the bee swarms are sweeping down upon us in envenomed fury. For a hundred millions years they have thwarted our dream of universal world dominion. Atasmas nodded, gestured, chanted. He understood. "You may use me as you will," he conveyed.

"I will have you carried to Agrahan where the bee swarms dwell in immense metallic hives," resumed the queen mother. "You are so small that you can creep unobserved between the legs of the soldier guardian bees. You will carry into the inmost core of the central hive a spore of flarraeson." Atasmas recoiled in horror. The color drained from his face and a tremor ran through him. Vague hints and rumors filtering down to the depths had obscurely revealed that flarraeson was a terrible vegetable petrifactive that fossilized all animal tissue.

By a process of intensive hybridization the small workers had intensified the petrifactive principle of certain chlorophyll-forming organisms of high evolutionary grade, and had produced a miscroscopic animal-like plant so deadly and swift-blossoming that it was a menace to the great dream itself. It was rumored that a single spore of properly planted flarraeson would overrun hives miles in extent and envelop in petrifaction a billion helpless bees in the course of a single terrestrial revolution. So prolific, indeed, was the growth of this malignant plant that its deadly course could not be checked by any means known to insects.

Though the servants of the great dream had created it, and knew its value as a war technique, they were not unaware that its successful use might envelop them in utter and abysmal ruin. Hitherto they had hesitated to employ it, just as long millenniums ago Atasmas' own race had refused to sanction certain deadly war gases in their hideous and sanguinary conflicts.

The queen mother noticed Atasmas' trepidation, and a note of reproach crept into her speech. "You will be destroyed, of course. But do you value your little life so highly?" Atasmas experienced a sudden tragic sense of shame and guilt. He made a gesture of frantic denial as the queen resumed:

"You will plant the spore and remain until you are consumed by the fossilizing growth. If you flee when you drop the spore, it may never blossom. The future of the great dream is in your little human hands." There ensued a pause.

Then the queen said: "There is something I must warn you against. You will meet the night shapes—millions and millions of night shapes."

Atasmas' pulses leaped with a sudden wild joy. "You mean I shall really see and touch the little ones who visit us in dreams?"

The queen assented. "You will see them, and touch them. They will light a great fire in your heart. But you must remember the dream and resist them. Millions of years ago, when we succored your poor frozen race, the night shapes seemed to us feeble, weak things. We refused to help them. We left them to perish beneath the weight of the antarctic glaciations, of the great flood of ice that swept equatorward from the pole. Only a few survived and were succored by the weak and sentimental bees." Atasmas' eyes were wide with wonder. He asked: "But why do these small weak shapes still haunt our dreams?"

"Because men will always be primitive creatures," replied the queen mother. "Even though we have multiplied you by laboratory techniques for millions of years, the old, primitive love of women still burns in your veins. We cannot eradicate it. It is a source of weakness in your kind, and in that respect you are inferior to the aphids."

Atasmas affirmed: "I will not forget the great dream. I will harden my heart." But something within him burst into song even as he promised. He would see the soft and consoling night shapes—see them, touch them.

He said with gestures: "I am ready to die for the great dream." The queen removed her flagellum from his forehead. She leaned backward, and a satisfied stridulation issued from her thorax.

* * * *

The little worker advanced, picked Atasmas up, and set him gently on its sack. For an instant it swayed reverently before the great mother. Then it backed swiftly out of the cell. When it had disappeared through the aperture the queen-preening ant leaped swiftly forward and healed the breach with a glutinous exudate from its swiftly moving mandibles.

The small worker carried its now precious burden up through long tunnels to the surface of the earth. At the central entrance of the nest, four great soldier ants with flattened heads moved reverently aside as the solemn pair came into view. The queen mother had laid upon her little emissary a peculiar and sanctifying scent. He was no longer a leader of his little race in the depths. He had become the potential savior of the immense dream; almost, an insect in his godlike selflessness and reverent dedication. He was conscious of immense forces at war within him as he gazed upward at the star-flecked sky. Martial dedication and tenderness fought for supremacy in his breast; an immense, overwhelming tenderness when he thought of the night shapes, a tenderness curiously tempered with superiority and disdain and a sense of loyalty to the dream. The night shapes were glorious, but did not the long night of extinction which would envelop him if he died in defense of the immense dream hold a greater glory?

The small worker turned on its side and Atasmas toppled to the earth. He arose in blinding moonlight, dazed and dazzled by the hard metallic brilliancy of the surface world. He stood waiting, scarcely daring to breathe, as the little worker rose on its hindmost legs and emitted a loud chordotonal stridulation by rubbing its elbowed feelers violently against its shins and abdomen.

For a moment as the queer chafing sound increased in volume, he saw only the towering forms of the soldier ants, dark and glistening in the moonlight, and of the little workers beside him. Then an immense dark form came sweeping down upon him out of the darkness. It had a wing span of a hundred feet and its barrel-shaped thorax shone with a luster as of frosted silver.

It came to rest a few yards from the earthern entrance with a loud, vibratory thrumming. Instantly the little worker approached and touched the summit of its globular head to the great bulging thorax of the aerial form. The form quivered and grew still.

With competent celerity the small worker picked Atasmas up, carried him to the waiting form, and deposited him gently in a tiny cavity at the base of the creature's abdomen. Touching Atasmas' forehead with its feeler, it spoke to him in rhythmic speech which surged coolly through his brain.

"You will be carried to Agrahan," it said. "It will be a long, perilous flight. If a storm arises on the southern ocean you will emerge and drop swiftly to your death. The great winged one cannot carry you in a storm.

If you perish, another spore of flarraeson will be prepared, and another winged one will carry another of your kind to Agrahan."

"Where is the spore?" asked Atasmas with excited gestures. Only his midget head and shoulders emerged above the dark, hair-lined cavity.

The little worker withdrew a few paces, turned upon its back, and fumbled for an instant with one of its foreclaws in the loose crevices of its underside. When it drew near again to Atasmas it was holding a small metallic cylinder. Atasmas took the cylinder with reverence and thrust it deeply into his gauze-fashioned tunic.

* * * *

The small worker touched its head again to the winged shape's thorax. A sudden, convulsive movement shook the great body. It moved spasmodically forward, reared with a roar and soared skyward. Fright and wild elation poured in ripples through Atasmas' brain. He had never before viewed the kaleidoscopic skies of the surface world from such a perilous vantage point. Looking down, he saw far beneath him the mottled surfaces of earth, and looking up he saw the stars in their remote and awful solitude and the planets in their wheeling courses. He saw the great white suns that would burn as brightly when the earth was a cinder, and suns that burned no more, but whose light would continue to encircle the pearshaped universe till the immense bubble burst, and time and space were merged in some utterly stupefying absolute for which neither Atasmas' kind nor the ants had any adequate symbol.

When Atasmas' gaze penetrated to the awful luminous fringes of the spiral nebula so great a pall enshrouded his spirit that he presently ceased to stare skyward. Far more reassuring was the checkerboard earth beneath with its dark and glistening lakes, ragged mountains, and valleys crammed with lush and multihued vegetation.

The checkerboard earth was soon replaced by the turbulent waters of the great southern ocean. For thousands of miles Atasmas gazed downward at the shining water, wonder and fear fighting for ascendancy in his little human breast. No storm arose to check the smooth southern flight of the great insect.

On and on it flew in the warm darkness, five miles above the turbulent dark sea. Belching volcanoes and white coral shoals passed swiftly before Atasmas' vision. He saw the barnacle colonies in their ocean-breasting splendor, terraces of iridescent shell rising in immense tiers beside the storm-lashed waves.

And suddenly as he gazed, the ocean vanished, and a dark plateau covered with gray-and-yellow lichens usurped his vision.

The great winged one swept downward then. In immense circles it approached the leaden earth and came to rest on a gray, pebble-incrusted plain. For an instant its wings continued to pulsate with a loud, vibratory throbbing. Then the vibrations ceased, and a moist foreclaw arose and fumbled in the cavity where Atasmas rested.

The midget voyager was lifted out, and deposited on the dark earth. As he stood staring wildly about him, a feeler fastened on his forehead.

"I will not return without you, little one," conveyed the great winged shape. "When you plant the spore, come back to me quickly. There is no need for you to die. The spore will blossom without supervision if you plant it in rich, dark soil. I pity you, little one. I wish to help you."

Atasmas was stunned and frightened. He started back in amazement and looked up dimly at the great shape. "Why do you disobey the great mother?" he asked with tremulous gestures. The winged form said: "We who fly above the earth do not obey the small ethics of your little world of tunnels. We have seen the barnacles in their majesty and the bees in their power, and we know that all things are relative. Go, and return quickly."

* * * *

Atasmas went. With the glimmering lights of the enormous hives of Agrahan to guide him, he went swiftly to fulfill his destiny. Over the dark earth he moved, an infinitesimal shape in a world of menacing shadows. And as he advanced the lights of Agrahan grew brighter till he was enveloped in their radiance as in a bath of living flame.

But no one observed him. The sentinel bees were asleep at their posts at the entrance of the central hive, and quickly he passed between their legs which towered above him like pillars of fire in the darkness. Inside the hive a luminous glow guided his footsteps. Moving with caution he ascended a terminus mound studded with several dozen yawning vents and entered one at random. The branching tunnel in which he found himself bore a superficial resemblance to the subterranean arteries of the ant people. For hundreds of feet it stretched. Its smoothly rounded earthen walls were gray-green in hue, and it had a flooring of moist, dark loam. Atasmas hugged the walls, taking every precaution to avoid being seen. He was tremulous with apprehension as he moved forward. It seemed incredible that the great central hive should be destitute of life, yet all about him silence reigned. From far ahead a dim bluish radiance illumined the walls of the passage, but no moving shape crossed his vision. He continued to move forward, little suspecting what lay ahead. The silence remained unbroken, and the only visible shadows were cast by his own insignificant form. It was not until he had advanced far into the tunnel that he encountered the dark mouth of the bisecting passage and the huge shape which filled it. As the shape burst on his vision he sprang back in instinctive alarm, and a cry tore from his throat. But before he could retreat, the thing was upon him. It fell upon him, and enveloped him. In frantic resistance Atasmas' little hands lashed out. They encountered a spongy surface bristling with hairs—a loose, gelatinous surface which gave beneath the assaults of his puny fists. Screeching shrilly, the bee larva twined itself about him and pressed the breath from his body. He shrieked and hammered and tore at it with his fingers in an agony of terror. His efforts were of no avail. The bulk of the maggot was too enormous to cope with.

He was dimly aware of a menacing yellow-lined orifice a yard from his face, spasmodically opening and closing. It drew nearer as he watched it and yawned above him. It twitched horribly with a dawning hunger.

Atasmas lost consciousness then. His senses reeled before the awful menace of that slobbering puckered mouth, and everything went dark about him.

He never knew what saved him until he found himself getting slowly to his feet in a confused daze. The first sight which usurped his blurred vision was the bee larva lurching cumbersomely away from him down the tunnel, emitting shrill screeches as it retreated. Then his gaze fastened in wonder on the night shape. She stood calmly in the center of the tunnel, a form as tiny as himself, but with a sweetness and grace about her that stirred inexplicable emotions within him. She was holding a long, many-thonged goad, which dripped with nauseaus yellow ichor.

As Atasmas stood staring, his clearing faculties apprehended with uncanny accuracy her true function in the colony of bees. She was obviously a kind of guardian of the large stupid maggot, and the goad in her hands was an implement of chastisement. In defense of Atasmas' little helpless person she had repudiated her function, had flailed the grub unmercifully. It was a triumph of instinctive over conditioned behavior.

In gratitude and awe, Atasmas drew near to her. She did not retreat, but raised the weapon in warning as he moved to touch her. Something snapped in Atasmas' brain. The wonder of her, standing there, awoke a great fire in his breast. He had to touch her, though he died for it. He touched her arm, her forehead. With a cry of utter dumfounderment she dropped the goad and her eyes widened. Without uttering a sound.

Atasmas moved even closer and took her in his arms. She did not resist. A great joy flooded Atasmas' being. For a moment he forgot the past and the sublime destiny toward which he moved. He stood there in silence, transfigured, transformed.

Then, suddenly, he remembered again. Even as ecstasy enveloped him he remembered the great queen, the nursery artery of the ant people, his selfless function as a servitor in the depths, and the great dream. Deep within him, in the dark depths of his little racial under-mind, the old loyalties flared up. His hand went to his tunic and emerged with the cylinder. With an effort he tore his gaze from the rapt, upturned face of the night shape and fastened it on the soft loam beneath his feet. With swift calculation he estimated the depth and consistency of the dark soil. For a brief, momentous instant he seemed to hesitate. Then, with a wrench, he unscrewed the cylinder and released the spore of flarraeson.

He continued to gaze deep into the woman's eyes in reverence and rapture as the tiny green spore took root, sprouted, and spread out in a dark petrifactive shroud.

Far away the great winged shape waited with thrumming wings as a green growth immortalized two lovers without pain in the central tunnel of the great hive of Agrahan.

The growth spread upward and enveloped the little human forms, darkly, greenly, and so absorbed was Atasmas in the woman in his arms that he did not know that he was no longer of flesh and blood till the transforming plant reached the corridors of his brain and the brain of his companion. And then the transition was so rapid that he did not agonize, but was transformed in an instant, and remained forever wrapped in glory and a shroud of deepest green.

CONES

They had never seen such skies. Glory beyond bright glory, wonder beyond wonder, in the black celestial vault above them. Earth the brightest of all the bright stars; Venus a small, watery green moon suspended in the bottomless depths of the sky; Mars a tiny reddish dot. And all the stars of the Galaxy shining in the brilliant whorls and angles of half-familiar constellations.

It was night on Mercury—cold night in a narrow world of infrequent night and day. Across a thin strip on the surface of the Sun's nearest neighbor there occurred at forty-four-day intervals the familiar alternations of sunlight and darkness which Gibbs Crayley and the other members of the First Mercury Exploration Expedition knew and loved on their home planet. The librations of the little celestial body, which rotated only once on its axis in its eighty eight-day journey about the Sun, splashed alternate bands of sunlight and dark over a relatively restricted strip of its metallic crust.

Where the face of Mercury was forever turned away from the Sun, the temperature was within a few degrees of absolute zero; there oxygen was a fine-white snow. On the bright side, continuously under the sun's rays, heat blighted and blasted the surface, and no alien shape of protoplasm could live there for long, no matter how well protected by the sciences of man. But on the strip where light and dark alternated, the conditions of climate and temperature were less extreme, and protected human life could exist there, if only for brief periods. Encased in a flexible metallic spacesuit surmounted by a rigid helmet, with fifty-pound weights attached to thighs, and oxygen tanks strapped to shoulders, a man could survive—and explore.

Gibbs Crayley, scientist-explorer, was leading the first expedition from Earth ever to land on the surface of Mercury. It was an invasion in force, spearheaded by the indomitable will and daring of the one man whose whole life had been directed toward this moment. Crayley was a representative of the small, select tribe of pure scientist-explorers, fanatics whose driving motivations were tempered only by the cautions of science. And now he led the way as he and his small band cautiously ventured out on the surface of the unknown planet.

Beside him was his wife, Helen. To her, the disciplines, exactions, and rewards of scientific exploration were a steadily sustaining flame; she made a magnificent complement to her husband's cold daring, his almost personal obsession with the mysteries of the Sunward planet.

William Seaton, trailing the Crayleys by a few feet, was impatient of natural wonders, preferring the cool precision of manmade instruments, a pattern of beauty an engineer could understand. Immediately behind him came Frederick Parkerson, a middle-aged biologist, and Ralph Wilkus, a tall, gangling youth who excelled in the arts of astrogation and cookery. These two, close friends as they had become, were alike absorbed by the fascinations and complexities of exploration in its more immediate aspects; they lived for what the next moment might bring that was new and strange.

Behind them trailed Tom Grayson, a metallurgist, and young Allan Wilson, an associate member of the National Biological Institute, essentially unimaginative men whose minds were occupied largely with the problems of movement and personal safety on this incredible planet. They completed the roster of the crew.

The explorers were setting out on their longest expedition since they had landed on Mercury. It was their hope to make it to the foothills of the high, craggy peaks which reared their angular shapes above the curiously near horizon. Behind them the immense, melon-shaped hull of their cobalt-glass spaceship loomed, flecked with Venus light. It was hardly more than half a mile away, yet its stern was already hidden by the abrupt curvature of the planet's surface.

Crayley led the way with slowly deliberate caution. With only his flash lamp to guide him, he walked slowly forward, step by step, testing every foot of the ground ahead of him with his electrodynamometer-tipped staff. The very surface on which the group trod was a treacherous mystery; in particular, they knew it to be spotted irregularly with shock patches of enormously high electrical potential. A step into one of them would crumple a man in his spacesuit and sear his body to a crisp.

These shock patches had been discovered several days before ("day" being defined in terms of an Earthian twenty-four hours, not in Mercury's own terms) when the Crayleys' dog had stumbled into one of them. Its body was now a charred cinder under the glittering Mercurian night sky. Crayley had provided a miniature spacesuit for the animal, complete with oxygen tank, heating coils, and weights, and it had run ahead a short distance to the end of its leash, as dogs will do, exploring on its own. Now Scottie was gone, a martyr to science.

After that, the explorers had thoroughly investigated the electromagnetic qualities of the crust, testing it until the full strangeness and menace of the phenomenon was apparent to all. It was because of the raging interference set up by the patches that they had to move in silence, for radio communication was obviously impossible.

Slowly the little group filed across the slightly luminous surface of the Mercurian plain. All around them surged an alien atmosphere tainted with heavy gases and ionized by cosmic rays. Their oxygen tanks were their sole protection against the corrosive horrors of this Mercurian air.

Gibbs Crayley, thinking of this and of the extended journey they were hoping to make, cut down the release gauge on his tank by two degrees, and signaled to the rest of the crew to do likewise. He knew that as the flow diminished they would all breathe less freely, but oxygen here was more precious than water on the deserts of Earth, and they could not afford to squander it.

A moment later Crayley noticed with some concern that, of all the group, his wife alone had not followed instructions. He stared at her and motioned to her oxygen gauge. She ignored him; and so, standing still, he raised his dynamometer-tipped staff from the ground and gave her tank a rap.

Behind the thick goggles of her helmet, Crayley could see Helen's eyes widen in momentary vexation. He knew she was convinced that there was more than enough oxygen in the tank to last the round trip; they had discussed it before they started out. Obviously she planned to leave her gauge alone; and apparently she had an impulse to rebuke her husband by tapping his tank in return.

In any event, she actually raised her own staff from the ground and swung it toward Crayley's encased form. But as the metal wand swung up and toward him, Crayley stopped abruptly and stiffened. His electrodynamometer had recorded a mountain-moving charge in the patch of glowing soil immediately before him. And as Helen's staff thumped against his shoulder, he swooped sideways, caught her about the knees, and in a running tackle carried her swiftly backward to safety.

Unfortunately, young Grayson let his attention be diverted by this odd action on his superior's part. Momentarily swinging his forgotten detector aside, he stepped forward into the shock patch while looking over his shoulder at the odd sight the Crayleys presented.

One moment he was walking in the bright circle cast by his electric torch. The next, only a tortured part of him could be seen, waving frantic hands in the faint Venus light. There was a burst of flame that blotted out the stars.

Like a dry leaf in a blast furnace, Grayson's limbs withered instantaneously into inert ash. Then the upper part of the youth's body crashed horribly in front of Seaton. For an instant the engineer was too appalled to move. He simply stood with his own staff extended, as though the fact that it was a man-made device could give him security when all else failed.

Behind him the other members of the group crowded forward in horror. Through their goggles they saw the hideous spectacle of a limbless torso, spacesuit blasted away, spinning upright on a blazing red field, light spiraling from sandy hair galvanically extended. Faster and faster spun the body—and then flame mercifully engulfed it.

Crayley set Helen down and threw one arm about her shoulder to steady her. For an instant she stood swaying, eyes lowered in sick comprehension. Then she stiffened and resumed her position beside her husband. There was no attempt at communication. Messages in sign languages could have been exchanged, but none were. There was nothing to say. The group moved on almost instantly, to avoid funking—like aviators going up immediately after a crash. The accident was due to human error, and they could not afford to stop for that. With slow steps they resumed their journey into the dark Mercurian night.

It was nearly half an hour later when Crayley halted again, staring intently ahead through his thick goggles. On the torchlit circle of soil before him, something had moved. Helen saw it, too, and threw out her right arm, waving back the men behind her.

Only Ralph Wilkus, perhaps missing the signal, moved forward into the region of dubious stirring. He did not recoil or shrivel but stepped right on through and continued to test his way with his staff on the featureless plain beyond.

Obviously, this was not a new type of shock patch; but what it was wanted investigation. Less foolhardy than Wilkus, the other explorers hesitated before advancing, their staffs waving experimentally above the region of stirring. Only the surface sand moved, as though blown by a faint, circularly whirling, breeze.

Crayley knew there was no breeze. The wind needle on Helen's helmet did not even vibrate. He raised his gloved hand and made signs in the torchlight.

"Something unknown here," he motioned. "Stay back."

They spread out, trying to measure the size of the whirling patch of particles. Several yards ahead, Wilkus, his back to them, was moving steadily forward, his dynamometer swinging in the light of his torch.

No one would ever know whether he had missed Crayley's signal or had ignored it: for suddenly, with shocking abruptness, a blinding purple light flared out in the darkness above him and to his right, and seemed to reach out and touch him. With a terrible wrenching, he doubled up, hands pawing at his stomach. His torch and staff fell to the ground.

For an instant the light hovered above him, pulsing with a greedy brilliance. Then it dimmed and whipped away into the darkness. Wilkus collapsed limply, like a deflating balloon.

When Crayley picked up the stricken youth he seemed to be holding a nearly empty suit. The light of his torch on Wilkus's helmet revealed two eyes that shone with the light of idiocy in a formless, boneless face.

Crayley clicked his torch off and stood for an instant in nearly total darkness, holding the awful burden. The others were coming toward him, swinging their lights in wide arcs.

Helen was the first to reach him. "What happened?" she gestured.

Crayley's helmet turned slowly in negation. He snapped on his torch again and focused it on Wilkus's helmet. Helen cried out involuntarily. The face of the stricken man was chillingly expressionless, the features like wax. But the twitching of his mouth showed he was still alive. By now the others had come up and clustered about the tall scientist and his limp burden. He motioned, "We've got to go back. Wilkus is seriously injured."

Parkerson stepped to Crayley's side and took part of his friend's weight upon his shoulders, although it was so negligible that Crayley could easily have borne it alone. Seaton picked up Wilkus's torch and staff, and with leaden hearts the group began retracing its steps.

Imbued with abnormal caution, they walked slowly, swinging their staffs in wide arcs before them, but they did not encounter any more shock patches until the vast, gleaming bulk of the spaceship loomed in reassuring relief against the sky. Then Helen's dynamometer recorded one about five hundred feet from the stern of the ship, and the party made a cautious circle about it.

A moment later they were ascending a metal ladder over the curving surface of cobalt glass. The little group crawled in beneath enormous hatches, down another short ladder inside, and along a narrow corridor that blazed with cold-light lamps. Then Helen threw a switch at the end of the passage and the hatches fell into place with a sharp clang. Air hissed in; another hatch opened before them.

They emerged into the ship's combined control room and bunkhouse. Crayley gently eased Wilkus down on one of the bunks and then sat down, fumbling with the screws of his helmet. Helen and the others also slumped down on their bunks, still wordless in the cold light of the room.

Crayley got his helmet off first and then shucked off his spacesuit, depositing it in inside-out disarray on one of the benches. As the others struggled out of their suits, he turned and began unscrewing Wilkus's helmet. His thoughts were under grim self-control; he half expected what he would find and was stoically prepared for it.

Not so the others. As Crayley stripped the spacesuit from the injured man, the other men took one shocked look and turned away. Helen saw the shriveled body with the drooling, idiot face moving, jerking about on the bench; for fully five seconds she stared without a sound, lips slack. Then she crumpled.

When she opened her eyes again she was lying on her bunk, concealed behind the automatic privacy screen that provided the only seclusion she had on the vessel. Parkerson was standing beside her. For a moment she could not recall where she was nor what had happened; then, with a little cry, memory returned and she swung her feet out and tried to stand up.

Parkerson sat on the edge of the berth and took her small hand in his, restraining her lightly.

"Frightened?" he asked.

She shook her head. "What happened to Wilkus?"

Parkerson avoided her gaze.

"Tell me," she insisted.

"He died."

Some of the strain went out of Helen's face; she moistened her dry lips with her tongue.

"I'm going to Gibbs," she said, struggling to her feet. "Where is he now?"

"In the laboratory," said Parkerson.

He stood regarding her for a moment with a troubled expression, still holding her hand. Helen looked in his eyes. "What's—what is it, Parky?"

"I—nothing…"

"Wilkus was your friend…"

Parkerson made an impatient gesture. "He was more than that. We grew up together. But that's not it. Forgive me, Helen; I'm upset. It's Gibbs…"

"Gibbs?"

"Yes. You're married to him. You know him better than any of us. I wonder if it ever occurs to you how he looks to other people." Parkerson looked away from her. "He's not human," he said in a strained voice. "He's a damned machine. Did you see his face when he took off Wilkus's suit? You'd think he was taking a clock apart!"

Helen touched his arm. "You know you're wrong, Parky. It's the situation we're in that's getting you. Gibbs Crayley wouldn't be what he is if he didn't have that kind of iron control. He's in charge, Parky. Wilkus and Grayson were out there on his orders. In spite of the fact that they were careless, both of them, Gibbs feels responsible. He always will; you know that. You've lost a dear friend; but at least you didn't acquire that kind of a burden at the same time." She squeezed his shoulder gently. "Think it over."

Parkerson managed a small smile. "You're right, of course. I guess— I guess I blew my top. Thanks, Helen."

Helen found her husband sitting motionless beside the covered body of Ralph Wilkus. He looked up and scowled when she entered the tiny laboratory and shut the sliding door behind her.

"Parkerson told me," she said, looking down at the narrow ledge where the dead man lay.

Crayley said nothing for a moment. He was grateful for the assurance of her hand seeking his and tightening in sympathy.

At last he said, "He died before I could etherize him."

"What did you find, darling?"

Crayley's lips tightened. "Something…incredible." He turned to the ledge and removed the sheet. "Let me show you."

Helen turned pale. Wilkus's body was flaccid and blue. It looked as though it had been poured on the ledge. The girl bit at her lower lip and dug her nails into her palms in her effort to maintain self-control.

"He should have died out there," said the calm man beside her. "His vitality must have been tremendous."

Helen said, "It's incredible, Gibbs."

Crayley looked down at the body before him. "Look, I'll show you something."

He put on his rubber gloves and raised the limp, bluish hand of the dead man. With the other he turned up a Bunsen burner standing on the table until the flame was blue-hot.

"Watch."

He sprayed the intense flame of the burner on the corpse's hand as far as the wrist. The flame flared, shot out fiery jets; its color turned greenish, then purple, then blue again, as Crayley moved the torch here and there over the lifeless member.

"I have dipped that arm in hydrochloric acid, dilute solution," he said. His tone was clinical, impersonal.

Helen's eyes widened as she grasped a little of what this meant. Crayley turned to the table again and picked up a thin glass slide. He held it before the flame-sheathed flesh.

"What color do you see through that glass, Helen?"

"Yellow," she whispered, awe-struck.

"Only the faintest tinge of orange in the flame," he said. "And when you view it through green glass it looks yellow, not green as it should."

Helen drew in a long breath. "Then there's no calcium at all. No calcium—even in the cells of his flesh! What—?"

Crayley shrugged. "I don't know. All I know is that when calcium compounds are moistened with hydrochloric acid, they turn the blue flame deep orange. Strontium also turns it orange-red, often concealing the characteristic calcium glow—but strontium shows yellow under green glass. The faintly orange tinge was undoubtedly imparted by strontium. Calcium would show finch-green under green glass."

He turned down the flame of the torch. "I used spectroscopic tests to make sure," he said. "The characteristic lines of calcium—orange and green and faint indigo—were wholly absent. Helen, something has extracted all the calcium from Wilkus's body!"

"But could a man live if—"

"A little while, apparently," said Crayley, anticipating his wife's thought. "I would have said no, but we can't dispute the evidence. The instantaneous withdrawal of calcium from his body must have left behind the neural patterns, temporarily at least. Motor and sensory nerves functioned, although the brain failed completely."

"But what could have caused it?" asked Helen.

"Only one thing. Radiation. Invisible-spectrum radiation, more intense than anything we have ever known on Earth. A terrific bombardment by ultraviolet. So-called black-sheep rays, perhaps, which would be deadly to all life on Earth."

He turned off the Bunsen burner. "Why, even the comparatively harmless members of the ultraviolet family will drain calcium from protoplasm. You know—single cells, amoebae, slipper animalcules, things like that, exposed to ultraviolet and whirled in a centrifuge become viscous blobs in a few seconds—blobs with a hardened core. The radiation drains the calcium from the outer surface of the cell and deposits it about the nucleus. Such radiation as I have suggested would do that to all the cells of the human body, drain off the external lime and—"

Crayley shivered for the first time. "It's pretty horrible, dear. Horrible. And yet there's something wonderful here, too. This looks like a directed, a purposeful, effect. Outside there in the darkness there may be living—perhaps intelligent—beings. Mercury is not a lifeless planet, as we thought!"

Helen shook her head in bewilderment. "But ultraviolet does not penetrate metal, Gibbs."

"You are forgetting that difolchrome is a silver alloy, Helen. Ultraviolet could penetrate our difolchrome suits if the radiation is sufficiently intense. And it must have been unimaginably intense to do what it did to Wilkus."

"You think it is a life form?" breathed Helen. "Why? Did you see anything?"

"Just that flash of purple light. And we both saw the moving sands. Something was resting on the sand, perhaps, and arose as we approached."

"You don't think the form was composed of invisible light itself?"

Crayley shook his head. "I hardly think so. I think it used the rays as a weapon. Something *tangible* moved out there."

He covered Wilkus's body again, and then slipped off his gloves. His fingers were shaking a little.

Helen said, "Are you going out again, Gibbs?"

Crayley nodded slowly. "I shall take the infrared stroboscopic camera with me, too," he said.

"Stroboscopic?—"

"Suppose the shapes are moving incredibly fast. Maybe that is why we couldn't see them with our own eyes. The stroboscopic camera can take dozens of swift images at intervals of ten-millionths of a second. The infrared plates will take care of the darkness, and the strobe will catch movements too swift for the eye to catch."

"But why do you think the objects are moving so fast, Gibbs?"

"They are invisible, or nearly so. That means either that they are composed of some alien form of energy which emits light waves too long or short for visual perception—or else that they are moving so fast that they can be seen only as faint blurs in bright light, and in darkness not at all."

The two started to walk from the laboratory. Helen took her husband's hand.

"It will be a terrible risk, Gibbs," she said quietly.

He looked down at her with a faint smile on his lips but said nothing.

The next two hours were to confirm Helen's fears more grimly than she had anticipated, but a perverse fate denied Crayley the privilege of sharing that risk in person. On the way up to the main observation chamber, the leader of the First Mercury Exploring Expedition wrenched a tendon in his right ankle atrociously on a ladder rung.

Parkerson, Seaton, and Wilson stood white-faced, listening to him curse and rave. For the first time during the trip, Crayley surrendered to his emotions with an explosive vehemence which did not even respect the presence of his wife. The ankle wrench had thwarted him at a vital point.

Helen suddenly found herself half smiling, catching Parkerson's shocked gaze. Slowly a half grin spread across his face, too, and she knew his thought: *Well, what do you know! The skipper's human, after all!*

The other men immediately volunteered to serve as proxies, and Crayley, after he had calmed down, selected Seaton and Wilson. Helen found herself wondering if the men would have volunteered so readily had she not been present in the passageway. Meeting Parkerson's half-disappointed gaze after the other two had been chosen, she suddenly realized that there was no doubt about it at all. A woman's presence did act as a catalyst, making lonely men more willing to endure hardship and heightening the intensity of their subconscious drives.

While the two men climbed into their spacesuits again, Parkerson went to get the stroboscopic camera from its storage compartment. It was a compact device, a small metallic cone about the size of an oxygen tank on top of a stroboscopic focusing panel and a curved, flexible carrier. Parkerson handed it to young Seaton, and then stood beside Crayley and Helen while the two men climbed awkwardly up the ladder to the airtight hatch above.

Crayley took a step, and a spasm of pain convulsed his features. Helen tried to restrain him, but with a muffled grunt he pulled free of her grasp and limped across the chamber to seat himself in a swivel chair before the control panel of the ship. For a moment he swayed in the chair, while the pain receded.

Then he threw a switch on the panel, and immediately a small opening appeared in the center of the wall above it. Swiftly the hole widened as the cobalt glass withdrew in overlapping crescents from an observation window of miraculously transparent glass.

Through the exposed window the three in the spaceship stared out into the black Mercurian night. Suddenly one torch flared out, then another, and into the cone of light thrown by the first the cumbersomely clad figure of Allan Wilson moved. Slowly, slowly he walked, with testing staff extended and his own torch focused on the soil before him.

Suddenly, for an instant, a purple light shone blinding clear above the plodding figure. Then it vanished, and as it did, Wilson seemed to stagger. For a full ten seconds the torches of both explorers continued to sweep across the terrain, but all at once it seemed as if Wilson was moving much too rapidly. Before any of the three could say a word, they saw the man pivot about, his legs kicking free of the surface, and abruptly disappear upward. With him went his torch, its beams dancing fantastically on objects far away.

Seaton's torch beam wavered, as if he had been shocked into indecision. It turned out later, however, that he had intrepidly set up the stroboscopic camera and was trying to take some pictures of the invisible horror that had captured his crewmate.

Inside the ship, Crayley manipulated a rheostat near the center of the panel, and instantly the plain was flooded with a blue-white light from an immense arc lamp set in the spaceship's entry hatch. In the light, the three in the ship saw a sight that none of them ever would forget. High above the rust-red plain the body of Wilson was dancing and bobbing about, arms thrown wide. He seemed spread-eagled against a field of star-flecked blackness—impaled upon empty air. Below the suspended man a vague, grayish blur seemed to intercept the light and dim the plain beyond.

Crayley turned to the other two, his fists clenched. "He's dead, I think," he said. "He couldn't live—"

But then Helen gave a low scream and pointed out the window. The suspended figure had been released and was falling leaf-like to the ground. It struck and bounced, then rolled over and over, careening along the plain until it collided with a boulder, when it disappeared in a burst of flame.

Seaton had turned and was racing headlong back to the ship. In one hand he held his torch, while his dynamometer staff, momentarily forgotten, jogged at his shoulder like a sheathed wagon. In the other hand he held the camera in a convulsive grip. Soon he disappeared into the ship's shadow.

Crayley swung about, shut off the arc-light control switch, and said in a coldly calm voice, "Seaton made it. Better help him in and get the camera, Fred."

Parkerson nodded and went up the ladder to the hatch, which soon opened, revealing a sagging Seaton still hanging on to the camera. Parkerson gently wrested it from his grasp, clicked open the wafer-thin steel cover, and thrust his hand deep into the protecting tube. The cold of space seemed to gnaw at his fingers as he grasped the little camera and drew it forth. He tossed it to Crayley and then helped Seaton down the ladder and unscrewed his helmet.

As soon as it was off, Seaton gasped, "God, God!... It went for me... I could almost feel it...and Wilson ran to me...tried to throw his light at it...to attract it...it—it *took* him!..."

Parkerson murmured, "I know, I know," helplessly, mechanically, as he unloosened the fastenings on the difolchrome suit. Wilson and Seaton had been the kind of buddies Parkerson and Wilkus were. "But Bill— you ran the camera, didn't you? You exposed some of the film? Maybe we can trap these—"

Seaton nodded wordlessly, then slumped into one of the bunks, his head in his hands.

Crayley broke open the camera and let fall from its interior a thin sheaf of automatically developed photographic plates. He handed these to Helen, whose fingers had not been chilled by the unbelievable cold of the camera.

With wordless apprehension, Helen lifted the topmost plate and turned it slowly about under one of the control-room lights.

The plate contained a clear image. Helen handed it to her husband, scarcely understanding what she saw. But Crayley took one glance and said:

"It's life, all right!"

With that, both Parkerson and Seaton rushed to stare over Crayley's shoulder. For a moment all that could be heard was the swift breathing of the four explorers.

Then Crayley spoke again. "Life, Helen—a sentient form, perhaps not intelligent, but certainly sentient. Seaton, did you *feel* anything—out there?"

Seaton said, "Feel?… Nothing… Nothing except…well, it was like a continuous electric shock, growing stronger and stronger… Horrible!…"

Crayley studied the picture more closely. By comparing it with the metallic pebbles on the ground, he concluded that the shape was very large, perhaps four times as tall as a man, and proportionately huge in its other dimensions.

It was cone-shaped, mathematically clean in line and yet disturbingly vital. From its broad base a single long rod descended to the ground, and four smaller rods projected sideways from its pointed summit. Where the base of the rod rested on the soil there were many little flares, as though the shape were standing on a surface which constantly reacted to it with electrical coruscations.

Crayley said quietly, "The second plate, Helen."

Helen looked at it, gasped. "Three of them."

Crayley seized the plate and studied it. "Three—and see how they are grouped!"

"Five on this one," said Helen, extending the third plate.

Crayley swiftly went through the rest of the plates without another word. When he had finished examining the twelfth and last, he looked up slowly, his lips set in a tight line.

"The ship is in danger," he said.

Parkerson stared. "What do you mean, Gibbs?"

"Simply this. These cones are sentient entities. I think they are energy shapes, moving fields of force, endowed with intelligence and purpose. My guess is that they are connected in some way with the electromagnetic fields, the shock patches."

He stood up, wincing as the wrenched tendon reminded him of its presence. "I think these cones generate ultraviolet and nourish themselves on the electromagnetic resources of the shock patches. Remember that protoplasm itself is an electrical phenomenon, shaped by energy and radiation. But protoplasm is the product of an environment only lightly charged with solar energies. Mercury is different."

He handed the pictures to Parkerson. "Note this series, Fred. I think they prove that these cones are planning to attack. They seem to be forming some kind of a wedge-shaped formation. There are at least fifteen cones in the last shot—*and all of them are pointing toward this ship!*"

Crayley pivoted and stared out through the view port. Below was blackness, save for the faintest glimmerings of light where the tenuous Venus rays glittered on tiny pebble points. But the explorer knew that strange shapes of power were there, though he could not see them. And he also suspected that the cones were assembling on the immense shock patch which lay less than five hundred feet from the stern of the ship.

Time for action, Crayley thought regretfully. The odds were too great—this time. He sat again in his control seat, and turned to activate the starting motors of the great vessel.

Before he could do so, a violent glare pierced through the ship. A roar drowned out all other sound. A shaking detonation vibrated every object in the control room. The floor seemed to rise up, suddenly and horribly. Then came the familiar crushing weight of acceleration, and Crayley blacked out momentarily, despite the fact that he was cupped in the cushions of the control chair.

He regained consciousness by a feat of buried will, coming up hand over hand out of the mists of blackout. There was an ominous silence in the ship, punctured by eerie creaks and cracklings from the tortured cobalt-glass plates. Crayley glanced then at the vision port. The haunted plain, the distant, twisted hills of Mercury were gone, and in their place was black space and wheeling stars.

Instantly his trained eyes flicked over the dials and gauges of the control panel. The great atomic motors were still. The only operating machinery was the auxiliary plant—light, heat, atmosphere. A red light glowed above one gauge, indicating the firing of two of the chemical jets which were used to give nonradioactive thrust at takeoff.

Crayley's quick mind assimilated and computed the evidence. The strange cones of the plain unquestionably had loosed a blast of energy which had fired the chemical jets and had sent the ship screaming upwards from the face of the planet. An occurrence so unlikely as to seem providential—except that Crayley knew that statistically it lay high in the realm of probability.

His fingers played the switches on the panel with a controlled frenzy. The silence ended with a dull thunder from the atom motors, and the ship steadied as they took hold. Crayley let out a noisy sigh of relief: The atomic fuels were immune even to the fantastic temperatures of the cone's ultraviolet radiation. Artificial gravity and running lights came on, and at last the great cobalt-glass ship was under full control.

Only then did Crayley permit himself to look around.

Parkerson was huddled in a broken heap by the after bulkhead. Next to him lay Seaton, his head turning slowly, his eyelids fluttering. And—

"Helen!"

He limped to her, unconscious of his own wrenching pain; touched her body swiftly, deftly, in a frantic mixture of caresses and skillful probing for injuries. She moaned.

"Are you all right? Helen! Helen…"

She opened her eyes, moaned again, and then gave him the tiniest of smiles. "Wh-what…"

He helped her up. She was badly shaken but relatively unhurt. She had apparently hurtled back and struck Parkerson, and his body had cushioned the impact when they struck the bulkhead.

Crayley gently lowered Helen onto one of the benches and turned to Parkerson. He was unconscious, breathing painfully. A trickle of blood oozed from the corner of his mouth.

"Ribs broken," said Crayley tersely. "Possible puncture. See to Seaton if you can, darling. I'll take care of Fred."

An hour later they were droning through the dark, building up acceleration for the long loop back to Earth. Seaton, his arm in a sling, crouched over the computer, checking their flight line. Helen sat by Parkerson's bunk, watching the flow of plasma from a plastic container into his veins. The automatic privacy screen was partly drawn, concealing the front of the control room from Parkerson's view.

"Home…" Parkerson said weakly. "It's going to be good, Helen."

She nodded. "Try not to talk, Parky."

Ignoring her, Parkerson said, "Wilkus, Wilson, Grayson. Scottie, too. All dead. For what? Bloody unnecessary business. What has anyone gained because they're dead?" Tears appeared under his lids. He shook them away angrily. "Sorry, Helen. But it's such a waste."

With a strange, tight smile, Helen rose and raised the automatic screen. "Look," she said softly.

Parkerson slowly turned his head, following her gaze. Crayley was there in the control chair. His shoulders were squared, his hands quiet on the ledge of the panel before him, his face lifted to the spangled immensities of space. He did not move.

She came back and sat down, her eyes first on the plasma bottle and then on the injured man. "Parky," she whispered, "you wondered once whether he was human. Look at him now. We were driven off. They killed our men and hurt our ship. We were defeated. We cut and ran." She smiled wryly. "But—look at him, Parky. He's an explorer. He's the new frontiersman, in an age which knows the greatest frontier of all."

She pushed back her hair with a tired motion. "Maybe he isn't human. Maybe he's just humanity. Look at him, Parky. In spite of death and in spite of danger, in spite of life forms which have all the advantage of their own mystery—he'll be back. Don't you see it?"

Parkerson gazed at the still, strong figure and then at the woman.

"He'll be back," he whispered. "Yes—that's it." And as the full realization of what Helen Crayley had been saying flooded him, he said, "*We'll* be back!"

THE SKY TRAP

Lawton enjoyed a good fight. He stood happily trading blows with Slashaway Tommy, his lean-fleshed torso gleaming with sweat. He preferred to work the pugnacity out of himself slowly, to savor it as it ebbed.

"Better luck next time, Slashaway," he said, and unlimbered a left hook that thudded against his opponent's jaw with such violence that the big, hairy ape crumpled to the resin and rolled over on his back.

Lawton brushed a lock of rust-colored hair back from his brow and stared down at the limp figure lying on the descending stratoship's slightly tilted athletic deck.

"Good work, Slashaway," he said. "You're primitive and beetle-browed, but you've got what it takes."

Lawton flattered himself that he was the opposite of primitive. High in the sky he had predicted the weather for eight days running, with far more accuracy than he could have put into a punch.

They'd flash his report all over Earth in a couple of minutes now. From New York to London to Singapore and back. In half an hour he'd be donning street clothes and stepping out feeling darned good.

He had fulfilled his weekly obligation to society by manipulating meteorological instruments for forty-five minutes, high in the warm, upper stratosphere and worked off his pugnacity by knocking down a professional gym slugger. He would have a full, glorious week now to work off all his other drives.

The stratoship's commander, Captain Forrester, had come up, and was staring at him reproachfully. "Dave, I don't hold with the reforming Johnnies who want to re-make human nature from the ground up. But you've got to admit our generation knows how to keep things humming with a minimum of stress. We don't have world wars now because we work off our pugnacity by sailing into gym sluggers eight or ten times a week. And since our romantic emotions can be taken care of by tactile television we're not at the mercy of every brainless bit of fluff's calculated ankle appeal."

Lawton turned, and regarded him quizzically. "Don't you suppose I realize that? You'd think I just blew in from Mars."

"All right. We have the outlets, the safety valves. They are supposed to keep us civilized. But you don't derive any benefit from them."

"The heck I don't. I exchange blows with Slashaway every time I board the Perseus. And as for women—well, there's just one woman in the world for me, and I wouldn't exchange her for all the Turkish images in the tactile broadcasts from Stamboul."

"Yes, I know. But you work off your primitive emotions with too much gusto. Even a cast-iron gym slugger can bruise. That last blow was—brutal. Just because Slashaway gets thumped and thudded all over by the medical staff twice a week doesn't mean he can take—"

The stratoship lurched suddenly. The deck heaved up under Lawton's feet, hurling him against Captain Forrester and spinning both men around so that they seemed to be waltzing together across the ship. The still limp gym slugger slid downward, colliding with a corrugated metal bulkhead and sloshing back and forth like a wet mackerel.

A full minute passed before Lawton could put a stop to that. Even while careening he had been alive to Slashaway's peril, and had tried to leap to his aid. But the ship's steadily increasing gyrations had hurled him away from the skipper and against a massive vaulting horse, barking the flesh from his shins and spilling him with violence onto the deck.

He crawled now toward the prone gym slugger on his hands and knees, his temples thudding. The gyrations ceased an instant before he reached Slashaway's side. With an effort he lifted the big man up, propped him against the bulkhead and shook him until his teeth rattled. "Slashaway," he muttered. "Slashaway, old fellow."

Slashaway opened blurred eyes, "Phew!" he muttered. "You sure socked me hard, sir."

"You went out like a light," explained Lawton gently. "A minute before the ship lurched."

"The ship *lurched*, sir?"

"Something's very wrong, Slashaway. The ship isn't moving. There are no vibrations and—Slashaway, are you hurt? Your skull thumped against that bulkhead so hard I was afraid—"

"Naw, I'm okay. Whatd'ya mean, the ship ain't moving? How could it stop?"

Lawton said. "I don't know, Slashaway." Helping the gym slugger to his feet he stared apprehensively about him. Captain Forrester was kneeling on the resin testing his hocks for sprains with splayed fingers, his features twitching.

"Hurt badly, sir?"

The Commander shook his head. "I don't think so. Dave, we are twenty thousand feet up, so how in hell could we be stationary in space?"

"It's all yours, skipper."

"I must say you're helpful."

Forrester got painfully to his feet and limped toward the athletic compartment's single quartz port—a small circle of radiance on a level with his eyes. As the port sloped downward at an angle of nearly sixty degrees all he could see was a diffuse glimmer until he wedged his brow in the observation visor and stared downward.

Lawton heard him suck in his breath sharply. "Well, sir?"

"There are thin cirrus clouds directly beneath us. They're not moving."

Lawton gasped, the sense of being in an impossible situation swelling to nightmare proportions within him. What could have happened?

* * * *

Directly behind him, close to a bulkhead chronometer, which was clicking out the seconds with unabashed regularity, was a misty blue visiplate that merely had to be switched on to bring the pilots into view.

The Commander hobbled toward it, and manipulated a rheostat. The two pilots appeared side by side on the screen, sitting amidst a spidery network of dully gleaming pipe lines and nichrome humidification units. They had unbuttoned their high-altitude coats and their stratosphere helmets were resting on their knees. The Jablochoff candle light which flooded the pilot room accentuated the haggardness of their features, which were a sickly cadaverous hue.

The captain spoke directly into the visiplate. "What's wrong with the ship?" he demanded. "Why aren't we descending? Dawson, you do the talking!"

One of the pilots leaned tensely forward, his shoulders jerking. "We don't know, sir. The rotaries went dead when the ship started gyrating. We can't work the emergency torps and the temperature is rising."

"But—it defies all logic," Forrester muttered. "How could a metal ship weighing tons be suspended in the air like a balloon? It is stationary, but it is not buoyant. We seem in all respects to be *frozen in*."

"The explanation may be simpler than you dream," Lawton said. "When we've found the key."

The Captain swung toward him. "Could *you* find the key, Dave?"

"I should like to try. It may be hidden somewhere on the ship, and then again, it may not be. But I should like to go over the ship with a fine-tooth comb, and then I should like to go over *outside*, thoroughly. Suppose you make me an emergency mate and give me a carte blanche, sir."

Lawton got his carte blanche. For two hours he did nothing spectacular, but he went over every inch of the ship. He also lined up the crew and pumped them. The men were as completely in the dark as the pilots and the now completely recovered Slashaway, who was following Lawton about like a doting seal.

"You're a right guy, sir. Another two or three cracks and my noggin would've split wide open."

"But not like an eggshell, Slashaway. Pig iron develops fissures under terrific pounding but your cranium seems to be more like tempered steel. Slashaway, you won't understand this, but I've got to talk to somebody and the Captain is too busy to listen.

"I went over the entire ship because I thought there might be a hidden source of buoyancy somewhere. It would take a lot of air bubbles to turn this ship into a balloon, but there are large vacuum chambers under the multiple series condensers in the engine room which conceivably could have sucked in a helium leakage from the carbon pile valves. And there are bulkhead porosities which could have clogged."

"Yeah," muttered Slashaway, scratching his head. "I see what you mean, sir."

"It was no soap. There's nothing *inside* the ship that could possibly keep us up. Therefore there must be something outside that isn't air. We know there *is* air outside. We've stuck our heads out and sniffed it. And we've found out a curious thing.

"Along with the oxygen there is water vapor, but it isn't H_2O. It's HO. A molecular arrangement like that occurs in the upper Solar atmosphere, but nowhere on Earth. And there's a thin sprinkling of hydrocarbon molecules out there too. Hydrocarbon appears ordinarily as methane gas, but out there it rings up as CH. Methane is CH_4. And there are also scandium oxide molecules making unfamiliar faces at us. And oxide of boron—with an equational limp."

"Gee," muttered Slashaway. "We're up against it, eh?"

Lawton was squatting on his hams beside an emergency 'chute opening on the deck of the Penguin's weather observatory. He was letting down a spliced beryllium plumb line, his gaze riveted on the slowly turning horizontal drum of a windlass which contained more than two hundred feet of gleaming metal cordage.

Suddenly as he stared the drum stopped revolving. Lawton stiffened, a startled expression coming into his face. He had been playing a hunch that had seemed as insane, rationally considered, as his wild idea about the bulkhead porosities. For a moment he was stunned, unable to believe that he had struck pay dirt. The winch indicator stood at one hundred and three feet, giving him a rich, fruity yield of startlement.

One hundred feet below him the plummet rested on something solid that sustained it in space. Scarcely breathing, Lawton leaned over the windlass and stared downward. There was nothing visible between the ship and the fleecy clouds far below except a tiny black dot resting on vacancy and a thin beryllium plumb line ascending like an interrogation point from the dot to the 'chute opening.

"You see something down there?" Slashaway asked.

Lawton moved back from the windlass, his brain whirling. "Slashaway there's a solid surface directly beneath us, but it's completely invisible."

"You mean it's like a frozen cloud, sir?"

"No, Slashaway. It doesn't shimmer, or deflect light. Congealed water vapor would sink instantly to earth."

"You think it's all around us, sir?"

Lawton stared at Slashaway aghast. In his crude fumblings the gym slugger had ripped a hidden fear right out of his subconsciousness into the light.

"I don't know, Slashaway," he muttered. "I'll get at that next."

* * * *

A half hour later Lawton sat beside the captain's desk in the control room, his face drained of all color. He kept his gaze averted as he talked. A man who succeeds too well with an unpleasant task may develop a subconscious sense of guilt.

"Sir, we're suspended inside a hollow sphere which resembles a huge, floating soap bubble. Before we ripped through it it must have had a plastic surface. But now the tear has apparently healed over, and the shell all around us is as resistant as steel. We're completely bottled up, sir. I shot rocket leads in all directions to make certain."

The expression on Forrester's face sold mere amazement down the river. He could not have looked more startled if the nearer planets had yielded their secrets chillingly, and a super-race had appeared suddenly on Earth.

"Good God, Dave. Do you suppose something has happened to space?"

Lawton raised his eyes with a shudder. "Not necessarily, sir. Something has happened to *us*. We're floating through the sky in a huge, invisible bubble of some sort, but we don't know whether it has anything to do with space. It may be a meteorological phenomenon."

"You say we're floating?"

"We're floating slowly westward. The clouds beneath us have been receding for fifteen or twenty minutes now."

"Phew!" muttered Forrester. "That means we've got to—"

He broke off abruptly. The Perseus' radio operator was standing in the doorway, distress and indecision in his gaze. "Our reception is extremely sporadic, sir," he announced. "We can pick up a few of the stronger broadcasts, but our emergency signals haven't been answered."

"Keep trying," Forrester ordered.

"Aye, aye, sir."

The captain turned to Lawton. "Suppose we call it a bubble. Why are we suspended like this, immovably? Your rocket leads shot up, and the plumb line dropped one hundred feet. Why should the ship itself remain stationary?"

Lawton said: "The bubble must possess sufficient internal equilibrium to keep a big, heavy body suspended at its core. In other words, we must be suspended at the hub of converging energy lines."

"You mean we're surrounded by an electromagnetic field?"

Lawton frowned. "Not necessarily, sir. I'm simply pointing out that there must be an energy tug of *some* sort involved. Otherwise the ship would be resting on the inner surface of the bubble."

Forrester nodded grimly. "We should be thankful, I suppose, that we can move about inside the ship. Dave, do you think a man could descend to the inner surface?"

"I've no doubt that a man could, sir. Shall I let myself down?"

"Absolutely not. Damn it, Dave, I need your energies inside the ship. I could wish for a less impulsive first officer, but a man in my predicament can't be choosy."

"Then what *are* your orders, sir?"

"Orders? Do I have to order you to think? Is working something out for yourself such a strain? We're drifting straight toward the Atlantic Ocean. What do you propose to do about that?"

"I expect I'll have to do my best, sir."

Lawton's "best" conflicted dynamically with the captain's orders. Ten minutes later he was descending, hand over hand, on a swaying emergency ladder.

"Tough-fibered Davie goes down to look around," he grumbled.

He was conscious that he was flirting with danger. The air outside was breathable, but would the diffuse, unorthodox gases injure his lungs? He didn't know, couldn't be sure. But he had to admit that he felt all right *so far*. He was seventy feet below the ship and not at all dizzy. When he looked down he could see the purple domed summits of mountains between gaps in the fleecy cloud blanket.

He couldn't see the Atlantic Ocean—yet. He descended the last thirty feet with mounting confidence. At the end of the ladder he braced himself and let go.

He fell about six feet, landing on his rump on a spongy surface that bounced him back and forth. He was vaguely incredulous when he found himself sitting in the sky staring through his spread legs at clouds and mountains.

He took a deep breath. It struck him that the sensation of falling could be present without movement downward through space. He was beginning to experience such a sensation. His stomach twisted and his brain spun.

He was suddenly sorry he had tried this. It was so damnably unnerving he was afraid of losing all emotional control. He stared up, his eyes squinting against the sun. Far above him the gleaming, wedge-shaped bulk of the Perseus loomed colossally, blocking out a fifth of the sky.

Lowering his right hand he ran his fingers over the invisible surface beneath him. The surface felt rubbery, moist.

He got swayingly to his feet and made a perilous attempt to walk through the sky. Beneath his feet the mysterious surface crackled, and little sparks flew up about his legs. Abruptly he sat down again, his face ashen.

From the emergency 'chute opening far above a massive head appeared. "You all right, sir," Slashaway called, his voice vibrant with concern.

"Well, I—"

"You'd better come right up, sir. Captain's orders."

"All right," Lawton shouted. "Let the ladder down another ten feet."

Lawton ascended rapidly, resentment smouldering within him. What right had the skipper to interfere? He had passed the buck, hadn't he?

* * * *

Lawton got another bad jolt the instant he emerged through the 'chute opening. Captain Forrester was leaning against a parachute rack gasping for breath, his face a livid hue.

Slashaway looked equally bad. His jaw muscles were twitching and he was tugging at the collar of his gym suit.

Forrester gasped: "Dave, I tried to move the ship. I didn't know you were outside."

"Good God, you didn't know—"

"The rotaries backfired and used up all the oxygen in the engine room. Worse, there's been a carbonic oxide seepage. The air is contaminated throughout the ship. We'll have to open the ventilation valves immediately. I've been waiting to see if—if you could breathe down there. You're all right, aren't you? The air *is* breathable?"

Lawton's face was dark with fury. "I was an experimental rat in the sky, eh?"

"Look, Dave, we're all in danger. Don't stand there glaring at me. Naturally I waited. I have my crew to think of."

"Well, think of them. Get those valves open before we all have convulsions."

A half hour later charcoal gas was mingling with oxygen outside the ship, and the crew was breathing it in again gratefully. Thinly dispersed, and mixed with oxygen it seemed all right. But Lawton had misgivings. No matter how attenuated a lethal gas is it is never entirely harmless. To make matters worse, they were over the Atlantic Ocean.

Far beneath them was an emerald turbulence, half obscured by eastward moving cloud masses. The bubble was holding, but the morale of the crew was beginning to sag.

Lawton paced the control room. Deep within him unsuspected energies surged. "We'll last until the oxygen is breathed up," he exclaimed. "We'll have four or five days, at most. But we seem to be traveling faster than an ocean liner. With luck, we'll be in Europe before we become carbon dioxide breathers."

"Will that help matters, Dave?" said the captain wearily.

"If we can blast our way out, it will."

The Captain's sagging body jackknifed erect. "Blast our way out? What do you mean, Dave?"

"I've clamped expulsor disks on the cosmic ray absorbers and trained them downward. A thin stream of accidental neutrons directed against the bottom of the bubble may disrupt its energies—wear it thin. It's a long gamble, but worth taking. We're staking nothing, remember?"

Forrester sputtered: "Nothing but our lives! If you blast a hole in the bubble you'll destroy its energy balance. Did that occur to you? Inside a lopsided bubble we may careen dangerously or fall into the sea before we can get the rotaries started."

"I thought of that. The pilots are standing by to start the rotaries the instant we lurch. If we succeed in making a rent in the bubble we'll break out the helicoptic vanes and descend vertically. The rotaries won't backfire again. I've had their burnt-out cylinder heads replaced."

An agitated voice came from the visiplate on the captain's desk: "Tuning in, sir."

Lawton stopped pacing abruptly. He swung about and grasped the desk edge with both hands, his head touching Forrester's as the two men stared down at the horizontal face of petty officer James Caldwell.

Caldwell wasn't more than twenty-two or three, but the screen's opalescence silvered his hair and misted the outlines of his jaw, giving him an aspect of senility.

"Well, young man," Forrester growled. "What is it? What do you want?"

The irritation in the captain's voice seemed to increase Caldwell's agitation. Lawton had to say: "All right, lad, let's have it," before the information which he had seemed bursting to impart could be wrenched out of him.

It came in erratic spurts. "The bubble is all blooming, sir. All around inside there are big yellow and purple growths. It started up above, and—and spread around. First there was just a clouding over of the sky, sir, and then—stalks shot out."

For a moment Lawton felt as though all sanity had been squeezed from his brain. Twice he started to ask a question and thought better of it.

Pumpings were superfluous when he could confirm Caldwell's statement in half a minute for himself. If Caldwell had cracked up—

Caldwell hadn't cracked. When Lawton walked to the quartz port and stared down all the blood drained from his face.

The vegetation was luxuriant, and unearthly. Floating in the sky were serpentine tendrils as thick as a man's wrist, purplish flowers and ropy fungus growths. They twisted and writhed and shot out in all directions, creating a tangle immediately beneath him and curving up toward the ship amidst a welter of seed pods.

He could see the seeds dropping—dropping from pods which reminded him of the darkly horned skate egg sheaths which he had collected in his boyhood from sea beaches at ebb tide.

It was the *unwholesomeness* of the vegetation which chiefly unnerved him. It looked dank, malarial. There were decaying patches on the fungus growths and a miasmal mist was descending from it toward the ship.

The control room was completely still when he turned from the quartz port to meet Forrester's startled gaze.

"Dave, what does it mean?" The question burst explosively from the captain's lips.

"It means—life has appeared and evolved and grown rotten ripe inside the bubble, sir. All in the space of an hour or so."

"But that's—*impossible*."

Lawton shook his head. "It isn't at all, sir. We've had it drummed into us that evolution proceeds at a snailish pace, but what proof have we that it can't mutate with lightning-like rapidity? I've told you there are gases outside we can't even make in a chemical laboratory, molecular arrangements that are alien to earth."

"But plants derive nourishment from the soil," interpolated Forrester.

"I know. But if there are alien gases in the air the surface of the bubble must be reeking with unheard of chemicals. There may be compounds inside the bubble which have so sped up organic processes that a hundred million year cycle of mutations has been telescoped into an hour."

Lawton was pacing the floor again. "It would be simpler to assume that seeds of existing plants became somehow caught up and imprisoned in the bubble. But the plants around us never existed on earth. I'm no botanist, but I know what the Congo has on tap, and the great rain forests of the Amazon."

"Dave, if the growth continues it will fill the bubble. It will choke off all our air."

"Don't you suppose I realize that? We've got to destroy that growth before it destroys us."

* * * *

It was pitiful to watch the crew's morale sag. The miasmal taint of the ominously proliferating vegetation was soon pervading the ship, spreading demoralization everywhere.

It was particularly awful straight down. Above a ropy tangle of livid vines and creepers a kingly stench weed towered, purplish and bloated and weighted down with seed pods.

It seemed sentient, somehow. It was growing so fast that the evil odor which poured from it could be correlated with the increase of tension inside the ship. From that particular plant, minute by slow minute, there surged a continuously mounting offensiveness, like nothing Lawton had ever smelt before.

The bubble had become a blooming horror sailing slowly westward above the storm-tossed Atlantic. And all the chemical agents which Lawton sprayed through the ventilation valves failed to impede the growth or destroy a single seed pod.

It was difficult to kill plant life with chemicals which were not harmful to man. Lawton took dangerous risks, increasing the unwholesomeness of their rapidly dwindling air supply by spraying out a thin diffusion of problematically poisonous acids.

It was no sale. The growths increased by leaps and bounds, as though determined to show their resentment of the measures taken against them by marshalling all their forces in a demoralizing plantkrieg.

Thwarted, desperate, Lawton played his last card. He sent five members of the crew, equipped with blow guns. They returned screaming. Lawton had to fortify himself with a double whiskey soda before he could face the look of reproach in their eyes long enough to get all of the prickles out of them.

From then on pandemonium reigned. Blue funk seized the petty officers while some of the crew ran amuck. One member of the engine watch attacked four of his companions with a wrench; another went into the ship's kitchen and slashed himself with a paring knife. The assistant engineer leapt through a 'chute opening, after avowing that he preferred impalement to suffocation.

He *was* impaled. It was horrible. Looking down Lawton could see his twisted body dangling on a crimson-stippled thornlike growth forty feet in height.

Slashaway was standing at his elbow in that Waterloo moment, his rough-hewn features twitching. "I can't stand it, sir. It's driving me squirrelly."

"I know, Slashaway. There's something worse than marijuana weed down there."

Slashaway swallowed hard. "That poor guy down there did the wise thing."

Lawton husked: "Stamp on that idea, Slashaway—kill it. We're stronger than he was. There isn't an ounce of weakness in us. We've got what it takes."

"A guy can stand just so much."

"Bosh. There's no limit to what a man can stand."

From the visiplate behind them came an urgent voice: "Radio room tuning in, sir."

Lawton swung about. On the flickering screen the foggy outlines of a face appeared and coalesced into sharpness.

The Perseus radio operator was breathless with excitement. "Our reception is improving, sir. European short waves are coming in strong. The static is terrific, but we're getting every station on the continent, and most of the American stations."

Lawton's eyes narrowed to exultant slits. He spat on the deck, a slow tremor shaking him.

"Slashaway, did you hear that? *We've done it.* We've won against hell and high water."

"We done what, sir?"

"The bubble, you ape—it must be wearing thin. Hell's bells, do you have to stand there gaping like a moronic ninepin? I tell you, we've got it licked."

"I can't stand it, sir. I'm going nuts."

"No you're not. You're slugging the thing inside you that wants to quit. Slashaway, I'm going to give the crew a first-class pep talk. There'll be no stampeding while I'm in command here."

He turned to the radio operator. "Tune in the control room. Tell the captain I want every member of the crew lined up on this screen immediately."

The face in the visiplate paled. "I can't do that, sir. Ship's regulations—"

Lawton transfixed the operator with an irate stare. "The captain told you to report directly to me, didn't he?"

"Yes sir, but—"

"If you don't want to be cashiered, *snap into it.*"

"Yes—yessir."

The captain's startled face preceded the duty-muster visiview by a full minute, seeming to project outward from the screen. The veins on his neck were thick blue cords.

"Dave," he croaked. "Are you out of your mind? What good will talking do *now?*"

"Are the men lined up?" Lawton rapped, impatiently.

Forrester nodded. "They're all in the engine room, Dave."

"Good. Block them in."

The captain's face receded, and a scene of tragic horror filled the opalescent visiplate. The men were not standing at attention at all. They were slumping against the Perseus' central charging plant in attitudes of abject despair.

* * * *

Madness burned in the eyes of three or four of them. Others had torn open their shirts, and raked their flesh with their nails. Petty officer Caldwell was standing as straight as a totem pole, clenching and unclenching his hands. The second assistant engineer was sticking out his tongue. His face was deadpan, which made what was obviously a terror reflex look like an idiot's grimace.

Lawton moistened his lips. "Men, listen to me. There is some sort of plant outside that is giving off deliriant fumes. A few of us seem to be immune to it.

"I'm not immune, but I'm fighting it, and all of you boys can fight it too. I want you to fight it to the top of your courage. You can fight *anything* when you know that just around the corner is freedom from a beastliness that deserves to be licked—even if it's only a plant.

"Men, we're blasting our way free. The bubble's wearing thin. Any minute now the plants beneath us may fall with a soggy plop into the Atlantic Ocean.

"I want every man jack aboard this ship to stand at his post and obey orders. Right this minute you look like something the cat dragged in. But most men who cover themselves with glory start off looking even worse than you do."

He smiled wryly.

"I guess that's all. I've never had to make a speech in my life, and I'd hate like hell to start now."

It was petty officer Caldwell who started the chant. He started it, and the men took it up until it was coming from all of them in a full-throated roar.

> *I'm a tough, true-hearted skyman,*
> *Careless and all that, d'ye see?*
> *Never at fate a railer,*
> *What is time or tide to me?*
>
> *All must die when fate shall will it,*
> *I can never die but once,*
> *I'm a tough, true-hearted skyman;*
> *He who fears death is a dunce.*

Lawton squared his shoulders. With a crew like that nothing could stop him! Ah, his energies were surging high. The deliriant weed held no terrors for him now. They were stout-hearted lads and he'd go to hell with them cheerfully, if need be.

It wasn't easy to wait. The next half hour was filled with a steadily mounting tension as Lawton moved like a young tornado about the ship, issuing orders and seeing that each man was at his post.

"Steady, Jimmy. The way to fight a deliriant is to keep your mind on a set task. Keep sweating, lad."

"Harry, that winch needs tightening. We can't afford to miss a trick."

"Yeah, it will come suddenly. We've got to get the rotaries started the instant the bottom drops out."

He was with the captain and Slashaway in the control room when it came. There was a sudden, grinding jolt, and the captain's desk started moving toward the quartz port, carrying Lawton with it.

"Holy Jiminy cricket," exclaimed Slashaway.

The deck tilted sharply; then righted itself. A sudden gush of clear, cold air came through the ventilation valves as the triple rotaries started up with a roar.

Lawton and the captain reached the quartz port simultaneously. Shoulder to shoulder they stood staring down at the storm-tossed Atlantic, electrified by what they saw.

Floating on the waves far beneath them was an undulating mass of vegetation, its surface flecked with glinting foam. As it rose and fell in waning sunlight a tainted seepage spread about it, defiling the clean surface of the sea.

But it wasn't the floating mass which drew a gasp from Forrester, and caused Lawton's scalp to prickle. Crawling slowly across that Sargasso-like island of noxious vegetation was a huge, elongated shape which bore a nauseous resemblance to a mottled garden slug.

Forrester was trembling visibly when he turned from the quartz port. "God, Dave, that would have been the *last straw*. Animal life. Dave, I—I can't realize we're actually out of it."

"We're out, all right," Lawton said, hoarsely. "Just in time, too. Skipper, you'd better issue grog all around. The men will be needing it. I'm taking mine straight. You've accused me of being primitive. Wait till you see me an hour from now."

Dr. Stephen Halday stood in the door of his Appalachian mountain laboratory staring out into the pine-scented dusk, a worried expression on his bland, small-featured face. It had happened again. A portion of his experiment had soared skyward, in a very loose group of highly energized wavicles. He wondered if it wouldn't form a sort of sub-electronic macrocosm high in the stratosphere, altering even the air and dust particles which had spurted up with it, its uncharged atomic particles combining with hydrogen and creating new molecular arrangements.

If such were the case there would be eight of them now. *His* bubbles, floating through the sky. They couldn't possibly harm anything—way up there in the stratosphere. But he felt a little uneasy about it all the same. He'd have to be more careful in the future, he told himself. Much more careful. He didn't want the Controllers to turn back the clock of civilization a century by stopping all atom-smashing experiments.

WOBBLIES ON THE MOON

CHAPTER I

Cry in the Lunar Night

"John, John, wake up!" Vera Dorn screamed, pounding on the door of Carstairs' sleeping turret. "The wobblies have broken loose!"

The Curator of the Interplanetary Botanical Gardens stirred, yawned, turned over and buried his head in the bedclothes. "Ahhhh—" he sighed.

"John, let me in! Open the door! The wobblies—"

Carstairs leapt up in consternation, throwing back the bedclothes so violently that they wrapped themselves around his long legs and sent him sprawling. Shivering, he groaned, rolled over and struggled to a sitting position.

"Take it easy, Vera," he muttered, knuckling sleep from his eyelids. "The blasted things aren't flesh-eaters."

"Oh, but, darling, if we should lose them! Our rarest specimens, walking around loose! Can you blame me for getting excited?"

"No, I suppose not," Carstairs grunted. "Open the door yourself. It isn't locked." The door opened a crack, and the pale face of John Carstairs' attractive, coppery-haired secretary came into view. Wrapping the bedclothes tightly around his rangy bulk, Carstairs arose and crossed to the window. When he pulled up the shade a glint of Earthlight from the Lunar Apennines grazed his pupils, dazzling him. He blinked and stared out at the towering peaks which he had been contemplating with awe for several days now.

Vera was sitting on the edge of the bed when he turned, her hands clasped around her knees.

"It will be a shock to Gleason," she said. "One of them came into my room and climbed out the window. I encountered another in the corridor. When I tried to catch it, it hurled a nettle at me. It's still here, in my shoulder."

She turned and bared a portion of her right shoulder. Half-buried in her flesh was a huge, downy nettle. It was strawberry-colored, and five or six inches in diameter. It brought a shiver to Carstairs' spine.

"We'll get it out," he said. "They are loathsome creatures, but worth their weight in platinum."

"You don't seem very upset about losing them," Vera retorted. "They're probably streaking back to the mountains by now."

Carstairs shrugged. "We're Gleason's guests, aren't we? We're spending the weekend with him. The right kind of host doesn't let his guests down. If I'm any judge of character, he won't rest until he's tracked down some more specimens for us."

Vera Dorn's freckled face crimsoned with indignation. "John Carstairs, you're the most cynical, ungrateful person I've ever known. Gleason is an extremely wealthy man. He doesn't *have* to collect specimens for you."

"He's a good egg," Carstairs grunted. "But vain. Endowing our lunar expeditions and collecting for us puffs him out like a kid's toy balloon. He likes to pose as a scientific big shot. If *I* had a glassite-walled palace on the moon, decked out with seven black plastic bathrooms, I'd forget about science with a capital S. I'd just be myself."

"What makes you think a wealthy man can't be a humble soldier in the army of science?" Vera flared.

"Heck, we're not fighting anything," Carstairs snorted. "Am I a soldier? All I do is collect unhealthy looking plants, and hold down a dull job on Earth. Utterly nightmarish plants, from `glowing Venus to Neptune's chill domain'—to quote from a book of bum poems I once read."

"John, what are you driving at?"

"Well, do our expeditions save human lives? Is our work really important? Vera, I'm just a tired old man killing a dull weekend with an elderly playboy in his pleasure palace on the moon. If he hadn't sent me a space-o-gram telling me he had an extraordinary new specimen, and would I call for it, I'd be killing a duller one on Earth. Oh, heck."

"You got up on the wrong side of the bed, all right," Vera sneered. "Old man, indeed! You're a few hours past twenty-eight, on account of this is your birthday. But you're not so old, and all you need to pep you up is a nice, juicy, murder."

She wrinkled her nose. "You're just disgruntled because you can't help the New York police department crack down on the criminal element. You're as sore as the dickens because you can't neglect your research work and go rushing around like a turkey with its neck stretched out for the chopping block." Carstairs gnawed at his underlip and glared at the attractive university graduate who had wangled a job for herself at the Interplanetary Botanical Gardens solely on her nerve. Bitterly Carstairs recalled that she had walked into his office on a rainy Sunday, pretending to be a research botanist of established reputation. Actually she had merely majored in botany at college, and had the softest eyes.

"You're a botanist eight days out of seven," he flung at her. "But right now I'm fed up. Fed up, you hear?"

"But, John—"

"All right, wobblies are rare, wobblies *are* valuable. And Gleason is a resourceful collector. We didn't even know wobblies existed on Luna until he hoisted three adult specimens out of a mountain crevice, and sent me that space-o-gram. I was elated at first, but it's worn off. I'm bored, peeved, and if we've lost them, I just don't give a Neptunian peso."

Vera Dorn's lips tightened ominously. "Botanical Detective John Carstairs is going to eat crow," she said.

"He's going to apologize to the most gracious host a man ever had for putting those valuable specimens in a fragile glass herbarium. And if you think he'll go out, and collect some more wobblies for you—"

She stiffened in sudden horror. A piercing, long-drawn scream had reverberated across the glassite-walled sleeping turret, congealing her vocal chords, and turning Carstairs' blood to ice. It was followed by a silence so cloying that it seemed to muffle the tick of Carstairs' Greenwich-synchronized wrist watch.

With a startled oath, he snatched an oxygen mask from an overnight bag, clamped it on his face and rushed to the window. Throwing the casement wide, he strode out on the railed observation platform which half-encircled Gleason's towerlike dwelling.

* * * *

Beneath him stretched the foothills of the mightiest mountain range on Luna. Coruscating in the light of brittle stars, they arose precipitously from an ash-strewn plain, and though the smallest of them would have dwarfed a full-fledged mountain on Earth they seemed of pygmy dimensions when his gaze swept upward over the Gargantuan peaks beyond.

A strangled sound came from behind him. He swung about, his lips tightening. Vera was standing just outside the window.

"John," she choked. "That scream came from downstairs. You can't see anything from here. The wobblies wouldn't be visible in this glare."

The scream came again. It was audible now on the platform, a hideous, tormented wailing which seemed to drift up from below.

"It's coming from Gleason's sleeping turret," Carstairs said. "He sleeps with his oxygen mask on and his windows flung wide. I just wanted to make sure."

"Then why are we standing here?" Vera choked. "Oh, he's dying!"

"Get back inside," Carstairs rapped. "You ought to have more sense than to come out here without a mask."

"John, are the wobblies attacking him?"

"It couldn't be the wobblies. They're not carnivorous, and their nettles merely irritate the skin a little. Now get back, before your lungs buckle into folds."

Vera obeyed. She didn't stay in Carstairs' turret, but ran breathlessly through the door, and down a cold-lighted corridor to a spiraling flight of black plastic stairs. Down them she raced, oblivious to the torment in her lungs. Carstairs descended in slower strides, but the length of his legs kept him constantly at her side. With almost simultaneous movements he had thrown off the blankets, pushed the oxygen mask back over his forehead and wrapped a dressing gown around his rangy bulk.

"Take it easy, Vera," he cautioned. "If you drop dead, you'll be sorry later on." On dim walls on both sides of the stairway loomed imaginative paintings. Segrelles' *Mountains of theMoon* and Degrasse's *Seas of Saturn.* The tower was richly furnished, dark and awesome from its observatory roof to the deep cellars underground where Gleason's choicest wines were stored. In one aspect of his personality Gleason was an epicure, almost a sybarite. A scientific Gleason had welcomed the director of the Interplanetary Gardens to the Lunar Apennines, but Carstairs knew that there were other, more riotous Gleasons. There was a Gleason who devoutly admired chorus girls from the Twenty-first Century follies, a Gleason who went on periodic binges, and a Gleason who liked to gamble for high stakes over stacked chips at midnight.

Gleason's sleeping turret was at the end of a long, winding corridor on the third floor of the tower. Vera got to the door a split second ahead of Carstairs. Although it did not seem to be locked, the barrier creaked noisily and resisted her frantic tuggings.

"John, you'd better put your shoulders to it," she whispered hoarsely. "It seems to be stuck. Oh, John, I'm frightened."

Carstairs needed no urging. Bracing himself, he hurled his massive shoulders against the portal. There was a grinding crunch, and something clattered to the floor inside the turret. His face purpling, Carstairs pushed the door vigorously inward.

Vera pressed in after him, so closely that her breath fanned his neck. His shoulders half-blocked her view, but she could see chairs, a dresser and the upper portion of Gleason's bed. She could see Gleason sitting upright in his bed.

Her vision was superior to Carstairs', and wider in scope. She could see obscurely in the dark, and sharply in a dim light. The turret was bathed in a pale, sickly radiance. A cry rasping in her throat, she reeled forward and gripped Carstairs' shoulders with both hands.

CHAPTER II

Flight and Pursuit

In the center of the turret stood three huge wobblies. Their tendrils were weaving about in the gloom, and they had grouped themselves in a semicircle around the rigidly distorted figure of Gleason. Like plant ghosts they hovered above him, their body-roots glowing with a faint, spectral radiance. Unutterably terrifying they seemed, but what drove the blood in torrents from Vera's heart was Gleason's bulging eyes, and gruesomely sardonical grin.

"John, he's dead," she husked, her voice like a whisper from the tomb. A convulsive contraction twisted Carstairs' rough-hewn face. Swiftly he strode to the bed, ignoring the nettles which the tallest of the three wobblies instantly flung at him. One grazed his right cheek, another embedded itself in his shoulder.

He winced, and clawed at his flesh with his fingers, as though the downy "strawberry" had been dipped in acid, and was corroding his skin. Actually the gesture was instinctive, and on a par with nail-gnawing in a crisis.

Although Carstairs was no stranger to post-mortem appearances, his examination of the still figure was brief. Nothing can be done for a corpse, and Gleason had unmistakably stopped breathing. The risus sardonicus which distorted his features seemed to relax a little as Carstairs drew the sheets up over him. Shuddering, he turned from the bed. Vera was staring at the wobblies with terror stenciled on every lineament of her twitching face.

"John, did these ghastly things attack him?" she husked.

Carstairs shook his head. "How many times must I tell you that wobblies are not flesh-eaters," he said chokily. "They hurl nettles to protect themselves from their natural enemies, but otherwise they're harmless. When Gleason observed them on the mountains he took copious notes. They're freakish, but harmless perambulating plants."

The appearance and behavior of the wobblies seemed to belie Carstairs' words. They now hurled themselves across the dead man's bed, plucking with quivering tendrils at the sheets which covered him. Hideously manlike they seemed, with their gray and eroded-looking body-roots writhing against the sheets.

Tall they were, at least seven feet in height, and proportionately broad of shoulder. The fact that they had three tendrils on each side of their torsolike bodies in lieu of arms, and that they moved, when erect, on stumpy legs which caused them to wobble grotesquely did not detract from the illusion of humanness which their appearance conveyed.

Staggeringly weird they seemed when they used their nettles, for the flabby sacks in which the prickly "strawberries" grew resembled the belly pouches of kangaroos, and the nettles had to be plucked out, and hurled. Jocularly, Gleason had called Carstairs' attention to the fact that a wobbly with its tendril arm extended, and its body twisted sharply in the act of hurling a nettle looked not unlike a pitcher in the old Earth game called baseball.

But now Gleason was no longer capable of jocularity, and Carstairs' expression was as grim as death. He was sniffing at the air and staring at his hands, as though bewildered by his ability to flex his fingers when his spine was a column of ice, his tongue a swollen mass of jelly.

"John, what is it?" Vera whispered hoarsely. "I don't smell anything."

"It would be better if you did," Carstairs husked. "Vera, this is devilish. Something utterly diabolic has occurred here. Yet there isn't a mark on him."

"What, John? What is it?"

"It—it defies reason. There are unmistakable evidences of foul play. Brownish mucous membranes, dilated pupils."

He returned to the bed and bent over the still figure lying there. His nostrils quivered, flared.

"The characteristic odor," he grunted. "But only his body exhales it."

"Uncle always was eccentric," said a cynical voice from the doorway. "In death as in life—peculiar, different."

Carstairs turned about on his heels, his jaw hardening.

The youth standing in the doorway had a sickly leer on his face. He was wearing black silk pajamas and he had thrown a monogrammed bath towel about his shoulders and knotted it foppishly in front.

* * * *

Carstairs had met Gleason's weak-chinned, dissolute nephew several times on Earth, and had hardly been able to stomach the youth's exaggerated mannerisms, and air of knowing he would someday inherit his uncle's wealth.

Henry Gleason Showalter was unmistakably intoxicated, but his sneering manner did not seem to emanate from the alcohol in his brain. His gaze was steady enough, and his voice had a quality of smirking contempt for the living and the dead which chilled Vera to the depth of her being. Before she could draw away from him he patted her arm. "You're right in your element, aren't you?" he sneered. "Helping him with his police work."

Carstairs saw red. He advanced upon the youth in three long strides, grabbed him by the shoulders and shook him until his jaw sagged.

"You cold-blooded little rotter," he grated. "Your uncle is *dead*. Doesn't that mean anything to you?"

"In his present condition, how could it mean anything?" asked a silky voice from the doorway. "He's been drinking steadily for hours."

Mona Clayton looked hard, cynical. She looked infinitely more cynical than Gleason's nephew, but she had more strength of character than the weak-chinned youth, and knew when and how to keep her thoughts to herself. The fact that she was that youth's fiancée had amazed Carstairs at first, but after conversing with her in Gleason's presence he had decided she was nobody's fool. She was marrying young Showalter for the money he'd eventually inherit. A gold-digger, if ever there was one. A hard, calculating little minx.

Behind her in shadows hovered Lee Chan, Gleason's Chinese butler, his once yellow face drained of all color.

"The master is dead," he wailed, wringing his hands. "He was the kindest man I ever knew. The very kindest man."

Vera crossed to Carstairs' side and tugged urgently at his arm. "John, control yourself!" she pleaded thickly. "Set him down."

"Would you rather I *squeezed* the rottenness out of him?" Carstairs grunted. "Just say the word." There was a sudden, deafening roar, and an energy pellet thudded into the wall behind Carstairs' head, shaking the entire turret. Mona Clayton screamed, and Carstairs leaped backward with a startled oath, carrying the youth with him.

Two more blasts came in staccato sequence. The window flamed orange, and a thin ribbon of smoke drifted into the turret from the darkness beyond.

Carstairs knew that a Gierson automatic pistol held five energy pellets. He also knew that Interplanetary Patrol regulations prohibited fancy weapons on the moon. The chances seemed to favor a Gierson, and a nearly exhausted clip.

Carstairs hurled Showalter from him with a snort of disgust. Three furious strides carried him to the window; a raised right foot and a leverage jounce from his left heel lifted him over the sill into the cold lunar night.

From the ventilator turbines at the base of the tower thin currents of scorching air ascended, to be instantly moderated by the cold of space. His shoulders etched in Earthlight, a cloaked figure was running along the observation platform toward what appeared to be a mistily weaving spiral of light. Pulling his oxygen mask down over his face, Carstairs pounded after him, his breath congealing on the frosty air. His energy carried him on with incredible speed. The moon's light gravity put wings on his heels, and lengthened his strides till his dressing gown swirled up about his shoulders, and streamed out behind him like a wind-lashed cloak.

His lips were contorted with savage mutterings when the spiral resolved itself into the stern light of a small vacuum plane. The machine was poised at the edge of the platform, its forward struts gleaming in the Earthlight, its magnetic traction vanes humming.

* * * *

Even as Carstairs' gaze swept over it, the fleeing figure heaved itself into the pilot's seat and bent sharply forward. There was a sudden, vibrant roar, and the plane zigzagged along the edge of the platform, and took off so abruptly that Carstairs nearly lost his grip on the strut toward which he had literally dived.

Clinging with both hands, he let his long legs dangle, and cursed himself for a madman. The plane rose sharply and then swooped, descending toward the foothills below in a graceful, hawklike glide. Carstairs looked down, his spine congealing. Sheer height, when viewed from a solid structure, is seldom terrifying, but it is quite otherwise when the observer is clinging to the thrumming struts of a circling plane. Beneath him yawned a dizzying gulf of emptiness, walled with darkness and substructured with peaks which looked like stalactites in reverse, each one of which seemed capable of impaling him, and rotating him in squirming agony till the end of time.

"Maybe it wasn't such a good idea," he muttered between clenched teeth, tightening his grip on the strut. Down the plane swooped and down. It had ceased to descend gracefully, had begun to gyrate. Like a wounded bladder-bird, it swooped to right and left and quivered from beak to stern. Carstairs' nerves were shrieking when it settled to the ground in a deep gulch between two peaks and glided to a halt with a barely perceptible jolt. White-lipped, he dropped to the ground, and tore around the front of the plane to the pilot compartment.

It was a reckless thing to do, for the emerging pilot blasted from the hip the instant he discovered that he had a passenger. He stood half-out of the pilot seat, grasping the strut with one hand, and emptying his automatic in Carstairs' direction.

Two blasts echoed between hollow peaks as Carstairs clambered over a heated vane, and gripped the wrist of his assailant. "You're a bum pilot, Bowles," he panted. "You're also a bum marksman. It stands to reason, doesn't it, that you can't be good at *this?*"

He struck the other on the jaw as he spoke, rocking his head back. To his amazement the eyes opposite him did not glaze. Instead, fury flamed in them, and the jaw that he had jolted seemed to stiffen.

"That's what you think!" came in a hoarse bellow.

Limbs interlocked, the two men dropped to the ground and rolled over. The fact that Carstairs' had recognized his assailant as George Bowles, Gleason's huge and taciturn gardener, was no help to him. The man was six feet six, and as strong as an ox.

He twisted Carstairs' arm back, and bit him in the shoulder.

"Fight clean, Bowles," Carstairs gibed, concealing his agony with a grin which increased the other's rancor. Furiously he pummeled Carstairs, ignoring the angular knee which the still grinning botanist rammed into his stomach and the shower of fisticuffs which spattered against his close-cropped head, rocking it to and fro.

Bitterly Carstairs realized that he had underestimated his adversary. The man could take it, and he could ladle it out. He could absorb so much punishment that Carstairs' plight was not an enviable one. He was flat on his back, and Bowles was trying viciously to break his arm, and almost succeeding. Worse, the big gorilla's punches were packed with dynamite, and coming faster and faster. Carstairs fought with all his strength, but gradually he felt himself growing weaker. In desperation he squirmed and twisted, dragging himself over the ground, his shoulders jerking. He reached a jagged outcropping of rock on the slightly sloping floor of the ravine, where he furiously endeavored to raise his shoulders when Bowles began violently to shiver. The half-Nelson which he had thrown about Carstairs relaxed, and a convulsive shudder shook him.

Stunned, Carstairs wrenched his arm free, twisted about and raised his fist for a crushing blow that wasn't needed. Bowles had rolled over on his side, and was lying utterly rigid, a bubbling froth on his lips. Clinging to his neck was a small, strawberry-colored nettle.

Horror struck, Carstairs stared at it, unable to believe his eyes. It was in all respects an exact duplicate of the one which was still clinging to his own shoulder, except for one thing. It was scarcely one-fourth as large.

CHAPTER III

Blood Pressure of a Plant

A shrill ululation caused Carstairs to raise his eyes and glance star- tlingly about him. The wobbly he saw was one-fourth the normal size.

A baby wobbly, an unmistakable fledgling of the species which Gleason had captured and studied was standing a few feet away, its tendrils fluttering in the hot air currents from the tower's turbines which were swirling down into the gulch in erratic gusts, its small root-body quivering in infantile panic.

Lifting Bowles' limp body in his arms, and carrying it to the vacuum plane was a nerve-racking ordeal, because Car-stairs was sure he had another corpse on his hands. It wasn't until he was back in the tower, with a stirring and groaning Bowles clutching at his sleeve, that the truth struck him like a bolt from the blue, rocking him back on his heels and shedding dazzlement in all directions. The big, pugnacious bruiser was *allergic* to nettles! So allergic that the shock of one entering his flesh had brought on a convulsion and laid him out limp. It wasn't such a rare mishap from a medical point of view, but it left Carstairs stunned and gasping. That big, husky giant—brought low by a nettle flung by a baby wobbly!

Carstairs deposited Bowles on the floor of Gleason's sleeping turret, directly under a dim cold light bulb. The big, rectangular chamber had quieted down, for Vera Dorn had not been idle in Carstairs' absence. She had sprayed a narcotizing vapor over the three wobblies, and locked them up in a metal herbarium. She had sent Mona Clayton back to her sleeping turret on the floor below, and turned on Showalter a glance so withering that he had slunk furtively into shadows. The nephew was standing now in a dim recess behind Gleason's bed, his eyes boring holes in the gloom.

Bowles raised himself on his elbow, trying desperately to talk his way back into Carstairs' good graces. His voice was husky, and all the pugnacity had gone out of him.

"I lost my head when you swung at me," he muttered. "I've nothing against *you,* Carstairs, but when you came at me like that I had to defend myself, didn't I? I'm hot-tempered, sure. But I didn't kill Gleason. It was that little hyena there."

Mentally Carstairs docketed for reference the astonishing fact that everyone referred to Gleason's nephew as a hyena, skunk, or snake. He gnawed at his underlip, and fixed Bowles with an accusing stare.

"You blasted *before* I clipped you," he said. "You tried to shoot me down in cold blood. You tried to shoot Showalter down. Why did you crouch in darkness outside that window and try to drill him?"

"I'll tell you why," Bowles choked. "I took my job here seriously. I like flowers. That may seem sort of screwy to you, but I mean it."

"It doesn't," Carstairs assured him.

"Well, you've seen Gleason's orchids. Glass-encased, sure, with air pumped in. Tropical terrestrial plants—nothing fancy about 'em. But I took a personal pride in them."

"You did a good job," Carstairs admitted. "Raising *perfect* plants under artificial sunlight is a tough assignment."

"That's it—*perfect,*" Bowles cried eagerly. "My orchids were perfect. Perfect, you hear? I liked my job, and I wanted to keep it. But *he* didn't want me too."

He gestured toward the shadows where Gleason's nephew stood. Showalter had lit a cigarette and was puffing on it furiously.

"He came stumbling into the greenhouse last night as high as a kite," Bowles muttered accusingly. "He tore my flowers up by the roots. He upset trays, and turned a hose on my finest bed. Did you ever see fine blooms flattened into a mud soup?"

Carstairs nodded sympathetically. "I would have perhaps killed him myself. We're all savages when something rasps us in a vital spot. But you had a few hours to calm down in."

"Yeah, but he ran to his uncle like a dirty little schoolboy sneak. He accused me of tanking up, and throwing my own trays around. Gleason gave me my notice before he turned in at midnight. He called me a liar, refused to hear me out."

"He wouldn't listen to *any* honest man or woman," shrilled a quavering voice from the doorway. "He deserved to die. He was a hard man— cold and unjust. There was no compassion in him. I'm glad he's dead!"

Carstairs swung about. A frail, white-haired old woman had slipped into the room and was standing by Vera's side. As Carstairs stared at her in consternation she raised a clawlike, veined hand and pointed at the still figure on the bed.

"May you rest in torment, James Gleason," she shrilled.

Carstairs had had about enough. He crossed to the door in three long strides, turned the old woman about, and guided her gently but firmly into the corridor.

"Go back to your room," he said. "And stay there. If I need you, I'll send for you. You've been a good housekeeper to James Gleason. Why should you hate him so much?"

The old woman shook her head. "It's not for me to be telling you," she muttered. "You'll find out soon enough."

Returning to the sleeping turret, Carstairs swabbed sweat from his forehead and spoke crisply to Vera Dorn.

"I said that something diabolic had occurred here. I'm afraid it's worse than that. Listen carefully, Vera. I'm going to take one of the wobblies up to my turret. I want you to bring me Gleason's notes. All of them, you understand? His day-by-day observations, the complete record of what he saw on the mountains when he studied the wobblies from behind a blind. His speculations as to their feeding habits, the chemical and osmotic tests which he made on the three specimens which are now our guests."

"But you've almost memorized those notes," Vera protested.

"I know, but there are minor details I may have overlooked. One thing more—give me fifteen or twenty minutes' leeway before you snap to it."

Twelve minutes later Vera Dorn tapped apprehensively on the door of Carstairs' sleeping turret.

"Come in," a grim voice said.

Vera obeyed, shivering. She knew John Carstairs. He was never so unpredictable as when he asked her to do something for him when he had all the pieces in an unspeakably terrifying case. She knew that he was at the crucial stage. The glint in his eyes, his air of repressed excitement, and his willingness to permit four vengeful people to remain at liberty indicated that he was prepared to act swiftly and inexorably. Vera Dorn had steeled herself to encounter an unusual manifestation of Carstairs' genius at work, but the sight which she saw when she shut the door firmly and turned to face her employer was so completely ludicrous that it chilled her more than a gruesome exhibit would have done. In a way, it was a little gruesome—comically so, perhaps, like a child's rag doll dangling from a hangman's noose—but unspeakably nightmarish in its implications.

One of the wobblies was sitting upright in a chair by the window, its tendril-arms bound by thin wires and its stumpy legs interlocked. The anesthetic vapor which Vera had sprayed over it had worn off, and it was squirming about and emitting shrill ululations.

Clamped to its rugose, tapering head was a semi-circular metal disk, somewhat resembling an aluminum eye-shield. From the disk a thin glass tube descended to the creature's "waist" and branched off at right angles to its body-root. A few inches beyond the bent section of the tube the glass terminated in a flexible rubber extension which carried the tubular portion of the apparatus across the floor to Carstairs' hand. Carstairs was sitting on the edge of his bed, pressing a large rubber bulb at five-second intervals. Every time he gave the bulb a squeeze a pale, greenish fluid bubbled and frothed in the glass portion of the tube, occasionally ascending to the half-disk on the plant creature's head.

"Good Lord!" Vera Dorn choked.

"Quiet, Vera," Carstairs cautioned. "If the pressure goes any higher we'll have a dead wobbly on our hands."

"John, are you out of your mind? Why did you truss that poor thing—*pressure!* John, what do you mean?"

"I'm taking its blood pressure," Car-stairs said. "To be strictly accurate, its *sap* pressure, although the fluid which circulates in its veins contains actual blood-plates, and mononuclear cells containing basophilic granules. Its blood pressure is unbelievably high now. So high that—" He stared at her steadily. "Well, it will be labeled Exhibit A, Vera. And I wouldn't want to be in the shoes of a certain party when I lay my findings before a jury."

Vera Dorn's jaw sagged. "John Carstairs, how can you take the blood pressure of a plant? I never heard of such a thing."

"Vera, I thought you majored in botany at college," Carstairs said acidly. "Perhaps you'd better go back for another semester of intensive osmotic research. You know, summer course for girls with low I.Q.s who can't quite make the grade."

Vera flushed scarlet. "What has osmosis to do with taking the blood pressure of a plant?"

"Plenty," Carstairs grunted. "Most plants, as you know suck nourishment from the soil through their roots by osmosis, and draw it up through the woody part of their stems by capillary attraction and a process known as transpiration. All these processes are accelerated by the pressure of sugar and salt in the sap."

"But—"

"Let me finish, Vera. In terrestrial plants the nutrient fluid is an amalgam of common minerals. But in lunar plants a different kind of nourishment is sucked up, and their veins are filled with specialized chemicals capable of accelerating its absorption.

"When osmosis is accelerated to an abnormal extent a plant's blood pressure begins to rise. It may reach twenty or thirty atmospheres. On Earth many plants exhibit the symptoms of high blood pressure, but leaf or tendril evaporation drains off the excess nourishment and keeps them from going into convulsions.

"Here on the moon there is no such safety valve. Plants scarcely perspire at all, due to environmental factors. They have to eat sparingly, or else."

"But no plant or animal ever eats sparingly," Vera protested. "A dog, for instance, never knows when to stop, and the same rule applies all down the biological scale."

Carstairs nodded. "True. But you're forgetting that living creatures gorge themselves only when there is an *abundance* of nourishment. Wobblies feast on a substance which is rare on Luna. Being perambulating plants, they have to suck it in from the nearly airless vacuum which is the moon's atmosphere through their body roots, and it costs them a tremendous effort. Ordinarily their blood pressure remains low because they have adapted themselves to an environment in which nourishment is scarce.

"But nourishment wasn't scarce here in the tower last night. I've a very sick wobbly on my hands, a wobbly that is going to put a noose around somebody's neck. That wasn't Gleason we heard screaming last night. It was three wobblies with high blood pressure, ululating together in his sleeping turret." Vera's lips were white. "Whose neck, John?"

Carstairs shook his head. "No, you don't. Vera. You'll know when I'm sure. I've got to get answers to a couple of space-o-grams first. If what I suspect is true, the murderer is no ordinary criminal. He—or she—must possess a mind of the first order of malign cunning."

He shuddered. "It gives me a sick feeling in the pit of my stomach."

"It does me, too," Vera flared, biting her lip. "Although you won't tell me a darned thing about it. I'm that way—sympathetic when my boss gets a tummyache."

Carstairs scowled. "All right, Vera, I asked for it. You're hard and unsympathetic, but you understand me. I feel sort of helpless when I close in for the kill. I like to be—well, coddled." Vera kissed him, patting his cheek. "Sure, I know. That's why I'm supposed to be in love with you."

"Aren't you?"

"I think maybe I am." She looked at him hopefully.

Carstairs' eyes narrowed. "All right, then you can do something for me. I want you to get them all together in Gleason's turret—Bowles, Showalter, the Chinese butler, Mona Clayton, and that sweet, white-haired grandmother, Miss Newton. Get them together, and give me twenty more minutes. When I come down I'll try to satisfy your curiosity."

"John Carstairs, if you got romantic for once in your life and whispered sweet nothings to me without an ulterior motive," Vera declared, "do you know what I'd do?"

"No, what?"

"Turn into a wobbly. I'd have to do that to keep my blood pressure down." She went out, slamming the door so violently that the wobbly emitted a long-drawn ululation, and squirmed violently in its chair.

CHAPTER IV

Botanical Stoolpigeon

When John Carstairs appeared in the doorway of Gleason's sleeping turret the five white-lipped people gathered there stared at him as though he were a visitor from Saturn. His expression was utterly inscrutable, and an almost godlike detachment seemed to emanate from him. He hoped that none of the five suspected that he felt like a scared kid with one exploratory thumb poised above a high-voltage electric wire.

Nodding at Vera, he crossed in silence to the bed where Gleason's sheet-covered body lay, made sure that the cold light did not fall directly on his head and shoulders, and swept the five suspects with his gaze.

He began to talk at once, fixing Henry Showalter with an accusing stare. The nephew began instantly to tremble. His air of vicious cynicism had dropped from him, like a cloak that he had found much too costly to wear.

"If there is any crime you would not have committed to get your hands on your uncle's wealth, Showalter," Carstairs said, "it would have to be mentioned in whispers by anyone with an ounce of decency in him. You were quite capable of killing your uncle, and you would have experienced no remorse. I've a pretty complete account here of your—well, I'll be charitable, and call them escapades—on Earth.

"I sent a space-o-gram to the New York Police Department, *Mr.* Showalter. You've a record of seven arrests, ranging from drunkenness to arson. You're a thorough rotter, but—" He frowned. "You did not kill him. You are neither a chemist or a genius." Carstairs turned his gaze to Gleason's housekeeper with a shudder of disgust. The white-haired old woman quivered. "Why are you staring at me like that? Do you think I killed him?"

"No," Carstairs said. "But you are suffering from the same disease, I'll be charitable and call it ungratefulness. Gleason raised your salary every time you came to him with a hard luck story. The last time you rasped his patience a little, and he didn't give you as much as you thought you deserved. Consequently, you hated him."

He shrugged, turning to the Chinese butler. "You're a pretty good guy," he said. "You didn't kill him, did you, Lee Chan?"

The yellow man shook his head. "He was a pretty good guy himself," he singsonged. "The kindest man I've ever known."

"Yes, there are still a few kindly people left in the world," Carstairs agreed, swinging suddenly toward George Bowles and Mona Clayton. They were standing close together, their faces drained of all color, their eyes fastened on Carstairs.

"Sulphuretted hydrogen, Bowles," Carstairs said softly, "causes symptoms which end rapidly in death. It is one of the deadliest gases known, comparable only to cyanide fumes in the swiftness with which it acts. If the concentration is marked, fatal effects by inhalation are immediate." His jaw muscles tightened. "Oh, you were clever, Bowles. Posing as a humble lover of flowers, an eccentric with only one consuming passion in life. A simple gardener, living for his plants."

"You're crazy, Carstairs," Bowles choked. "What are you driving at?"

"You were not only interested in orchids, Bowles," Carstairs continued relentlessly. "You were interested in wobblies, and you persuaded Gleason to let you see his notes. Your thumbprints are on the sheets Miss Dorn brought to me. You are also a toxicologist, Bowles. You worked in a chemical laboratory on Earth, and you knew that sulphuretted hydrogen has one disadvantage as a killing agent.

"It leaves an odor, the strongest odor of any lethal chemical, one which hovers in the air and impregnates the flesh of the victim."

Mona Clayton's agitated voice rang out across the chamber. "He lies! Oh, darling, defend yourself, tell him—"

"Darling, is it?" Carstairs rasped. "I thought so. Bowles, you knew that sulphuretted hydrogen leaves an unmistakable odor, but you also knew that the wobblies feast on it. It is their natural source of nourishment. It clings to the walls of deep gulches in the mountains, and they suck it in by osmosis through their permeable body-roots!"

* * * *

Mona Clayton uttered a faint moan. But the botanical detective went on relentlessly.

"Last night you treated the three wobblies which Gleason had captured to a feast. You smashed the glass herbarium and released them, after pumping sulphuretted hydrogen into Gleason's sleeping turret through a sprayer from outside the window to kill him. You knew that wobblies can scent sulphuretted hydrogen half across the moon, and you figured they would streak like starved bloodhounds to Gleason's turret.

"They did. Vera Dorn encountered one in the corridor and one in her sleeping turret, but wobblies are like that. They know that a roundabout way is often the quickest distance between two points on the Moon. They climbed down outside, and entered through the window which you had purposely left open. When their blood pressure rose and they ululated, Miss Dorn and I raced downstairs, to discover they had sucked up all the sulphuretted hydrogen in the air leaving it crisp and odorless.

"Gleason usually slept with his windows thrown wide, but last night you must have had to raise the pane to pump the gas in. Although we found the casement the way you had left it, there was still air in the room. The wobblies would have sucked that giveaway odor out of Gleason himself, but we got to him in time, and a little of it lingered when I bent over him. You thought the wobblies would clear away every trace of the gas, and make it look as though Gleason had died of natural causes." Carstair's eyes were steely slits. "When you saw I had it tabbed as murder you tried to throw suspicion on Showalter by accusing him of upsetting your trays last night, and subtly hinting that maybe Gleason hadn't quite believed his nephew's version of the affair either. In other words, you implied that Showalter was in danger of being cut off without a cent."

"That's a lie," Bowles muttered hoarsely. "You're trying to frame me, Carstairs."

"Think so? I've got a space-o-gram here from Earth which says that you and Miss Clayton have been partners in crime for a decade, and are wanted for blackmail and homicide by the San Francisco police.

"It was beautifully planned, Bowles. All you had to do was murder Gleason and the rest would unwind like a carefully oiled spring. Showalter would inherit a fortune, Mona would marry Showalter, and then you and Mona would take a vacation together, with Showalter's inheritance in an overnight bag to brighten the trip."

Carstairs looked straight at Mona Clayton. Her hands were clenched and her features seemed all wrenched apart. "You should have picked a less allergic partner, Mona. I suspected him from the first, but what really clinched it was his aversion to nettles. He plucked most of the nettles out of the wobblies with tweezers before releasing them.

"It was just blue funk, I guess—he couldn't bear the thought of being in the same tower with nettle-hurling wobblies running around loose."

"But one of those wobblies hurled a nettle at me, John," Vera said. "And at you. You've one in your shoulder now."

Carstairs nodded and held up his hand. "I said most of the nettles, Vera. When I examined the wobblies a half-hour ago I couldn't find a nettle in them. I knew then that I had him, and I could see the noose tightening about his neck. The fact that he must have overlooked three nettles deep in the pouch of the tallest wobbly won't influence the jury much. Three nettles! One for you, one for me, and this one for evidence of—"

Before he could finish Bowles dived for the window. There was a splintering crash as his gigantic bulk tore a hole in the pane and vanished.

Carstairs crossed the room in a flying leap. For the barest fraction of a second he paused to hurl the casement open and clamp on his oxygen mask. Mona Clayton screamed, and Vera grasped her arms from behind and held on tight.

Cursing himself for a sissy, Carstairs tore out into the lunar night. His reluctance to tear his face to ribbons had proved a costly mistake. Bowles was thirty feet away, and running along the edge of the platform toward a weaving spiral of light.

Instantly Carstairs had a vision of himself descending once again into the foothills on the thrumming strut of a vacuum plane. It was an appalling vision and it chilled his heart like ice. It also stopped him in his tracks.

He hurled the nettle with surprising ease, his body twisting a little like a pitcher in a game called baseball. Bowles shrieked. Spinning about on his toes, he tottered for an instant at the edge of the platform and then plunged downward, his body revolving as he fell toward peaks which looked like stalactites in reverse, each one of which seemed capable of impaling him and rotating him in screaming agony to the end of time.

Carstairs turned away, shaken, and a little sick.

* * * *

"Darling," Vera said, eternities later, "you'll have to operate on both of us. There is still one nettle in my shoulder and one in yours. You can't just pluck them out."

"No, I suppose not," Carstairs grunted, reaching for a bottle of antiseptic and a cotton pad. "But next time you bump into a wobbly in the dark, try talking to it. It will quiet right down."

"You mean my voice would calm it down?" exclaimed Vera Dorn, her eyes glowing. "John, how sweet of you."

Carstairs smiled, dabbing at her shoulder. "When you pay a woman a compliment, she always stays put for a minute. I've never known it to fail."

"Then you didn't mean that—about my voice?"

"Oh, certainly, but I wanted to get you to hold still."

The silence in the big, rectangular turret was broken by the sound of a slap.

THE CRITTERS

"Inertia is what saves us, young fellow," Traubel said. "Malignancy, human or otherwise, wilts under its own weight."

He was sitting on a jagged granite outcropping on the crest of his land, his sagging shoulders and straddle-legged posture giving him the aspect of a dejected steeplechase rider about to come a cropper. But suddenly as he spoke his shoulders straightened, and the rusty garden rake in his gnarled, blue-veined hands began to vibrate like a whip.

Morley watched a rapt possessiveness creep into the steel-gray eyes and found himself wondering how a man so gaunt and ill-colored could have turned the sloping mountainside into a garden plot so riotously ablaze with color that it dazzled his vision.

On the sloping acres below were russet patches, and emerald patches, and a solid acre of pumpkins gleaming in the sunlight opposite a field of waving corn.

And suddenly the old man was nodding, his eyes sweeping all of the wide green acres he'd refused to yield up to the alien hordes. His acres were green because he'd gone right on plowing and seeding and hoeing. Not all of Joel Traubel's neighbors had been as brave.

"Perhaps 'brave' isn't the right word," Morley thought aloud. "Perhaps 'foolhardy' would be a better word."

"Come again, young fellow?"

Morley took off the glasses he'd found by rummaging through the charred debris of an optical display case—he'd tried on sixty pairs—and his stare seemed to take on an added sharpness before he returned them to his nose.

He wasn't a "young fellow" but a lean, haggard-faced man of forty-two, with his years etched as indelibly into his face as the whorls on the shell of a mossback.

But then—Traubel had been on Earth. A man as virile as Traubel still would naturally lie a little about his age.

He'd lop off a few years as a sop to his vanity and a few out of sheer cussedness, but the way the old man's memory kept harking back to the closing years of the twentieth century was a dead giveaway.

The winding procession of armed Venusians in the blue-lit defile far below would have checked the loquacity of an ordinary man in midstream. But Traubel just kept talking about his young manhood, and his mental processes were not those of a hunted man, but of an imaginative lad with a well-ordered, well-regulated life looming ahead of him through the hazy mountain vista up which he'd been climbing for forty years.

"Didn't catch what you said, young fellow. Funny thing, no one thought it would be like this when the first spaceship landed on Venus, and Fleming and Pregenzer were massacred. We just didn't realize we'd supplied the malignant critters with a blueprint. They couldn't build spaceships before they'd seen one, naturally. But when we plunked a ship down in the pea soup right before their nostril slits—"

"I wouldn't want the job," Morley said.

"Come again, young man?"

"Oh, I mean—the job of splitting the hair that separates an imitative from a constructive faculty."

Traubel nodded. "They built thousands of ships as alike as peas in a pod," he reminisced grimly. "And now there's a blight on the Earth and all the people have to look forward to is the time when they'll be buried together. If they're married, that is.

"Funny thing about that. The cities have been leveled and all the folks I see are just marking time. But it's the green fields turning black I feel the worst about. A city you can toss away without an awful lot of grief, but the earth of a man's own plowing under his feet, the smell of fresh-turned earth when it's been raining up and down the mountainside—"

"So you've stayed on," Morley said, jerking his bronze-haired head at the fertile acres beneath, "year after year, minding your own business, wresting a living from the land."

"That's right, young fellow. Up and down the Earth you young fellows go with your bellies pulled in, hiding in caves from dawn to dusk, picking up scraps of food like turkey buzzards."

The old man bent and scooped up a handful of dirt. "Scavenger beetles," he amended, his nostrils wrinkling as he picked out a fat white grub, and crushed it between his thumb and forefinger. "No offense, son, but that's what you are. There are a few cracked mirrors left. Did you ever try standing off and taking a long, sober look at yourself? I'll wager those black leather boots you're wearing came from—"

Traubel checked himself. "Oh, well, where they came from is no business of mine. But *I* wouldn't want to die with a dead man's boots on, son."

"I have died," Morley said. "I died yesterday; today and tomorrow I'll die again. A man is dead when he's caught like a fly in a web, and he's dead—and he dies. They kill swiftly, erratically, for no reason at all. They kill for the sheer pleasure of killing. It's like…well, you see a grub…no a mosquito…and suddenly, there's a little red smudge on your thumb. You don't hate the mosquito—"

"No, they don't hate us," the old man agreed. "That's what I've been trying to make you see. You wouldn't go out of your way to kill a mosquito. You or I wouldn't and they're no different from us in that respect. My land's so high up on the mountain they just don't bother to turn aside and bother me."

"Not in forty years, old man?"

"Not more than four times in forty years," Traubel said. "And each time I made myself scarce. Just hiding in a cave for one day, even if it means crouching over a decaying carcass, doesn't harm a man when he knows he'll have his own land to come back to."

Traubel laughed harshly. "They set my fields ablaze, but a burning harvest now and then sweetens the labors of a man. You plow and you sow again, bringing a greenness out of the ash layer."

"It's like living on the edge of a volcano," Morley said.

"The law of averages is on my side," Traubel reminded him. "Four times in forty years is a pretty good batting average, as we used to say when we could move about freely enough to play games. Baseball—"

"You can flip a coin, and it comes heads fifty times," Morley reminded him. "Perhaps you've just been trading on your luck."

"Maybe so, young fellow, maybe so. But I just can't picture myself inviting a gift horse to kick me in the face."

Three thousand feet below red sunlight glinted on the hooked beaks of marching Venusians, glinted on their scaly bodies and tentacled limbs.

"And in the background of a man's mind there is always a vision of the little towns, driving him on, giving him the will to remain a man—"

"There are no more little towns," Morley reminded him.

"There *were* little towns," the old man said, raising his rake, and scraping rust from one of the prongs. "And I wouldn't want the job of splitting the hair that separates here and now from something I can still see and smell and touch just by stretching out a hand."

He nodded. The steely hardness had gone out of his eyes. His eyes looked now like a kid's on Christmas morning, sliding down the banisters with his head aureoled in a golden haze.

"A rake resting against a barn door, pigs—if you like pigs—all splashed with mud down one side, and pumpkins and wood smoke in October. Even the swill trough smells sweet, and you and the missus, you put on your Sunday best and go chugging into town in a converted jeep roadster, and the missus says…shucks, it's all so close in my mind I just have to stretch out a hand.

"Come tomorrow, the missus will have been gone exactly fourteen years," he added, thoughtfully.

"I don't know whether I've been standing here a long time or a short time talking like an idiot," Morley heard himself saying. "Tell me, did you feel the same way when you and your wife were facing this together? Did you feel like a man who has gone out with his last penny and doesn't know whether to gamble it or not?"

Traubel turned and looked at him sharply. "You're not alone, young fellow? You weren't just passing by—alone?"

"No." Morley shook his head. "We…we passed your hut-house on the way up. We thought you mightn't mind if we put up with you for—" He hesitated. "I guess you'd call it a spell."

"Home burned down with the wheat," Traubel said, raking some dry leaves toward the outcropping. "Four times right down to the soil. The big trees had to be felled, and dragged up from the valley. My path almost crossed theirs."

He raked through the leaves, and uncovered a chestnut bur.

"If you saw a mosquito groaning beneath a log, would you crush it? They saw me, all right, following a winding trail up through the timber line. But shucks, crushing a mosquito carrying a log would take a kind of special double effort. Inertia—"

He wouldn't have thought of mosquitoes if I hadn't put the idea into his head Morley thought. Aloud he said: "Is it all right, then—if we stay on for a spell? You know that queer old notion about a house? A house isn't a home until it's really been lived in. You give something to the house and the house gives something back to you. It's sort of partnership, if you know what I mean—a symbiosis."

Traubel said: "Young man, I don't quite see—"

"She's going to have a baby," Morley said.

Traubel was silent for a full minute. Then he said: "Oh!" Then after a pause: "Hut's above the timber line, high enough up to be as safe as the rock we're sitting on. You'd better get back to her, son."

Morley reached out and gripped the old man's arm, a curious wetness glistening on his cheekbones.

"Thanks," he said.

"Don't mention it son. If you don't mind I'll just sit here a moment longer where I can see all of my land spread out beneath me like a chessboard. Sort of makes me feel good to know I can still move the pieces around. That wheat field down below reminds me of a queen with corn-silk hair arguing with a bishop decked out in cabbage leaves.

"You've played chess, son? The hut's my castle. You set out a lot of pawns to protect your rook or castle, and—"

Morley left him nodding in the gathering dusk, and went on down the mountainside, his trouser legs sticking out from the back of his boots.

Halfway down the mountain—exactly halfway as Morley's accurate eye measured the distance—he halted in his stride and his hand went under his coat to emerge with a small, flat object that caught and held the sunlight.

The object measured roughly four inches by seven and its general appearance was somewhat like that of the flattish, large-lensed cameras which had been so popular in the middle years of the twentieth century.

In all of the crumbling yellow optical catalogues which Morley had thumbed through such immense, metal-embedded "eyes" were euphemistically listed as "candid cameras"!

Did that mean that they caught men and women in their unguarded moments, and presented a more accurate picture of humanity's frailties than the more primitive visual recording installments of an earlier period?

With fingers that trembled a little he loosened his shoulder pack, and a small metal tripod fell to the ground. He screwed the camera-like object on the tripod with a grim urgency in his stare.

Almost he wished that the object were a camera.

Perhaps his belief in himself was no more than a fantastic nightmare which had mushroomed in his brain.

No—he really didn't believe that. He had a natural bent for *improving* things, and the camera-like object had taken shape so inevitably that he could not doubt his ability to bring the invention to full fruition in another two years. Two years? God, he'd settle for seven months—six—Morley wiped the sweat from his face. His hands were trembling so that they seemed all thumbs. He had all the needed, delicate parts now, but freedom from fear, freedom from strain, the opportunity to work unmolested in a small, hastily improvised laboratory might well spell the difference between success and failure.

A mountain laboratory? Well, he'd know in a moment whether he could achieve effective results by training the instrument straight down the mountain at a *marching* column.

Oh, it wasn't a vain hope, for he was the only man left on Earth with a surgical technique worth developing.

There was a brackish taste in Morley's mouth. Deep therapy was what it amounted to, but, if it couldn't be adapted to the peculiar structure of Venusian brains, humanity would do better to stick to hand-blasters. What he desperately needed now was more time—time to work on the skillful interlocking of high-frequency wave transmission with the destructive intracranial vibrations set up by the controlled use of subsonics.

In the last years of the twentieth century beam surgery could make babbling infants of men, but not even a cyclotron beam of alpha particles could destroy the brains of Venusians. Convulsive idiocy in humans, yes. The forebrain and cortex destroyed, nothing left but the thalamus—all in the last six years of the twentieth century!

Morley had watched a few experiments go wrong. Himself a fifteen-year-old kid, his uncle a surgeon, and letting the beam get out of control because with all the great accumulation of knowledge and experience at his disposal that grand old man couldn't control the trembling of his hands.

Well, he, Morley, could control the trembling but—the transmitter just wasn't powerful enough. When he trained it on the Venusians there was a brief pause like the petit mal of human epilepsy. For the barest fraction of a second the beam worked, but—For an instant there stirred within Morley a foreboding born of years of acute fear and blind sensation. Then—he heard something click beneath his fingers.

Instantly he slammed the dread in his mind back against a mental wall—held it there.

Two thousand feet below a moving shadow stopped. The sunlight seemed to deepen, and monstrously between walls of blueness there spread the penumbra of a beast with many beaked heads that *had ceased utterly to weave about.*

A dislodged stone rasped against Morley's heel and went bounding down the slope like a startled hare.

Bounding, zigzagging—If a man didn't smoke, it could be because—he had no matches. If a man didn't breathe, it could be because the air about him had become thick, viscid.

Ten minutes later Morley was standing very still, a thin trickle of blood running down his chin.

Ten full minutes, he thought wildly. The whole blasted column sent mindless. It halted and then—moved on *without remembering.* I've got them, I've got them—in the palm of my hand! Give me seven months—a mountain laboratory—I'll settle for four!

"He asked me if I played chess," Morley said, when he'd scrubbed the dirt from his hands and dried them with a towel.

The woman on the bunk raised her face and stared at her husband across the rafter-hung hut, the hair above her brow a tumbled mass of gold.

For an instant she seemed almost pretty, despite her wind-coarsened skin and the harsh lines which hunger and deprivation had etched into her flesh.

"Do you really think he's just been lucky, Jim? Or is it something we—" she hesitated, as though visualizing the begrimed, misery-laden millions who trudged the waste places of the Earth—"is it some hidden power he has which we could use too, if he'd tell us about it?"

Morley sat down on the edge of his bunk, and leaned forward, hands on knees. "I don't know," he said. "It may be he's caught up in what used to be called an infinity cycle of lucky runs."

"An infinity cycle?"

Morley nodded. "I told him a flipped coin can fall the same way fifty times in succession. But that's not remarkable. It happens so often it doesn't even do violence to the law of averages. What I didn't tell him— perhaps I didn't need to—was that a flipped coin can come heads fifty million times. In a cycle of luck which begins and ends in infinity—"

Morley rose and adjusted the wick on a grimy oil lamp, his hands trembling.

"The opponents of extrasensory perception used to claim that we're all at the receiving end of dozens of such cycles, where all the lucky runs just happen to come together in the little segment of space-time we've been caught out in. For all we know Traubel may be at the receiving end of a cycle that has 'luck-with-Venusians' stamped all over it."

Arline Morley half-rose, her eyes bright with a dawning hope. "Then if that's true, Jim, he'll be *safe* here. Your son and mine!—safe in a green mountain land that's protected by something no power on Earth can break!"

Morley's face was grim. "No, I...I don't think so. The introduction of an extraneous factor would invalidate the probability factor. Just our being here would...well, we've jarred the hand that does the flipping. Our presence here may bring down the thunder!"

"But that's just a theory, isn't it? It can't be proved."

Morley said, "Just a wild guess, of course. I didn't mean to sound so dogmatic. There's probably no such thing as an infinity cycle of lucky runs anyway. Traubel claims it's just inertia which keeps the critters—he calls them critters—from climbing the mountain and laying waste to his land. Just inertia."

"Maybe he's right," Arline said. "Remember how the others were all cut down? Then remember how it stopped, an instant before it reached us, and—went off down the road."

White-lipped, Morley nodded.

"The road was a shambles. We had to stumble over their bodies to get to the cave, the bodies of men and women cut in two by—"

"Stop that!" Morley's palms were sweating. "Stop it, you hear?"

"Twisted, crushed," Arline said tonelessly. "Limbs torn off—"

She began to sway from side to side, her nostrils quivering. "Our son will never know a safer world. We won't be his real parents. He'll be cradled in the lap of terror and when he cries—Death will suckle him. If he doesn't cry, if he's born dry-eyed, so much the worse for him. Tears are a coward's refuge, but we have to be cowards or—go mad. He'll curse the day he was born!" Morley started to move toward her across the hut.

Before he'd advanced a foot his scalp began to tingle, and he felt a coldness start up his spine.

For an instant he stood utterly motionless, staring at his wife. Then terror began to tug at his wrists, tug at his mouth. For perhaps a full minute it was an ambiguous sort of terror. He thought at first his wife's features were distorted because his own were.

He'd lost control over his features, especially his lips. He couldn't stop the twitching of his lips. But mercifully for a moment he was permitted to believe that the terror which he felt had simply communicated itself to his wife. Then he saw that it was much more than that. She was feeling it, too. Her palms were pressed to her temples and she was staring past him at the slowly opening door of the hut.

The pattern never varied. It was always the same—a coldness, a fullness, a tightness, holding the muscles rigid, paralyzing the will to resist.

The nearness of a Venusian did something to the human brain that could not be explained by any of the known laws of nature. There were unknown laws, patterns dimly suspected to exist and laws which had almost been grasped and dragged out into the light.

But compared to that power, whatever it was, telepathy was like a tiny wax candle sputtering in the glow of a billion candle power light.

It was a power which could flatten a human body in a split second of time, flatten it as though by a blow from a gigantic mace. It was a power which no ordinary human weapon could withstand, or ever hope to withstand. It could twist, maim, tear, rend, crush. It could move slantwise like a buzzsaw across a column of men; it could rip holes in the earth, it could pile up the dead in stiffening rows like cordwood—Morley tried vainly to moisten his lips. The patient, his mind seemed to be saying, should be kept in a dark room and nutrient enemata administered. That, according to an old medical book he'd read once, was the prescribed treatment for—rabies. Never a recorded cure, in all the history of rabies, but the patient had to be fed, the agony had to be prolonged, in order to exhaust all the nonexistent possibilities of a cure.

The compact little energy weapon in Morley's clasp had never destroyed a Venusian. It never could destroy a Venusian. It was as useless as a "cure" for rabies.

But instinctively his hand had traveled under his begrimed oversuit, grasped the weapon, and drawn it forth. He knew he'd be caught up, mauled, twisted before he could blast. And if he were caught up with his work uncompleted, there could be no cure for a disease which had blotted out the sunlight for the entire human race. No cure—no cure—worse than rabies. *Slam!* An opening door closes, a leaf is torn from a book and perhaps there is a breath-taking instant when a man does what he can— Goodbye, he thought. Goodbye darling, goodbye James Morley, Jr. Why did a man instinctively assume that his first-born would be a boy?

Morley suddenly saw that the door had swung so wide there was no longer a barrier between his straining eyes and the night without.

The form looming in the doorway conveyed an illusion of having laboriously impressed itself upon the sky. It was faintly rimmed with light, and the stars which glimmered on both sides of it seemed to be rushing together, as though its bulk had torn a rent in the warp-and-woof stuff of the physical universe.

Even in broad daylight the bulk of the Venusian would have blotted out the natural brilliant green of the mountainside up which it had come. Now it seemed to blot out more than the mountainside, seemed to catch at the starlight and distort the sky itself, so that the light-threaded firmament above and behind it reminded Morley of a collapsing shroud.

There was an awful instant when time seemed to miss a beat. Morley felt his fingers tighten on the blaster, felt his scalp tighten all over his head.

Then as in a dream from which he had been rudely awakened by something to which he could not give a name, he heard a ghostly faint fluttering behind him, and a voice said: "Cuckoo! Cuckoo! Cuckoo! Cuckoo! Cuckoo! Cuckoo!"

Slowly Morley turned his head. As he did so the fluttering was resumed, and the door of the clock banged shut on a feathered mite!

Morley had noticed the clock hanging on the wall, but now he seemed to be staring at it through the wide, stationary eyes of a madman. A magical clock! Morley had heard of such things, gadgets which dated back to the middle years of the nineteenth century.

He had noticed this one in particular because weighted bellows under glass had always held a peculiar fascination for him. By the push of a wire given to the body of a bird it could be bent forward, the wings and tail raised, the beak opened.

The bulkiness in the doorway must have shared Morley's interest in the clock, for it crossed the hut so rapidly that a light-rimmed after-image appeared to hover in its wake.

There was a moment of silence while it stared at the clock, all of its malignancy humped together in a towering, overwhelming wave that could be felt in every part of the room.

Then, slowly, methodically, the Venusian began to dismantle the clock.

There was a metallic clatter, a ripping sound, and something that looked like the intestines of a robot gleamed for an instant between its scaly hands. Then the door behind which the cuckoo had taken refuge was lifted out on a dangling filament, its neck distended, its white breast feathers flecked with grease.

The Venusian departed without uttering a sound. It simply swung about, re-crossed the room, and went clumping out into the night, half the clock dangling from the amorphous limb-like structure which jutted from its breast.

After what seemed like an eternity the back door of the hut opened a crack and a familiar voice said: "I forgot to tell you, son, that I have a few solitary visitors. Now and again one of the critters will leave the line of march and come clumping up the mountainside. If you saw a mosquito across the room, and your thumb began to itch you'd cross the room on a sudden impulse, maybe, and smash it."

The door opened wider, and a rusty garden rake clattered against the jamb.

"But you wouldn't have to cross the room, son. You'd almost as soon as not, and if when you're raising your thumb a hand reaches out from the wall and says: 'Clasp me,' or the wallpaper turns from green to pink your interest shifts and there's time for inertia to set in. You become interested in the wallpaper, and the mosquito just doesn't get crushed."

The rake made a rasping sound on the floor. "Pawns. That clock was a pawn, and I've set other pawns out on the mountainside to protect my rook just in case one of the critters turns aside and starts up. I've been playing a game with them for more than thirty years now, son. It isn't often one of them gets as far as the hut."

A low chuckle came from the doorway. "Interested? You bet it was interested. A cuckoo clock is about the rarest mechanical gadget on Earth. Not many of 'em left, not one Venusian in fifty thousand has seen one—no, make that fifty million. And they do like to imitate things; they like to pull gadgets apart. There's just that little interval between impulse and inertia which has to be bridged."

"Good Lord!" Morley choked.

"It came in through the front door, didn't it? You came in through this door, I guess, or you'd have heard the birdie too. 'Cuckoo, cuckoo'—because just coming in through the front door activates the clock. You see, son, there's a photo-electric beam in the front door, and the poisonous critter brought the birdie out the instant it stepped into my parlor."

Morley wiped the sweat from his face. *He had all the needed, delicate parts, and freedom from fear, freedom from strain, the opportunity to work unmolested in a small, hastily improvised laboratory might well spell the difference between success and failure.*

Might? Would. And he wouldn't have to settle for four months now. He'd have all the time he needed to perfect the instrument.

The door made a rasping sound as it was thrown wide.

Traubel stumbled a little as he crossed the hut. He crossed to the wash-stand, poured out some water and started fumbling around for a cake of soap on the cluttered shelf where he kept his shaving kit, a few necessary drugs, and a dog-eared calendar dating back to the late years of the twentieth century.

"I'm glad you and the missus are going to stay for a spell, son," he said. "You've no idea how lonely it gets up here when the crickets stop chirping, and the nights start getting longer. You see, son, I've been stone blind now going on eighteen years."

FILCH

All Griscom had to show for his eighteen months on Rigel's third planet was a haunted stare, and a storeroom littered with rubbish. He felt walled in, beaten down, and spiritually suffocated. He felt angry and resentful and victimized. He felt like a stooge and a zany. He couldn't even—well, it was hard to put into words, but when he eavesdropped on his own subconscious he couldn't be sure the code numerals were the ones he'd put there.

Not that he was in any danger of cracking up physically. So far he'd maintained his footing despite a physical environment which was all wet in patches. Everything he touched was either streaked with damp, or drier than the rasp of pumice on a revolving metal cylinder. Everything—for all seven of the Rigel sun planets were drymoist and had a checkerboard quilt sort of atmosphere.

There were patches of damp green rot on the metal-sheeted walls of the company buildings, and when he walked his shoes spurted dust and a haziness swirled up about him. But so far he'd squared off, and taken the arid tundra and night-heavy clouds in his stride. He hadn't even beefed to the home office.

He wasn't beefing now. Having pulled off his boots, he sat squinting through a haze of tobacco smoke at a much younger man than himself, his long face a sickly brown study.

"You smoke shag?" the youth asked, wrinkling his nose.

The gaunt skeleton that was Griscom turned slightly, and ladled up a spoonful of the unsavory stew which was dawdling to a boil on the small magneto-grill at his elbow.

"Yeah," he grunted. "It's about the only thing out here I like. The coarser the better."

Griscom sniffed at the stew as he spoke, blew upon it, and forced himself to take a sip. He shuddered as the spoon caressed his palate, a hot resentment in his stare. Then it occurred to him that a schizoid would have felt no such repugnance and relief swept into his eyes.

He laughed harshly. "I'm afraid smoking is becoming an obsession with me. Strong tobacco is a powerful disinfectant, you know."

The youth smiled nervously. "I still think—"

"I know what you're going to say," Griscom interposed, with a wry grimace. "I should have gone native. When in Rome do as the Romans do, eh? Well, we're not in Rome, and you'll find out what going native means quickly enough. When you do, there's one thing I can promise you. It won't smell like shag, or anything you've ever met."

The young man—his name was Richard Bosworth—seemed bewildered. "But, sir, I thought—"

"You thought, because I O.K.'d your ideas on a sidereal communication disk, I'd stay on and be your father-confessor? No, my dear chap—no. I played a scurvy trick on you. In theory your ideas are appealing, even brilliant, but if I had to be here when they really take hold of you—"

He shrugged, and knocked the dottle from his pipe.

"I'm sorry if my record misled you. When you've lived as long as I have, you'll know that the greatest human gifts have about as much relation to a man's integrity as the color of his hair. And I'm just a shrewd company haggler. I tell you, I'm fed up, and—you'd better get spruced up. We've a redhead here who hopes I'll stay on. When she sees you I can fade out with better grace."

Bosworth stroked his chin, which was covered with a three days growth of stubble. "Yeah, I guess I could do with a shave and a tubbing. In space you sort of neglect—"

"You'll have plenty of time to look your worst," Griscom assured him. "Besides, the natives can't grow hair, and beards don't set well with them. They're just human enough to resent what they can't imitate."

The redhead was an unbelievable phenomenon so far from the Solar System, her eyes especially. It had taken Bosworth a full hour to recover from the shock of Griscom's ultimatum. Now, moving about the storeroom, he could hear her fast, staccato breathing, and felt suddenly rudderless again.

In a clash of masculine wills there was always a rapier-like give and take to give a man a feeling of confidence. But how could he defend himself against the scorn of a frail, trembling girl who regarded him as a pariah?

He knew she was following his every movement with the same dark eyes she had used to drill holes in his self-assurance. Griscom had delivered a body blow to his chances of taking refuge behind a barrier of reticence by the informality of his introduction.

"Joan, this is Dick Bosworth. You know why he's here, so it shouldn't come as too great a shock to you."

Horror and loathing had flared in Joan Mallory's stare, and she had looked away quickly.

If only she'd kept her gaze averted he might have endured the mounting tension, the feeling that she resented having him near her, and would have screamed if he touched her.

It came suddenly, in a vehement whisper so laden with scorn it completely unnerved him.

"I'd rather a struvebeast clawed out my throat," she said bending over a miserable shard of something that looked like a bullet-riddled tea kettle. "Jim never would, and I've always respected him for it."

Anger is a strange emotion. Bosworth had never known just how strange till he felt it take complete possession of his vocal cords, and heard himself saying in a voice which he scarcely recognized as his own: "If you expect to trade with an alien race, you've got to find out what makes them tick. You've got to get as close as possible to bedrock by living as they do. What if their inner springs do vibrate to nonhuman rhythms? So do the springs inside a clock, but you can get a clock to cooperate if you understand the winding mechanism.

"You may get a little greasy, but you can pretty well master the mechanism of a clock if you keep taking it apart and putting it together again. Any clock—and the same goes for the psychology of an alien race. The reason Griscom found himself tricked and out-guessed at every turn was because he adopted a superior, standoffish attitude. Griscom's a great proctor, but these Rigel System planetarians are so totally unlike—"

"You'll never know how unlike till you've sat down to eat with them," the girl interposed, with passionate conviction. "Eat, carouse with them. You'll find out."

"Will I?"

"That's what they wanted Jim to do. If he had, we'd have something more valuable to pack and ship back to Terra than a few wretched crockery fragments. Earthern potsherds are a credit a dozen. Oh, the company can sell this rubbish to the Institute of Galactic Archaeology for enough fluid currency to pay your salary and mine. But Jim could have filled the sheds with jeweled ornaments and urns of beaten gold. Once he went just far enough to—"

She shuddered, and stared at him out of eyes that seemed to fill her face. "Jim told me about it. It was a ghastly, a completely sobering experience. You were just now talking about clocks. Suppose you were to open up a big, old grandfather clock—just to see what makes it tick, just to steady the winding mechanism. Your hands are inside and you are fumbling around and suddenly—it grabs hold of you! Instead of wheels and pulley something reaches out and grabs you. Suppose it is all alive inside, and not even three-dimensional."

"It was as bad as that, was it?"

"It was worse than that, a simplicity of evil beyond anything I could have imagined. I can't even—talk about it."

Bosworth stared at her levelly. "You mean you don't want to talk about it."

"I can't, I won't. Jim knows what may happen to you, and in a way, he'd give his right arm to prevent it. But right now his decent human instincts an waging a terrible struggle with his loyalty to the company. He knows how kind the natives would be; how generous they'd be. They wouldn't haggle with you for wretched potsherds. Oh, no—they'd shower you with presents."

"And Griscom knows what that could mean to the company?"

She nodded. "He can't go native himself," she said firmly. "His pride, his inner integrity would be outraged. The shame would never wear off. But when you volunteered, when the home office beamed you were young and confident and eager he O.K.'d your appointment."

"Go on."

"You know how company reprimands creep into your skin when you're talking into a sidereal communication disk. The light-years fall away, and you feel you're actually on Terra. Yet just talking across such a vast distance makes you unsure of yourself, makes you...well, it warps your perspective."

"I get it. Griscom wants the natives to trot out their best silverware. So I stick my neck out, I put my head on the chopping block, and he looks the other way. He's a grand guy—but squeamish. He doesn't want to watch the blade descend."

"You didn't have to stick your neck out!" the girl retorted, her color rising. "You didn't have to, you *didn't*—"

Bosworth narrowed his eyes. "No-o," he said slowly, "I suppose not." Clumping away from the trading post over the moistdry plain Bosworth found himself wondering why his thoughts kept fluttering back and forth like prismatic mayflies over the stagnant marsh-moss inside his head.

He was feeling the strain now, he told himself grimly. Rigel wasn't exactly an easy sun to get to, and the long journey through space had strained his nerves to the breaking point.

His eyes swept the arid plain, roamed over everything. The frown on his face showed the uneasiness he felt. Space-warp travel had an advantage over mere planet-hopping in a rocket-driven ship, but when a man came out through the yawning gravity-port of a spiral-nosed sidereal cruiser he had to expect to feel shaken up a bit.

It was curious, but his brain felt limpid somehow, as though the long journey had melted it down and catalyzed it with little floating grains of lunacy. Everything about the Rigel System planet seemed off key and subtly out of alignment. What was even more disturbing, he couldn't seem to shake off an inner sense of foreboding, as though something he couldn't even begin to visualize were getting ready to lay an egg directly in his path. An egg filled with explosive possibilities, an egg—He checked himself abruptly. What was the matter with him? Was he running a fever, or was it just the effect of the harsh, bright sunlight slanting down through rifts in the clouds, and glittering in crazy-quilt patches on the moistdry soil?

There were no winds to dispel the intermittent humidity, but off to his left the receding company buildings were smoldering in a deep, purple haze which was soothing to his vision. With a shudder he fastened his gaze on the distant, metal-sheeted walls of the compound, and plunged on doggedly. He wasn't going to allow himself to think such thoughts, he told himself grimly. Not while his strength held out, and he could keep on walking.

He knew that natives would seek him out if he just kept on walking. They were probably watching him now from a distance, for their telescopic eyes could discern a walking human before their sensitive nostrils could detect one.

Somehow the thought rankled. They were watching him, and he couldn't watch back. He couldn't even smell back. He couldn't—there it was again—that light-headed feeling, as though he'd been given a thousand nursery rhymes, a thousand meaningless jingles to repeat with Socratic inflections. Don't stop, don't leave out a single line, or *you'll be sorry!*

Suddenly—Bosworth caught on! Griscom had warned him to anticipate this. They were feeling out his thoughts from a distance! His light-headedness was caused by a stream of almost formless thoughts flowing into his brain, and mingling with the thoughts already there. Thoughts like fluid scalpels, twisting, turning—setting up a mental whirring.

He wished they'd stop. They were violating the privacy of his mind in a very disturbing way, because he had no way of knowing just how deeply they could probe. He wondered a little wildly how much Griscom knew. How much had Griscom kept back, how much—Thoughts couldn't hurt him. After all, he wasn't a child. Sticks and stones could break his bones, but thoughts couldn't touch him. They'd have to stop soon because they were drawing closer, and he was sure the instant he saw them the probing would stop. They'd know by then why he had walked out to meet them.

Griscom had warned him he'd get a shock when he saw them. He'd looked at a few photographs and returned them to Griscom with a slight shrug, as though he hadn't been at all put out.

Actually, he'd been shocked, and—revolted? No, that was too strong a word. Square the shade of difference between repulsion and revulsion, and the right word would emerge. It wasn't disgust, exactly, but the human race has never quite reconciled itself to exposed digestive organs. Perhaps it would be more correct to say it has never overcome a deep, instinctive horror, shared by all primates, of unsanitary housing facilities.

In appearance the Rigel System planetarians were close enough to humanity to be repulsive on that account alone. Griscom had warned him there were aspects of skin texture and expression which no photograph could capture, but—the photographs had been the opposite of vague.

It was curious, but when he shut his eyes he could see them now, stalking the gray tundra like Fuseli nudes, their owlish faces thrust sharply forward, and their skeleton-thin bodies glinting in the harsh sunlight.

The visualization seemed as natural as breathing. What he did not know was that he was seeing them in his mind's eye when he might just as well have been staring straight before him.

Like most contagious diseases, fear has a brief incubation period.

Even when Bosworth opened his eyes and saw them squatting on the moist-dry soil in a semicircle about him his immediate reaction was merely one of surprise.

Though a dark current was sweeping into his mind he told himself simply that they were much uglier than he'd imagined they would be. Much, much uglier. Their flesh was caked with dust, their lips were cracked and blistered, and the series of collapsing lenses which enabled them to telescope their vision at will overlapped in concentric ridges, giving to their faces in repose a distinctly goggle-eyed appearance.

For the barest instant fear convulsed Bosworth, and then—ceased to have an influence over him. There swept in upon him instead an immense calmness, a feeling of gratitude and deliverance. It was like—being intoxicated. It was even partly physical. He could feel a warmth creeping up inside him—bridging a gap, breaking down a barrier.

Surely there could be very little difference between a human and the creature who sat directly in his path, regarding him with an expression vaguely reminiscent of—a stuffed pig's head, he thought idiotically. How could there be, when he could share that creature's inmost thoughts and emotions?

"You are the new young proctor?" the creature asked, elevating its haunches and waving its claw-like hands at him.

"I am nothing if I am not your friend," Bosworth heard himself replying.

"Then you will feed with us?" the creature asked.

"Yes. I...I would be honored."

"Then come, my friend, my brother. We will feast together."

The food gagged Bosworth, but he forced himself to eat it. Everything else was so agreeable it wouldn't have seemed right to refuse the food. Thick chunks of something that certainly wasn't meat, floating in an evil-smelling gravy, had been set before him in a shallow earthen pan, and he was doing his best to ladle it up, plunk it in his mouth, and forget about it.

He couldn't quite forget the taste, which had a way of lingering on despite a fluid intake far in excess of his customary drinking habits.

The beverage certainly wasn't bad. It set up a wet tingling on his palate, and brought a glow to his vision when he raised his eyes to the sloping stone roof of the hut.

Phonetically his host's name was Glu-gub-gun, but Bosworth had found it more convenient to slur the middle syllable, and address the dear chap merely as Glugun. There was no way of evading the friendliness which Glugun exuded. There flowed from him a continuous solicitude which took the form of replenishing the earthen platter with more chunks of the unsavory goulash, and refilling Bosworth's goblet till a giddiness swept over him.

He looked at Glugun across the eating board, noticed how emaciated he seemed, and felt an overwhelming pity for him.

"You don't eat enough, Glugun," he wanted to say.

It was curious how many things he wanted to tell Glugun. Things he wouldn't have dreamed of confiding to Joan Mallory, and certainly not to Griscom. Things all humans would like to confide to other humans, but didn't dare for fear of something which was a little difficult to define.

In general all humans shared the same frailties, but if you let down your hair and the other chap didn't you were at a disadvantage. With Glugun he just didn't feel that way at all. Was it because he felt so superior to Glugun that no advantage which the Rigel System planetarian might snatch could alter the nature of their relationship? Was it because he just couldn't imagine Glugun assuming a gloating, superior attitude?

It wasn't so much the really bad things about themselves that humans kept from one another. It was all the little, fleeting mean thoughts and inane thoughts which surged through their minds in a continuous stream from dawn to dusk. All humans were zanies in their thoughts, but that was all right so long as nobody got caught with his mental pants down.

If you were feverish and babbled, or became intoxicated and babbled, you were just out of luck. Humans lived and breathed and had their
beings behind a triple-piled barrier of deceit, a smokescreen which had
to be maintained, or else—Even the little ridiculous posturings which
all humans struck in the privacy of their homes couldn't be exposed to
public view without provoking mirth, astonishment or a lifting of eyebrows. That inane little song you sang while shaving. Suppose you had
to repeat it before an audience? Or the way you hogged your food when
you thought no one was looking.

Or the time you spanked the cat, not cruelly, but a little more vigorously than the offense warranted, and with appropriate expletives. Or
the scribblings you made on the margins of a book while waiting for a
shuttle-plane—meaningless little curlicues with just enough symbolism
in the twists and turns to damn you in the eyes of a psychiatrist.

With Glugun he just didn't feel that way. With Glugun there was no
need for secrecy—He was suddenly aware that the Rigel System planetarian was leaning sharply toward him. There was a bright and shining
something in Glugun's taloned clasp, and the thin lips were moving.

"Now we shall feast in a different way. Stare steadily, and tell me
what you see!"

The crystal cube was about eight inches square, and just holding it
made Bosworth feel strange. It had passed so unobtrusively from Glugun's claw-like hands to his own trembling ones that it was hard for him
to realize he was staring into it with an insistence that seemed to pluck at
his eyeballs and draw his vision down—and down.

"Stare steadily," he heard Glugun reiterating, as though from a great
distance.

At first there was nothing but a milky opacity in the depths of the
cube. Then the milkiness cleared a little and he saw—something that
glittered. The cube grew brighter, and the glitter resolved itself into a line
of metal-sheeted poles, very tiny and far away, as though he were staring
down at them through the wrong end of a telescope.

For a fractional second Bosworth thought that his temples would
burst. Standing in front of the compound shading her eyes, was a tiny
human figure. There was no longer any opacity inside the cube, and he
could see the sunlight glinting in Joan Mallory's hair, and the thin film
of dust which had swirled up about her knees. After a moment Griscom
came clumping out to stand beside her.

Bosworth squeezed the cube between his palms, and as he did so it
seemed to contract a little. He could make out the girl's troubled frown,
the tilt of Griscom's pipe. The girl's head was sun-aureoled, and a thin

ribbon of smoke—he wrinkled his nose—was arising from the bowl of Griscom's pipe into the moist-dry air.

Suddenly Joan Mallory moved her head a little, and her brow seemed to take on a deeper redness, as though a crimson desert flower had blossomed in the tangled wilderness of her hair.

"Draw them closer, draw them toward you!" a far-off voice urged. It wasn't difficult: it was not even necessary for Bosworth to increase the intensity of his stare. About the two tiny figures there had crept a translucent glimmering, and they swayed in it like—the image came unbidden into his mind—two minikin corpses afloat in a luminous tide.

Abruptly as he stared the stockade seemed to recede, and they were swirling up toward him over a tilted plain. Larger they grew and larger, swirling up as though propelled by an invisible wind. They hardly seemed to move their limbs as they drew near, and their faces were no longer mobile.

Suddenly they were quite astonishingly large, as though a magnification had taken place inside the cube. Their eyes were closed, and they appeared to be asleep. There was a pulsing at the girl's temples, and a brightening and a dimming of the glowing dottle in Griscom's pipe.

He saw them for an instant and then—he didn't see them. His faculties seemed to expand, and into him there swept a vitality such as he had never known. He wasn't staring into the cube any more. He wasn't staring at anything at all.

There was a darkness in his brain—a vast, tumultuous pulsing which filled him with a soaring sense of power. The darkness and the pulsing were like a carousal. Winey was the darkness, bubbling and intoxicating, and with all his senses he drank deep of it until his temples swelled and something seemed to burst in his brain.

When he opened his eyes he seemed to be outside his own body. Remote and cold his body seemed—no longer a part of himself. He could look down over his drawn-up legs, could see also his hands which were folded in front of him. But a gray opacity swirled where his chest should have been, and he felt that he could not move his head. There was a sucked-in feeling about his eyes, and he couldn't—seem to—blink them.

Then he saw Glugun. The Rigel System planetarian was slumped down opposite him, his spindly legs drawn up grasshopper fashion on both sides of his thin body, his anemone-like digestive orifice concealed by the cube which he was clasping to his chest with rigidly contracted talons. He eyes were lidded and upon his owlish face there was a slumberous expression.

Bosworth thought he knew what his mind had done to the minikins in the crystal. He was a bright boy—bright enough to pry out the ghastly rind of the fruit which Glugun had offered him. He'd taken a mental bite, and it had—intoxicated him. Glugun had then snatched the cube back, and was now intoxicated himself.

Cold sweat oozed out on Bosworth's brow, and his teeth came together. He'd feasted on—human vital energies? Astral images? Occultism? Vampirism? On Terra crystal spheres and cubes were associated with the trappings of occultism. But on a Rigel sun planet—Might there not be something entirely physiological in the human body, some as yet undetected vital emanation which could be trapped and imprisoned? If the cube were a kind of magnetized flytrap, composed of matter so sensitized it could absorb protoplasmic auras, and release them to a mind craving nourishment—

He stopped, appalled by the direction his thoughts were taking. Were the trappings and legends of occultism—crystal balls, abnormal mental states, the vampire and werewolf myths—simply the expression of a kind of psychic cannibalism, innate in humanity, but denied fulfillment on Terra, and groping blindly for the right answer?

Humans fashioned little wax figurines and pierced them with nails. Humans looked into crystals. An organism with an innate but unsatisfied craving would be guided by intuition, for evolution had a mysterious way of transforming blind drives into hunches.

Was the crystal cube which Glugun was now clasping something which humans had always longed to clasp? Had the Rigel System planetarians the same urge, and worked out a scientific means of gratification?

With considerable effort Bosworth fought back a desire to retch. He was back inside his body now. He couldn't move his limbs yet, but he could see his chest, blink his eyes, and corporeality had returned to his stomach.

How long had Glugun slept, he wondered wildly. How long had *he* slept. Seven hours—ten? Beyond the open door of the hut there was now a redness, as though the dry air outside had caught fire, and—Bosworth's thoughts congealed. The Rigel System planetarian had changed his position. He had lowered the cube and was leaning sharply forward, and out of the owlish face two slitted eyes were parrying Bosworth's stare with unmistakable derision.

In the spherical control room of the sidereal cruiser Joan Mallory's coppery hair seemed to set up a blaze.

"You should have told him the truth," she said, raising her voice to make herself heard above the droning of the atomotors. "He didn't know what he was letting himself in for."

"He knows now," Griscom grunted, drawing on his pipe, and staring out through the viewpane across a wet-dry plain that was already a blur in the wake of the thrumming vessel.

There was nothing out there he was sorry to be bidding good-by to, he told himself savagely. Six company sheds, smoldering in dry rot. Three smoldering in wet. The metal-sheeted posts of the stockade, mottled green and pink. Eighteen wasted months, receding like spectral horsemen over the hump of the plain. He'd know what to say to anyone who tried to claim you couldn't visualize a month. He'd have an answer ready.

He swung about with an angry gesture. "Why should I have alarmed him with a lot of vague suspicions. I've been getting weaker for months and you've been feeling it, too. They have a crystal cube, and when I looked into it I saw you. That's absolutely all I know. I fell into a drugged sleep and when I woke up I felt…all right, I'll say it…sluggish and all warm inside like a satiated vampire bat."

Griscom drew on his pipe. "I didn't feel like a Dracula in the flesh, you understand. It wasn't as gross as that. But ta-ra-ra boom-de-ay. Sing it out loud and I don't see how it can add up to anything but a kind of mental vampirism."

"Yes, I think so," the girl agreed.

"You want to know why I didn't warn him. I'll tell you. He happens to be the youngest son of the President of the Intergalactic Trading Co. He's an ambitious young whelp, and he wanted to prove to papa he could make good on his own. If I'd laid my cards on the table, a realistic report telling the truth about a planet is the one thing I couldn't have wheedled out of him. He *had* to see for himself. He had to think he was improving our chances of pulling urns of beaten gold out of a very rank hat."

The girl looked at him. "You mean he had to be a guinea pig," she said. "That's what you mean, isn't it?"

Griscom reddened. "He got back all right, didn't he? He's safe on his bunk in the cuddy, isn't he? A bit white around the gills, but safe. I tell you, I had to make sure the post will stay abandoned. Now that he's actually seen what's inside the hat he'll back me to the hilt. The company won't just pigeonhole my report, and send another proctor out."

Griscom strode to the control board and studied the estimator. He manipulated a rheostat. He tested the synchronization of the automatic drive controls with a wet thumb and forefinger.

Then it came: "When I was a kid, we had a pirate's den in the back-yard. We hung toy effigies from the yardarm of a little wooden ship. But when I grew up I put such things behind me. Rigel System planetarians may not be criminals. They may simply have failed to grow up."

Joan said slowly: "Just what does that mean?"

"Nothing, except that I'd rather live in a six by eight room with an Irrawaddy cobra."

The girl directed a startled glance at Griscom's stooped shoulders. "Jim, I thought you were a thoroughgoing materialist. If the crystals—"

Griscom straightened heavily. "The crystals are dangerous, but not in the way you think. Any bright and shining object would be dangerous—if *you had what it takes.*"

He nodded. "It's as clear as a pikestaff. When the vision becomes fixed on a bright and shining object the subconscious leaps into the saddle, and believes everything it's told. There is no actual outside compulsion—people hypnotize themselves. But if the operator had telepathic powers, and could get *inside* our minds—"

Griscom's face was grim. "Hypnosis might not be a self-induced state at all. Look at it this way. There may be something in the human mind which can be—manipulated. A kind of inhibiting sixth sense, perhaps, a faculty which keeps us from hopscotching it back down the shoreline into the pelagic muck. Perhaps that faculty, that inhibiting something can be *filched.*"

"Filched?"

Griscom nodded. "You know what filch means—petty pilfering, the sly taking away of something that's not likely to be missed. Apparently Rigel System planetarians can drain organic vital energies from a distance, and most effectively, perhaps, with the aid of a shining object. Perhaps if our brains were properly manipulated we could, too. Telepathic hypnosis, however induced, should be potent and pervasive enough to overcome an evolutionary quirk."

"Jim!"

Griscom frowned. "It would be an extra-sensory faculty, of course. But it could go back to a very early form of terrestrial life. For all we know even unicellular organisms may have extra-sensory endowments. Long ages ago some lowly form of life may have acquired the power and handed it on to us. Cilio-telepathy. Some primitive Cambrian—sea jelly, perhaps, or a fleshy, fat worm with a blood-red proboscis. But such a power would have to be sidetracked, or the species would end by destroying itself. So natural selection built up a barrier, an inhibiting sixth sense—"

"Just a minute, Jim!" Joan was pressing her palms to her temples. "I don't feel I can stand any more. I don't believe it, it's too revolting, I… Jim, why did you have to talk about it? Why couldn't you have left it the way it was?"

Griscom looked at her for a long time. "Nothing nature does or fails to do should surprise you," he said. "Her sins of commission are bad enough, but her sins of omission—"

His voice sharpened and became tinged with rancor, as though he were airing a grievance. "Half blind she is, a lazy and unscrupulous strumpet, but she never fails to pocket the tip, and walk off with her chin in the air. With just a little extra trouble she could have doubled our life spans, given us telescopic vision—or microscopic, for that matter—and a much richer enjoyment of scents."

Bosworth sat up. There was a dryness in his throat, and his brain was ticking like a clock. He tried to go to sleep, but sleep wouldn't come. Now he wasn't trying any more. Now he was only interested in stopping the shaking of his limbs, and getting the cobwebs out of his brain.

With a shudder he moved to the edge of the berth and felt around with his bare toes for his slippers on the thrumming deck. He couldn't sleep because certain memories were much too fresh in his mind. But by tomorrow or the next day they'd begin to recede, to shrink and shrivel up, and he wouldn't have to keep reminding himself he was in danger of cracking up.

He was going to be all right. When he poured himself a stiff one the cobwebs which kept creeping under his eyelids would cease to trouble him. There just wouldn't be any cobwebs and he might feel calm enough to make out a report backing Griscom to the hilt. If he couldn't sleep, writing steadily would help to calm his nerves, and—He had only a confused recollection of descending to the deck, lurching across the cuddy and flinging open the metal cabinet which stood against the opposite bulkhead. But that he had stooped and reached inside the cabinet he could not doubt, for he suddenly found himself pouring amber fluid into a glass that mirrored his face in all its haggardness.

Although the cobwebs were creeping under his eyelids again he could see the glass clearly. His hand had trembled a little, and a thin film of spilled fluid encircled the glass. In the cold light from the lamp-studded overhead the deep-toned Scotch had a very pleasing aspect.

He grasped the edge of the cabinet and stared down as though fascinated.

At first there was nothing but a weaving opacity in the depths of the glass. Then the filminess cleared a little, and he saw something that glittered. The glass grew brighter and the glitter resolved itself into a gleaming control panel, very small and far away, as though he were staring down at it through the wrong end of a telescope.

Standing in front of the panel was a tiny human figure. There was no longer any opacity inside the cube, and he could see the cold light glinting in Joan Mallory's hair.

Bosworth's temples tightened, and his eyes began to shine.

THE TRAP

It was a beautiful morning. The mist had come up deep and blue, the air was not too cold, and out of the blueness a great ship loomed, its hull outlined in garish radiance against a shimmer of light so vast and tumultuous it seemed to span the Galaxy.

"She's sure coming in fast!" called a voice from the star station.

William Hanley knocked the dottle from his pipe, and scowled at a rent in the mist where a few truant stars still hung like droplets of flame. At first the ship had loomed up soundlessly, but now the landing strip was vibrating, and the drone of the huge vessel's motors had become a deep, throbbing roar overhead.

"She'll take the station with her!" Hanley groaned. Then, as though his mind rejected the thought: "She'll veer—she'll have to. No astragator this side of the Coal Sack could be *that* malicious!"

As if in confirmation a sudden, vibrant clang rang out in the stillness. Not the resonant crash of buckling gravity plates, but the more reassuring sound of magnetic mooring cables clattering against a smooth metal hull.

Hanley stood perfectly motionless, his mouth hanging open. For an instant he had the distinct and awful feeling that he had parted company with his sanity. That the forward ends of mooring cables—a scant half-dozen magnetically groping strands—could steady and slow down a ship three hundred meters in length was against all reason.

Yet it was happening. From the great vessel's bow there projected a notched metal half-moon which gathered up the questing strands and bound them into a stabilizing skein a hundred yards from the mooring mast. Faster and faster, more and more incredibly, until the ship hung completely motionless—an immense, blue-black ellipsoid agleam with winking lights.

"Bill! Did you see that? Did you *see* it?"

Peering back over his shoulder, Hanley could make out the startled face of his assistant hovering like a plucked owl's head in the station's mist-filled doorway. As he stared in consternation young Gregg withdrew his head, and the mist which swirled in the doorway brightened. A moment later the station's one window glowed.

Hanley swore softly, aware of a stirring of panic deep down in his consciousness. Mingling with his alarm was an angry realization that Gregg was turning on all the lights in the station.

On a Rigel System refueling station a million light-years from nowhere time could hang heavy with uneventfulness. A process of desensitization could set in so profound that even the coming and going of trans-Galactic cruiser flotillas—"great old ships in sidereal splendors veiled"—impinged on the mind with a mirage-like vagueness. Yet now, in a few brief moments, the pattern of months had been shattered.

Hanley knew what was happening, of course.

He was slowly going crazy.

A ship with a bowsprit that gobbled up mooring cables was on par with young Gregg's habit of yodeling to the ogreish shadow-shapes which haunted the mist-draped planetoid from dawn to dusk. And Gregg was crazy, had been for months.

The youth hadn't been told yet, but he *was* crazy. How could he be sane and want to play a saxophone into the small hours, wrenching from that utterly base instrument music that made Hanley physically ill. Most of the time he stayed by himself at the far end of the dingy station, and that, too, was a bad sign.

Was lunacy contagious?

Behind Hanley there loomed four cyclopean fuel tanks, their conical summits bathed in a fuzzy glow. The star station, which was also conical, had been constructed out of discarded scraps of metal in great haste by a Galactic Commission engineer bent on getting back to Terra in time for Christmas holidays.

"The tanks' young 'un," Gregg had ironically dubbed it.

There was no law, of course, to prevent Gregg from coining names for objects which got on his superior's nerves. But as Hanley swung about and strode into the wretched structure he told himself that Gregg was more case-hardened than the average run of criminals. He was forever committing breaches of simple decency by refusing to keep his thoughts to himself. He—

Hanley shuddered, and stood blinking at the personification of all his woes regarding him from the depths of the station's dingy, blank-walled interior, the train of his thoughts derailed by something in the youth's stare which infuriated him to the core of his being.

The bright but rapidly disintegrating personality that was Gregg was not incapable of a kind of fish-cold sympathy which verged on condescension, verged on pity, and all because—Well because Gregg was forever insisting that he, Hanley, had no poetry in his soul, and no appreciation of what it meant to be an artist. Sporadically the youth painted, wrote poetry, and thought of himself generally as a misunderstood and maladjusted man of genius.

Actually there was no lazier youth this side of Betelgeuse. When something showed signs of blowing he could be a competent grease monkey, could climb all over the big tanks till sweat dripped from him. But that didn't mean he wasn't lazy. Things had to come to an almost calamitous pass before he'd exert himself.

Gregg now sat now on a narrow cot with his hands locked across the back of his head, a slight frown creasing his handsome face. Having helped himself to one of Hanley's cigars, he was keeping his feet firmly planted on the floor, so that his superior would not suspect that he was wearing holes in a borrowed pair of cello socks.

"Well, Bill?" he said.

"Why did you duck out of sight just when I needed your advice?" Hanley flared.

Gregg looked startled. "You needed *my* advice?"

"Certainly." Hanley was bitter. "When you disagree with me, I know I'm right. When you don't, I have to watch my step."

Gregg took the cigar out of his mouth and stared hard at the glowing tip. "I don't think we should ignore the message just because there were no code numerals on the tape," he said. "I've a feeling it will be followed by an official message."

He looked up, serious concern on his face. "That's my honest opinion, and I'd advise you not to shrug it off just because you don't like the cut of my jib."

"That's for me to decide," Hanley snorted. Then his features softened: "The cut wouldn't matter so much if we had more elbow room. Shut two or six or a dozen men up together in a station this size for six months running and any one of ten million personality traits can produce downright hostile reactions. You get so you resent the way a guy draws on his socks."

He smiled bitterly. "Even when they're *your* socks."

"Holes in mine," Gregg said, shamelessly. "You borrowed my magnetorazor, didn't you?"

"Yeah, and your second best pipe. It stank up the whole planetoid."

Hanley fumbled in his pocket, drew out a crumpled tele-message. "It doesn't mean a thing to me that this came in over a sidereal communication circuit," he said, defensively. "Any screwloose could have sent it."

He read aloud: "Ship of peculiar design and unknown origin, recently triangulated in Eridanus, is now believed to be approaching Orion. Vessel refuses to communicate."

"And that's all," Hanley grunted, crumpling the flimsy message for the twentieth time. "No description of the ship, no—"

"How about 'peculiar design'?" Gregg asked.

"Do you call that a description?"

"Perhaps whoever sent that message wanted *you* to fill in the gaps," Gregg suggested, with a twisted smile. "If he'd said there was a ship loose in space with a cable-eating bowsprit, you know where you'd have tossed that message."

"It wouldn't have cost him anything to describe the ship!" was Hanley's embittered response.

"No, it wouldn't." Gregg admitted. "But perhaps some sympathetic little minor official somewhere knew there's nothing quite so unnerving as a terse, carefully-phrased understatement. Perhaps—"

"Stop right there!" Hanley snapped. "I'm sick and tired of your circumlocutions."

"But don't you see? He could be trying to warn you without stepping on official toes. The Commission may not want to commit itself—yet. So far the ship hasn't made port. The Commission may be waiting to see what happens when it does. A clever man would use just that approach—throw out a hint without seeming to do so."

"Anything more?" Hanley exploded.

"Only that we ought to thank our lucky stars the message came through when it did. We might have permitted her to refuel."

Hanley started across the room. Gregg's eyes following him. He swung about before he reached the door.

"Just a minute, Gregg. What do you suggest we do?"

Gregg's brooding gaze hovered between his superior and the glowing tip of his cigar.

"Well, nothing inside that ship can come out and descend to our peaceful little Utopia unless it suits our convenience. She may or may not have an antimagnetic hull, but the force-field she's nesting against couldn't be busted open by a runaway star with a core of pure deuterium."

"Go on."

Gregg blew a smoke ring and watched it ascend toward the ceiling. "We built that field up as a protection against piracy. If the crew refused to image themselves in on the disk, we won't dissolve the field. We'll be within our rights unless—" Gregg hesitated. "Unless their papers are in order, and a human face comes through. Even then we could tell them we're in quarantine. I've often thought that a human face *could* be simulated. On the disk, I mean—"

Hanley passed a hand over his brow. "Maybe we'd better start making arrangements now," he said.

"For what?"

"Your incarceration."

Gregg watched his superior swing about. This time Hanley did not pause or look back.

He's not telling me, Gregg thought, *but he'll be inside that ship in ten minutes.*

He started toward the door and then—inertia enfolded him like a winding sheet. Lord, how he hated to act, to make decisions, to do anything which went counter to the immense indolence which was his most outstanding character trait.

In some respects he was like those pioneer fossil amphibians, the lobefins. Not as good as reptiles, better than fishes, the lobefins had been caught up in a backwash of inertia on the eve of what might have been their greatest evolutionary triumph.

Compared to men of really vibrant energies he was a lobefin. He couldn't quite climb up over the bank because he liked to stretch himself out in the tidal muck, and bask in the warm sunlight.

He moved in a radiant little orbit of his own inside the immense, bustling beehive of activity which homo sapiens had set up.

Some day anthropologists were going to discover that the genus homo embraced six distinct species of men. Extinct were homo heidelbergensis, homo neanderthalensis, homo rhodesiensis and homo soloensis. Living were homo sapiens, and—homo indolensis.

Fortunately very few people suspected the existence of homo indolensis.

Gregg moved languidly to a bookcase and pulled out Hargrave's "Third Stage of Interstellar Expansion." It was a fascinating book because Hargrave, too, had been capable of deriving the most intense emotional satisfaction from just sitting sprawled out in a chair and letting his imagination run riot.

There could be no doubt that the impulse to sit and dream, to forego all exertion, was a progressive, specialized derivation from a much earlier attempt on the part of primitive man to shuffle off the immense responsibility of—fire and flint making, the pursuit of game, and the upbringing of a family.

An artist who could sit and paint lovely pink bison on the walls of the communal rock cavern didn't have to worry much about any of those things. When game was plentiful his needs were supplied by other, less imaginative members of the tribe. But when the development became too specialized—A bitterness tightened Gregg's lips. He could, of course, have forcibly prevented Hanley from sticking out his neck. He had the edge on Hanley in physical strength and could have restrained him with very little effort. Why hadn't he?

Within the scope of his inertia he was not incapable of exerting himself in a dramatic, forceful way. He shrank only from making long-range decisions, from shouldering great, dull burdens, from becoming enmeshed in aggressive arguments with people who did not possess enough intelligence to argue imaginatively about anything.

A lobefin? Why did he persist in kidding himself? He was in all respects the exact opposite of a lobefin. His inertia was the inertia of a tremendous creativeness anchored in the pleasure principle, a creativeness that had to be stimulated in just the right way, or—it wouldn't play ball. It was a physiological fact that when creative impulses were thwarted inertia enveloped the body, a sluggishness crept into the brain.

He didn't feel exactly sluggish now, however. Not mentally sluggish. He had a feeling that out in the mist something might very well be taking place which would have stripped his inertia from him—could he have but seen it.

His head felt suddenly cold. Not just his face, but his entire head, the top of his skull especially.

Why hadn't he tried to stop Hanley? Was it because, subconsciously, he'd known that Hanley feared nothing he could not come to physical grip with? The one thing Hanley couldn't do was sit and dream. And when a practical man goes forth to take a bull by the horns, half-expecting to be gored, a practical man, a dreamer, had no right to interfere.

Gregg opened "The Third State of Interstellar Expansion," and removed the bookmark he'd placed opposite Chapter 2. He began, slowly, to read: "As for the possibility of life on other worlds—"

He has taken the first step. There were two. Why did the other not come?

The thought moved slowly along the passageway, and hovered above Hanley. The thought pulsed, and moved down the wall and across the floor of the passageway. It hovered above Hanley from the opposite wall, comprehending him.

Hanley stood just inside the air lock examining a passageway which seemed covered with the dust of centuries, his heart thudding against his ribs.

In the narrow swath of radiance cut by his glow torch he could see the dust clearly. It was greenish-yellow, mildewed over with moist threads of fungus growth which adhered to his shoes when he lifted first his right foot, then his left.

He does not need the light he is carrying. Surely he can see without the light.

A dull radiance suffused the passageway, so that when Hanley clicked off the torch he was not in darkness.

There was a musty smell in the passageway, and in the wider corridor which branched off from it. The walls of the ceiling were covered with mildew, and when he moved, his head felt suddenly cold. Not just his face, but his entire head, the top of his skull especially.

The corridor startled Hanley, not because it was empty, but because it was so full of strange, angular shadows. The room at the end of the corridor startled him still more.

The room wasn't empty. In the dim light Hanley could make out a circular metal chair, and the dim outlines of a seated figure. The chair was faintly luminous, and seemed not so much an article of furniture as an extension of the floor which had mushroomed into a chilling circularity in the precise middle of the room.

Touch him. He was once like yourself.

The seated figure bore an unmistakable resemblance to a shrunken old man with thinning hair and a greenish-yellow beard. But when Hanley reached out and touched the beard, it crumpled, leaving a dampness on his palm. Mildew, dust came away, revealing a gleaming clavicle, and hollow eye sockets which seemed to be staring past Hanley at something on the opposite wall.

The wall. If you would know more, scrape—scrape away the dust.

For a terrifying instant Hanley had an apprehension that something in the room was trying to communicate with him. It was as though there were a living presence in the room which could force him to obey its unspoken commands.

Could force him? With a convulsive shudder Hanley turned, and stumbled from the room. Out in the corridor another heart-stopping spasm shook him. For an instant he was on the verge of giving way completely to his terror.

Then—anger flooded into his brain. Nothing he couldn't see could force him to do something he didn't want to do. Nothing—nothing—

He was standing in another room. The chair was larger and more disturbingly circular, more disturbingly *shaped* than the chair in the room from which he had fled. The seated figure was larger too.

He is beginning to understand. This was a very ancient one of his own kind. Will he scrape away the dust?

The seated figure was vaguely humanoid in appearance, but its teeth were very large, and enormous brow ridges arched above its hollow eyes. Sweat was trickling down Hanley's face, and something seemed to be pressing against his mind, blurring his thought processes. Like a skull he'd seen somewhere. Unutterably remote, behind glass in a dim shadowed hall. A pug-faced ape that had decided to become a man, in the vaguest way shambling through a forest primeval. Ugly, snarling—

Hanley forced his mind back to awareness. He wasn't standing in a museum on Terra. All through his body he could feel a tension mounting. There was a dense coating of dust on the creature's heavy, almost chinless jaw and its limbs were so thickly coated with dust they seemed enmeshed in the cobwebs.

Scrape—scrape away the dust.

Hanley turned, and stumbled from the room.

It was a very large and silent room, and the light was so dim that Hanley had to strain to see the back of the seated figure's head. The chair was squarish rather than circular, and so high that the figure's short, spindly legs barely touched the floor. The skull was massive—more birdlike than apelike.

Hanley groped his way out of the room.

It was a skeleton, but the head grew out from the middle of the squat torso, and long, translucent talons curved about the arms of the chair.

The crusted suns spawned him/her in the night of a long begetting. The wall. Scrape away the dust.

When at last Hanley found himself scraping away the dust on the wall of a very dim, circular chamber deep within the bowels of the ship his lips were twitching, and he could no longer control the trembling of his hands.

Behind him loomed a chair which had seemingly mushroomed up out of the floor in a frenzied attempt to support and contain a growth so prolific that not even death could prevent it from sprawling. The many-tubed occupant of the chair was not a skeleton. There were no articulations, nothing but a dotted mass of tendrils spilling over the arms of the chair, and snaking out across the floor. Its young lay scattered about the chamber—tiny medusa-heads, desiccated and loathsome.

A chair in which to sit and dream.

Hanley started, for the words had come unbidden into his mind, and had no relation at all to the frantic scrapings he was making with his pocket knife on the smooth metal wall.

The design, when it came into view, did not startle him as much as he had anticipated it would.

He was conscious that his palms were sweating. How—how had he known he was going to uncover a design? He hadn't known, couldn't have known.

It wasn't important anyway. Only the design was important. It was engraved deeply on the metal and almost it seemed geometrical, an overlapping series of circles superimposed on triangles.

He has taken the second step. A chair in which to dream and die.

The design was sharply-etched, and yet it seemed to possess a kind of physi-mathematical mobility. As Hanley stared the corners of the triangles blurred, and the circles dissolved into a pinwheeling blur of radiance.

Then—

Gaze deeply on that which is now a stillness, now a dreaming—forever and forever a dreaming and a stillness.

Hanley was shivering convulsively when he left the room.

The room was quite brightly illumed, and there was no dust at all on the wall. And the chair was like the first chair he'd seen, designed to support and contain not an alien inhabitant of a planet encircling some distant sun, but a man of about his own height and weight—

Hanley knew that he had found the *right* chair even as he seated himself. There was no dust on the wall, and he could see the design clearly. At first he saw only the design and then—a strange beauty danced on the wall. A beauty and a growing wonder that he could have so quickly progressed from a childish reluctance, a childish drawing back to the all-embracing glory of—

The music was faint at first, but gradually, as Hanley stared, it grew louder. But even when it filled the room it seemed to come from distances immeasurably remote.

It was like no music Hanley had ever heard. It throbbed and it pulsed, and there were times when it seemed cruel, almost torturing, and times when it was a sweetness ineffable which kept company with his thoughts as he voyaged mathematically afar, through stellated caverns of stillness and aisles of incredibly converging prisms—

Thomas Gregg sat on the edge of the cot, with "The Third Stage of Interstellar Expansion" spread out on his knees. It was a very large and bulky book, and one of the folding illustrations had come unhinged, so that a filmy tar field seemed to float between his waist and the floor. He was reading aloud, in a voice that trembled a little with the intensity of his emotion.

"We are far too prone to think of life as exclusively a biological phenomenon. If a creature moves about and absorbs nourishment and reproduces itself, we say that it is alive. But pure form, pure design, may also be a manifestation of life.

"In the dim infancy of our race, when it was believed that the soul of a dead man could leave the buried body by night to suck the blood of living persons, a curious expression gained currency, *the blood is the life.*

"In a coldly scientific sense it may be said that even the most primitive superstitions bear a casual relation to reality, for without their aid certain ideas could not be easily expressed or explained, or a satisfying mind picture built up. For instance, a thing is shaped in a certain way, and it lives. Destroy the pattern and it dies. How can we be sure that on some far planet that has not yet known the tread of man the *form* may not be the life?

"*The form is the life*!

"...neither should we assume that such a life would stay confined to the planet of its origin, for it is not in the nature of life to forego all questing. In the course of ages a decorative-locomotive synthesis would doubtless be built up. In the course of ages a far-voyaging synthesis—perhaps in certain superficial aspects not unlike the slender stellar craft which have carried our own kind to the farthest star—might well seek out new worlds to conquer.

"As to what form that questing would take, who can say? A life that is decorative, a life that is pure form, pure design, would have a tendency, perhaps, to seek above all things *appreciation.*"

Gregg snapped the book shut, stood up, yawned, and walked to the door of the star station.

It was a beautiful morning. The mist had come up deep and blue, the air was not too cold and out of the blueness a great ship loomed, its hull outlined in garish radiance against a shimmer of light so vast and tumultuous it seemed to span the Galaxy.

On a Betelgeuse System refueling station a million light-years from nowhere time could hang heavy with uneventfulness.

But now somehow Gregg was strangely stirred.

Not that the ship was even remotely like the one he'd dragged a babbling and completely demoralized Hanley from a decade before. But somehow, just reading Hargrave's book, of course, with that very memorable passage inserted *after* he, Gregg, had explored three or four of the rooms inside the vessel.

Shutting his eyes, Gregg could see again the great ship regurgitating her mooring cables, slipping out into the void with a vibrant droning.

It seemed only yesterday that he'd proved to himself that an impractical man, a dreamer, could be stronger inwardly than a hard-bitten extrovert. He'd saved Hanley without succumbing himself, and now soon he'd be going back to Terra to bask in the affluence which "The Third Stage of Interstellar Expansion" had brought him.

After ten years of lonely exile, five under Rigel, five under Betelgeuse, the world had at last discovered that William Hargrave, alias Thomas Gregg, poet, musician, painter, and, in his more energetic moments, star station grease monkey par excellence, was an astra-historian of the first rank, and a man of tremendous creative energies.

Smiling a little, Gregg passed through the narrow doorway and out across the landing strip with his arms upraised, partly as a welcoming gesture to the crew of the incoming vessel, partly in sheer exuberance because the dawn was so beautiful.

GUEST IN THE HOUSE

Roger Shevlin set down his bags, shook the rain from his umbrella and wondered just how long it would be before he found himself consulting a psychiatrist. He'd made mistakes before—plenty of them. But he was essentially a man of sound judgment, and it was hard to believe he could have allowed himself to be talked into renting a twenty-room house.

He was amazed at his own incredible stupidity; the lack of judgment he'd shown right up to the instant he'd signed the lease and returned the pen to the renting agent with a complacent smirk.

A huge and misshapen ogre of a dwelling it was, with ivy-hung eaves and a broken-down front porch, and as Shevlin stood in the lower hallway staring up the great central staircase a shudder went through him. There was always a chance, of course, that the place would shed some of its ugliness amidst the changing colors of autumn and the sweet-warbled songs of meadowlarks and grasshopper sparrows.

But Shevlin knew that no one would ever refer to the place he'd leased as a "house." It would always be "that place the Shevlins settled in—the poor chumps!" or "Johnny, run over to the Shevlin place and see if Mrs. Shevlin has any butter to spare."

To add to Shevlin's woes, the children had brushed right past him, and were losing no time in making themselves at home. Children could take root and sprout almost anywhere and the Shevlin youngsters were hardy perennials six and nine respectively. Already the house was beginning to resound with yells, shrieks and blood-curdling whoops.

A man should be proud to be the father of two such sturdy youngsters, Shevlin thought, and glared at his wife.

"The place won't look half so bad when I get those new curtains ironed out and hung up," Elsie said, and could have bitten her tongue out.

"Thanks," Shevlin said, dryly. "I was waiting for that. Now, if you don't mind, I'll go down in the cellar and mix myself a rum collins."

"Why pick on the cellar," Elsie said, miserably. "There's nothing down there but a lot of rusty machinery which we'll have to pay someone to rip out and cart away. The renting agent said the last tenant was a professor of—what did he say he was a professor of, Roger?"

"Of physics," Roger grunted. "Perhaps if I go down in the cellar and surround myself with just the right atmosphere it will work with me."

Elsie stared at him. "What are you talking about?"

"The homeopathic system of therapeutics," Shevlin said. "If you have something bad, you dose yourself with more of the same until it either cures or kills you."

A queer feeling of insecurity took hold of Shevlin when he saw the cellar.

It was damper than he'd ever thought a cellar could be. And chillier.

The machinery was damp, too. It was studded with little blobs of moisture and under the wetness was a rustiness which made Shevlin think of tin cans rusting in the sun, and an ax half-buried in a chopping block in an abandoned woodshed.

Ah, well—a gloomy life and a stagnant one was better than being cooped up in a city apartment with two small kids running around in circles every time the doorbell rang.

The machinery was really quite elaborate. So elaborate, in fact, that if Shevlin had been writing a book about machinery he'd have gone out and hired a ghost writer solely to avoid describing it.

Shevlin took another sip of the rum collins and wished that he were out of the cellar and upstairs in the attic. Of one thing he was certain. It would be sheer insanity for him to remain in the cellar when he could roam all over the house without let or hindrance.

Once as a child Shevlin had almost tangled with a bulldozer and the experience had left an ineffaceable impression on his mind. He had no intention of touching the machinery, or becoming embroiled with it in any way.

Clumsy hands he had. Clumsy hands and a clumsy head, early to rise and early to bed.

He must have stumbled, though it was hard to see how he could have been so unsteady on his feet after just one rum collins.

He had a vague recollection of making a frantic clutch at something huge that glistened. He had a much sharper recollection of feeling that something move beneath his fingers.

The whirring began immediately and didn't stop. It was faint at first, very faint, but it increased so rapidly in volume that Shevlin had no time to leap back.

For one terrifying instant he seemed to be standing on the brink of a colossal sandstorm, his ears filled with a dull roar that was half a silence. Then there was a flurry of scintillating metal particles, and something seemed to lift him up, and hurl him backwards through a cyclone of motion toward a tumbled waste of emptiness.

When Shevlin struggled to a sitting position the floor was once more firm beneath him, and the machinery had ceased to gyrate. For an instant the walls had seemed to contract in fitful gusts, but now there was nothing to indicate that a convulsion of incalculable magnitude had taken place on the opposite side of the cellar.

He was beginning to think he'd suffered a vertigo attack and imagined the whole thing when he heard his wife's voice calling to him from the head of the stairs.

"Roger, come up here quick! I can't see out of the windows! Roger, hurry!"

Shevlin gasped, got swayingly to his feet, and mounted the stairs in five long bounds that carried him well past his wife, who had retreated into the lower hallway, and was staring at him out of eyes that seemed to fill her face.

"What do you mean, you can't see out?" he demanded.

"It's like a fine, dazzling mist," Elsie said, in a stunned voice. "You can see it best from the living room window."

The living room was filled with little dazzling dust motes that seemed to follow Shevlin as he crossed to the window, pressed his face to the pane and stared out with utter incredulity surging up in him.

"It can't be an ordinary fog," Elsie said. "It came up much too— Roger!"

"Yes, what is it?" Shevlin asked.

"The other pane!" Elsie almost screamed. "A little man with a horrible, *shrunken face looked right at me!*"

Shevlin swung about. "Oh, nonsense," he said anxiously. "You're making a mountain out of a fog bank."

"But I tell you, I saw him! Oh, I did, I did! You didn't, but I did!"

"All right," Shevlin said, his mouth tightening. "Shock does strange things to the mind. I most certainly didn't see him, but I'm going right out now and puncture him before we follow him over the hill to the madhouse."

He turned as he spoke and went striding toward the front door. Seemingly the door had soaked up a stickiness, for he had to tug and wrench at it, and the knob kept slipping out of his hand.

Bur it came open at last, and Shevlin found himself on the porch staring wildly about him. As far as he could see there wasn't anyone in sight. But he couldn't see very far, for the fog was thicker than he'd ever imagined a fog could be. "Oh, my stars!" he muttered, through clenched teeth.

"You're just not used to *our* kind of weather," a wheezy voice said. "Climatic conditions change quite a bit in a half million years."

Shevlin caught his breath.

Directly in front of him the fog had thinned a little, and—he could see the little man standing there.

The little man wasn't a dwarf exactly, but he was well below medium height and his cranium bulged so that his face seemed much more shrunken than it actually was. It was sufficiently shrunken, however, to resemble a tissue-paper mask which some besotted reveler had bought as a hand-me-down, daubed with rouge and worn once too often.

He didn't seem to be wearing much in the way of clothes. Or perhaps it would have been more correct to say he had been ill-advised in the matter of clothes. From his scrawny chest to just above the knees a thin, one-piece garment—not unlike a sarong—clung loosely to his mummy-thin body, obscuring what it couldn't conceal and taking a little of the curse off. But his shoulders were completely bare, his elbows stuck out and his legs were visible in their crookedness. He was entirely unshod.

"In another fifty years we'd have mastered time travel ourselves," the gnomish apparition said. "But now we shall have it right away."

"Yes, naturally," Shevlin said, blankly. "You'll have it—right away."

"I'm confident we will," the little man agreed. "You know the secret and will communicate it to us."

As though unaware that Shevlin had stiffened the little man bowed.

"Perhaps I'd better introduce myself. My name is Papenek, and I'm probably the only man on earth who could cope with a development like this. You see, the house didn't enter our time sector quite as fast as it left yours, so we had time to step up the beam and get a good look at it."

"You—"

"When we saw the house coming, Valt—he's our Chief Monitor—sent for me immediately. 'You can speak the language of First Atomic Age primitives as fluently as I can,' Valt told me. 'Take a tube and go right over there. If necessary, use persuasion.'"

The little man smiled. "Valt provides for every contingency. He wouldn't be where he is if he didn't. But I'm sure persuasion won't be necessary. You want to help us, don't you."

Shevlin had no clear recollection of leaping back through the front door and slamming it in the little man's face. But he must have done so, because he suddenly found himself inside the house with his back to the door and his stomach crawling with cold terror.

"Roger, what is it?" Elsie said, in a shrill, small voice. "What did you see out there? Why are you staring at me like that?"

Shevlin turned abruptly, and twisted the knob of the door to make sure it wouldn't open behind his back.

"The little man I didn't think was there is standing out on the front porch," he said. "He says the climate has changed a bit because we're a half million years ahead of the clock."

"A half million—"

"Apparently the professor wired the house for time travel," Shevlin said, moistening his dry lips. "Cruel and thoughtless people sometimes leave litters of unwanted puppies in damp cellars for the neighbors and the health department to worry about. I'm simply guessing, of course. But I've a hunch the professor just didn't realize how close to success he was. When that huge clutter of machinery down in the cellar wouldn't work he must have got disgusted and walked out on it."

Elsie screamed.

The little man was standing just inside the door, his eyes riveted on Shevlin's twitching face.

"Wood is an extremely hard substance to make permeable," he said, as though he were addressing a child. "It has never ceased to amaze me that the First Atomic Age could run its entire course without collapsing such dwellings in their entirety."

"It…it's just beginning," Shevlin muttered, a little wildly.

"You mean the First Atomic Age. Yes, I rather gathered you hadn't advanced very far into it. Certainly not as far as the Great Holocaust, which wiped out all but a pitiful remnant of the human race."

"One redeeming feature, though," he added, as though he'd just thought of it. "The mutations which made our race possible began to occur right after the first atomic bomb was dropped."

For the first time Shevlin noticed that Papenek was clasping a small glowing tube about five inches in length. It wasn't elaborate—in fact, a test tube filled with light wouldn't have looked any different, except that there was nothing inside the tube to account for the light.

"Don't be alarmed," Papenek said, with a deprecatory gesture. "The house won't collapse. I used the beam so sparingly that it didn't even destroy the wall when I came through. As you can see, all it did was make the wall permeable. I could walk out just as easily as I walked in, but—I've certainly no intention of leaving just yet."

Wide-eyed, Elsie turned sharply. "You hear that? He's going to *visit with us!*"

Papenek turned, and started at Shevlin's wife. "The tyranny of hysteria is the most crippling of all tyrannies because the normal mind has absolutely no defense against it," he said coldly. "Fortunately we now know how to deal with such aberrations. Women are so highly replaceable that we have no scruples about—"

He was interrupted by sudden clatter on the great central staircase.

Down it came first Shevlin's only son and heir, Roger J. Shevlin, Jr., pulling after him a toy locomotive and three streamlined pullman cars. The cars bumped and careened perilously on every step and for an instant Shevlin was sure they would come uncoupled. It was curious, but just watching the train descend steadied Shevlin, so that his daughter's noisy appearance at the top of the stairs armed with his son's air rifle did not unnerve him too much.

What horribly unnerved him was the expression on Papenek's face when Petty Lou Shevlin screwed up her face, and aimed the rifle straight down the banisters at the little man from the future.

BBBRRUPP

Though the bb shot hit Papenek in the most delicate part of his anatomy he didn't budge an inch. Surprisingly he just stood very still, his lips sucked in and a doughy knobbiness sprouting from his face. Then, slowly, his features picked themselves up from where they had landed and regrouped themselves where the doughiness was most pronounced, giving him the aspect of a tormented half-wit.

"Children!" he said, icily.

"Y-you still have them, d-don't you?" Shevlin asked, a coldness encircling his scalp.

"Oh, yes, we still have them," Papenek said.

"I...I suppose you treat them differently than we do, though. Give them haywire toys to play with that turn them into pitiful little adult lunatics before they're six."

Being an imaginative man Shevlin had often tried to imagine what the children of the far distant future would be like. Despite his terror, despite the fact that Betty Lou was now tripping down the stairs in the wake of his son he couldn't repress a certain curiosity as to the young of the species which his own descendants had sired.

"No, we don't," Papenek said, a malevolent resentment in his stare. "The human infant has a long learning period. We...we don't try to telescope it. All we do is utilize it to teach a child the rudiments of civilized behavior. What amazes me is that you haven't utilized it at all. Your children are far more primitive than young orangutans or chimpanzees."

"Are they?" Shevlin said, and something in his tone made Papenek tighten his hold on the tube and take another swift step backward.

"I didn't mean to seem patronizing," Papenek said. "You First Atomic Age primitives must have had a quite astonishing grasp of scientific imponderables in some respects. Perhaps I should say 'hit-or-miss techniques.' In a crude way you've outdistanced us. Possibly a barbaric, not to say, savage childhood has given you a certain mental resilience which—"

He was not permitted to finish. Betty Lou had dropped the air rifle, seized her brother by the arm, and was dragging him toward Papenek as though she wanted something confirmed which she didn't dare refer to in the presence of her parents.

"I tell you he has!" she shrieked. "He has, he has, *he has!*"

"Aw, he's just a dwarf," Junior protested. "Let him alone and he'll sing 'happy birthday to you' from the Western Union."

It all seemed like a dream, but Shevlin knew it wasn't. The bright and shining faces of his brats were far too real and earnest.

And now Betty Lou was coming right out with it, accusing Papenek of having little knobby outgrowths at the base of his skull. Like horns they were, jutting out a good inch and a half on both sides of his neck.

Shevlin hadn't noticed them before. But now Papenek was fingering the growths, causing Elsie to squirm in horror.

"Directional organs," Papenek said, almost belligerently. "I'm not surprised those little savages should be upset by them."

"Directional—"

"They're vestigial in you," Papenek explained impatiently. "Cats, dogs and birds have a highly developed directional sense which our own ancestors lost far back in the Miocene. In fact, the bodies of all animals contain vestigial homologues of organs that were once functional. Certain snakes, for instance, have tiny skeletal legs buried under their skins, so incredibly minute as to present anatomical difficulties to a taxonomist."

"If he used any bigger words he'd choke himself," Junior said.

"If you're talking about snakes you needn't bother to tell us," Elsie muttered. "Just show us. Turn your back, Betty Lou. He wants to show us his buried legs."

"Directional organs are vestigial in you," Papenek said, ignoring the interruption. "But we've redeveloped them."

"Oh," replied Shevlin, his hands traveling to the bumps at the base of his own skull.

"Oh, don't," Elsie pleaded wildly.

PLOP

Just why Junior should have seen fit to thrust out his leg and trip Papenek right at that moment was a riddle which the child psychologists of the future might have been capable of unraveling. But Shevlin doubted that.

He doubted it still more when he saw the look of fury on Papenek's face. The little man's features were so convulsed with rage that Shevlin feared his temples would burst.

A scream from Elsie warned him that there was no time to be lost.

Grabbing his son by the coat collar, Shevlin swung him about and started toward the stairs with him. He had little hope of reaching the top of the stairs before Papenek could regain his feet. It was more an act of appeasement than anything else, and like most such acts it failed utterly to achieve its purpose.

He saw Papenek's hand go out, but he wasn't prepared for the blinding flash of radiance which shot from the tube.

He himself wasn't touched. Only Junior was touched.

For an instant Shevlin's son was bathed in an unearthly refulgence. Then—Elsie was babbling and clawing at Papenek's face, and a little wisp of smoke was hovering above a moist spot on the floor that might or might not have been Junior.

"No, no—don't," Papenek shouted, squirming and writhing under Elsie's merciless assault. "He'll come back. I just punished him a little. Do you think I'd extinguish a *child!*"

"He'll *come back?*" Elsie's voice was a shriek. "He'll—"

"Certainly. I just stepped up the beam a bit. Right now his body has the same refractive index as the air about him, but he'll waver back in about five…why, she seems to have fainted!"

Five minutes later Shevlin stood with his arm about his wife's sagging shoulders, watching his son wavering back.

Not all of Junior came back immediately. First his face materialized, pale and startled, and then the back of his head, and then his small body, and finally his feet. His feet took their time in coming back.

"I just didn't realize what a shock it would be to you," Papenek said. "You Atomic Age primitives had abnormally developed parental instincts. When *we lose* children we certainly don't lose any sleep over it. We—"

Something in Shevlin's stare caused him to break off abruptly.

Miraculously Junior didn't seem to be any worse for his experience. Though the punishment had surpassed a sound spanking in severity there was nothing to indicate that it had left a lasting impression on his mind.

As though to prove that it hadn't he bent over and stuck out his tongue at Papenek the instant he was himself again.

The little man seemed to reach a decision then. He moved closer to Shevlin and said, very quietly: "Perhaps you'd better take your children upstairs and put them to bed—or wherever you put them when you want to discuss serious matters in a quiet way."

"I'll take them up," Elsie said, just as quietly. "Stay here and talk to him, dear. Find out just how long he intends to stay. Before we make any plans we've got to find out what our chances are of staying alive in this house."

The next fifteen minutes were for Shevlin the most unnerving of all, for the instant Elsie's footsteps died away the little man asked him the sixty-four dollar question.

He'd been afraid all along that Papenek wouldn't believe he knew no more about time travel than the man in the moon. If he told Papenek the truth—He decided to stake everything on Papenek's capacity for recognizing the truth when he heard it. He avoided looking at the tube as he make his reckless bid for survival. He kept nothing back, even though it meant sacrificing the niggardly respect which Papenek had for the resourceful primitive he'd pretended to be.

It was a long moment before Papenek spoke.

For the first time the little man seemed visibly shaken, as though the bottom had dropped out of something that had flared with a blinding incandescence for him.

"I've been incredibly blind," he said. "I should have known that the father of such children would be incapable of inventing a time-traveling house."

Shevlin no longer felt angry—only cold. He suddenly realized that he'd put his cards on the table without weighing the advantages which might have accrued from playing them close to the chest. Not that he'd held a trump hand, exactly, but—

Startlingly Papenek said: "My mind works better on a full stomach. Before we go down in the cellar and have a look at the machinery perhaps we'd better have something to eat. Have you any eggs or fresh meat I could heat up?"

"Eggs?" Shevlin said, dazedly. "You mean you still eat—"

Papenek blinked. "Naturally we still eat. What gave you the idea we could live without food?"

"I…I took it for granted vitamin concentrates would be the food of the future. Even in our age—"

"Good earth, no!" Papenek said, impatiently. "It may take me a week—or a month—to learn the correct way of sending the house backwards and forwards in time. If I'm to be your guest I've no intention of foregoing the pleasures of the table."

Shevlin's face looked a little abnormal, as though it were reflecting his thoughts in an illicit way and not at all along the lines laid down by nature.

"You'll occupy the guest room, I suppose?"

"Why not?" Papenek said. "Oh, and while I think of it. I hope you have soft feather beds. If there's anything I detest it's a coarse hair mattress."

* * * *

Elsie looked down the long table, and pressed her palms to her temples. "He must have had specialized training in eating," she said.

Shevlin followed his wife's stare, wondering how he'd managed to live through the past three days.

Papenek had tucked a paper napkin under his chin, and was busily engaged in sucking his fifth egg. Having cooked the egg by stepping down the tube to its lowest potential, he seemed to consider it his duty to savor its flavor to the utmost.

"There isn't a great deal you can do to help me, Shevlin," he said, looking up. "But you might at least stop whispering to your wife while I'm eating. It upsets my digestion."

Shevlin shut his eyes, ground his teeth together and thought back seventy-two hours.

Papenek climbing into bed, after first bouncing up and down in the middle of the bed to make sure it would sustain his weight. Papenek drawing up the sheets, demanding a heating pad, and telling Elsie to get out.

"Your husband will see that I'm made comfortable. If there's anything I detest it's a woman standing in the doorway wringing her hands while I'm getting into bed. Get out! GET OUT!"

Elsie slamming the door, screaming back through the door: "Roger, there's some chloroform in the medicine cabinet! If you don't come out smelling of chloroform, you can start looking around for another wife!"

Papenek down in the cellar, very wide awake, bending over the machinery.

Hour after hour after hour. His lean and competent little hands working feverishly away in the glow which came from the tube as he stepped it up and down at ten-second intervals. Papenek using both his hands and the beam, turning occasionally to nod at Shevlin, gloating over this progress and making statements which filled Shevlin with steadily mounting dread.

Papenek saying: "Of course we'll go back immediately to your age and find the man and destroy him. If the secret leaked out, you First Atomic Age primitives might construct dozens of time machines and destroy our world completely. You almost destroyed your own world, so how can you be trusted with such knowledge?"

"But when you've found him—" Shevlin shuddered. "When you've done that you'll return to your age?"

"No, I can't promise you that. It may be necessary for us to police your world for a while. In fact, you may be sure we shan't allow anything to exist in the past which could possibly injure us here in the future. Even a minor infection should be cleansed at the source. Otherwise it will spread and fester."

Papenek was smacking his lips now, and rising from the table. "My work is so exacting I need a great deal of food to ward off fatigue," he said. "But you certainly don't need an egg apiece. Next time scramble one and divide it. You want the eggs to last, don't you?"

"If they were filled with cyanide, I'd want them to last," Elsie mumbled under her breath. "I'd even settle for roach poison."

"The little man who came for dinner," Shevlin whispered, "is eating us out of house and home. Perhaps we could sprinkle arsenic on the wall paper."

"Be careful, Shevlin," Papenek warned. "I shouldn't care to *really* step up the beam, but—I must warn you! Remarks like that disturb me because I know you mean them."

Shevlin's features darkened. "All right," he said, loudly. "I'll consider myself warned. Now what?"

"Back to work," Papenek said. "Success is almost within my grasp now, Shevlin. It might even come this morning."

He turned abruptly and went hobbling from the room.

Elsie waited until she heard him descending the cellar stairs before she took her husband's cold hands in her feverish ones and said, anxiously: "Roger, if it should come this morning, are we prepared for it?"

"About as prepared as the dodo was when the early Dutch navigators peppered his hide with a blunderbuss and blasted his nest right out from under him," Shevlin said.

He stood up as he spoke, pulling his hands free and shoving his chair back.

"That all-purpose tube he's toting doesn't merely alter electronic orbits. It controls atomic chain reactions in a way we've never dreamed they could be controlled. You might say it makes monkeys out of atoms."

Elsie nodded. "They'll overrun our age, Roger. They'll regulate, remold everything and everyone. They'll give us lessons in cooking, eating, mating and—dying. They'll complain, they'll be petulant. They'll be capricious and fretful. Sour little spinsters armed with glowing darning needles they are, male and female. I haven't seen the females, but—"

"We've seen Papenek. He's been our guest."

"Yes, we've seen Papenek."

A moment later Shevlin was descending the cellar stair. He moved cautiously, because he hoped to surprise Papenek in one of his unguarded moments and perhaps learn just how close to success he really was. Shevlin knew that not too much reliance could be placed on Papenek's words, but Papenek's expression would be a dead giveaway if he could be surprised in the very act of making a connection bright with promise.

It wouldn't have to be the final connection. It could be the one before the last or the one before that. What it boiled down to was that if Papenek was about to succeed the mounting tension would show up in his features.

Shevlin was halfway down the stairs when he saw Papenek kneeling in shadows a little to the left of the beam cast by the tube, which was lying on a circular metal stand about twenty feet from the base of the stairs.

Shevlin's breath caught in his throat. It was the first time Papenek had ever turned his back on the tube or allowed it to stray so far from his person.

It was Shevlin's chance, and he knew it.

According to present ideas of motion a moving body can't be in two places at the same time. But almost Shevlin seemed to be crossing the cellar floor while his feet were still clattering on the stairs.

Probably it was simply a case of unbelievably speeded up reflexes. At any rate, he had the tube and was clasping it firmly when Papenek turned.

For perhaps five seconds Papenek's expression remained completely blank. Then, slowly, his mouth tightened and a purplish flush suffused his features.

"Put it down," he said.

Shevlin shook his head. "No. Remember what you said about an infection? It should be cleansed, you said, at the source."

For an instant Shevlin had feared that the tube might be completely smooth, precluding any attempt to step up its energies. But that fear, he now perceived, had been ill-grounded. The part he was clasping was slightly flattened, and he could detect beneath his thumb a double row of tiny protuberances, like musical stops on a child's toy flute.

"I'm afraid you don't realize just what the potential of that tube is," Papenek warned. "It could destroy the earth."

Shevlin was suddenly aware that his knees were shaking. He'd suddenly remembered that the ancients had believed that a flute could go completely bad, piping shrill mysterious music that could bring down the keystone of matter itself, could topple the very universe into an abyss.

Perhaps it was just thinking about that guess which further unnerved Shevlin, causing him to tighten his clasp on the tube. Or perhaps he'd been exerting too much pressure from the first. At any rate, there was a dull flare, and—total darkness came sweeping across the cellar like a moving wall, obliterating everything in its path.

Then out of the darkness came a voice, filled with utter hate.

"You've inverted the beam, Shevlin. Steady pressure, evenly applied, will do that. I can't see in the dark, but my directional organs will enable me to find you."

There was a sudden, metallic clatter.

"W-what are you doing?" Shevlin asked.

"Looking for a sharp, cutting instrument," Papenek replied, with startling candor. "With all these tools you'd think…ah, this will do very nicely. Before I kill you, Shevlin, there's something you may as well know.

"I can send the house back now, to your age or any age. You know that straining blade unit at the base of the central shaft—the one I was re-assembling yesterday? Well, you just swing the blade completely around the neutral pole of the magnetic wave arrester and groove it into the third notch from the top. The third notch will carry the house completely back to your age."

Shevlin felt a sudden prickling at the base of his scalp. Under the guise of talking to him Papenek had moved very close to him in the darkness. He could hear the little man's harsh breathing, the shuffling scrape of his unshod feet.

Shevlin clenched his jaw. He'd often wondered just how much self-control he'd have if someone in a *position* to kill him was a murderer by choice or necessity. Now he knew.

He didn't have *any* self-control. But there were forms of fear which could paralyze—"I've got him, Pop! I'VE GOT HIM!"

The voice tore out of the darkness, exuberant, lusty, springy with confidence. It swelled into a mouthing of syllables that ran together as syllables are prone to do in the mouth of a nine-year-old almost beside himself with the joy of battle.

"I tripped him up, Pop! Pop, quick—turn on the lights!"

Mentally Shevlin poured himself a stiff one, swallowed it and went staggering blindly around the cellar in search of a dangling light bulb that continually seemed to elude his grasp.

He was still making frantic clutches at the air when the entire cellar blazed with light.

For an instant Shevlin thought that he'd collided with the bulb and jarred it on. Then he saw that by some distortion of pressure he'd energized the tube again, causing it to brim with more than its wonted share of light.

Papenek, armed with a very long and wicked-looking drill, was trying to get up. But Junior was sitting on Papenek's chest, swinging his legs and digging his thumbs into the little man's eye sockets, so remorselessly as almost to justify what Papenek had said about the savagery of children.

"You murderous little savage," Papenek shrieked. "Let me up, you hear? You primitive little—"

"Enough of that!" Shevlin said, clasping the tube very firmly and aiming it at Papenek's bulging brow. "One more word out of you and I'll step up the beam so high you'll be just a little wisp of smoke drifting off into limbo. Perhaps less than that."

Papenek quieted down.

"That's better," Shevlin said.

Very deliberately he unfastened his wrist watch and handed it to his son.

"What goes, Pop?"

Shevlin looked at his son. "Junior, just how long have you been down here?" he asked.

"Since before breakfast, Pop," Junior said. "I've been spying on him ever since he started dismantling that straining blade unit yesterday afternoon. I was hiding in the coal bin, so I didn't miss a thing. Y'know, Pop, there's a make-or-break ignition factor involved that's only partly magnetomotive. A regular manual pinion shift movement it is, Pop."

"Hm-m-m," Shevlin said. "Are you sure you can handle it, Junior. You didn't seem like a prodigy to me when you tripped him three days ago for no reason at all. Not a prodigy born a year after the New Mexico experiment, at any rate."

"Ah, that was just a gag, Pop. Betty Lou dared me. Besides, I wanted him to think that all I had inside my head was an elaborate arrangement of knocking tubes."

Shevlin nodded at Papenek. "Remarkable boy in some respects. I.Q. of 270. It disturbs my wife more than it does me. Maturity will bring emotional balance, and we'll need a few young *mutant* geniuses to handle the difficult tasks ahead. He can see in the dark too. Dark sight is common enough in Eskimos, but before 1945 extremely rare in Caucasoids. It's more effective than directional organs, don't you think?"

Papenek seemed to be having trouble with his face. It kept darkening and whitening in patches, and—his jaw had begun to twitch.

"If the house returns as fast as it came, we should be back in time for lunch," Shevlin said. "Give me five minutes, Junior. Then notch in the thingamajig and let the straining blade…aw, shucks, I don't have to tell *you* how to handle a machine. The Los Alamos radiations took care of that."

"Just leave everything to me, Pop. I won't even get grease on my hands."

Shevlin flourished the tube a trifle menacingly.

"Start moving, Papenek," he said.

Up the cellar stairs Papenek stumbled, his face a twitching mask. Down the lower hallway into the living room, and then out through the living room to the front porch. The permeable patch was just wide enough to enable Shevlin to pass through in Papenek's wake. He had to stoop a little, but he didn't mind because he knew that another ten seconds would see the last of Papenek.

Out on the porch he spoke sharply. "All right, jump!" he ordered. "Get on with you! Right out into the mist, little man!"

Papenek jumped from the porch.

Shevlin waited until he'd disappeared in the mist before he turned and went striding back into the house.

It was curious, but he'd grown quite fond of the house just in the last fifteen minutes. No—it went back further than that. The house, too, had gone through a lot, and like a faithful old collie dog that has shared man's trials and tribulations—He was suddenly aware that Elsie was standing in the living room door, her face distraught.

"Roger, I've searched everywhere for Junior," she said. "Do you suppose—"

Shevlin smiled and crossed to her side in three long strides.

"Don't worry," he said, kissing her. "Junior's at the helm and everything's under control. In just about five seconds now—"

There was a sudden, dazzling flash of light.

LAKE OF FIRE

Steve found the mirror in the great northwestern desert. It was lying half-buried in the sand, and the wind howled in fury over it, and when he bent to pick it up the sun smote him like a shining blade, dividing his tall body into blinding light and wavering shadow.

I knew it was a Martian mirror before he straightened. The craftsmanship was breathtaking and could not have been duplicated on Earth. It was shaped like an ordinary hand mirror; but its glass surface was like a lake of fire, with depth beyond depth to it, and the jewels sparkling at its rim were a deep aquamarine which seemed to transmute the sun-glow into shimmering bands of starlight.

I could have told Steve that such mirrors, by their very nature, were destructive. When a man carries a hopeless vision of loveliness about with him, when he lives with that vision night and day, he ceases to be the undisputed master of his own destiny—

"She's alive, Jim," Steve said. "A woman dead fifty thousand years. A woman from a civilization that flourished before the dawn of human history."

"Take it easy, Steve," I warned. "The Martians simply knew how to preserve every aspect of a mirrored image. Say howdy-do to her if you like. Press your lips to the glass and see what happens. But don't mistake an imitation of life for the real thing."

"An imitation of life!" Steve flared. "Man, she just smiled at me. She's aware of us, I tell you."

"Sure she is. Her brain was mirrored too, every aspect of its electro-dynamic structure preserved forever by a science that's lost forever. Get a grip on yourself, Steve."

I was hot and tired and dusty. My throat was parched and I didn't feel much like arguing with him. But I had my reasons for being stubborn.

"Men have found Martian mirrors and gone mad," I said. "Don't take any chances, Steve. We don't know yet what it's rigged with. Why not play it safe? A thousand cycles of direct current should melt it down."

"Melt *her* down!" Steve's eyes narrowed in sudden fury. "Why, it would be murder!"

Steve got up and brushed sand from his knees. He held the mirror up so that the red Martian sunlight caught and aureoled the splendor of a face that offered a man no chance of help if he ever let go.

A pale, beautiful face, the eyes fringed with long, dark lashes, the lips parted in a mocking smile. A living image capable of mercurial changes of mood, unnaturally still one moment, smiling and animated the next.

One thing at a time, I thought. *Don't drive him too hard.*

"Some men have carried them about for years," I said. "But just remember what falling in love with an image can mean. You'll never hold her in your arms, Steve. And compulsions can kill."

"She's alive as flesh-and-blood is alive," he said, glaring at me.

"Easy, Steve!"

I could see that I was going to have trouble with my stout-hearted buddy, Captain Stephen Claymore.

He could have stared at a mountain of gold unmoved. He could have knelt with a wry chuckle, and let a handful of diamonds trickle through his wiry, bronze-knuckled hands, in utter contempt for what diamonds could buy on Earth.

He could have thrown back his head and laughed, at wealth, at glory, at anything you want to name that men prize highly on Earth. But a beautiful woman was a temptation apart A beautiful woman—

Steve grabbed my arm. "Look out, Tom!" he cried. "Watch it!"

The bullet whizzed past like a heat-maddened insect. Steve leapt back, and I flattened myself.

The attack was no great surprise. When people take up a new way of life, when they pull up stakes and go striding into the sunrise, strife paces after like a ravenous hound, red tongue lolling. When the first colonists from Earth swarmed into the crumbling Martian cities a good third of them ended up in stony desolation with their hearts drilled through.

They danced to riotous tunes, calling for louder music and stronger wine, and they fought savagely to set up little kingdoms of tyranny eighty feet square.

Everywhere anarchy reigned, and haggard-eyed, desperate men crouched behind smoke-blackened ruins and held off other men as greedy as themselves. They fought and died by dozens, by hundreds, their minds inflamed by the quickly-made discovery that the Martian cities were vast treasure troves.

You had to go prospecting, you had to search, and when you found your own shining treasure you didn't want to share it with any man alive.

Steve had his gun trained on the wall ahead when he ducked down at my side.

"Yes, sir," I whispered, half to myself. "This is going to be rough!"

"They asked for it!" Steve said.

His gun roared twice.

From the wall ahead came a burst of gunfire in reply.

"If they think they're going to get this mirror away from me—"

I looked at his grim, sweat-beaded face. "I'll help you fight for it," I said.

"So nice of you," he grunted.

"Then maybe you'll have sense enough to bury it face down in the sand."

Guns went off thirty feet directly in front of us. Red sand geysered up, granite cracked and splintered. You could feel the awful heat of the blazing exchange of bullets.

I could see faces between the chinks. Malignant faces moving from peep-hole to peep-hole like scavenger birds hopping about in the desert.

I was aiming at one of the peep-holes when Steve groaned and sagged against me. His gun arm sagged, and I could see that a bullet had pierced his shoulder high up.

"I'm sorry, Tom," he whispered, hoarsely. "I was careless, damn it I"

"Never mind, Steve," I said.

"Now they'll close in and get you. Better take my gun. You can use two guns."

"I won't need two guns, Steve," I said. "I'm walking into the open with my hands raised."

"You're crazy!" he breathed, his eyes, on my face. "We're outnumbered five to one. They'll drop you the instant you step out from behind this wall."

My gun was hot and smoking. I smiled and tossed it to the sand.

"I'll be back in a minute and fix up that shoulder," I said.

"You'll be walking to your death," he said. "They've been trailing us for days, hoping we'd stumble on something. They must have seen me pick up that mirror."

"They trailed us because they thought we looked experienced, rugged," I said. "They thought we were following a map. They just haven't got what it takes to go prospecting for themselves. They're hyenas of the desert, Steve."

"All right—hyenas. That means they won't respect a white flag. If you walk out with your hands raised they'll burn you down before you've taken five steps."

I steadied my helmet and unloosed my collar so that I wouldn't feel cramped.

"Don't worry, Steve," I said.

I knew they saw me the instant I stepped out from behind the wall.

The silence was ominous, and I could feel their eyes upon me, hot and deadly.

I didn't raise my hands. It didn't seem quite right to let them think I was seeking a truce. A man may be a fool to play fair with killers, but something made me change my mind about raising my hands.

I'd give them their chance—ten seconds. I wouldn't try to bargain for those ten seconds by walking toward them under false colors. I'd just trust to luck and—

Steve had never seen the weapon I held in my palm. It was a tiny electrostatic accelerator tube, capable of flexible, high precision control of ions with energies up to twelve million electron-volts.

It was a simple thing—and unbelievably destructive. It made no sound at all. But ten seconds after I clicked it on, the desert directly in my path was glowing white hot.

Just a glow, white, dazzling for an instant. Then a dull rumbling shook the ground and the wall opposite blackened and crumbled. The heat was like a blast of incandescent helium gas from a man-made sun.

I turned and walked back to where Steve was lying.

"I didn't want to do it that way," I said. "But I had no choice. It was them—or us."

Steve seemed not to realize we were no longer in danger. There was fear in his eyes, and he was staring at me as if I'd just returned from the dead.

In a way I had. A man may die fifty deaths while counting off ten seconds in his mind.

"I'll give you something to help you sleep, Steve," I said.

It didn't take me long to dress and bind up his wound. He winced once or twice, but he never took his eyes from the mirror.

"You promised to bury it face down in the sand," I said.

He looked at me. "You know better than that," he said. "I promised nothing of the sort."

"It's like falling in love with a ghost, only worse," I said.

"That's where you're wrong. There's nothing ghostly about her."

I mixed him a sleeping draught, using the little water we had left.

In five minutes he was snoring. I pried the mirror from his fingers and propped it up against a rock, so that he could see her face when he woke up.

Then I stretched myself out in the sand, kicked off my shoes and stared up at the sky. The sun was just sinking to rest, and there was a thin sprinkling of stars in the middle of the sky.

The stars seemed cold and immeasurably remote.

Would it work out?

Could it possibly work out? Was I sticking out my neck in a gamble so big it was like attempting to pierce the sun, and hammer out a new humanity on a great blazing anvil heated to millions of degrees centigrade?

I laughed, alone with my thoughts. Nothing dared, nothing gained. What does a man gain by striking bargains with the mouse in himself?

* * * *

I awoke in the cool dawn. The morning mists had rolled back and the red desert looked almost beautiful in the sun glow.

Steve was sitting up, staring at the mirror. The light shifted suddenly, and I could see the radiance which smoldered in the depths of the glass.

I got up, walked to the wall and peered over Steve's shoulder. The girl was looking at him, her face so beautiful it fairly took my breath away. It was as though after a lifetime of wandering she'd found the only man in the world for her.

Her face was bright with sympathy, with compassion, for Steve. But Steve sat slumped in utter dejection, his eyes burning holes in his face. He didn't even look up when I spoke to him.

"She knows, Tom," he whispered, hoarsely. "She turned pale when that bullet hit me. She was relieved when you dressed the wound. She's been watching over me all night, like an angel of mercy."

"You'll need her more and more," I said. "You know what the end will be, Steve. Complete hopelessness in an empty room."

He stood up, his face savage.

"I never asked your advice," he ground out. "I'm not asking it now."

"I've got to save you, Steve," I said.

"I love her, do you hear? I don't care what happens to me!"

I picked up the mirror before he could guess my purpose. I swung about and I brought that rare and beautiful object down on the rock Steve had been sitting on.

There was a splintering crash, a crackling burst of white flame.

Steve gave a great despairing cry. He stood for an instant staring down at the shattered fragments of the mirror. Then he came at me like a charging bull, his eyes bloodshot.

I clipped him lightly on the jaw. "That's all I wanted to know, Steve," I said. "Thanks, pal."

I looked down at him, lying in a crumpled heap at my feet

I was glad he hadn't fallen on his wounded side. He was plenty sturdy, and he came from a long-lived family, and I didn't think a little clip on the jaw could hurt him. I hoped he'd forgive me when he woke up. That was important, because I thought a lot of Steve.

When you've been to Mars, when you've fought your way through the red and raging dust storms, and labored beneath the naked glare of the sun, and juggled with men and ships and supplies like some tremendous Herculean figure in the morning of the world, you'll never really feel at home on Earth. You'll see the world of ordinary men and women as a vision of Lilliput, too small to be measurable in terms of human worth. You'll be lost and helpless, blind and staggering beneath the weight of a memory you can't throw off. A memory of bigness, too much bigness, integrated into your every fiber, as much a part of you as the beating of your heart.

You'll lurch and over-reach yourself, you'll never feel at home on Earth, never really at home. You'll find a way to come back to Mars.

I smiled down at Steve.

So Steve had come back to go prospecting, like an ordinary greed-driven man, and only I knew he was one of the scant dozen great constructive geniuses who had made possible man's conquest of space.

He was an engineer, a physicist and—a man in need of a partner. So I'd just stepped up and introduced myself. Tom Gierson, who knew every square foot of Mars. For my purpose one Earth name was as good as another, and Tom Gierson had a sturdy ring.

Hard-bitten Toni Gierson, bronzed by the harsh Martian sunlight, as much at home in the desert as the sturdy little spiked plants that thrust their way up through the parched soil when the spring begins to break.

Steve's finest achievement was years in the past, but he was a young man still, with a young man's need of a woman as great as himself to share every moment of his waking life. That woman was waiting for him, but I had to be sure that he'd really go berserk if I smashed the glass.

I was sure now.

I raised my arm, and out of the ruins the Martians came.

Steady hands lifted Steve up, and a hushed silence ringed Steve round.

"Azala," I said. "Where is she—"

Then I saw her. She was advancing straight toward me through the glare of sunset on desert sand, a shining eagerness in her eyes. The girl of the mirror, young and straight and alive, her hair the color of red sand and sunset glow, her eyes twin dark stars.

She paused before me and raised her eyes in questioning wonder.

"Go to him," I said. "He will never love another woman. I can promise you that."

She ran to Steve with a little glad cry and fell to her knees beside him. I wanted to break through the circle and slap Steve on the back, and wish him all the happiness on Mars. The first Earthian to wed a Martian, and it was tremendous, and I wanted to tell Steve—

But how could I tell him that Martians had numerous ways of watching Earthians, the very best being mirrors which were really two-way televisual instruments. How could I tell him that the alert Martian women had all been trained to watch and observe Earthians day and night? And all the while the Earthians thought they were carrying about with them, in beautiful jeweled artifacts of a dead culture, the living images of their heart's desire!

Steve was awake now and sitting up straight, and the image was warm and alive in his arms. But how could I make Steve understand? I had a wild impulse to say: "I'd change places with you if I could, Steve. She's just about the cutest kid I know."

You get to thinking that way when you've mingled with Earthians around desert campfires, studying them as you'd study a new neighbor who comes knocking at your door, the neighbor you fear at first and are never quite sure of until you really get to know and like him.

You see, we had so much to offer one another. A young race, constructive, brawling, shouting its defiance to the stars. And an old race, imaginative, sensitive, heirs to a civilization on the wane, but needing just a few Steves to make it young and great again.

I'd picked Steve because he was one of the shining ones of Earth. I'd known from the start that persuading him to wed a Martian woman would take plenty of doing.

Earthians are funny that way. Love to them is a complex thing, a web that has to be skillfully woven right from the start. Beauty alone isn't enough. You have to say to them: "You'll never hold that woman in your arms. Can't you see how hopeless it is?"

Then the iron goes deep. If a love flies straight in the teeth of despair and comes out all right in the end, it will be as strong as death.

So I'd arranged for Steve to stumble on the mirror, to pick up that two-way televisual circuit into a very special paradise for two. And I'd opposed and warned him just to make sure he'd think of himself as a man facing hopeless odds to win through to an undying love.

On the other side, it was easier. Azala had fallen in love with Steve before we put her on the other end of that televisual circuit. But seeing him wounded and in need of her had turned it into what Earthians call a great love.

Perhaps Earthians would someday smash the aura that had flamed about the heads of the Martian rulers for fifty thousand years.

I'd done my best to smash it. I had gone simply and humbly among Earthians, seeking a fresh wind to trundle the cinders of a dying culture.

I dreamed of Martians and Earthians standing equal and strong and proud, hands linked in friendship, cemented by bonds of kinship, separated by no gulfs such as now yawned before me, separating me from Steve.

I wanted to shout: "Good luck, Steve, Azala. You're good kids and you deserve the best."

Then I remembered that Steve was nearly forty, not quite a kid by Earthian standards. But, looking at Azala, I was pretty sure that Steve still had his best years ahead of him.

I wanted to go up to him and shake his hand for the last time. But now the hands of my people were tugging at my shoulders, stripping off the Earthian garments I'd worn so long with scant respect for my desire to be as human and regular as the next guy.

They got the suit off, and then I saw the old familiar cloak, purple and billowing out with shimmering star images, and I shuddered a little because I knew I'd never really feel at ease wearing it from that moment on.

They got me into the cloak and they bent down and straightened the stiff imperial folds and I was suddenly bored and deathly weary.

A chill wind from the stars seemed to blow over me, but I stood straight and still, and allowed them to fasten on the cloak the great glowing jewel I'd worn from childhood.

Steve saw me then. He was sitting up very straight, his hand on Azala's tumbled, red-gold hair, and I heard him say: "Holy smoke."

I stared down at the jewel, blazing and shuddering and shivering in the desert air, and I shut my eyes tight, wishing for the first time in my life that it did not proclaim me Tulan Sharm, the Glorious One, Temporal Ruler of the Seven Cities before Whom the Stars Bowed.

THE WORLD OF WULKINS

Molly Denham was scornful and made no attempt to hide her sentiments.

"Antique shops!" she exclaimed. "What do children see in them?"

"Incredible things!" Ralph Denham replied, winking at his son and giving his small daughter's hand a squeeze. "The past through rose-colored glasses and—thingummies!"

Molly Denham smiled mischievously. Her bamboo-colored hair whipped by the wind, her hat tilted at a rakish angle, she moved up close to her husband and shook a reproving finger at his reflection in the window.

"Conspiring again and leaving me out of it," she complained. "Just you three. Winking and whispering together. Ye canna do that, laddie."

"For the last time," Denham said. "Will you put another nickel in Johnny's sun glasses before the polarization clicks off?"

"People who like gadgets should carry their own change," Molly challenged. "Renting sun glasses for a boy of eight! If you want the nickel—you'll have to catch me first."

Denham let go of his daughter's hand and made a frantic grab for his wife. Molly leapt nimbly to one side. Denham missed his footing and went crashing into the shop window, his long arms outflung.

Fortunately he didn't go very far into the window. The shatterproof plastiglass sagged under his weight, and bounced him back to his feet on the long boardwalk with scant respect for his dignity.

Denham turned slowly, a big man with keen gray eyes and gray-streaked hair—a man well past his first youth, but happy in his marriage, happy in his work.

Denham liked to think of himself as an easy-going family man—an anchor of security to his children, a gay sweetheart to his wife. But sometimes it was a little difficult, especially when the woman he'd married became a radiant water sprite with the puckish impulses of a willful child.

He suddenly realized that his daughter was plucking at his sleeve. "Daddy, look! It's a rabbit! One of the olden kind—a little one. I bet you could buy him cheap, daddy. He's all rusty."

"She means a robot!" Johnny Denham said.

Denham avoided looking at his daughter. There was no need for him to look at her. He'd gotten over his surprise long ago. Betty Anne Denham was big for her age, saucer-eyed and insatiably curious—but what child of seven wasn't?

"Tell her you like stores like that too, Pop. G'wan, tell her! *Tell her!* She thinks it's just me."

Molly Denham grimaced and spoke directly to her son. "Don't take off your hat, Johnny. Your father's had a sunstroke. There are dozens of stores like that on Maiden Row. But we came to the beach to *get away* from cobwebs and musty antiques."

"Aw, Pop knows what he's doing," Johnny said.

Good lad, Denham thought. If he went away and never came back, his children would remember him and stand up for him. They'd—"You could buy it *cheap,* daddy," Betty Anne insisted.

Denham turned with a shrug and stared into the antique shop window at the musty relics which time's relentless tides had washed up from a past that was best forgotten. To an imaginative man like Denham, a teacher of advanced semantics, the last years of the Twentieth Century loomed through the mists of time with all the fascination of a vast dust bin infested with black widow spiders.

Nightmarish was the word for it. From behind the plastiglass there stared out at Denham a goggle-eyed horror which sent a chill coursing up his spine. Robot manufacturers had experimented with dozens of different models between 1985 and 2025, but rust-green Mr. Small was certainly an odd one!

The robot was big-little and ugly, with a perfectly square head, bulging sea-green eyes and a globular body case. Big-little in that it conveyed a disturbing impression of hugeness despite its size.

Just why that should be Denham couldn't imagine. But he came to a sudden decision. He knew that if Betty Anne turned sulky he'd have to buy her candies and dolls and everything nice—every day for a week. Not only would the robot save him money, it would amuse his guests when his occasional weekend parties came a cropper over an eccentric professor's collection of Duke Ellington hot jazz recordings, not to mention his more priceless Louis Armstrongs.

With this thought in mind he took hold of his daughter's hand again. "It won't cost us anything to ask the price of that robot!" he whispered. "Come on, honeybunch!"

The shopkeeper flashed one brief glance at Betty and shook his head. "You wouldn't want it," he said. "I put it in the window solely as an— eye-catcher. If I sold it to you, you'd come back and assassinate me. As you can see, it's clogged with rust inside and out. There's nothing inside its brain case but a lot of charred wires!"

The shopkeeper rapped the robot's ugly head sharply as he spoke, eliciting a hollow, jangling sound.

"Don't let him do that to you," Molly whispered. "What he doesn't know won't hurt him."

The shopkeeper was a gaunt, thin-lipped man with hair so sparse that it enmeshed the shiny contours of his skull like a cobweb. Denham momentarily expected that the spider which had spun the web would pop into view, eliciting a scream from Betty Anne.

He looked the shopkeeper straight in the eye. "Where did you get it?" he demanded.

"Ah, that's a story in itself. The man was a derelict—thin as a scarecrow. I felt sorry for him!"

"I see," Denham said, skeptically. "If you bought that little monstrosity from a seedy looking bum, you must have wanted it pretty badly!"

"No, I didn't," the shopkeeper protested, and there was a ring of sincerity in his voice. "But I couldn't help it—I felt sorry for the man! He—he told me he found it in the woods, covered with leaves, half buried in the earth!"

"Well, anyway, my daughter wants it!" Denham was insistent. "How much?"

The shopkeeper looked shocked. "But it isn't a toy! A child wouldn't—"

"Sev—six dollars!" the shopkeeper stammered, his eyes on Molly's accusing face.

Out in the warm, bright sunlight again, walking with his arm linked with Molly's, Denham was seized with misgivings. The robot dangled between his brats like a little, blue-green monkey, its segmented metal feet barely grazing the boardwalk.

It was easy to see that the children were in a world of their own now. As they walked on ahead of their parents, supporting the little monstrosity by its elbows, they kept grinning and whispering together.

Denham felt like an outsider, and a little out of humor with his wife. She had brought it on herself by accusing him of conspiring with his children.

Children never conspired with adults except when they wanted something. When they were accused of doing so they wriggled out from under, repudiating the entire adult world with a vehemence which could sunder a man from his offspring until—they needed him again.

It happened more quickly than Denham could have anticipated. Betty Anne shivered and came to an abrupt halt, as though she'd been hit by an idea that was causing her acute anguish.

"Daddy, could we take Wulkins for a ride on the roller coaster? Could we, Daddy?"

"Yeah, why not, Pop?" Johnny Denham chimed in, his tousled head jogging in the sunlight as only the head of an eight-year-old boy could jog when excitement swirled through it.

Wulkins! So the secret whispering had borne fruit, in the deep dark of a world no adult could enter. Denham was sure there were names for everything under the sun in that world. But why Wulkins? Why not Scheherazade? Oh, well—Wulkins.

Five minutes later Denham sat beside his wife in the back seat of a roller coaster, staring at the ugly head of the robot. Betty Anne and Johnny occupied the front seat, with Wulkins wedged securely between them on red plastic cushions that brought his entire brain case into view. Two round human heads flanking a square metal head for which Denham felt no affection.

The vista which stretched around them was one of enchantment. Above a cluster of carnival-bright concessions and fine-spun aerial traceries loomed the immense, stationary bulk of the roller coaster, its ascending rails enveloped in shafts of electric-blue magnetic energy. Something close to pure magic had been instilled into the scene by the architects who had designed the amusement park and the individual concessions.

But it was a magic which made Denham distinctly uneasy, as though some elusive, hard-to-pin-down aspect of danger had been added to the scheme without impairing its mechanical stability.

"Here we go, Pop!" Johnny yelled.

The car started off in a sinuous glide and picked up speed rapidly. Before Denham could get a firm grip on the sides of the car they were ascending through a dark tunnel at an almost perpendicular angle.

"We'll die a thousand deaths!" Molly whispered. "It gets progressively worse. They want to be orphans—just to see how it feels to cry their hearts out."

They were almost at the summit of the first loop, out in the sunlight again, when Betty Anne twisted about to stare back at her parents, the waist strap which held her to her seat giving her a feeling of superiority which she made no effect to conceal.

"You're not strapped in, Daddy!" she observed. "Aren't you nervous?"

"We'll talk about it in the ambulance," Denham gritted. "Why don't you ask Wulkins if *he* feels nervous? He—Ullp! *Here it comes!*"

The car seemed to hang for an instant motionless in the middle of the sky, a gleaming spiral of blackness falling away beneath it.

Then—it started down.

At first Denham felt nothing at all. Then something like a little breeze came into existence at the base of his spine and blew up through him.

He experienced a sudden, onrushing giddiness. The breeze became a hurricane, and the dizziness twisted his brain around so that he seemed to be moving back up the gleaming rails in the wake of the plunging car.

Suddenly—he realized that the front seat was slipping away from him. Not parting from the car, but unmistakably lengthening as it plunged downward with ever increasing velocity. It was as though—the car were stretching like an elastic band, carrying the children and the robot down the rails much faster than it was carrying him.

It wasn't an illusion spawned by the steepness of the drop. It wasn't, it wasn't—*it couldn't be!* He was dizzy, but not *that dizzy.* He wasn't deceived for one second. Despite his terror, despite the vertigo which plucked and tore at him, he could see that the children were leaving him.

Their heads were getting smaller. The robot's head too—dwindling as the car lengthened. The entire car was rocking furiously from side to side, its velocity threatening to carry it from the rails. But the lengthening was a thing apart.

As Denham tightened his grip on the sides of the car something like a wrinkled film of water seemed to float between himself and his dwindling children. For an instant the sheet remained translucent, glimmering in the sunlight above a converging blur of rails.

Then shapes loomed out of it—square-headed, metallic and hideous. The shapes resembled Wulkins but—were much larger. Enormous! Behind them he could see trees now, growing out of the water and something that looked like a bald-headed vulture sweeping low above the water.

He tried to cry out, but the shapes wouldn't let him. They were reaching out toward him with their segmented metal hands spread wide, and something about the hands constricted Denham's throat muscles, so that he couldn't utter a sound.

* * * *

The next instant the weird glimmering was gone. The car had reached the bottom of the spiral and was ascending again. And directly in front of Denham, so close he could have reached out and touched them, bobbed two small heads, dark against the clear, bright sky.

The car had contracted and the children had come back again! All in the length of a heartbeat—though Denham's heart had almost ceased to beat. It began to beat again as he stared, in great, tumultuous contractions that brought an ache to his throat.

The same instant there was a flurry of movement in the seat ahead, and Johnny's excited face popped into view.

"Gee, Pop, that was terrific! What made the light?"

"You—you saw the light?" Denham said, and choked.

Betty Anne squirmed about in her seat. "It got bright," she confirmed, breathlessly. "It got awful bright, Daddy. It got brighter faster when we went as fast as anything."

"Why didn't we turn upside down, Pop?" Johnny exclaimed. "If I put a train on a track standing straight up, it would fall off backwards, wouldn't it?"

"Not—if you stretched it!" Denham muttered.

It wasn't what he'd meant to say. On a roller coaster the impetus acted as a brake, gluing the car to the rails. Friction. It wasn't the steepness of the drop that had—"Daddy! Wulkin's waking up!"

Denham stiffened, a cold chill darting up his spine. The robot had turned its head and was staring at Johnny, its body was vibrating like a tuning fork!

Molly screamed. The car had reached the crest of the spiral and was starting down again.

The children went further this time and there was a frantic bobbing about that made Denham think of dead autumn leaves being carried by chill gusts into a city of dreadful night.

But there was no city beneath him. Merely a shifting landscape wrapped in filmy light. He saw more trees, and something huge and hideous with gauzy wings he couldn't quite make out.

As the car started up again a change came upon Denham. His eyes narrowed and his jaw tightened in savage fury. Leaning forward, he wrapped his arms about the robot and jerked it straight back into the seat beside him, wrenching another scream from Molly.

Call it desperation. Call it courage, or the fiercely protective instincts of a parent at bay. Whatever it was, Denham had been quick to sense that the robot was malign, something unnatural from a plane of existence alien to humanity which had reached out to enmesh his children—and was still reaching out.

Very deliberately Denham drew the little horror across his knees and turned it over on its back. Its movements were chillingly spiderlike. Its bulbous eyes twitched and its arms tried to wrap themselves around Denham as he struggled with it.

Denham felt the impact of cold, merciless metal, bruising his flesh, creeping upward toward his throat. But luckily the plates which protected the robot's vitals had worked a little loose.

Jabbing at the metal arms with his elbow, Denham wedged the fingers of his right hand beneath one of the plates, and pried it completely loose. Deep within him there squirmed a cold revulsion and a growing terror. But relentlessly he thrust his hand into a narrow opening in the robot's back, and grasped a tangle of quivering wires, cold to the touch.

Furiously Denham tugged at the wires. He was still tugging when the car reached the top of the loop and started down again. But the robot had ceased to quiver.

Five minutes later Denham stood facing his daughter on a firm plastiglass platform, the robot lying in a crumpled heap at his feet.

"Daddy, what did you do him?" Betty Anne shrieked. "He—he's dead. You killed him! You did! You *did!* I heard him scream."

Molly grabbed Betty Anne by the shoulder, and shook her vigorously. "He didn't make any noise—not a sound. Your father should have flung that horrible little monster out of the car. Now we'll have to use an ax on him."

Denham stood it as long as he could. Then he stepped forward and gave his daughter a resounding whack on her little behind.

"No recriminations, honeybunch," he said. "Your mother's right. I did what I thought was best. You'll just have to take my word for it because—I don't intend to discuss it!"

"Not even when we get home, Daddy?" Betty Anne said, oddly mollified by her father's forbearance. Not that he'd ever used a hairbrush but—there could always be a first time!

"Not until—Hades freezes over!" Denham said, firmly. "Perhaps not even then. So you can wipe that wheedling smirk off your face. It won't get you anywhere."

But Denham had spoken rashly, failing to take into consideration the tyranny which his daughter was capable of wielding. He discovered his mistake the following afternoon, when the children's hour brought her into his book-walled study and straight to the arm of his chair with a bad case of sulks.

Logs were crackling in the fireplace, Molly was out in the kitchen preparing dinner and late autumn sunlight was slanting in through the tall, antique windows at Denham's back.

Denham had made a deliberate effort to recapture for home consumption the serene, rose-petaled atmosphere of the middle Nineteenth century, which hadn't been half as feverish as the Twentieth.

Not only did he enjoy lecturing about the past, he liked to surround himself with objects from the past—a stuffed owl under glass, a china closet filled with rare porcelain bric-a-brac, a tasteful selection of Currier and Ives prints.

Beautiful, serene, decorative objects and not ugly ones like—hold on, he'd best stop right there!

It was Betty Anne who did the reminding. "You're not really going to destroy Wulkins, are you, Daddy?"

Denham was nettled. He sat up straight in his chair, flushing a little and glaring at his daughter.

"Look, honeybunch," he said slowly. "If I tell you all I know and suspect about Wulkins, will you keep out of my hair?"

"Daddy, couldn't we keep him? He's all broken up inside now, isn't he? We could make believe he's still alive—"

"Very well!" Denham capitulated. "I may as well tell you for you'd go right on talking about him anyway. But maybe you won't ask so many questions if I tell you."

"All right, Daddy. Tell me."

Denham ran his fingers through his hair. He reached for his pipe. A moment later he was squinting at his daughter through a haze of tobacco smoke. He knew that the smoke was bad for her. He wished she'd realize that and go away.

When she nestled closer to him he set the pipe down despairingly and put his arms about her.

"When we bought him he was all clogged with rust, remember? He wasn't vibrating. But that roller coaster ride—the jogging—must have started him up."

"Uh-huh!"

"Now don't get excited," Denham warned. "It isn't anything that will break out on you like a rash if you can't understand it. Here's what I think happened. When Wulkins started to vibrate he warped space in all directions. Very strongly in front of him and a little on both sides of him. De Sitter's soap bubble universe."

Denham scowled, rubbed his chin. "Physicists claim there are tensions which simply can't remain in ordinary space. They shoot right out of our space like—a cork from a champagne bottle. Something outside of our world creates them and, when they get into our world, they can't stay there."

Denham reached for his pipe again. "But if something came into our world from outside and built up tensions in itself, it could pop right back again, carrying a part of our world with it—perhaps."

Betty Anne stirred impatiently on her father's knee. "Are you talking to me, Daddy?"

"No!" Denham grunted. "Just thinking out loud. Here's how I'd tell it to you. The world's where we are. But there's another place—where we're not. Maybe a lot of other places, all pressed together close to where we are, with just a thin film of emptiness separating them. People live there too maybe, and, for all we know, they may be trying to come where we are. Sick to come where we are."

"And they can't?"

"So far as we know they've never been able to," Denham told her. "If they came at all, it would have to be in something pretty complicated. A machine of some sort. You see, it's a little like traveling into a far country at enormous speed. You've seen trains. They're complicated."

"Go on, Daddy!"

"Well—*Wulkins* is a machine and he's complicated. You don't know how complicated because you've never looked inside him. But you can take my word for it, he's as complex as you are."

"Complicated means all mixed up, doesn't it Daddy?"

"That's right. Sometimes it means mixed up in a rather simple way, and then you've really got something to worry about. But Wulkins is complicated in a dozen ways. Looking inside him is like looking into a big bare room and hearing a lot of noises below the threshold of sound, and seeing pictures on the wall that are there one minute and gone the next."

Denham's head had begun to ache. He put a hand to his brow and withdrew it quickly, as though he didn't really want to find out if he was running a fever.

"It's even worse than that. You can hear sounds outside the room, if you keep on staring and listening. And you don't need earphones. You can see colors, too, that never were on sea or land."

"Go on, Daddy!"

"Well, maybe the people couldn't come themselves. So they sent Wulkins to see what he could see. A dimension-traveling robot. And maybe he got clogged with rust before he could return to his world with samples of our world. Little things his makers have asked him to put into his knapsack, an old black bag, a peppermint stick, a tropical butterfly."

Denham smiled thinly at his daughter. "Or bigger things he'd have to *vibrate* back, like a little girl who was born curious and likes to torment older people for no reason at all. Or maybe she has a reason those other people would like to ask her about."

Betty Anne looked genuinely frightened. Denham said hastily: "Don't think it doesn't scare *me!* But it's tremendously important too! So

important a delegation of pompous screwballs—" Denham grimaced—
"world famous scientists to you, honeybunch—are coming to your father's house just to look at Wulkins."

"Unh—they *are?*"

"Tomorrow, honeybunch! Now do you understand why I can't let
you play with him?"

Betty Anne screwed up her face. "Well, if you don't want me to,
Daddy, I won't!"

* * * *

Several hours later two small, pajama-clad figures moved cautiously
down the central stairway of the Denhams' house. One of the figures was
Betty Anne, her hair braided for the night. The other was her brother,
whose manner was that of a sure-footed conspirator who had taken great
pains to dramatize himself.

Johnny's expression was Machiavellian and he spoke with an air of
mysterious authority, as though he were addressing not only his sister but
the sulking shadows as well.

"Know what I'm going to do when I fix Wulkins up?" he whispered.

"No, what?"

"Build a peep show in Freddy Gilroy's backyard and fit it so Wulkins
can't get out. We'll drill a hole in a board and watch him trying to get out
like we did with the snapping turtle!"

Betty Anne looked scared. "Freddy nearly got his hand bitten off,"
she whispered. "And Daddy was awful mad. You'll be good and sorry if
you do that to Wulkins."

"Aw, Pop never stays mad at me," Johnny told her. "I know how to
handle him."

"I wish I did."

There was a moment of silence. Then Johnny said pridefully: "I
know how to handle tools, too. I can fix anything, if I try hard enough.
Pop told me I looked like a little grease monkey the day I was born."

Betty Anne came to an abrupt halt, her hand on the banister. "When
did he tell you? The day you was born?"

"Don't be a dope! How could a baby understand a thing like that?"

"What's a grease monkey, Johnny?" Betty Anne asked, casting a
swift glance back up the stairs.

"A mechanic, you dope! Pipe down, willya? You want him to hear
us?"

The children were at the foot of the stairs now, tiptoeing through
shadows toward the rear of the house. Johnny moved a little faster than
his sister, his eyes shining with anticipation.

"Hurry up!" he urged. "What's the matter? Afraid!"

"No. But I just remembered something. You can't reach the light in the cellar. You're not tall enough."

"So what?" Johnny whispered. "I'll climb up on the workbench."

"We'll be all alone with Wulkins in the dark," Betty Anne exclaimed, a catch in her throat. "If I was a scarecat I'd be afraid. But I'm not."

"You are too," Johnny said. "Don't fool yourself."

There was a brief pause at the head of the cellar stairs, punctuated by an odd silence. Then down the stairs in total blackness the children crept. Down the stairs and across the cellar with their hearts fluttering wildly until—"Oh, Johnny, I'm scared. Johnny, where are you?"

Instantly the light came on, revealing Johnny crouching on the workbench, his eyes bright with alarm.

The alarm disappeared when he saw that his sister was unharmed. The robot was standing utterly motionless a foot from Betty Anne's outstretched hand, its long arms dangling, its globular body box half in shadows.

"Daddy left him standing up," Betty Anne said, as though aware of her brother's thoughts. "Didn't he tell you?"

"Naw!" Johnny muttered. "He said if he caught me down here he'd—"

Johnny colored to the roots of his hair. "Well, what are we waiting for? Hand me that screwdriver."

Tinkering is a specialized art. It is much more than that—it is an exact science. But every science, every art, no matter how specialized, has its mysterious short cuts. When the tinkerer is a child, soft spots occasionally open up in the hard mechanical cement which welds theory to practice.

For a child does not conform to any pattern in his tinkering. He ignores all the rules and relies on perseverance, curiosity and a semi-mystical legerdemain which has been known to empty orchards and whisk the frosting off cakes in a time interval too brief to be measured by the instruments of human science.

There is a right way of tackling every problem and there is a wrong way. But there is also a way which is neither right nor wrong, but just—a way.

With Johnny it was simply a matter of *knowing* he could get Wulkins running again, if he tried hard enough. There was no need for him to go before a delegation of world-famous scientists and justify his faith in himself. His confidence was boundless and completely beyond the reach of adult skepticism.

After fifteen minutes of tinkering the workbench was smeared with grease and bright with the tools which Johnny had used and discarded. But he wasn't discouraged—not by a long sight.

Wulkins was beginning to shine. Most of the rust had been removed by Betty Anne, who stood beside her brother with a bottle of metal polish in her hand. But Johnny had eyes only for the glitter of intricate mechanical parts. He was using his brain and his hands, all his skill, in a way that sent a surge of confidence spinning through him.

"Stop jarring him, Betty Anne!" he protested. "You've polished him enough. Hey cut it out!"

He whipped his hand from the robot's vitals as he spoke, a gleaming wire-cutter twisting in his clasp. "You want me to cut myself? I can't work on him unless you stop polishing him. What's the big idea?"

"You want him to shine, don't you?" Betty Anne asked.

Johnny started to reply. He got out a single word, a clearly articulated "Aw—" Then—his speech congealed.

Wulkins had turned his head and was looking at Betty Anne. But he didn't reach for Betty Anne. He reached for Johnny. His segmented metal hand shot out and fastened on Johnny's arm before Johnny could leap back.

Betty Anne squealed with alarm and retreated into the middle of the cellar, her eyes darting to Johnny's face.

There was no hand over Betty Anne's mouth, but for an instant she remained as silent as Johnny. The floor spun under her, and her head whirled faster than the floor. The workbench whirled too, and the tools and Johnny.

Suddenly she was screaming, at the top of her lungs. But the robot paid no attention to her. Instead it fastened its bulbous eyes on Johnny and began to tug at his hair. It seemed amazed because—Johnny was Johnny! It grabbed one of Johnny's hands and turned it over and over, as though it had never seen a human hand before.

It tweaked Johnny's nose, tugged at his ear. Betty Anne stopping screaming suddenly, feeling all cold and ashamed inside because she couldn't do anything in keep the robot from treating Johnny like a—a limp rag doll.

The robot wasn't very rough with Johnny. But she didn't like it, she couldn't stand it, and she started to scream again.

She was still screaming when the robot shifted Johnny around until just his head emerged from under one stiff metal arm and started toward her across the floor…

Molly realized that the stars were changing before her husband did. It was like awakening in the still dark, and reaching out for something that wasn't there—a child's crumpled doll, or a warm little hand in a cot where a child's body had lain.

There was something in the room that wasn't right. It was nothing very tangible, nothing that could be seen. But it was there and she could sense it. Swiftly she got out of bed, threw a shawl about her shivering shoulders and darted to the window.

For an instant she stared out with her face pressed to the pane, her thoughts in a turmoil.

The stars *were* different! Beyond the black boughs which interlaced in the moonlight a yard from her face the far-flung splendor of the night sky had dwindled to a pallid glimmering. There was no Milky Way, no Great Dipper. Nothing but a sprinkling of very distant stars with a faint nebulosity behind them.

The moon had dwindled too. It was not only smaller, but it had a dull, coppery sheen, as though it were reflecting the light of a dying sun in a universe that had passed away.

Molly clenched her hands swiftly, utter horror in her stare. There's got to be *some* explanation she thought.

Suddenly her eyes widened and her hand went to her throat. Out of the house in the moonlight and across the lawn below there strode an enormous shadow. The shadow was angular, grotesque, and it moved with a convulsive trembling of its entire bulk.

As Molly stared she saw that there were two smaller shadows attached to it. The small shadows seemed to jut out from it and to move with it across the lawn. But the smaller shadows were also in violent motion, as though they were trying desperately to break loose from the larger shadow.

And then Molly saw what had cast the shadow! It must have been clumping toward the road at the very edge of the lawn, because when it came into view the moonlight struck down so sharply against it that it stood out instantly in all of its angular ugliness.

It was a robot! But not the hideous little robot her husband had refused to destroy. No! A colossal shape of metal, eight feet tall, its huge gleaming arms wrapped around two small, struggling human forms.

"Johnny—Betty Anne!" Molly screamed the names of her children as she rushed back across the room to her husband's side. It was a stricken cry, but it was also a cry of protest and fierce defiance.

She ripped the bedclothes from Denham, gripped his arm and gave it a furious wrench. "Ralph—*Ralph!* Wake up—get up! The *children!"*

Denham was out of bed so quickly his features had a tautly masked look, as though his reflexes had brought him to his feet while his brain was still asleep. But the queer thing about it was that he seemed to know that something horrible was taking place.

At first Molly had screamed in sheer panic and then at her husband to wake him. But now she spoke quietly, as she usually did when life turned cruel and ugly, tapping her reserves of strength.

"Go to the window and look out. Hurry, darling!"

When Denham reached the window the robot was disappearing into a weaving blur of vegetation at the edge of the lawn. But he caught one brief glimpse of the metal giant, a glimpse which galvanized him into instant action.

He started toward the clothes closet, then swung about, and ripped his dressing gown from the foot of the bed. He wrapped it around himself and sat down on the edge of the bed. Few men could have drawn on their shoes in exactly eight seconds. But Denham did it.

Beads of sweat were collecting on his forehead when he said: "I'm going after them. It's Wulkins! There's been some sort of dimension shift and Wulkins has grown larger. He must have vibrated himself back into his world, and the cottage with him."

"You're not going alone," Molly said, thrusting her husband's trousers into his lap. "Put those on. It won't take a second. You can't run in that dressing gown. Anything else you want? Is there?"

"Get me a flashlight and an automatic pistol. Downstairs in my desk!"

"I said I was going with you."

Denham sprang up. "All right, all right! I'll get the automatic. You get something on you."

When Denham and Molly emerged from the house, the night had taken on an alien aspect. Before them the lawn was a shining strip which stretched in a straight line to a quivering edge of darkness which seemed to recede as they plunged toward it.

In a moment they had crossed the lawn and were racing along an unfamiliar road beneath a canopy of heavily-scented vegetation. On both sides of them towered enormous trees, black against the pallid sky. They were different from any trees Molly had ever seen. Their boles glistened in the moonlight, and their branches seemed to tear and pluck at the night sky like the claws of rearing beasts.

The edge of darkness had moved on ahead of them and was still dividing the landscape, so that they seemed to be moving toward an ink-black, impenetrable void which had swallowed up everything in their path.

No, not quite everything. In the sheer walled immensity of the black-ness little glints kept appearing and vanishing, as though a few startled fireflies had become enmeshed in it and were trying to get out.

It was Denham who saw something beside the glints. Perhaps be-cause he was thirty feet ahead of Molly and the edge of darkness had receded further for him. But it may have been something else, a keener vision, or the courage to believe what he saw.

Not that Molly lacked courage, but there were times when it slipped away from her while fear drilled into the back of her mind.

As she ran she heard her husband shouting. *"Molly!* There's some-thing moving right up ahead—something bright!"

But though the words brought a catch to her throat she saw only the darkness, just the trees and the darkness stabbing down. Her heels lifted queerly as she ran and her hands were clenched so tightly it seemed her fingers must crack.

Then, suddenly, the edge of darkness seemed to dissolve, to float away, and she saw a thick clump of shrubbery bisecting the shadows at the edge of the road. Directly in front of the thicket the road turned sharply, circling out to sweep on past it.

Denham had stopped running. He was gripping the automatic pistol firmly, and advancing on the thicket with his shoulders hunched.

He called out: "Molly, turn on the flash. Keep it trained on that bush. You hear? On the bush! But try to sweep it past me."

For an instant Molly remained utterly rigid, the flash a lump of ice against her palm. Then, with a shudder, she clicked it on. As she did so a child's shrill scream sliced through the night.

"Run, Betty, run! Quick, before he catches you!"

Out of the thicket popped Betty Anne's small figure, her eyes dark pools of terror. She stood for an instant blinking in the beam, her elbows pressed to her side.

Then with a shriek she ran straight toward Molly, ignoring her fa-ther's intervening bulk. The next instant there was a straining tightness about Molly's neck, and a wet, cold cheek brushed her lips. As though from a great distance she heard her husband shout:

"He's still got Johnny! I'm going in after him!"

Then she heard another voice, shriller, edged with defiance: "He hasn't got me, Pop. I broke loose. But I—I can't get past him."

Molly leaped up, pushed Betty Anne around in back of her, and trained the flash on the thicket again. It was not only terror she felt, but shame, that she could have forgotten even for an instant that she had a son. She hadn't really forgotten, not deep in her mind, but her relief at finding Betty Anne in her arms had spilled over into the warm, bright little compartment reserved for her son. Now that compartment was as cold as ice.

From the thicket there was a scrambling sound. Then the boughs parted, and Johnny sprang into view, his terrified face twisting in the beam. His shoulders jerked, and there was a fright upon him so intense as to seem unnatural in a child.

Before Denham could move the robot parted the bushes directly behind his son with a single sweep of its long arms, as though it were stepping out from an annoying tangle of cobwebs.

It moved so swiftly it was towering over Johnny before Denham could scream a warning, its gleaming arms upraised. But some instinct warned Johnny that he was in mortal danger.

With a shriek, he swerved quickly to one side, pivoted about and raced toward his parents along the edge of the beam. Denham held his breath until Johnny was almost at his side.

Then the automatic pistol jerked in his hand, erupting in dull flame. The flash of light was accompanied by a harsh, metallic splintering, and a swirl of smoke which blotted the robot from view.

When the smoke cleared the robot was advancing on Denham in long, steady strides, its ponderous footsteps shaking the road. The blast had torn away half of its head, but it came on notwithstanding, its upraised right arm flailing the air like a gigantic mace.

Denham recoiled a step and took careful aim at the globular body case, his eyes so hot and dry they seemed to be burning holes in his flesh.

He was grateful for the beam which brought the monster into stark relief but the fact Johnny stood at his side, facing the horror in defiance of Molly, who was screaming at him to come to her, unnerved him so that his hand shook.

"Careful, Pop!" Johnny warned.

Denham fought to control his voice. "It's either him or us. If he gets me, don't yell or go down on your knees. You'll be in trouble if you do."

"I'm not leaving you, Pop."

Denham was grateful for something that brought a sudden steadiness to his arm.

He felt rather than heard the blast which spouted outward from his hand.

He blasted again and again and again—exhausting the energy load. The ground seemed to spiral beneath him with the dancing flare, and the smoke which swirled about the robot was so dense that it blotted out the sky.

When the smoke cleared the robot was still advancing.

It was a twisted, smoking mass of wreckage, its head a charred shell spilling metal pipes that glowed white hot. The atomic charge had also turned it radioactive, so that it glowed in a more dangerous way over every inch of its body case.

Denham's throat was so dry that swallowing was a torture. He knew that the robot was a deadly danger now, walking or just standing. It was drenched with radiations which could destroy every red blood corpuscle in Johnny's body if it came a yard closer.

The robot was within twenty feet of Denham when it halted. Slowly its shattered bulk began to sway, back and forth, back and forth, like an immense shuttlecock balanced on a wire. Then, just as slowly, it began to move backwards.

And as it moved away from Denham a yawning gulf of blackness which seemed as wide as the night swept toward it and swirled around it, obscuring its angular contours. It was suddenly small, a dwindling blur of spiraling light, weaving in and out between the trees. Then the darkness swallowed it up.

* * * *

Now they were castaways in an alien world, a world of dreadful shadows that kept lengthening on all sides of them.

The trees were gigantic, with pale, almost translucent boles wrapped in coiling tendrils of mist. The boles glistened in the wan moonlight, and the branches of the trees had heavily-veined, flat leaves which gave off a cloying perfume which clung to the nostrils like musk.

Others had foliage which swept the ground in long streamers and gleamed in the darkness with infinite gradations of color, like the sea-lashed tendrils of a Portuguese man-of-war.

On both sides of the road the earth was covered with huge, whorl-shaped fungus growths, scarlet-veined and rimmed with long, tapering tendrils as transparent as glass. Between the flat whorls the ground was dotted with scarlet thistles and flowering shrubs, so fragile in structure they seemed woven of stardust and the even more elusive traceries of the glassblowers' art.

Molly had sensed the alienness back in the cottage, leaping out of bed, and staring out in terror at a sky that had changed. Sharing that knowledge with her husband had made it seem worse, perhaps because it was a knowledge that could not be sanely shared. But now that they all knew, it chilled their hearts like ice, so that they hardly dared discuss it with another.

Other dimensions, Ralph had said. There were other dimensions impinging on the warm, secure world they'd always known. And now they were in one, stumbling back toward the cottage, a fearful purposefulness in their silence.

Silence was a protection. It was the only safeguard, the only sure anchor in a world where nothing was sure.

It was Betty Anne who shattered it. "Daddy! There's something big and black standing right beside the house. If it's Wulkins, he's grown bigger."

Denham came to an abrupt halt. His lips whitening, he reached out and grabbed his daughter's wrist—just in case. Children had been known to dash straight toward terrifying objects, for no reason an adult could fathom.

He stood very still, staring past the cottage at the object which had frightened Betty Anne. He could see at once that it wasn't—Wulkins! It was almost as tall as the cottage and it didn't have a square head.

It bulged out chillingly in the shadows, but—a building with over-size foundations which anchored it to the earth. And everything about the object proclaimed that it was just that—a building. It had a massive, architectural look, a firmly rooted look!

He turned to Molly. "All right! Stay put—and keep the kids off my neck. I'm going to take a look."

A moment later Denham turned to wave in the darkness, the strange structure looming above him. "Molly, come here. It's a big stone vault."

When Molly arrived at her husband's side he was crouching at the base of the structure, training the flashlight on a massive slab of rock heavily overgrown with weeds.

"It's made of solid blocks of rock, cemented together a little un-evenly!" he exclaimed. "Each block must weigh tons. But the stone's beginning to crumble. I could probably force this entrance slab, if I put my shoulder to it."

"Oh, no!" Molly breathed.

"I'm going to try," Denham said, straightening.

Molly started to protest, but something in his expression silenced her.

Five minutes later Denham was advancing alone into the vault, the entrance slab standing ajar behind him, a narrow shaft of light slicing through the darkness ahead of him. The light sliced through the darkness without dispelling it, like a luminous and expanding wire cutter.

The odors which filled the vault were unnerving. The smell of stale air and earth mold mingled with a fainter exhalation which might well have been the smell of age itself. It did not seem to be the odor of cor-ruption. There was no fleshly taint to it, no lingering reek such as a desiccated shape of flesh might have spread through the darkness, even after millenniums.

For a moment the extremity of the beam wavered on a discolored surface of stone as rough as the exterior of the vault. Then it came to rest on a long stone slab, projecting straight out from the wall on a level with Denham's knees.

The slab was—occupied.

Denham sucked in his breath sharply. The thing on the slab looked like nothing so much as an enormous cicada! Its gauzy wings, which were folded on its chest, glowed with a dull, metallic sheen, and its huge corpse-white eyes stared blankly, as though after thousands of years, it had given up trying to see in the dark.

The thing conveyed pure horror in its attitude, as though it had been rolled on the shelf and left there to rot. For it had begun to rot, all down one side. Something chillingly like tomb mold was spilling from its vitals.

As Denham steadied the flash a dizziness swept over him. Had the thing on the slab been unmistakably an insect Denham might have endured the sight of it. What unnerved him completely was his inability to put it into any category that did not make for unadulterated horror.

For it seemed alive even in death, as though it might at any moment get up and go stumbling blindly about in the darkness.

There was something hideously functional about it, something that was hard to associate with the slow, sure decay which time brings to fleshly creatures whether they be high or low in the scale of evolution.

There was a silence, thick, cloying, ghastly. Denham fought down his revulsion, and then he saw the small, spindle-like objects which lay scattered at the horror's feet and under its gauzy wings at the edge of the slab.

His vision had become blurred from too much staring. But when he moved closer to the slab, and trained the flash directly on its weathered surface the spindles ceased to quiver and he found himself staring down in stunned incredulity at eight tiny, gleaming spools of photo-film with perforated edges.

After a moment Denham's amazement ebbed a little. His common sense told him there was nothing more functional than a threaded spool of photofilm. Projected images were inseparable from civilization. In fact, it was impossible to think of any advanced culture, in any age or dimension, without cinematographic recordings.

As Denham turned from the slab, shoving the spools into his pocket, he found himself wondering a little wildly if the spools would fit his own cinema projector.

Suddenly his heart pounded in his throat. Something was moving toward him across the floor. Rolling straight toward him from out of the shadows, with the brittle impetus of an autumnal puffball caught in a sudden gust of wind.

The instant the object came to rest at Denham's feet he stiffened, his senses touched queerly. The object was a fragile-looking crystal globe faintly suffused with light. As Denham stared down at it the light brightened, blazed with a radiance that dazzled his vision and held him rooted.

After a moment the radiance dimmed a little, but still Denham's gaze remained riveted on the globe. The skin crawled at the base of his scalp. Try as he might, he could not wrench his gaze from its gleaming convexity.

As Denham stared something began to stir in the depths of the crystal. A dark insect-like face with bulging eyes and moving mouth parts came slowly into view, grew swiftly larger.

For an instant the hideous face filled the globe, and then, just as slowly, it began to dwindle, moving further back into the glow until Denham could see its entire body, enmeshed in a blur of fluttering wings.

Denham knew instantly that he was staring at a moving image of the ghastly shape on the slab. And—at something else! Behind the cicada-shape towered the angular, stationary bulk of Wulkins.

The robot's mirrored image was intact, and it was staring at Denham behind the cicada with its enormous eyes riveted on his face. It seemed to be reproaching him for what he had done to it, a cold malignity in its stare.

Somehow Denham got the impression that he was gazing at something that no longer existed in reality, the cicada shape restored to a living vigor that belied its immobility on the slab; the robot restored to a mechanical vigor that was like a thought projected from *its* mind to him, through the medium of that hypnotic crystal.

For if the crystal was not hypnotic why was he powerless to move, why did his thoughts seem to float up through his brain and out toward the glow as though drawn by a compulsion outside of himself.

Torment can take many forms, but the worst kind of torture does not come from pain undergone in a physical struggle. It is subjective—a slow, merciless crushing of a man's will to struggle. And Denham was feeling that torment now.

Not only was his mind being invaded, its innermost secrets were laid bare.

He felt himself regressing to a more primitive level of consciousness, where everything stood starkly revealed—the red, hideous impulses and rages he had inherited from the jungle, the heritage of humanity's buried apehood—and thoughts no human mind could endure and remain sane.

Abruptly, as Denham stared, sickened to the depths of his mind, another crystal ball came spinning toward him across the vault. The second sphere was much larger than the first and as it came to rest at Denham's feet the light in the first globe went out.

But the second crystal brought no relief to Denham, no cessation of the torment. Instead as it brimmed with radiance his anguish and terror increased, for he saw himself lying stretched out on the slab, with the cicada shape hovering over him, its wings vibrating, a long, gleaming scalpel twisting in its upraised claw.

As Denham stared transfixed the cicada shape bent, and plunged the scalpel into his vitals! Denham screamed.

The scream brought a sudden easing of the tension, shattering the unnatural hypnosis and enabling him to wrench his gaze away.

Afterwards, he was unable to remember whether Wulkins was standing or crouching above the still larger crystal globe which it was just about to push toward him. He only knew that he saw Wulkins clearly for the barest instant, the Wulkins he had maimed, its head still shredded and glowing.

The robot had moved out from a horizontal slab of stone a few yards from the slab and was facing him in the shadows, a mind-numbing assortment of objects at its back.

The objects were indescribable in that they became increasingly nightmarish the longer Denham stared at them. Cubes without foundations, crisscrossing metal pipes set in frames that seemed to melt and run in all directions, and at least a dozen shapes of crystal that became square one instant, spherical the next.

Some of the crystals were tiny, others were enormous, and a few were massed together in formations that gave the lie to the painstaking edifice of mathematical science which humanity had erected on the premise that parallel lines cannot meet.

If lightning had diffused itself through all the vault in the second that Denham stood frozen he could not have acted with greater presence of mind.

His feet were heavier than they should have been and his fingers felt numb. Yet he managed to switch off the flash and stood facing imminent destruction.

He knew that he had no chance at all of eluding the robot with the light on. By its own glow it could see him faintly, even in the darkness. But with the light off he could see it clearly. By so thin a margin did his safety hang, but the small advantage was all he needed.

He was suddenly in weaving motion, his eyes fastened on the robot as he backed away toward the entrance of the vault. It was terrible enough before the robot emerged from behind the slab and started after him. When it made blind clutches in the darkness, its feet scraping the floor, Denham almost succumbed to panic.

But something he hadn't realized until that instant kept him backing toward the entrance. To give Molly and his children a fighting chance to survive in a world that was black and horrible, he'd have grappled with Wulkins in a death struggle.

No struggle took place. Yet the culmination of Denham's desperate retreat across the vault was just as terrifying in a different way. Three paces from the entrance he stubbed his toe, and went reeling.

Instantly the robot lunged, its glowing arms sweeping straight toward him through the darkness. Just in time Denham regained his balance, leaping so swiftly aside that the robot went crashing into the wall with a harsh, metallic clatter. Then Denham was outside the entrance slab, shouting at Molly:

"It's Wulkins! He was hiding in there! Quick, Molly! Head for the cottage. There's another automatic load in my desk. Hurry, *hurry!* I can't hold this slab much longer!"

Molly stood rigid between her children, holding on tight to them.

"Get away from that slab," she said, almost without moving her lips. "If he wants to come out, let him!"

"Molly, are you crazy?"

"I don't want to be a widow! That's how crazy I am. You're coming with us. We can make it, if we don't stop to argue!"

"Sure we can, Pop!" Johnny urged, his eyes shining in the darkness.

* * * *

Five minutes later Denham was crouching by a thrown-open window on the ground floor of the cottage, a recharged automatic gleaming in his hand. Behind him in shadows loomed the walls of his study, and in front of him stretched a wide lawn.

The robot was advancing across the lawn toward the cottage, its long arms swinging, its shredded head against the sky.

Denham was aware of a warm, reassuring stir of movement behind him. Everything he'd have died to protect made itself felt in that stir, steeling his muscles, steadying his aim.

He waited until the robot's dark bulk blotted out the red moon. He waited until it became edged with a dull glow that brought all its angular contours into stark relief.

Then, and only then, he blasted.

The redness which came from his weapon matched the redness which spilled out from the robot's body as the blast ripped through it. For the barest instant the heat of the blast fanned the air about it into violent motion. Then the smoke of the blast swirled over it, blotting it from view.

When the smoke cleared there rested on the lawn a smoking, stationary metal torso, a half giant with its legs shot away, its globular body box flush with the grass.

And behind Denham, in the warm shadows Johnny was yelling: "He's shrinking, Pop! He's getting small again."

The lawn seemed to tilt then and everything beyond the window spun dizzily. The robot shrunk in erratic jerks. For an instant it seemed to expand as well as shrink, so that parts of it became very large while the rest of it shriveled.

But after a moment even the larger parts began to shrink. Smaller and smaller it became, until it was no longer a half giant, but a small metal shape which was all too familiar.

But Wulkins did not remain merely small. He did not remain even a shattered, blackened parody of his antique shop self. He continued to shrink as Denham stared, a cold prickling running up his spine.

The lawn had ceased to gyrate and the glimmering beyond the window had subsided. But Wulkins continued to shrink. Smaller he became and smaller. He became tiny so quickly that the grass around him seemed to grow up about him, so that he resembled for an instant an inch-high luminous elf shape sparkling in the middle of the lawn, half buried in the long, upsweeping blades.

But it was only an illusion, for Denham could see that the grass wasn't really moving. Only Wulkins was moving, and suddenly Wulkins was gone. A firefly enmeshed in the grass, its lantern sparking out, would have looked no different from Wulkins vanishing. A tiny pinpoint of light in the middle of the lawn glowing brightly and then—nothing, nothing at all. Not even Wulkins, not ever again, Wulkins.

When Denham sank into a chair by the fireplace he was so shaken that his voice sounded like a cracked record jarringly enunciating harsh syllables from a broken down sound track.

"He vibrated the cottage back! We're back, Molly, kids. We're back in our own world. We're back—we're back!"

Both arms of Denham's chair were instantly occupied by his children. At almost the same instant there was a heaviness on his lap, and he was holding Molly tightly and smoothing her hair while his voice, like a cracked record, droned raucously on: "I know we are—because the vault's gone. I could just see it from the window and it's not there. We're back."

Johnny had no difficulty with his voice. He was trembling a little and he started off pale, but when the questions came tumbling from his lips, thick and fast, the color flooded back into his face. "What d'you suppose happened, Pop? What made Wulkins shrink? Why didn't he stop?"

"There are two possible explanations," Denham managed to say. "You can take your pick." He was still having trouble with his voice, but he found to his relief that he could enunciate less harshly now. "Either the atomic blast set his dimension-warp mechanism in motion erratically, so that he was powerless to control it."

Denham wet his dry lips. "Or he deliberately chose to destroy himself. His way of committing suicide may have been to go into a still smaller dimension, and vibrate right out of our space too. If that's what happened, we can thank our lucky stars his power to warp the cottage stopped when he became as small as he was when we bought him."

"But why should he want to kill himself, Daddy?" Betty Anne asked.

"There was something in the vault with him," Denham told her. "His maker, perhaps. All desiccated, shriveled up, as dead as a doornail. When he came back and found the *human*—" Denham gagged a little over the word. "When he found the equivalent of a human being in his world lying dead, despair may have overwhelmed him, and then, when I blasted away his legs, he realized that his number was up!"

"Gee, you really think that's what happened, Pop?" Johnny asked.

"I said you could take your pick," Denham reminded him. "Now that he's gone, it doesn't really matter."

He straightened as he spoke, gently elevating Molly until she was sitting on his knee, facing him.

"It's an ungodly hour for your children to be up!" he reminded her. "I've got a few films I'd like to examine, but I can't concentrate when I'm on the witness stand!"

Molly's eyes widened. "Films?"

"Films, Pop?" Johnny said.

"I'd rather have that than a nightcap," Denham said. "Both the kids, tucked in for the night!"

Molly smiled and kissed him. "All right," she said.

An hour later Denham and Molly stood in the upper hallway, staring into a shadowed room at the tousled head of their son.

"And Johnny's back in his own little bed again!" Molly whispered.

She shut the door almost reverently. "He's a good boy! He's never made any trouble for us."

"As good as they come!" Denham said.

The instant the door closed Johnny sat up straight in bed. "He'll never know if you don't tell him!" he whispered.

In the bed opposite the sheets heaved up. "Go to sleep," Betty Anne murmured drowsily. "I'm not a tattletale! Besides—I helped you, didn't I?"

Back in their own bedroom, Denham turned to face his wife. "The projector wouldn't take those films," he said. "The perforations were all out of alignment."

"Then you didn't—"

"Don't worry," Denham said. "I examined them. But I had to project them as stills. It was a tedious process, but there's something to be said for stills. Animation would have turned my hair white."

"What did you find out?"

Denham was silent for a moment. "You'll have to make an imaginative effort to understand," he said, at last. "A very resolute effort. You see, life in a completely alien world would be—completely alien!"

"Well, that makes sense," Molly said. "But it's a little obvious, isn't it?"

"No, it isn't! Nothing's obvious when all analogies break down."

"What are you trying to say?"

"There's one analogy that might apply," Denham said, as though it were being dragged out of him. "The cobwebby old legend of the Sorcerer's Apprentice!"

"The Sorcerer's—"

"Cells," Denham said. "Monastic-like stone cells, scattered throughout that ghastly dimension. Each cell occupied by a sorcerer and his apprentice. They're not really that, but I can't think of a better analogy."

"Well...go on!"

"Each cell a focus of intense intellectual activity. Each sorcerer and his apprentice exploring the mysteries of time and space, of other worlds and other dimensions, spurred on by curiosity, seeking to extend the boundaries of non-human knowledge."

Molly blinked and thought that over for a minute or two. "Go on!"

"That's the picture I got from the films," Denham told her. "Wulkins occupied one of those cells, with the cicada-like shape. The sorcerer and his robot apprentice. Both distinctly on the malign side."

"Then you were right!" Molly exclaimed excitedly. "You said that when Wulkins came back and found the sorcerer dead, his maker dead, he succumbed to despair."

"Exactly," Denham said. "Only Wulkins didn't find the sorcerer dead!"

"What do you mean?"

"Dimension travel," Denham said. "A robot might be able to travel in a space warp, but it would be easier for a trained intellect. That intellect occupied a body so highly functional, so perfectly adjusted to its world, that it looked *mechanical* to us. If that intellect made certain adjustments in its body—"

Molly's eyes were so wide now they seemed to fill her face. "You mean—"

"Exactly!" Denham said. "The cicada-like shape was the robot apprentice. Wulkins was—the sorcerer himself!"

THE MISSISSIPPI SAUCER

Jimmy watched the *Natchez Belle* draw near, a shining eagerness in his stare. He stood on the deck of the shantyboat, his toes sticking out of his socks, his heart knocking against his ribs. Straight down the river the big packet boat came, purpling the water with its shadow, its smokestacks belching soot.

Jimmy had a wild talent for collecting things. He knew exactly how to infuriate the captains without sticking out his neck. Up and down the Father of Waters, from the bayous of Louisiana to the Great Sandy other little shantyboat boys envied Jimmy and tried hard to imitate him.

But Jimmy had a very special gift, a genius for pantomime. He'd wait until there was a glimmer of red flame on the river and small objects stood out with a startling clarity. Then he'd go into his act.

Nothing upset the captains quite so much as Jimmy's habit of holding a big, croaking bullfrog up by its legs as the riverboats went steaming past. It was a surefire way of reminding the captains that men and frogs were brothers under the skin. The puffed-out throat of the frog told the captains exactly what Jimmy thought of their cheek.

Jimmy refrained from making faces, or sticking out his tongue at the grinning roustabouts. It was the frog that did the trick.

In the still dawn things came sailing Jimmy's way, hurled by captains with a twinkle of repressed merriment dancing in eyes that were kindlier and more tolerant than Jimmy dreamed.

Just because shantyboat folk had no right to insult the riverboats Jimmy had collected forty empty tobacco tins, a down-at-heels shoe, a Sears Roebuck catalogue and—more rolled up newspapers than Jimmy could ever read.

Jimmy could read, of course. No matter how badly Uncle Al needed a new pair of shoes, Jimmy's education came first. So Jimmy had spent six winters ashore in a first-class grammar school, his books paid for out of Uncle Al's "New Orleans" money.

Uncle Al, blowing on a vinegar jug and making sweet music, the holes in his socks much bigger than the holes in Jimmy's socks. Uncle Al shaking his head and saying sadly, "Some day, young fella, I ain't gonna sit here harmonizing. No siree! I'm gonna buy myself a brand new store suit, trade in this here jig jug for a big round banjo, and hie myself off to the Mardi Gras. Ain't too old thataway to git a little fun out of life, young fella!"

Poor old Uncle Al. The money he'd saved up for the Mardi Gras never seemed to stretch far enough. There was enough kindness in him to stretch like a rainbow over the bayous and the river forests of sweet, rustling pine for as far as the eye could see. Enough kindness to wrap all of Jimmy's life in a glow, and the life of Jimmy's sister as well.

Jimmy's parents had died of winter pneumonia too soon to appreciate Uncle Al. But up and down the river everyone knew that Uncle Al was a great man.

* * * *

Enemies? Well, sure, all great men made enemies, didn't they?

The Harmon brothers were downright sinful about carrying their feuding meanness right up to the doorstep of Uncle Al, if it could be said that a man living in a shantyboat had a doorstep.

Uncle Al made big catches and the Harmon brothers never seemed to have any luck. So, long before Jimmy was old enough to understand how corrosive envy could be the Harmon brothers had started feuding with Uncle Al.

"Jimmy, here comes the *Natchez Belle*! Uncle Al says for you to get him a newspaper. The newspaper you got him yesterday he couldn't read no-ways. It was soaking wet!"

Jimmy turned to glower at his sister. Up and down the river Pigtail Anne was known as a tomboy, but she wasn't—no-ways. She was Jimmy's little sister. That meant Jimmy was the man in the family, and wore the pants, and nothing Pigtail said or did could change that for one minute.

"Don't yell at me!" Jimmy complained. "How can I get Captain Simmons mad if you get me mad first? Have a heart, will you?"

But Pigtail Anne refused to budge. Even when the *Natchez Belle* loomed so close to the shantyboat that it blotted out the sky she continued to crowd her brother, preventing him from holding up the frog and making Captain Simmons squirm.

But Jimmy got the newspaper anyway. Captain Simmons had a keen insight into tomboy psychology, and from the bridge of the *Natchez Belle* he could see that Pigtail was making life miserable for Jimmy.

True—Jimmy had no respect for packet boats and deserved a good trouncing. But what a scrapper the lad was! Never let it be said that in a struggle between the sexes the men of the river did not stand shoulder to shoulder.

The paper came sailing over the shining brown water like a white-bellied buffalo cat shot from a sling.

Pigtail grabbed it before Jimmy could give her a shove. Calmly she unwrapped it, her chin tilted in bellicose defiance.

As the *Natchez Belle* dwindled around a lazy, cypress-shadowed bend Pigtail Anne became a superior being, wrapped in a cosmopolitan aura. A wide-eyed little girl on a swaying deck, the great outside world rushing straight toward her from all directions.

Pigtail could take that world in her stride. She liked the fashion page best, but she was not above clicking her tongue at everything in the paper.

"Kidnap plot linked to airliner crash killing fifty," she read. "Red Sox blank Yanks! Congress sits today, vowing vengeance! Million dollar heiress elopes with a clerk! Court lets dog pick owner! Girl of eight kills her brother in accidental shooting!"

"I ought to push your face right down in the mud," Jimmy muttered.

"Don't you dare! I've a right to see what's going on in the world!"

"You said the paper was for Uncle Al!"

"It is—when I get finished with it."

Jimmy started to take hold of his sister's wrist and pry the paper from her clasp. Only started—for as Pigtail wriggled back sunlight fell on a shadowed part of the paper which drew Jimmy's gaze as sunlight draws dew.

Exciting wasn't the word for the headline. It seemed to blaze out of the page at Jimmy as he stared, his chin nudging Pigtail's shoulder.

NEW FLYING MONSTER REPORTED BLAZING GULF STATE SKIES

Jimmy snatched the paper and backed away from Pigtail, his eyes glued to the headline.

* * * *

He was kind to his sister, however. He read the news item aloud, if an account so startling could be called an item. To Jimmy it seemed more like a dazzling burst of light in the sky.

"A New Orleans resident reported today that he saw a big bright object 'roundish like a disk' flying north, against the wind. 'It was all lighted up from inside!' the observer stated. 'As far as I could tell there were no signs of life aboard the thing. It was much bigger than any of the flying saucers previously reported!'"

"People keep seeing them!" Jimmy muttered, after a pause. "Nobody knows where they come from! Saucers flying through the sky, high up at night. In the daytime, too! Maybe we're being *watched*, Pigtail!"

"Watched? Jimmy, what do you mean? What you talking about?"

Jimmy stared at his sister, the paper jiggling in his clasp. "It's way over your head, Pigtail!" he said sympathetically. "I'll prove it! What's a planet?"

"A star in the sky, you dope!" Pigtail almost screamed. "Wait'll Uncle Al hears what a meanie you are. If I wasn't your sister you wouldn't dare grab a paper that doesn't belong to you."

Jimmy refused to be enraged. "A planet's not a star, Pigtail," he said patiently. "A star's a big ball of fire like the sun. A planet is small and cool, like the Earth. Some of the planets may even have people on them. Not people like us, but people all the same. Maybe we're just frogs to them!"

"You're crazy, Jimmy! Crazy, crazy, you hear?"

Jimmy started to reply, then shut his mouth tight. Big waves were nothing new in the wake of steamboats, but the shantyboat wasn't just riding a swell. It was swaying and rocking like a floating barrel in the kind of blow Shantyboaters dreaded worse than the thought of dying.

Jimmy knew that a big blow could come up fast. Straight down from the sky in gusts, from all directions, banging against the boat like a drunken roustabout, slamming doors, tearing away mooring planks.

* * * *

The river could rise fast too. Under the lashing of a hurricane blowing up from the gulf the river could lift a shantyboat right out of the water, and smash it to smithereens against a tree.

But now the blow was coming from just one part of the sky. A funnel of wind was churning the river into a white froth and raising big swells directly offshore. But the river wasn't rising and the sun was shining in a clear sky.

Jimmy knew a dangerous floodwater storm when he saw one. The sky had to be dark with rain, and you had to feel scared, in fear of drowning.

Jimmy was scared, all right. That part of it rang true. But a hollow, sick feeling in his chest couldn't mean anything by itself, he told himself fiercely.

Pigtail Anne saw the disk before Jimmy did. She screamed and pointed skyward, her twin braids standing straight out in the wind like the ropes on a bale of cotton, when smokestacks collapse and a savage howling sends the river ghosts scurrying for cover.

Straight down out of the sky the disk swooped, a huge, spinning shape as flat as a buckwheat cake swimming in a golden haze of butterfat.

But the disk didn't remind Jimmy of a buckwheat cake. It made him think instead of a slowly turning wheel in the pilot house of a rotting old riverboat, a big, ghostly wheel manned by a steersman a century dead, his eye sockets filled with flickering swamp lights.

It made Jimmy want to run and hide. Almost it made him want to cling to his sister, content to let her wear the pants if only he could be spared the horror.

For there was something so chilling about the downsweeping disk that Jimmy's heart began leaping like a vinegar jug bobbing about in the wake of a capsizing fishboat.

Lower and lower the disk swept, trailing plumes of white smoke, lashing the water with a fearful blow. Straight down over the cypress wilderness that fringed the opposite bank, and then out across the river with a long-drawn whistling sound, louder than the air-sucking death gasps of a thousand buffalo cats.

Jimmy didn't see the disk strike the shining broad shoulders of the Father of Waters, for the bend around which the *Natchez Belle* had steamed so proudly hid the sky monster from view. But Jimmy did see the waterspout, spiraling skyward like the atom bomb explosion he'd goggled at in the pages of an old *Life* magazine, all smudged now with oily thumbprints.

Just a roaring for an instant—and a big white mushroom shooting straight up into the sky. Then, slowly, the mushroom decayed and fell back, and an awful stillness settled down over the river.

* * * *

The stillness was broken by a shrill cry from Pigtail Anne. "It was a flying saucer! Jimmy, we've seen one! We've seen one! We've—"

"Shut your mouth, Pigtail!"

Jimmy shaded his eyes and stared out across the river, his chest a throbbing ache.

He was still staring when a door creaked behind him.

Jimmy trembled. A tingling fear went through him, for he found it hard to realize that the disk had swept around the bend out of sight. To his overheated imagination it continued to fill all of the sky above him, overshadowing the shantyboat, making every sound a threat.

Sucking the still air deep into his lungs, Jimmy swung about.

Uncle Al was standing on the deck in a little pool of sunlight, his gaunt, hollow-cheeked face set in harsh lines. Uncle Al was shading his eyes too. But he was staring up the river, not down.

"Trouble, young fella," he grunted. "Sure as I'm a-standin' here. A barrelful o' trouble—headin' straight for us!"

Jimmy gulped and gestured wildly toward the bend. "It came down *over there*, Uncle Al!" he got out. "Pigtail saw it, too! A big, flying—"

"The Harmons are a-comin', young fella," Uncle Al drawled, silencing Jimmy with a wave of his hand. "Yesterday I rowed over a Harmon jug line without meanin' to. Now Jed Harmon's tellin' everybody I stole his fish!"

Very calmly Uncle Al cut himself a slice of the strongest tobacco on the river and packed it carefully in his pipe, wadding it down with his thumb.

He started to put the pipe between his teeth, then thought better of it.

"I can bone-feel the Harmon boat a-comin', young fella," he said, using the pipe to gesture with. "Smooth and quiet over the river like a moccasin snake."

Jimmy turned pale. He forgot about the disk and the mushrooming water spout. When he shut his eyes he saw only a red haze overhanging the river, and a shantyboat nosing out of the cypresses, its windows spitting death.

* * * *

Jimmy knew that the Harmons had waited a long time for an excuse. The Harmons were law-respecting river rats with sharp teeth. Feuding wasn't lawful, but murder could be made lawful by whittling down a lie until it looked as sharp as the truth.

The Harmon brothers would do their whittling down with double-barreled shotguns. It was easy enough to make murder look like a lawful crime if you could point to a body covered by a blanket and say, "We caught him stealing our fish! He was a-goin' to kill us—so we got him first."

No one would think of lifting the blanket and asking Uncle Al about it. A man lying stiff and still under a blanket could no more make himself heard than a river cat frozen in the ice.

"Git inside, young 'uns. *Here they come!*"

Jimmy's heart skipped a beat. Down the river in the sunlight a shantyboat was drifting. Jimmy could see the Harmon brothers crouching on the deck, their faces livid with hate, sunlight glinting on their arm-cradled shotguns.

The Harmon brothers were not in the least alike. Jed Harmon was tall and gaunt, his right cheek puckered by a knife scar, his cruel, thin-lipped mouth snagged by his teeth. Joe Harmon was small and stout, a little round man with bushy eyebrows and the flabby face of a cotton-mouth snake.

"Go inside, Pigtail," Jimmy said, calmly. "I'm a-going to stay and fight!"

* * * *

Uncle Al grabbed Jimmy's arm and swung him around. "You heard what I said, young fella. Now git!"

"I want to stay here and fight with you, Uncle Al," Jimmy said.

"Have you got a gun? Do you want to be blown apart, young fella?"

"I'm not scared, Uncle Al," Jimmy pleaded. "You might get wounded. I know how to shoot straight, Uncle Al. If you get hurt I'll go right on fighting!"

"No you won't, young fella! Take Pigtail inside. You hear me? You want me to take you across my knee and beat the livin' stuffings out of you?"

Silence.

Deep in his uncle's face Jimmy saw an anger he couldn't buck. Grabbing Pigtail Anne by the arm, he propelled her across the deck and into the dismal front room of the shantyboat.

The instant he released her she glared at him and stamped her foot. "If Uncle Al gets shot it'll be your fault," she said cruelly. Then Pigtail's anger really flared up.

"The Harmons wouldn't dare shoot us 'cause we're children!"

For an instant brief as a dropped heartbeat Jimmy stared at his sister with unconcealed admiration.

"You can be right smart when you've got nothing else on your mind, Pigtail," he said. "If they kill me they'll hang sure as shooting!"

Jimmy was out in the sunlight again before Pigtail could make a grab for him.

Out on the deck and running along the deck toward Uncle Al. He was still running when the first blast came.

* * * *

It didn't sound like a shotgun blast. The deck shook and a big swirl of smoke floated straight toward Jimmy, half blinding him and blotting Uncle Al from view.

When the smoke cleared Jimmy could see the Harmon shantyboat. It was less than thirty feet away now, drifting straight past and rocking with the tide like a topheavy flatbarge.

On the deck Jed Harmon was crouching down, his gaunt face split in a triumphant smirk. Beside him Joe Harmon stood quivering like a mound of jelly, a stick of dynamite in his hand, his flabby face looking almost gentle in the slanting sunlight.

There was a little square box at Jed Harmon's feet. As Joe pitched Jed reached into the box for another dynamite stick. Jed was passing the sticks along to his brother, depending on wad dynamite to silence Uncle Al forever.

Wildly Jimmy told himself that the guns had been just a trick to mix Uncle Al up, and keep him from shooting until they had him where they wanted him.

Uncle Al was shooting now, his face as grim as death. His big heavy gun was leaping about like mad, almost hurling him to the deck.

Jimmy saw the second dynamite stick spinning through the air, but he never saw it come down. All he could see was the smoke and the shantyboat rocking, and another terrible splintering crash as he went plunging into the river from the end of a rising plank, a sob strangling in his throat.

Jimmy struggled up from the river with the long leg-thrusts of a terrified bullfrog, his head a throbbing ache. As he swam shoreward he could see the cypresses on the opposite bank, dark against the sun, and something that looked like the roof of a house with water washing over it.

Then, with mud sucking at his heels, Jimmy was clinging to a slippery bank and staring out across the river, shading his eyes against the glare.

Jimmy thought, "I'm dreaming! I'll wake up and see Uncle Joe blowing on a vinegar jug. I'll see Pigtail, too. Uncle Al will be sitting on the deck, taking it easy!"

But Uncle Al wasn't sitting on the deck. There was no deck for Uncle Al to sit upon. Just the top of the shantyboat, sinking lower and lower, and Uncle Al swimming.

Uncle Al had his arm around Pigtail, and Jimmy could see Pigtail's white face bobbing up and down as Uncle Al breasted the tide with his strong right arm.

Closer to the bend was the Harmon shantyboat. The Harmons were using their shotguns now, blasting fiercely away at Uncle Al and Pigtail. Jimmy could see the smoke curling up from the leaping guns and the water jumping up and down in little spurts all about Uncle Al.

There was an awful hollow agony in Jimmy's chest as he stared, a fear that was partly a soundless screaming and partly a vision of Uncle Al sinking down through the dark water and turning it red.

It was strange, though. Something was happening to Jimmy, nibbling away at the outer edges of the fear like a big, hungry river cat. Making the fear seem less swollen and awful, shredding it away in little flakes.

There was a white core of anger in Jimmy which seemed suddenly to blaze up.

He shut his eyes tight.

In his mind's gaze Jimmy saw himself holding the Harmon brothers up by their long, mottled legs. The Harmon brothers were frogs. Not friendly, good natured frogs like Uncle Al, but snake frogs. Cottonmouth frogs.

All flannel red were their mouths, and they had long evil fangs which dripped poison in the sunlight. But Jimmy wasn't afraid of them no-ways. Not any more. He had too firm a grip on their legs.

"Don't let anything happen to Uncle Al and Pigtail!" Jimmy whispered, as though he were talking to himself. No—not exactly to himself. To someone like himself, only larger. Very close to Jimmy, but larger, more powerful.

"Catch them before they harm Uncle Al! Hurry! *Hurry!*"

There was a strange lifting sensation in Jimmy's chest now. As though he could shake the river if he tried hard enough, tilt it, send it swirling in great thunderous white surges clear down to Lake Pontchartrain.

* * * *

But Jimmy didn't want to tilt the river. Not with Uncle Al on it and Pigtail, and all those people in New Orleans who would disappear right off the streets. They were frogs too, maybe, but good frogs. Not like the Harmon brothers.

Jimmy had a funny picture of himself much younger than he was. Jimmy saw himself as a great husky baby, standing in the middle of the river and blowing on it with all his might. The waves rose and rose, and Jimmy's cheeks swelled out and the river kept getting angrier.

No—he must fight that.

"Save Uncle Al!" he whispered fiercely. "Just save him—and Pigtail!"

It began to happen the instant Jimmy opened his eyes. Around the bend in the sunlight came a great spinning disk, wrapped in a fiery glow.

Straight toward the Harmon shantyboat the disk swept, water spurting up all about it, its bottom fifty feet wide. There was no collision. Only a brightness for one awful instant where the shantyboat was twisting and turning in the current, a brightness that outshone the rising sun.

Just like a camera flashbulb going off, but bigger, brighter. So big and bright that Jimmy could see the faces of the Harmon brothers fifty times as large as life, shriveling and disappearing in a magnifying burst of flame high above the cypress trees. Just as though a giant in the sky had trained a big burning glass on the Harmon brothers and whipped it back quick.

Whipped it straight up, so that the faces would grow huge before dissolving as a warning to all snakes. There was an evil anguish in the dissolving faces which made Jimmy's blood run cold. Then the disk was alone in the middle of the river, spinning around and around, the shantyboat swallowed up.

And Uncle Al was still swimming, fearfully close to it.

The net came swirling out of the disk over Uncle Al like a great, dew-drenched gossamer web. It enmeshed him as he swam, so gently that he hardly seemed to struggle or even to be aware of what was happening to him.

Pigtail didn't resist, either. She simply stopped thrashing in Uncle Al's arms, as though a great wonder had come upon her.

Slowly Uncle Al and Pigtail were drawn into the disk. Jimmy could see Uncle Al reclining in the web, with Pigtail in the crook of his arm, his long, angular body as quiet as a butterfly in its deep winter sleep inside a swaying glass cocoon.

Uncle Al and Pigtail, being drawn together into the disk as Jimmy stared, a dull pounding in his chest. After a moment the pounding subsided and a silence settled down over the river.

Jimmy sucked in his breath. The voices began quietly, as though they had been waiting for a long time to speak to Jimmy deep inside his head, and didn't want to frighten him in any way.

"Take it easy, Jimmy! Stay where you are. We're just going to have a friendly little talk with Uncle Al."

"A t-talk?" Jimmy heard himself stammering.

"We knew we'd find you where life flows simply and serenely, Jimmy. Your parents took care of that before they left you with Uncle Al.

"You see, Jimmy, we wanted you to study the Earth people on a great, wide flowing river, far from the cruel, twisted places. To grow up with them, Jimmy—and to understand them. Especially the Uncle Als. For Uncle Al is unspoiled, Jimmy. If there's any hope at all for Earth as we guide and watch it, that hope burns most brightly in the Uncle Als!"

The voice paused, then went on quickly. "You see, Jimmy, you're not human in the same way that your sister is human—or Uncle Al. But you're still young enough to feel human, and we want you to feel human, Jimmy."

"W—Who are you?" Jimmy gasped.

"We are the Shining Ones, Jimmy! For wide wastes of years we have cruised Earth's skies, almost unnoticed by the Earth people. When darkness wraps the Earth in a great, spinning shroud we hide our ships close to the cities, and glide through the silent streets in search of our young. You see, Jimmy, we must watch and protect the young of our race until sturdiness comes upon them, and they are ready for the Great Change."

* * * *

For an instant there was a strange, humming sound deep inside Jimmy's head, like the drowsy murmur of bees in a dew-drenched clover patch. Then the voice droned on. "The Earth people are frightened by our ships now, for their cruel wars have put a great fear of death in their hearts. They watch the skies with sharper eyes, and their minds have groped closer to the truth.

"To the Earth people our ships are no longer the fireballs of mysterious legend, haunted will-o'-the-wisps, marsh flickerings and the even more illusive distortions of the sick in mind. It is a long bold step from fireballs to flying saucers, Jimmy. A day will come when the Earth people will be wise enough to put aside fear. Then we can show ourselves to them as we really are, and help them openly."

The voice seemed to take more complete possession of Jimmy's thoughts then, growing louder and more eager, echoing through his mind with the persuasiveness of muted chimes.

"Jimmy, close your eyes tight. We're going to take you across wide gulfs of space to the bright and shining land of your birth."

Jimmy obeyed.

It was a city, and yet it wasn't like New York or Chicago or any of the other cities Jimmy had seen illustrations of in the newspapers and picture magazines.

The buildings were white and domed and shining, and they seemed to tower straight up into the sky. There were streets, too, weaving in and out between the domes like rainbow-colored spider webs in a forest of mushrooms.

* * * *

There were no people in the city, but down the aerial streets shining objects swirled with the swift easy gliding of flat stones skimming an edge of running water.

Then as Jimmy stared into the depths of the strange glow behind his eyelids the city dwindled and fell away, and he saw a huge circular disk looming in a wilderness of shadows. Straight toward the disk a shining object moved, bearing aloft on filaments of flame a much smaller object that struggled and mewed and reached out little white arms.

Closer and closer the shining object came, until Jimmy could see that it was carrying a human infant that stared straight at Jimmy out of wide, dark eyes. But before he could get a really good look at the shining object it pierced the shadows and passed into the disk.

There was a sudden, blinding burst of light, and the disk was gone.

Jimmy opened his eyes.

"You were once like that baby, Jimmy!" the voice said. "You were carried by your parents into a waiting ship, and then out across wide gulfs of space to Earth.

"You see, Jimmy, our race was once entirely human. But as we grew to maturity we left the warm little worlds where our infancy was spent, and boldly sought the stars, shedding our humanness as sunlight sheds the dew, or a bright, soaring moth of the night its ugly pupa case.

"We grew great and wise, Jimmy, but not quite wise enough to shed our human heritage of love and joy and heartbreak. In our childhood we must return to the scenes of our past, to take root again in familiar soil, to grow in power and wisdom slowly and sturdily, like a seed dropped back into the loam which nourished the great flowering mother plant.

"Or like the eel of Earth's seas, Jimmy, that must be spawned in the depths of the great cold ocean, and swim slowly back to the bright highlands and the shining rivers of Earth. Young eels do not resemble their parents, Jimmy. They're white and thin and transparent and have to struggle hard to survive and grow up.

"Jimmy, you were planted here by your parents to grow wise and strong. Deep in your mind you knew that we had come to seek you out, for we are all born human, and are bound one to another by that knowledge, and that secret trust.

"You knew that we would watch over you and see that no harm would come to you. You called out to us, Jimmy, with all the strength of your mind and heart. Your Uncle Al was in danger and you sensed our nearness.

"It was partly your knowledge that saved him, Jimmy. But it took courage too, and a willingness to believe that you were more than human, and armed with the great proud strength and wisdom of the Shining Ones."

* * * *

The voice grew suddenly gentle, like a caressing wind.

"You're not old enough yet to go home, Jimmy! Or wise enough. We'll take you home when the time comes. Now we just want to have a talk with Uncle Al, to find out how you're getting along."

Jimmy looked down into the river and then up into the sky. Deep down under the dark, swirling water he could see life taking shape in a thousand forms. Caddis flies building bright, shining new nests, and dragonfly nymphs crawling up toward the sunlight, and pollywogs growing sturdy hindlimbs to conquer the land.

But there were cottonmouths down there too, with death behind their fangs, and no love for the life that was crawling upward. When Jimmy looked up into the sky he could see all the blazing stars of space, with cottonmouths on every planet of every sun.

Uncle Al was like a bright caddis fly building a fine new nest, thatched with kindness, denying himself bright little Mardi Gras pleasures so that Jimmy could go to school and grow wiser than Uncle Al.

"That's right, Jimmy. You're growing up—we can see that! Uncle Al says he told you to bide from the cottonmouths. But you were ready to give your life for your sister and Uncle Al."

"Shucks, it was nothing!" Jimmy heard himself protesting.

"Uncle Al doesn't think so. And neither do we!"

* * * *

A long silence while the river mists seemed to weave a bright cocoon of radiance about Jimmy clinging to the bank, and the great circular disk that had swallowed up Uncle Al.

Then the voices began again. "No reason why Uncle Al shouldn't have a little fun out of life, Jimmy. Gold's easy to make and we'll make some right now. A big lump of gold in Uncle Al's hand won't hurt him in any way."

"Whenever he gets any spending money he gives it away!" Jimmy gulped.

"I know, Jimmy. But he'll listen to you. Tell him you want to go to New Orleans, too!"

Jimmy looked up quickly then. In his heart was something of the wonder he'd felt when he'd seen his first riverboat and waited for he knew not what. Something of the wonder that must have come to men seeking magic in the sky, the rainmakers of ancient tribes and of days long vanished.

Only to Jimmy the wonder came now with a white burst of remembrance and recognition.

It was as though he could sense something of himself in the two towering spheres that rose straight up out of the water behind the disk. Still and white and beautiful they were, like bubbles floating on a rainbow sea with all the stars of space behind them.

Staring at them, Jimmy saw himself as he would be, and knew himself for what he was. It was not a glory to be long endured.

"Now you must forget again, Jimmy! Forget as Uncle Al will forget—until we come for you. Be a little shantyboat boy! You are safe on the wide bosom of the Father of Waters. Your parents planted you in a rich and kindly loam, and in all the finite universes you will find no cosier nook, for life flows here with a diversity that is infinite and—*Pigtail!* She gets on your nerves at times, doesn't she, Jimmy?"

"She sure does," Jimmy admitted.

"Be patient with her, Jimmy. She's the only human sister you'll ever have on Earth."

"I—I'll try!" Jimmy muttered.

* * * *

Uncle Al and Pigtail came out of the disk in an amazingly simple way. They just seemed to float out, in the glimmering web. Then, suddenly, there wasn't any disk on the river at all—just a dull flickering where the sky had opened like a great, blazing furnace to swallow it up.

"I was just swimmin' along with Pigtail, not worryin' too much, 'cause there's no sense in worryin' when death is starin' you in the face," Uncle Al muttered, a few minutes later.

Uncle Al sat on the riverbank beside Jimmy, staring down at his palm, his vision misted a little by a furious blinking.

"It's gold, Uncle Al!" Pigtail shrilled. "A big lump of solid gold—"

"I just felt my hand get heavy and there it was, young fella, nestling there in my palm!"

Jimmy didn't seem to be able to say anything.

"High school books don't cost no more than grammar school books, young fella," Uncle Al said, his face a sudden shining. "Next winter you'll be a-goin' to high school, sure as I'm a-sittin' here!"

For a moment the sunlight seemed to blaze so brightly about Uncle Al that Jimmy couldn't even see the holes in his socks.

Then Uncle Al made a wry face. "Someday, young fella, when your books are all paid for, I'm gonna buy myself a brand new store suit, and hie myself off to the Mardi Gras. Ain't too old thataway to git a little fun out of life, young fella!"

LESSON IN SURVIVAL

School was out. The dismissal bell tolled, and the children rushed in delight from the classroom, and went careening and shouting down garden paths bright with blue and yellow flowers. Overhead a cheery noonday sun beamed down on the emerging schoolmaster, a tall, dark-haired young man whose eyes followed his retreating charges with a warm and eager gratefulness.

Brian Andrews enjoyed teaching, but not on such a day as this. It is a strain to change one's occupation at a moment's notice, but fishing was not an occupation to Brian. It was as natural as breathing.

There were red and yellow trout flies pinned to his hat, and a supple bamboo rod had come to life in his hand. He flicked it as he strode along, counting his blessings one by one. He was free, and independent, and young. He liked his job, and the quiet, dreamy little town with its cloistered air of belonging to an earlier, less mechanized age. He liked to cross the village green and slap the big antique fire-bell opposite the war monument, eliciting a hollow boom, and he liked to go padding along Main Street in his moccasin shoes.

"There's the new young schoolmaster! A college man, but you'd never think it to look at him."

Then there was Jenny Fleming. It hadn't taken him long to get to know Jenny well enough to tease her about her freckles while she unwrapped sandwiches on a shady bank, and made light of his attempts to kiss her.

He supposed he'd soon have to write off "free" and be content to remain resolutely independent.

The best thing about the trout stream was its nearness. He had only to cross a deep-elbowed road and ascend a red clay bank to plunge into the leafy green solitude of a truly enchanted stretch of woodland. Enchanted in every way. Jenny would be waiting for him with a luncheon basket beside a willow-shadowed pool, and further down the stream the children would be fishing with worms.

He was quite sure the laughter of the children wouldn't bring the schoolroom back. It would be the completely natural laughter of youngsters at play, freed for the moment from all adult stuffiness and tyranny.

He caught his breath when he actually saw her, waiting for him by the pool. She'd removed her stockings and gone wading in the cool, sparkling water, and now she was sitting on the bank drawing her stockings on again.

He went whistling up to her, picked up the lunch basket and looked inside.

"Ham sandwiches," he said. "What could be nicer?"

She did not get up to snatch the basket from him and mingle her laughter with his. She simply leaned back against, a slanting willow tree, her eyes searching his face in troubled concern.

"Sit down, Brian," she said. "I want to talk to you."

Surprised, he sat down beside her on the sloping bank. "Hungry men make poor listeners, honeybunch." He smiled in mock distress. "Don't say I didn't warn you."

She said without smiling: "Brian, the planes went over again yesterday."

All of the levity went out of Brian Andrews' eyes. He stared down at the shadowed pool, his mouth suddenly dry.

"I didn't hear them," he said, quickly. "I was busy all day."

"Not too busy to know that every man, woman and child in Fairview is under sentence of death. How can you make yourself forget we're living on borrowed time."

"Just a minute now—"

"It's true, isn't it?" she persisted.

"True or false, you've got to shut your mind to it. If you don't it will darken the sunlight for you."

"Is that your secret, Brian? Have you shut your, mind?"

"I can avoid thinking about it for days at a stretch," he told her. "I keep remembering I came to Fairview to take a teaching job, and go fishing, and fall in love with you. The simple truth keeps me sane."

"How sane, Brian? Subconsciously you're in bad shape, just us, the rest of us are. It doesn't really help not to be honest about it."

"You're forgetting, what a big country this is," he told her. "The planes can't bomb every isolated village, every tiny cluster of houses. Even if they could, bombing on that scale would boomerang. They'd expose themselves to retaliation on a scale which would make interesting source material for future historians—of another intelligent species."

She looked at him steadily for a moment, with understanding and a kind of pity, as if she herself had once clung as tenaciously to hope, and believed quite as firmly that the smaller villages would be spared.

"It may not come tomorrow," she said. "It may not come for a year. Yes, we'll have time to pretend. Tell, me—what in the future would you prize most highly? A single long month of waiting? Two?"

He said with stubborn pride: "Fairview itself. If we cling with courage to what we have here, we can face the future without fear. That in itself is a victory—perhaps the only true victory mankind can ever know."

"We've lived in Fairviews too long!" she said. "We did not see the danger until it was too late."

"What good would seeing the danger have done?" he asked. "We know now that man will never succeed in controlling his own destiny. What would you have had our best minds do?"

She laughed suddenly. Her laughter rang out defiant and challenging in the peaceful wood.

"Every age brings a new approach to reality, Brian," she answered. "The Atomic Age brought tools so bright we should have found in them the answer to all of our problems. We should have used our genius to banish war forever."

He looked at her, amazed by her vehemence, sensing for the first time a depth of eloquence in her thinking which challenged his own reasoned convictions at a vital point.

"You'll have to admit we've tried," he said. "We've tried desperately hard to—follow through."

"Not hard enough," she said. "A race can only be judged by its success."

"Then our race has been judged," he said. "It has failed, and the judgment is in, and nothing can be changed. I still say that Fairview can give us courage."

Jenny shook her head. "Only because, when you walk in its quiet streets, you think of the men who once struggled to build ten thousand other Fairviews, each new and each different. If you go back and try to stand where your ancestors stood, your illusions will start to crumble."

"I take it you don't think Fairview is the answer." He forced laughter into his voice. "I haven't noticed any crumbling. Honestly I haven't. If I dropped a trout fly lightly, on that pool, and caught a two-pounder, my happiness would be complete."

"You only think it would. You can never shut out the roar of the planes going over, Brian. We had the tools, but we lacked the boldness really to try."

Brian stood up suddenly, staring down at Jenny Fleming sitting on the bank, the sunlight bright on her berry-brown shoulders.

"I still say that Fairview is a positive good in itself. His voice had lost none of its confidence. "We're lucky to be young, and in Fairview.

Let the great bombers come. Their wings will cast no shadow for me while I can go on remembering there are speckled trout in that pool, and that you are very beautiful."

"Brian—"

"I have my work, and it is good work. Teaching eager young minds to explore the buried past of the earth, to grasp the almost, miraculous beauty of its mountains, rivers and fossils. That's what I like most about Fairview. We still have blackboards. We still have reading, writing and arithmetic. But you can also start early on the really important things.

"Every kid in Fairview with an eager, inquiring mind can use the classroom telescope, and look out across space at the tunneling stars and the Great Nebula in Andromeda."

"It is good work, Brian. But if Fairview should be bombed—"

He bent suddenly, and helped her to her feet. "Fairview will not be bombed," he said.

She laid a finger on his lips. "We've argued enough," she said.

He nodded in quick agreement. "Come on, let's dance!"

"If we had some music—"

"We'll dance anyway. Shall we make it a waltz?"

"All right, Brian."

It was no more than a faint, distant humming—at first, like the drowsy murmur of bees in a noonday glade. Bees drowsy with nectar, too sluggish to be dangerous.

They danced on the cool bank, around and around in mock solemnity, hardly aware of the sound, never associating it with danger until it was suddenly thunderous in their ears.

They looked up then and saw the flight of jet bombers screaming across the sky, huge and vulture-black and wobbling a little with the weight of their bomb loads. They looked up and saw the bomb descending. Incredibly tiny it seemed, like a flickering dust mote that persisted in its dancing until the sun's glare claimed it.

They flattened themselves just as the silence gave way to a rumbling and then to a roaring. There were flashes of light between the trees, a vast flickering, a reddening of the entire forest. Then silence again, complete, mind-numbing.

In stunned horror Brian raised himself, and saw Jenny Fleming's limp body lying motionless at his feet. He was aware of pain, and a tumultuous stirring deep within his own body as if something imprisoned in his flesh were struggling furiously to free itself.

Shivering, he closed his eyes, then opened them quickly. The body of his companion had begun to shatter, to break into many gleaming pieces. Like a brittle mold of over-hardened clay it crumbled and flew apart, the arms splintering into fragments, the face separating itself from the rest of the head, and rolling down the bank into the pool. The face did not immediately sink, but continued to stare up masklike for an instant through a deepening film of water, as if puzzled by something it could not quite understand.

From the fragments on the bank a long, glistening shape crawled its bulging, many-faceted eyes probing the forest gloom. Had there been human eyes to watch, the shape would have seemed to move with a dignity and grace absurd in a creature so lowly.

But there were no human eyes in the forest shadows. Neither were there human ears to hear it say: "The play is over, Chica Maca. You are inflicting upon yourself quite unnecessary torment."

The creature paused, then went on: "You gave a magnificent performance! You lived the part as it was meant to be lived!"

Chica Maca awoke, to reality then, completely: He detached himself from the many manipulative props controlling the eyes, lips, vocal organs and limbs of the artificial man body, and crawled swiftly forth. For a moment he lay motionless in the shadows, his many-faceted eyes acknowledging with pleasure the admiration of his teaching associate Raca Clacan. Then he moved with a dignity and a grace peculiarly masculine to the edge of the stage, and stared down over the bright lights at his student audience. The students were just beginning to stir, to-awaken as he had done, from the bright compelling magic of the stage to prosaic reality. They lay motionless in their classroom tunnels, a glistening sea of upturned heads, and supine bodies, packed so closely into the vast hall they, seemed almost to be one great crawling organism.

Chica Maca stared down with a deep satisfaction. The drama reconstruction had taken many days, of patient research, but certainly it had been worth the effort. In education there could be no substitute for the archaeological drama. Act it out! When the characters were those of a long-vanished intelligent species, debating great issues of survival, the historical lesson could not fail to be spectacularly high-lighted.

A Masterpiece of reconstruction, truly a masterpiece! He thought of the sound recordings of man speech excavated from caverns in the earth sealed from within by a heat so terrific it had melted the surface rocks. He remembered how difficult it was to preserve all of the semantic overtones and fine shadings when such recordings were revamped as passages of dramatic dialogue couched in the infinitely more subtle speech idioms of a more advanced species.

He looked about the immense revolving stage, and in his mind's eye saw the schoolhouse once more turned toward the audience and himself emerging in the artificial man body, the smaller bodies with their child actors skipping away before him into the woods.

He had lived the man part so completely he had actually believed in the village all through the play. The village had existed as a richly experienced reality in his own mind, and in that way he had made the village seem real to the audience, had saved the extra cost of an actual stage reconstruction.

Even without the village, the school-house and the stretch of woodland had made the production a costly one. But surely, surely, it had been worth the cost! His students now knew more about the last days of man than they could have learned from twenty or thirty carefully prepared lectures.

Chica Maca's eyes quivered, and he half-arose on his twentieth pair of legs, assuming an almost manlike posture on the stage. It seemed only fitting to him that, at the end of such a play, a species that had conquered should thus pay its respects to a species that had passed.

THE MAN THE MARTIANS

I

There was death in the camp.

I knew when I awoke that it had come to stand with us in the night and was waiting now for the day to break and flood the desert with light. There was a prickling at the base of my scalp and I was drenched with cold sweat.

I had an impulse to leap up and go stumbling about in the darkness. But I disciplined myself. I crossed my arms and waited for the sky to grow bright.

Daybreak on Mars is like nothing you've ever dreamed about. You wake up in the morning, and there it is—bright and clear and shining. You pinch yourself, you sit up straight, but it doesn't vanish.

Then you stare at your hands with the big callouses. You reach for a mirror to take a look at your face. That's not so good. That's where ugliness enters the picture. You look around and you see Ralph. You see Harry. You see the women.

On Earth a woman may not look her glamorous best in the harsh light of early dawn, but if she's really beautiful she doesn't look too bad. On Mars even the most beautiful woman looks angry on arising, too weary and tormented by human shortcomings to take a prefabricated metal shack and turn it into a real home for a man.

You have to make allowances for a lot of things on Mars. You have to start right off by accepting hardship and privation as your daily lot. You have to get accustomed to living in construction camps in the desert, with the red dust making you feel all hollow and dried up inside. Making you feel like a drum, a shriveled pea pod, a salted fish hung up to dry. Dust inside of you, rattling around, canal water seepage rotting the soles of your boots.

So you wake up and you stare. The night before you'd collected driftwood and stacked it by the fire. The driftwood has disappeared. Someone has stolen your very precious driftwood. The Martians? Guess again.

You get up and you walk straight up to Ralph with your shoulders squared. You say, "Ralph, why in hell did you have to steal my driftwood?"

In your mind you say that. You say it to Dick, you say it to Harry. But what you really say is, "Larsen was here again last night!"

You say, I put a fish on to boil and Larsen ate it. I had a nice deck of cards, all shiny and new, and Larsen marked them up. It wasn't me cheating. It was Larsen hoping I'd win so that he could waylay me in the desert and get all of the money away from me.

You have a girl. There aren't too many girls in the camps with laughter and light and fire in them. But there are a few, and if you're lucky you take a fancy to one particular girl—her full red lips and her spun gold hair. All of a sudden she disappears. Somebody runs off with her. It's Larsen.

In every man there is a slumbering giant. When life roars about you on a world that's rugged and new you've got to go on respecting the lads who have thrown in their lot with you, even when their impulses are as harsh as the glint of sunlight on a desert-polished tombstone.

You think of a name—Larsen. You start from scratch and you build Larsen up until you have a clear picture of him in your mind. You build him up until he's a great shouting, brawling, golden man like Paul Bunyon.

Even a wicked legend can seem golden on Mars. Larsen wasn't just my slumbering giant—or Dick's, or Harry's. He was the slumbering giant in all of us, and that's what made him so tremendous. Anything gigantic has beauty and power and drive to it.

Alone we couldn't do anything with Larsen's gusto, so when some great act of wickedness was done with gusto how could it be us? Here comes Larsen! He'll shoulder all the guilt, but he won't feel guilty because he's the first man in Eden, the child who never grew up, the laughing boy, Hercules balancing the world on his shoulders and looking for a woman with long shining tresses and eyes like the stars of heaven to bend to his will.

If such a woman came to life in Hercules' arms would you like the job of stopping him from sending the world crashing? Would you care to try?

Don't you see? Larsen was closer to us than breathing and as necessary as food and drink and our dreams of a brighter tomorrow. Don't think we didn't hate him at times. Don't think we didn't curse and revile him. You may glorify a legend from here to eternity, but the luster never remains completely untarnished.

Larsen wouldn't have seemed completely real to us if we hadn't given him muscles that could tire and eyes that could blink shut in weariness. Larsen had to sleep, just as we did. He'd disappear for days.

We'd wink and say, "Larsen's getting a good long rest this time. But he'll be back with something new up his sleeve, don't you worry!"

We could joke about it, sure. When Larsen stole or cheated we could pretend we were playing a game with loaded dice—not really a deadly game, but a game full of sound and fury with a great rousing outburst of merriment at the end of it.

But there are deadlier games by far. I lay motionless, my arms locked across my chest, sweating from every pore. I stared at Harry. We'd been working all night digging a well, and in a few days water would be bubbling up sweet and cool and we wouldn't have to go to the canal to fill our cooking utensils. Harry was blinking and stirring and I could tell just by looking at him that he was uneasy too. I looked beyond him at the circle of shacks.

Most of us were sleeping in the open, but there were a few youngsters in the shacks and women too worn out with drudgery to care much whether they slept in smothering darkness or under the clear cold light of the stars.

I got slowly to my knees, scooped up a handful of sand, and let it dribble slowly through my fingers. Harry looked straight at me and his eyes widened in alarm. It must have been the look on my face. He arose and crossed to where I was sitting, his mouth twitching slightly. There was nothing very reassuring about Harry. Life had not been kind to him and he had resigned himself to accepting the slings and arrows of outrageous fortune without protest. He had one of those emaciated, almost skull-like faces which terrify children, and make women want to cry.

"You don't look well, Tom," he said. "You've been driving yourself too hard."

I looked away quickly. I had to tell him, but anything terrifying could demoralize Harry and make him throw his arm before his face in blind panic. But I couldn't keep it locked up inside me an instant longer.

"Sit down, Harry," I whispered. "I want to talk to you. No sense in waking the others."

"Oh," he said.

He squatted beside me on the sand, his eyes searching my face. "What is it, Tom?"

"I heard a scream," I said. "It was pretty awful. Somebody has been hurt—bad. It woke me up, and that takes some doing."

Harry nodded. "You sleep like a log," he said.

"I just lay still and listened," I said, "with my eyes wide open. Something moved out from the well—a two-legged something. It didn't make a sound. It was big, Harry, and it seemed to melt into the shadows. I don't know what kept me from leaping up and going after it. It had something to do with the way I felt. All frozen up inside."

Harry appeared to understand. He nodded, his eyes darting toward the well. "How long ago was that?"

"Ten—fifteen minutes."

"You just waited for me to wake up?"

"That's right," I said. "There was something about the scream that made me want to put off finding out. Two's company—and when you're alone with something like that it's best to talk it over before you act."

I could see that Harry was pleased. Unnerved too, and horribly shaken. But he was pleased that I had turned to him as a friend I could trust. When you can't depend on life for anything else it's good to know you have a friend.

I brushed sand from my trousers and got up. "Come on," I said. "We'll take a look."

It was an ordeal for him. His face twitched and his eyes wavered. He knew I hadn't lied about the scream. If a single scream could unnerve me that much it had to be bad.

We walked to the well in complete silence. There were shadows everywhere, chill and forbidding. Almost like people they seemed, whispering together, huddling close in ominous gossipy silence, aware of what we would find.

It was a sixty-foot walk from the fire to the well. A walk in the sun— a walk in the bright hot sun of Mars, with utter horror perhaps at the end of it.

The horror was there. Harry made a little choking noise deep in his throat, and my heart started pounding like a bass drum.

II

The man on the sand had no top to his head. His skull had been crushed and flattened so hideously that he seemed like a wooden figure resting there—an anatomical dummy with its skull-case lifted off.

We looked around for the skull-case, hoping we'd find it, hoping we'd made a mistake and stumbled by accident into an open-air dissecting laboratory and were looking at ghastly props made of plastic and glittering metal instead of bone and muscle and flesh.

But the man on the sand had a name. We'd known him for weeks and talked to him. He wasn't a medical dummy, but a corpse. His limbs were hideously convulsed, his eyes wide and staring. The sand beneath his head was clotted with dried blood. We looked for the weapon which had crushed his skull but couldn't find it.

We looked for the weapon before we saw the footprints in the sand. Big they were—incredibly large and massive. A man with a size-twelve shoe might have left such prints if the leather had become a little soggy and spread out around the soles.

"The poor guy," Harry whispered.

I knew how he felt. We had all liked Ned. A harmless little guy with a great love of solitude, a guy who hadn't a malicious hair in his head. A happy little guy who liked to sing and dance in the light of a high-leaping fire. He had a banjo and was good at music making. Who could have hated Ned with a rage so primitive and savage? I looked at Harry and saw that he was wondering the same thing.

Harry looked pretty bad, about ready to cave in. He was leaning against the well, a tormented fury in his eyes.

"The murderous bastard," he muttered. "I'd like to get him by the throat and choke the breath out of him. Who'd want to do a thing like that to Ned."

"I can't figure it either," I said.

Then I remembered. I don't think Molly Egan really could have loved Ned. The curious thing about it was that Ned didn't even need the kind of love she could have given him. He was a self-sufficient little guy despite his frailness and didn't really need a woman to look after him. But Molly must have seen something pathetic in him.

Molly was a beautiful woman in her own right, and there wasn't a man in the camp who hadn't envied Ned. It was puzzling, but it could have explained why Ned was lying slumped on the sand with a bashed-in skull. It could have explained why someone had hated him enough to kill him.

Without lifting a finger Ned had won Molly's love. That could make some other guy as mad as a caged hyena—the wrong sort of other guy. Even a small man could have shattered Ned's skull, but the prints on the sand were big.

How many men in the camp wore size-twelve shoes? That was the sixty-four dollar question, and it hung in the shimmering air between Harry and myself like an unspoken challenge. We could almost see the curve of the big question mark suspended in the dazzle.

I thought awhile, looking at Harry. Then I took a long, deep breath and said, "We'd better talk it over with Bill Seaton first. If it gets around too fast those footprints will be trampled flat. And if tempers start rising anything could happen."

Harry nodded. Bill was the kind of guy you could depend on in an emergency. Cool, poised, efficient, with an air of authority that commanded respect. He could be pigheaded at times, but his sense of justice was as keen as a whip.

Harry and I walked very quietly across a stretch of tumbled sand and halted at the door to Bill's shack. Bill was a bachelor and we knew there'd be no woman inside to put her foot down and tell him he'd be a fool to act as a lawman. Or would there be? We had to chance it.

Law-enforcement is a thankless job whether on Earth or on Mars. That's why it attracts the worst—and the best. If you're a power-drunk sadist you'll take the job just for the pleasure it gives you. But if you're really interested in keeping violence within bounds so that fairly decent lads get a fighting chance to build for the future, you'll take the job with no thought of reward beyond the simple satisfaction of lending a helping hand.

Bill Seaton was such a man, even if he did enjoy the limelight and liked to be in a position of command.

"Come on, Harry," I said. "We may as well wake him up and get it over with."

We went into the shack. Bill was sleeping on the floor with his long legs drawn up. His mouth was open and he was snoring lustily. I couldn't help thinking how much he looked like an overgrown grasshopper. But that was just a first impression springing from overwrought nerves.

I bent down and shook Bill awake. I grabbed his arm and shook him until his jaw snapped shut and he shot up straight, suddenly galvanized. Instantly the grotesque aspect fell from him. Dignity came upon him and enveloped him like a cloak.

"Ned, you say? The poor little cuss! So help me—if I get my hands on the rat who did it I'll roast him over a slow fire!"

He got up, staggered to an equipment locker, and took out a sun helmet and a pair of shorts. He dressed quickly, swearing constantly and staring out the door at the bright dawn glow as if he wanted to send both of his fists crashing into the first suspicious guy to cross his path.

"We can't have those footprints trampled," he muttered. "There are a lot of dumb bastards here who don't know the first thing about keeping pointers intact. Those prints may be the only thing we'll have to go on."

"Just the three of us can handle it, Bill," I said. "When you decide what should be done we can wake the others."

Bill nodded. "Keeping it quiet is the important thing. We'll carry him back here. When we break the news I want that body out of sight."

Harry and Bill and I—we took another walk in the sun. I looked at Harry, and the greenish tinge which had crept into his face gave me a jolt. He's taking this pretty hard, I thought. If I hadn't known him so well I might have jumped to an ugly conclusion. But I just couldn't imagine Harry quarreling with Ned over Molly.

How was I taking it myself? I raised my hand and looked at it. There was no tremor. Nerves steady, brain clear. No pleasure in enforcing the law—pass that buck to Bill. But there was a gruesome job ahead, and I was standing up to it as well as could be expected.

Ever try lifting a corpse? The corpse of a stranger is easier to lift than the corpse of a man you've known and liked. Harry and I lifted him together. Between us the dead weight didn't seem too intolerable—not at first. But it quickly became a terrible, heavy limpness that dragged at our arms like some soggy log dredged up from the dark waters of the canal.

We carried him into the shack and eased him down on the floor. His head fell back and his eyes lolled.

Death is always shameful. It strips away all human reticences and makes a mockery of human dignity and man's rebellion against the cruelty of fate.

For a moment we stood staring down at all that was left of Ned. I looked at Bill. "How many men in the camp wear number-twelve shoes?"

"We'll find out soon enough."

All this time we hadn't mentioned Larsen. Not one word about Larsen, not one spoken word. Cheating, yes. Lying, and treacherous disloyalty, and viciousness, and spite. Fights around the campfires at midnight, battered faces and broken wrists and a cursing that never ceased. All that we could blame on Larsen. But a harmless little guy lying dead by a well in a spreading pool of blood—that was an outrage that stopped us dead in our legend-making tracks.

There is something in the human mind which recoils from too outrageous a deception. How wonderful it would have been to say, "Larsen was here again last night. He found a little guy who had never harmed anyone standing by a well in the moonlight. Just for sheer delight he decided to kill the little guy right then and there." Just to add luster to the legend, just to send a thrill of excitement about the camp.

No, that would have been the lie colossal which no sane man could have quite believed.

Something happened then to further unnerve us.

The most disturbing sound you can hear on Mars is the whispering. Usually it begins as a barely audible murmur and swells in volume with every shift of the wind. But now it started off high pitched and insistent and did not stop.

It was the whispering of a dying race. The Martians are as elusive as elves and all the pitiless logic of science had failed to draw them forth into the sunlight to stand before men in uncompromising arrogance as peers of the human race.

That failure was a tragedy in itself. If man's supremacy is to be challenged at all let it be by a creature of flesh-and-blood, a big-brained biped who must kill to live. Better that by far than a ghostly flickering in the deepening dusk, a whispering and a flapping and a long-drawn sighing prophesying death.

Oh, the Martians were real enough. A flitting vampire bat is real, or a stinging ray in the depths of a blue lagoon. But who could point to a Martian and say, "I have seen you plain, in broad daylight. I have looked into your owlish eyes and watched you go flitting over the sand on your thin, stalklike legs? I know there is nothing mysterious about you. You are like a water insect skimming the surface of a pond in a familiar meadow on Earth. You are quick and alert, but no match for a man. You are no more than an interesting insect."

Who could say that, when there were ruins buried deep beneath the sand to give the lie to any such idea. First the ruins, and then the Martians themselves, always elusive, gnomelike, goblinlike, flitting away into the dissolving dusk.

You're a comparative archaeologist and you're on Mars with the first batch of rugged youngsters to come tumbling out of a spaceship with stardust in their eyes. You see those youngsters digging wells and sweating in the desert. You see the prefabricated housing units go up, the tangle of machinery, the camp sites growing lusty with midnight brawls and skull-cracking escapades. You see the towns in the desert, the law-enforcement committees, the camp followers, the reform fanatics.

You're a sober-minded scholar, so you start digging in the ruins. You bring up odd-looking cylinders, rolls of threaded film, instruments of science so complex they make you giddy.

You wonder about the Martians—what they were like when they were a young and proud race. If you're an archaeologist you wonder. But Bill and I—we were youngsters still. Oh, sure, we were in our thirties, but who would have suspected that? Bill looked twenty-seven and I hadn't a gray hair in my head.

III

Bill nodded at Harry. "You'd better stay here. Tom and I will be asking some pointed questions, and our first move will depend on the answers we get. Don't let anyone come snooping around this shack. If anyone sticks his head in and starts to turn ugly, warn him just once— then shoot to kill." He handed Harry a gun.

Harry nodded grimly and settled himself on the floor close to Ned. For the first time since I'd known him, Harry looked completely sure of himself.

As we emerged from the shack the whispering was so loud the entire camp had been placed on the alert. There would be no need for us to go into shack after shack, watching surprise and shock come into their eyes.

A dozen or more men were between Bill's shack and the well. They were staring grimly at the dawn, as if they could already see blood on the sky, spilling over on the sand and spreading out in a sinister pool at their feet. A mirage-like pool mirroring their own hidden forebodings, mirroring a knotted rope and the straining shoulders of men too vengeful to know the meaning of restraint.

Jim Kenny stood apart and alone, about forty feet from the well, staring straight at us. His shirt was open at the throat, exposing a patch of hairy chest, and his big hands were wedged deeply into his belt. He stood about six feet three, very powerful, and with large feet.

I nudged Bill's arm. "What do you think?" I asked.

Kenny did seem a likely suspect. Molly had caught his eye right from the start, and he had lost no time in pursuing her. A guy like Kenny would have felt that losing out to a man of his own breed would have been a terrible blow to his pride. But just imagine Kenny losing out to a little guy like Ned. It would have infuriated him and glazed his eyes with a red film of hate.

Bill answered my question slowly, his eyes on Kenny's cropped head. "I think we'd better take a look at his shoes," he said.

We edged up slowly, taking care not to disturb the others, pretending we were sauntering toward the well on a before-breakfast stroll.

It was then that Molly came out of her shack. She stood blinking for an instant in the dawn glare, her unbound hair falling in a tumbled dark mass to her shoulders, her eyes still drowsy with sleep. She wore rust-colored slippers and a form-fitted yellow robe, belted in at the waist.

Molly wasn't beautiful exactly. But there was something pulse-stirring about her and it was easy to understand how a man like Kenny might find her difficult to resist.

Bill slanted a glance at Kenny, then shrugged and looked straight at Molly. He turned to me, his voice almost a whisper, "She's got to be told, Tom. You do it. She likes you a lot."

I'd been wondering about that myself—just how much she liked me. It was hard to be sure.

Bill saw my hesitation, and frowned. "You can tell if she's covering up. Her reaction may give us a lead."

Molly looked startled when she saw me approaching without the mask I usually wore when I waltzed her around and grinned and ruffled her hair and told her that she was the cutest kid imaginable and would make some man—not me—a fine wife.

That made telling her all the harder. The hardest part was at the end—when she stared at me dry-eyed and threw her arms around me as if I was the last support left to her on Earth.

For a moment I almost forgot we were not on Earth. On Earth I might have been able to comfort her in a completely sane way. But on Mars when a woman comes into your arms your emotions can turn molten in a matter of seconds.

"Steady," I whispered. "We're just good friends, remember?"

"I'd be willing to forget, Tom," she said.

"You've had a terrible shock," I whispered. "You really loved that little guy—more than you know. It's natural enough that you should feel a certain warmth toward me. I just happened to be here—so you kissed me."

"No, Tom. It isn't that way at all—"

I might have let myself go a little then if Kenny hadn't seen us. He stood very still for an instant, staring at Molly. Then his eyes narrowed and he walked slowly toward us, his hands still wedged in his belt.

I looked quickly at Molly, and saw that her features had hardened. There was a look of dark suspicion in her eyes. Bill had been watching Kenny, too, waiting for him to move. He measured footsteps with Kenny, advancing in the same direction from a different angle at a pace so calculated that they seemed to meet by accident directly in front of us.

Bill didn't draw but his hand never left his hip. His voice came clear and sharp and edged with cold insistence. "Know anything about it, Kenny?"

Strain seemed to tighten Kenny's face, but there was no panic in his eyes, no actual glint of fear. "What made you think I'd know?" he asked.

Bill didn't say a word. He just started staring at Kenny's shoes. He stood back a bit and continued to stare as if something vitally important had escaped him and taken refuge beneath the soggy leather around Kenny's feet.

"What size shoes do you wear, Jim?" he asked.

Kenny must have suspected that the question was charged with as much explosive risk as a detonating wire set to go off at the faintest jar. His eyes grew shrewd and mocking.

"So the guy who did it left prints in the sand?" he said. "Prints made by big shoes?"

"That's right," Bill said. "You have a very active mind."

Kenny laughed then, the mockery deepening in his stare. "Well," he said, "suppose we have a look at those prints, and if it will ease your mind I'll take off my shoes and you can try them out for size."

Kenny and Bill and I walked slowly from Molly's shack to the well in the hot and blazing glare, and the whispering went right on, getting under our skin in a tormenting sort of way.

Kenny still wore that disturbing grin. He looked at the prints and grunted. "Yeah," he said, "they sure are big. Biggest prints I've ever seen."

He sat down and started unlacing his shoes. First the right shoe, then the left. He pulled off both shoes and handed them to Bill.

"Fit them in," he said. "Measure them for size. Measure *me* for size, and to hell with you!"

Bill made a careful check. There were eight prints, and he fitted the shoes painstakingly into each of them. There was space to spare at each try.

It cleared Kenny completely. He wasn't a killer—this time. We might have roused the camp to a lynching fury and Kenny would have died for a crime another man had committed. I shut my eyes and saw Larsen swinging from a roof top, a black hood over his face. I saw Molly standing in the sunlight by my side, her face a stony mask.

I opened my eyes and there was Kenny, grinning contemptuously at us. He'd called our bluff and won out. Now the shoe was on the other foot.

A cold chill ran up my spine. It was Kenny who was doing the staring now, and he was looking directly at my shoes. He stood back a bit and continued to stare. He was dramatizing his sudden triumph in a way that turned my blood to ice.

Then I saw that Bill was staring too—straight at the shoes of a man he had known for three years and grown to like and trust. But underlying the warmth and friendliness in Bill was a granite-like integrity which nothing could shake.

It was Bill who spoke first. "I guess you'd better take them off, Tom," he said. "We may as well be thorough about this."

Sure, I was big. I grew up fast as a kid and at eighteen I weighed two hundred and thirty pounds, all lean flesh. If shoes ran large I could sometimes cram my feet into size twelves, but I felt much more comfortable in a size or two larger than that.

What made it worse, Molly liked me. I was involved with her, but no one knew how much. No one knew whether we'd quarreled or not, or how insanely jealous I could be. No one knew whether Molly had only pretended to like Ned while carrying a torch for me, and how danger-ously complex the situation might have become all along the line.

I stood very still, listening. The whispering was so loud now it drowned out the sighing of the wind. I looked down at my shoes. They were caked with mud and soggy and discolored. Day after day I'd trudge back and forth from the canal to the shacks in the blazing sunlight with-out giving my feet a thought until the ache in them had become intoler-able, rest an absolute necessity.

There was only one thing to do—call Kenny's bluff so fast he wouldn't have time to hurl another accusation at me.

I handed Bill both of my shoes. He looked at me and nodded. I waited, listening to the whispering rise and fall, watching him stoop and fit the shoes into the prints on the sand.

He straightened suddenly. His face was expressionless, but I could see that he was waging a terrible inward struggle with himself.

"Your shoes come pretty close to filling out those prints, Tom," he said. "I can't be sure—but a wax impression test should pretty well clear this up." He gripped my arm and nodded toward the shacks. "Better stick close to me."

Kenny took a slow step backward, his jaw tightening, his eyes searching Bill's face. "Wax impression test, hell!" he said. "You've got your murderer. I'm going to see he gets what's coming to him—right now!"

Bill shook his head. "I'll do this my way," he said.

Kenny glared at him, then laughed harshly. "You won't have a chance," he said. "The boys won't stand for it. I'm going to spread the word around, and you'd better not try to stop me."

That did it. I'd been holding myself in, but I had a sudden, over-powering urge to send my fist crashing into Kenny's face, to send him crashing to the sand. I started for him, but he jumped back and started shouting.

I can't remember exactly what he shouted. But he said just enough to put a noose around my neck. Every man and woman between the shacks and the well swung about to stare at me. I saw shock and rage flare in the eyes of men who usually had steady nerves. They were not calm now—not one of them.

IV

It all happened so fast I was caught off balance. In the harsh Martian sunlight human emotions can be as unstable as a wind-lashed dune.

A crazy thought flashed through my mind: Will Molly believe this too? Will she join these madmen in their wild thirst for vengeance? My need for her was suddenly overwhelming. Just seeing her face would have helped, but now more men had emerged from the shacks and I couldn't see beyond them. They were heading straight for me and I knew that even Bill would be powerless to stop them.

You can't argue with an avalanche. It was rolling straight toward me, gathering momentum as it came—not one man or a dozen, but a solid wall of human hate and unreason.

Bill stood his ground. He had drawn his gun, and he started shouting that the prints couldn't have been made by my shoes. I chalked that up to his credit and resolved never to forget it.

I knew I'd have to make a dash for it. I ran as fast as I could, keeping my eyes on the glimmer of sunlight on rising dunes, and deep hollows which a carefully placed bullet could have quickly changed into a burial mound.

A sudden crackling burst of gunfire ripped through the air. Directly in my path the sand geysered up as the bullets ripped and tore at it. Somebody wasn't a good marksman, or had let blind rage unnerve him and spoil his aim. A lot of somebodies—for the firing increased and became almost continuous for an instant, a dull crackling which drowned out the whispering and the sighing of the wind.

Then abruptly all sound ceased. Utter stillness descended on the desert—an unnatural, terrifying stillness, as if nature herself had stopped breathing and was waiting for someone to scream.

I must have been mad to turn. A weaving target has a chance, but a target standing motionless is a sitting duck and his life hangs by a hair. But still I turned.

Something was happening between the well and the shacks which halted the pursuit dead in its tracks. One of the shacks was wrapped in darting tongues of flame, and a woman was screaming, and a man close to her was grappling with something huge and misshapen which loomed starkly against the dawn glow.

A human shape? I could not be sure. It seemed monstrous, with a bulge between its shoulders which gave a grotesque and distorted aspect to the shadow which its weaving bulk cast upon the sand. I could see the shadow clearly across three hundred feet of sand. It lengthened and shortened, as if an octopus-like ferocity had given it the power to distort itself at will, lengthening its tentacles and then whipping them back again.

But it was not an octopus. It had legs and arms, and it was crushing the man in a grip of steel. I could see that now. I stared as the others were staring, their backs turned to me, their blind hatred for me blotted out by that greater horror.

I suddenly realized that the shape was human. It had the head and shoulders of a man, and a torso that could twist with muscular purpose, and massive hands that could maul and maim. It threw the hapless man from it with a sudden convulsive contraction of its entire bulk. I had never seen a human being move in quite that way, but even as its violence flared its manlike aspect became more pronounced.

A frightful thing happened then. The woman screamed and rushed toward the brutish maniac with her fingers splayed. The swaying figure bent, grabbed her about the waist, and lifted her high into the air. I thought for a moment he was about to crush her as he had crushed the man. But I was wrong. She was hurled to the sand, but with a violence so brutal that she went instantly limp.

Then the brutal madman turned, and I saw his face. If ever monstrous cruelty and malign cunning looked out of a human countenance it looked out of the eyes that stared in my direction, remorseless in their hate.

I could not tear my gaze from his face. The hate in it could be sensed, even across a blinding haze of sunlight that blotted out the sharp contours of physical things. But more than hate could be sensed. There was something tremendous about that face, as if the evil which had ravaged it had left the searing brand of Lucifer himself!

For an instant the madman stood motionless, his ghastly brutality unchallenged. Then Jeff Winters started for it. Jeff had come to Mars alone and grown more solitary with every passing day. He was a brooding, ingrown man, secretive and sullen, with a streak of wildness which he usually managed to control. He went for the madman like a gigantic terrier pup, shaggy and ferocious and contemptuous of death.

The big figure turned quickly, raised his arm, and brought his closed fist down on Jeff's skull. Jeff collapsed like a shattered plaster cast. His body seemed to break and splinter, and he sprawled forward on the sand.

He did not get up.

Frank Anders had guns on both hips, and he drew them fast. No one knew what kind of man Anders was. He hardly ever complained or made a spectacle of himself. A little guy with sandy hair and cold blue eyes, he had an accuracy of aim that did his talking for him.

His guns suddenly roared. For an instant the air between his hands and the maniac was a crackling wall of flame. The brute swayed a little but did not turn aside. He went straight for Anders with both arms spread wide.

He caught Anders about the waist, lifted him up, and slammed his body down against the sand. A sickness came over me as I stared. The madman bashed Anders' head against the ground again and again. Then suddenly the big arms relaxed and Anders sagged limply to the ground.

For an instant the madman swayed slowly back and forth, like a blood-stained marionette on a wire. Then he moved forward with a terrible, shambling gait, his head lowered, a dark, misshapen shadow seeming to lengthen before him on the sand like a spindle of flame.

The clearing was abruptly tumultuous with sound. The fury which had been unleashed against me turned upon the monster and became a closed circle of deadly, intent purpose hemming him in—and he was caught in a crossfire that hurled him backwards to the sand.

He jumped up and lunged straight for the well. What happened then was like the awakening stages of some horrible dream. The madman shambled past the well, the air at his back a crackling sheet of flame. The barrage behind him was continuous and merciless. The men were organized now, standing together in a solid wall, firing with deadly accuracy and a grim purpose which transcended fear.

The madman went clumping on past me and climbed a dune with his shoulders held straight. With a sunset glare deepening about him, he went striding over the dune and out of sight.

* * * *

I turned and stared back at the camp. The pursuit had passed the well and was headed for me. But no one paid the slightest attention to me. Twelve men passed me, walking three abreast. Bill came along in their wake, his eyes stony hard. He reached out as he passed me, gripping my shoulder, giving me a foot-of-the-gallows kind of smile.

"We know now who killed Ned," he whispered. "We know, fella. Take it easy, relax."

My head was throbbing, but I could see the big prints from where I stood—the prints of a murderer betrayed by his insatiable urge to slay.

I saw Kenny pass, and he gave me a contemptuous grin. He had done his best to destroy me, but there was no longer any hate left in me.

I took a slow step forward—and fell flat on my face....

I woke up with my head in Molly's lap. She was looking down into my face, sobbing in a funny sort of way and running her fingers through my hair.

She looked startled when she saw that I was wide awake. She blinked furiously and started fumbling at her waist for a handkerchief.

"I must have passed out cold," I said. "It's quite a strain to be at the receiving end of a lynching bee. And what I saw afterwards wasn't exactly pleasant."

"Darling," she whispered, "don't move, don't say a word. You're going to be all right."

"You bet I am!" I said. "Right now I feel great."

My arm went around her shoulder, and I drew her head down until her breath was warm on my face. I kissed her hair and lips and eyes for a full minute in utter recklessness.

When I released her her eyes were shining, and she was laughing a little and crying too. "You've changed your mind," she said. "You believe me now, don't you?"

"Don't talk," I said. "Don't say another word. I just want to look at you."

"It was you right from the start," she said. "Not Ned—or anyone else."

"I was a blind fool," I said.

"You never gave me a second glance."

"One glance was enough," I whispered. "But when I saw how it seemed to be between you and Ned—"

"I was never in love with him. It was just—"

"Never mind, don't say it," I said. "It's over and done with."

I stopped, remembering. Her eyes grew wide and startled, and I could see that she was remembering too.

"What happened?" I asked. "Did they catch that vicious rat?"

She brushed back her hair, the sunlight suddenly harsh on her face. "He fell into the canal. The bullets brought him down, and he collapsed on the bank."

Her hand tightened on my wrist. "Bill told me. He tried to swim, but the current carried him under. He went down and never came up."

"I'm glad," I said. "Did anyone in the camp ever see him before?"

Molly shook her head. "Bill said he was a drifter—a dangerous maniac who must have been crazed by the sun."

"I see," I said.

I reached out and drew her into my arms again, and we rested for a moment stretched out side by side on the sand.

"It's funny," I said after a while.

"What is?"

"You know what they say about the whispering. Sometimes when you listen intently you seem to hear words deep in your mind. As if the Martians had telepathic powers."

"Perhaps they have," she said.

I glanced sideways at her. "Remember," I said. "There were cities on Mars when our ancestors were hairy apes. The Martian civilization was flourishing and great fifty million years before the pyramids arose as a monument to human solidarity and worth. A bad monument, built by slave labor. But at least it was a start."

"Now you're being poetic, Tom," she said.

"Perhaps I am. The Martians must have had their pyramids too. And at the pyramid stage they must have had their Larsens, to shoulder all the guilt. To them we may still be in the pyramid stage. Suppose—"

"Suppose what?"

"Suppose they wanted to warn us, to give us a lesson we couldn't forget. How can we say with certainty that a dying race couldn't still make use of certain techniques that are far beyond us."

"I'm afraid I don't understand," she said, puzzled.

"Someday," I said, "our own science will take a tiny fragment of human tissue from the body of a dead man, put it into an incubating machine, and a new man will arise again from that tiny shred of flesh. A man who can walk and live and breathe again, and love again, and die again after another full lifetime.

"Perhaps the Martian science was once as great as that. And the Martians might still remember a few of the techniques. Perhaps from our human brains, from our buried memories and desires, they could filch the key and bring to horrible life a thing so monstrous and so terrible—"

Her hand went suddenly cold in mine. "Tom, you can't honestly think—"

"No," I said. "It's nonsense, of course. Forget it."

I didn't tell her what the whispering had seemed to say, deep in my mind.

We've brought you Larsen! You wanted Larsen, and we've made him for you! His flesh and his mind—his cruel strength and his wicked heart! Here he comes, here he is! Larsen, Larsen, Larsen!

THE SPIRAL INTELLIGENCE

Donald Brewster was alone. From the blazing wreckage of his spaceship to the canopy of foliage overhead the forest itself seemed to be conspiring against him, to be whispering and protesting as only a forest can when its age-old privacy has been invaded.

An immense emerald prison was the forest, fragrant with growing things, strident with the cries of snowy-crested birds.

It was a prison without bars, beautiful and strange and frightening. It was a naturalist's paradise, and on Earth it would have challenged an explorer to take pride in loneliness and walk with squared shoulders. But what pain could be greater than the pain of loneliness light-years from Earth, what agony of frustration harder to endure than the crystallization of emotion which took place in a man when his heart whispered that he would never see Earth again.

Never again the russet-and-gold splendor of an autumn landscape or the gleam of sunlight on familiar meadows. Never again a journey by sea and land—a journey made for delight alone with a woman tender and yielding at the end of it.

Few would deny that the most desolate fate that can befall a man is the fate of the hermit. To be surrounded day and night by the unknown and the unknowable, to call out and hear no answering voice, to be cut off forever from all human sympathy—who can be blamed for preferring death to such a fate?

No man perhaps. Yet Brewster did not want to die, and as the first shock of bitter realization wore off he found himself accepting with gratitude the fact that he was still alive and in full command of his faculties. Whatever befell, he would fight to stay alive until his strength gave out. He inspected carefully the rations he had dragged from the burning ship, checking them item by item. Grim experience had taught him that strange fruits and berries were a major hazard, to be sternly shunned until hunger made a mockery of all caution.

He'd have to risk poisoning himself if his skill in setting traps failed him. But he refused to believe it would fail, and meanwhile, if he husbanded every scrap, he could make his food last for at least a week. He pulled a flask from his pocket and took a long drink. Then he gave the bottle a pat, corked it firmly, and returned it to his hip.

"First lesson in survival," he muttered to the jungle shadows. "A man's best friend is himself—first, last, and all the time."

Five minutes later he was threading his way through the forest in search of a place to camp. A sun much hotter than Sol burned down like an angrily pursuing eye, mocking his confidence and making him feel suddenly fearful, and less sure of himself.

It irked him to realize that the planet was down on the charts as an uninhabited world. There was an abundance of animal life, but no chance at all that he might be given food and shelter by friendly natives. He comforted himself with the thought that humanoid creatures were as often as not unfriendly. To see a creature intelligent enough to have mastered the use of fire come loping out of the jungle on eight stalk-like legs would not be a pleasant experience, and if a man were himself unarmed—

* * * *

Brewster's thoughts congealed. He stood utterly motionless, refusing to believe in the reality of what he saw, telling himself with a sudden, tremendous tensing of his muscles and nerves that he had escaped death too recently to have it confront him again in so horrible a form. It was against all reason, a twist of fate too cruel to accept at face value.

The lizard towered directly in his path. It had emerged from a tunnel of dark vegetation less than seventy feet ahead and it was staring straight at him—a scaly and vermilion-crested monster with a row of armored spikes running the length of its spine.

There were shadows where it stood, a mingling of sunlight and darkness which in some queer way made its swaying bulk seem even greater than it was.

A flicker of light gleamed on its bared teeth, and it was staring with the malign ferocity of a carnivorous beast aware of its own strength and agility, a beast that had come suddenly upon a prey that could not possibly escape.

Brewster was still frantically telling himself that it was an illusion— when a gun roared nearby. The roar was deafening, but its reverberation was almost instantly drowned out by the lizard's piercing scream as the monster went hurtling back into the underbrush, its body cut in two. There was an instant of silence, complete, mind-numbing. Then from the underbrush stepped a tall man with a smoking gun, his face peering mournfully into the shadows as if he felt pity for the beast he had been forced to slay.

Amazingly he wore a uniform which Brewster recognized, but had never expected to see again. His eyes were steel-gray and piercing, his cheekbones prominent, and his nose a sharp, bony ridge slightly flattened at the tip.

White-lipped, shaken, Brewster shifted his weight from one trembling leg to the other. He waited for the stranger to speak, but the tall man seemed in no hurry. He stood for a moment nodding at Brewster, as if to give the man whose life he had saved full opportunity to regain his composure. Then, suddenly, his ruggedly handsome features widened in a grin. "Ugly brutes, those lizards. For all I know they may be harmless. But the odds seem definitely against it."

"Harmless—"

The tall man chuckled. "Well, I've never been attacked by one. I've been careful to keep out of their way. At fifty feet or so a wrong guess might kill you. That's why I blasted when I saw how close you were." Brewster shivered. "I'm glad you didn't waste any time thinking it over!"

"So am I!" The stranger's grin was enlivened by a merry twinkle of voice and eye. "Guess I should introduce myself. I'm Captain James Emery, United States Interstellar Survey. We had a crackup some two months ago, and we've been living off the land ever since."

"You're not alone then?"

Brewster was still so shaken he was afraid the other might think him lacking in courage. But Emery answered his question in a tone which had nothing of contempt in it, only a warm friendliness.

"No, my wife came along to look after me. She's a Survey officer in her own right, but this is the first time we've explored a new planet together. The trip was to be a kind of second honeymoon for both of us." He nodded. "It's funny, you, know. When you emerge from overdrive tens of thousands of light-years from Earth you get a feeling of renewal, of rebirth. There's a brightness and newness about everything, and you're not weighed down with memories."

His eyes grew speculative. "The psychos could probably explain it. There was a character in one of Shakespeare's plays who lightly dismissed a crime he'd committed by claiming it happened long ago and in another country. It's easy to find that amusing—or viciously cynical. But I've always felt Shakespeare's scoundrel displayed profound insight. Time and distance does make a difference, even when you're not a scoundrel."

"That's an angle I didn't have time to think about," Brewster said. "My ship cracked up and caught fire. I was looking for a drier place to camp when that lizard appeared I thought I was having a nightmare."

"They're agile," Emery conceded. "First you see them, then you don't." Brewster did not smile. He was staring at the Survey officer as if amazed by the tricks of fate.

"Do you know—I wouldn't be here at all if my sensitive instruments hadn't analyzed every ounce of metal in your ship far out in space," he said. "I had no way of discovering that the metal was in a wrecked spaceship. I thought that there was a rich lode of Ullurian ore here in a natural state. That's why I headed straight for this vicinity and was probably wrecked by a repetition of the same ugly weather conditions that you ran into."

Emery nodded and gestured toward the forest gloom, his rugged features sympathetic.

"That's quite possible," he agreed. "Even those trees are no protection when the elements really cut loose here. But at least we've found a place to camp. You're welcome to share it with us if you don't mind taking pot luck with a man whose only specialty is hunting food animals. Without my instruments I'm just the bright lad who got himself shipwrecked without a compass or a guiding star."

"I don't mind at all," Brewster said.

"Fine! I forgot to ask your name—"

"Donald Brewster, I'm a rare-metal prospector, as I guess you've surmised!"

"Welcome to the third planet of the bright star Rugulius, sir. Welcome to a camping site that's distinctly on the unbelievable side."

He seemed amused by Brewster's puzzlement. "Believe it or not, we're camping in a circular limestone tower eighty feet high. It's not a ruin, exactly. It's more like a big sea-shell rising from the forest floor, scoured and glistening inside and out."

"You mean it really is a shell?"

Emery shook his head. "I wouldn't call it that. Only a highly intelligent creature could have built it. The individual limestone blocks are perfectly aligned, and the design as a whole is far too imaginative to be accidental. It could have been constructed only by some creature with an eye for beauty of design." He laid a friendly hand on Brewster's shoulder. "Come see for yourself," he said. "It's less than ten minutes walk, if we keep to this path."

It was an incredible walk. Butterflies as huge as dinner plates, vivid scarlet and aquamarine, rose in swirling clouds before them, and half-blinded them with their fluttering. Little fuzzy creatures with enormous ears peered from rifts in the foliage, and then shrieked and vanished like startled elves, leaving behind them a faint odor of musk.

Once the survey officer seized Brewster's arm and pulled him abruptly to one side. In the path a ten-foot snake reared, its viper-like head repulsive with jungle phosphorescence. They found their way blocked in another place by a hideous swarm of blood-red worms, and in still another by a brooding bird with iridescent plumes and a huge gular pouch.

The bird refused to budge until Emery bent and gave her a gentle prod. Then she arose and went screaming away through the forest, leaving behind two pale-blue eggs which Emery gratefully pocketed. The path changed direction, and the great trees thinned a little.

The clearing was visible for a full minute before they reached it, a glimmering oval in the foliage-choked jungle wall directly ahead, growing continuously brighter.

* * * *

Emery was the first to emerge. He swung about and watched his companion claw his way into the open. He was eager to observe Brewster's expression when he first set eyes on the tower. The Survey officer's curiosity was satisfied almost instantly, and in a wholly satisfying manner. Brewster had been told what to expect, but there was a look in his eyes as he stared which left no doubt that his imagination had left enormous gaps. The beauty and vitality of the tower had to be seen to be appreciated.

It did resemble a gigantic sea-shell, but its smoothly flowing whorls and convolutions bore the unmistakable stamp of intelligent artistry.

There was a circular opening at its base, visible clear across the clearing, and in the opening stood a woman whose face and figure, once seen, could not be readily forgotten. Helen Emery must have heard her husband coming and had gone to the door to meet him. Brewster could see her smile clearly, the flash of ivory-white teeth. The sun touched warm glints in her hair, and her dark eyes were bright with an eager questioning.

In a moment the two men were at the door, and Helen Emery was greeting her husband. Brewster could see that her love for him was both strong and elemental. It was in the caress of her fingers on his face, in the tenderness of her expression, in the very way she held herself when she kissed him. An instant of fulfillment it seemed, complete in itself, as if he had been gone from her for a whole lifetime. Then she turned quickly to Brewster, her eyes wide again with unspoken questions. Emery talked with her for a moment, raising his voice a little so that Brewster could hear everything that was said. When he had finished Helen Emery came forward and took Brewster's hand in hers.

"Welcome to Riddle Manor, Donald Brewster," she said. "It may be a long time before we see Earth again. I'm glad we're not alone, as we feared."

"I'm glad too," Brewster said.

"Where are you from, Donald?" Helen asked.

"New York," Brewster said.

A roaring seemed to fill his ears as he spoke. He saw sunlight bright on gigantic metal buildings, heard the scream of jet planes, the deep, never-ceasing drone of the underground. He saw the bright waters of New York Harbor, the tangled maze of shipping in the harbor, and the spaceports of New Jersey hugging the shores of the outer bay. He blinked, and the bright, tremendous vision was gone.

"I'm from Boston," Helen Emery said. "The Charles must be beautiful now. In the autumn, when the leaves start to fall, and you can see the golden dome of the capitol—"

* * * *

Emery put his arm about his wife's shoulder and together they entered the tower. Brewster followed—and halted abruptly. With a shock that almost made him doubt his sanity he stared up at a series of ascending platforms, each circular and slightly overlapping, the entire structure towering to the roof.

The staircase—if it were a staircase—rose like a burst of frozen energy, its summit a snowy disk, the individual platforms grooved and notched and scooped out in weirdly symmetrical fashion. Emery and his wife paused on the third platform, and Brewster saw two rude couches fashioned of boughs, an ammunition box, and another gun, its barrel, gleaming blue-black in the shadows. Scattered about were other articles of camping equipment—a tiny magnetic stove, metal eating utensils, and even a charred and badly-dented camera.

Helen turned, her eyes sweeping the platform. "This is all we could save from the wreckage," she said, with a wry grimace. "Luckily we've had good shooting. I've decided that Jim is the best marksman in the Survey, barring some white-mustached old colonel I've never even met." Emery laughed. "I'm no better marksman than she is a cook, Donald." He patted her shoulder. "She'll have dinner ready before this place can really start to haunt you." Emery never forgot his first dinner in the tower. It was like nothing he could have imagined, its goodness matching the hospitality of Jim and Helen—friends completely new. As they ate they talked.

"What's it like to be a rare-metal prospector, Donald?"

He told them, keeping many things back but wishing that he could find courage to be completely honest, for once in his life. He told them about the narrow escapes, the loneliness of the extragalactic planets, and the moments of wild joy and triumph when a ruined humanoid city or desolate crater yielded minerals unknown on Earth.

He matched shining stories with Emery, fire mountain with fire mountain, strange animal with strange animal, morning mist with sunset splendor. But fie forgot to mention how he had cheated and lied his way to wealth, how he had won and lost and won again with loaded dice. He was silent about the disloyalties and betrayals, the false salvage claims, the ships deliberately wrecked. Finally the shadows of evening crept into the tower, and the setting sun dyed the ascending spiral red, and they knew it was time to put an end to talk.

Brewster stood up. "Are the nights cool?" he asked.

"Cool enough," Emery said. "Why, Donald?"

"I was thinking it might be a good idea to bunk near the top. If you don't mind climb up and look."

"Sure, go ahead," Emery said. "Helen and I just picked a platter at random." He smiled. "We've got into the habit of calling those platforms `platters.' Just imagine how nice it would be to have one set before you at mealtime, filled to the brim with a steak-and-mushroom dinner." His smile increased in volume. "I can't promise you a bat won't fly in and wake you up. But it's cool and comfortable enough at any level. If it's privacy you're worried about—these overlapping, scallop-shell edges guarantee that."

"If you were right up above you couldn't see us," Helen said, laughingly. "We'd be hidden away in our own jungle paradise."

"You're making it tough for a lonely bachelor," Brewster complained. He drew a deep breath, and picked up his ration kit. Then he turned and looked up. "I might as well climb to the top anyway. If I don't like it up there I'll descend a few platters."

Emery chuckled. "Prefer to be lord of all you survey, eh?" Brewster started, and looked at the survey officer closely. He saw at once that there was no hidden meaning in the other's merriment and to hide his confusion he started quickly up the spiral. He turned once to call back. "That dinner was really special! Thanks again!"

"Glad you enjoyed it!" Emery shouted. "See you at breakfast." It took Brewster a full minute to reach the heights. The disk at the top was enormous, its edges curving upward. Breathing heavily, he sat down on a projecting limestone shelf, and dropped his ration kit. He looked up in awe. It was curious, but the oddly-fashioned grooves and hollows in the walls of the tower made him think of an old nursery story from childhood. Even a few of the words came back, although he wasn't sure of the exact phrasing.

And she slept in each of the three beds, and ate from each of the three bawls. The first bed was very small, and tine second not large at all. But the third bed was enormous.

* * * *

Brewster unlaced his boots, and leaned back with a weary sigh. The shadows were growing darker, and they seemed to cluster about him as if seeking to drain warmth from his body and mind. The sun no longer bathed the roof of the tower in a rosy light.

He shut his eyes and relaxed completely.

There is an interval between sleeping and waking which can be sensed by the dreamer even as the long night can be sensed. But Brewster could not even remember the numbing drowsiness which usually warned him of the approach of sleep. He had experienced neither the long night nor the surprise of awakening from a borderland state of half-slumber in which the firm contours of reality remained elusively remote.

Was it a dream that he was having, a terrifyingly dream? Or was he awake and in the grip of some strange power, some alien intelligence, which had seized control of his mind?

Of one thing only could he be sure. He was in another world. It was a world of tremendous contrasts, of sea and jungle, of rain and scorching sunlight. He seemed to be walking through it, but more slowly than he had ever walked before. He seemed almost to glide, to crawl over the ground. It was a world of thunder and tumult. You could stand by a sea-wall and stare out over rocky headland separated by miles of blowing spray. You could swing about, and glide inland through a flowering wilderness over paths of snow-white coral.

In the inland world there was no thunder and no tumult. If you listened carefully you could hear the furtive movements of little animals, the whir and drone of invisible insect life. But unless you were skilled in Nature's ways you might suppose yourself in a garden of enchantment, with each fruit-bearing tree and blue-and-vermilion flower artificially designed to create delight.

"The spaceship was a tiny dot at first in the depths of the sky. But it grew swiftly larger, sweeping straight down toward the sea wall like sweeping a wind-buffeted cocoon. It circled and wheeled and swept ever lower, the sunlight glistening on its cylindrical hull.

Then it was resting motionless in the garden wilderness, and all about it the startled wild life of the region was protesting the intrusion. Sea birds shrieked and circled, dipped and wheeled, and outraged lizards hissed and slithered like clockwork automatons into their burrows on the landward side of the sea wall. The ship burst suddenly into flame.

He watched the conflagration, saw the tremendous sheets of fire darting skyward. He watched, alone and appalled, and the slowness of his movement toward the ship was like the slowness which afflicts the terror-stricken in dreams.

Yet now more than ever he felt himself to be awake. The feeling remained when the immense white buildings and the glittering instruments of science came to replace what he had seen by the sea-wall, and he heard voices whispering hi his mind.

"I knew that we could heal them. But they were so close to death when we removed them from the wreckage I feared our task would be a difficult one."

"Even if they had died—we could have healed them," a second voice said. "Every living tissue carries within itself the somatic pattern of the organism as a whole. We could have restored and revitalized their bodies and their brains from a single living cell."

The voice paused, then went on. "Somatic death is never instantaneous. The brain dies more slowly than the body, as energy-discharge tests have shown, and there are always a few cells which survive for an incredible length of time. Even without the aid of a nutrient fluid we could have kept a few cells alive."

"That is true," the first voice agreed. "Had they died the vast complexity of their brains would have continued to survive in rudimentary form in a single neural filament. From a tiny living fragment of damaged brain tissue teeming with neurograms—the basic patterns of memory and inheritance—we could have reconstructed all of the perished stimulus-response circuits and linked memory-chains which are the wellsprings of thought, of imagination and desire.

"Life would have returned in all of its stormy splendor, for intelligent life is like a great sea in its restlessness. It may seem to have ebbed forever, but the slightest under-surge will lash it to hurricane violence and send it crashing across the beaches of eternity.

"You cannot confine life to a single planet of a single star, and even as it perishes it lights torch after torch on its stormy crests and hurls them afar to dazzle other worlds with its dreams of survival.

"Fortunately these two did not die, even though their injuries would have resulted in death if we had not healed them by a combined application of surgical techniques and somatic revitalizing rays.

"Every such victory over death is a milestone in the progress which science must make if intelligence is to increase its mastery over the blind forces of Nature. We have built a great and enduring civilization by holding fast to that one aim—the conquest of Nature by patient research alone. But we must never forget that our greatest victories lie ahead."

There was a swirl of brightness and Brewster became aware that he was inside one of the buildings, staring at moving shapes that loomed semitransparent in the gloom.

Standing side by side in what appeared to be a high-walled laboratory glittering with instruments of

'science such as he had never before seen were two white limestone slabs, each supporting an unmoving human form. Behind the slabs towered gleaming transparencies of metal and crystal, and a circular, mirrorlike object which reflected spots of light down ward on a man's drawn face and a woman's tousled, dark hair.

The man and the woman were naked in the glow. For a moment the downstreaming rays penetrated the shadows in steady shafts. Then they lit filaments of darting flame upon the woman's head and shoulders, and traced out a fiery circle about the torso of the man.

Slowly the light weaved back and forth, assuming changing patterns, and from behind the mirrorlike object something arose in the flame-streaked gloom that was not a machine. Something huge and white with protruding eyes and sluglike horns projecting from its head. It was quickly joined by another of its kind.

On the slab Helen Emery stirred and opened her eyes.

Then brightness again and the scene changed. There were dark clouds across the entire sky, obscuring the outlines of the white buildings. Lightning forked down, shafts of blinding radiance circled the sky. Did the radiance come from the buildings themselves? Brewster was never to know, for he fell at last into a deep sleep and did not awaken until dawn came to the tower.

Awakening, he felt for an instant a sense of unreality, a suspension of reason that made his temples throb. He arose in alarm, and stared down the enormous spiral that sloped away beneath him. In the cold gray dawn what had seemed merely incredible took' on a nightmare quality of fantastic madness. How could his mind interpret thoughts from a nonhuman brain? How could he see images and hear voices his memory had never recorded?

Did something dwell in the tower that could physically implant itself on its surroundings, as the sea could be tinted red by a sunset, or the jungle darkened by the shadow of a dangerous beast? Everything was quiet now. Everything was completely peaceful. Yet what he had seen and experienced could not have been a dream.

He knew what psychologists had discovered about the nature of dreams. It was a peculiarity of dreams that inner experiences were expressed in such a way that the mind was freed from the necessity of feeling deep concern for others. That had been positively established. Tests had been made which left no room for doubt. And in dreams the events which took place were subject to a special logic of their own which could seldom be justified on awakening.

But then—could the logic of what he had seen and heard be justified? Could an alien science cheat death on the planet of a distant star, light-years from Earth across the great curve of the universe? Could a greater science than man's restore the mortally injured to warmth and life and fire?

They'll know, he thought. If their ship circled a sea-wall they'll remember. I'll ask Jim and Helen to take me to the wreckage.

He looked up, and saw the dawn warming the sky through a window high in the tower. The sky was as bright as any dawn sky on Earth, and deep in the forest birds were singing. They'll know; they'll tell me.

* * * *

Helen Emery was bent above the tiny magnetic stove, her hair aureoled by the dawn light. She looked up quickly when she heard Brewster descending.

"Is that you, Donald?" she called out. "You're up early, aren't you?" He appeared suddenly before her, his face drawn.

"I hardly slept at all," he lied. "I was too tired, I guess. More badly shaken up than I realized. Where's Jim?"

"Taking an early morning dip," she said, brushing back a strand of hair that had fallen across her forehead. Dark hair, that had lain in a tumbled mass beneath shifting lights and shadows. She seemed embarrassed by his stare, and added quickly: "It's only a ten-minute walk to the sea-wall, I wish I enjoyed bathing in the sea as much as Jim does. I was born inland, on a farm, and I never saw the sea until I was eighteen."

The sea-wall!

He never quite remembered how he persuaded her to take him to the wreckage. The shock of her words had started a whirring in his brain, and he had only a confused recollection of giving her some very logical and plausible reason for wanting to make the trip. More sharply impressed on his mind was her quick nod of agreement.

It was an easy journey they made, along a path previously cleared. There was silence between them, broken only by the occasional crackle of a twig underfoot. They saw no birds or reptiles, but once a tiny mole-like creature darted across their path and vanished in the underbrush with an eerie screeching. A few minutes later they heard the roar and crash of the sea. The vegetation thinned and fell away, and they emerged into the open.

A startled cry burst from Helen Emery's lips. She stood staring, the blood draining from her face, her eyes wide with stark disbelief.

Suddenly she was running—running straight toward the bright new ship which stood by the sea-wall.

"It's our ship!" she cried. "Donald, it's the ship that brought us here! What could have happened? How could it have been rebuilt?"

Brewster stared at her still in motion, shouting the questions as she ran. Without replying he joined her beside the ship, a stunned horror in his eyes. He reached out and felt the cool, shining metal of the port locks. He looked in through a gleaming view-pane at an intricate cluster of navigational instruments. Fear came and stood beside him, and for a moment his eyes wondered to the sea-wall and came to rest on the shadows lurking there.

The dawn of understanding. It touched his mind, and retreated, and came back again. An intelligence so powerful that it could impress its thoughts on its surroundings would not find it difficult to rebuild a wrecked spaceship—even a ship gutted by fire. An intelligence of such power equipped with instruments of science could do…almost anything it wanted to do.

A trembling seized him and he could hardly trust himself to speak. The ship had been rebuilt for a purpose. What purpose? To study its construction, as human scientists would have studied a strange ship wrecked on Earth.

He had to be alone. To think—and reach a decision. An opportunity had presented itself and with opportunity had come a choice he would have to make. It was a decision which could not be put off, could not be delayed another instant.

He tried to speak calmly, tried to keep his voice from betraying him. "Get Jim," he said. "Jim must be back by now. He'll know if this is really your ship."

"I'll bring him as quickly as I can," she promised. "But I'm sure it's our ship. The instant I saw it I knew, I could tell."

She looked at him steadily for a long moment, as if trying to read his mind.

"I won't be satisfied until Jim is sure too," he said. "It means—there is intelligent life on this planet. It means that we're not alone, as we thought. We're being watched—studied." Her eyes widened in sudden alarm. "You really think that?"

"What other explanation is there? What other possible explanation?"

"I'll get Jim," she said.

She turned, and was gone.

Brewster stood for a moment listening to her footsteps die away. Then he turned hack to the ship, his mouth strangely dry.

He entered the ship through the open port-lock, and stared about him. Everything seemed incredibly new—new and bright and shining. He saw the double pilot seats, facing the controls. He went to the instrument board, tested the air pressure, and looked out through the viewpane at the green immensity of the forest.

In the small compact control room there was a security which could not be found in the forest, or by the sea wall. The forest could kill in a thousand cruel ways. And by the sea-wall lurked shadows which could threaten a man's sanity.

In the forest a man could die horribly, and his bones lie bleached and whitening under cold stars. There were two pilot seats, but one man could pilot the ship. There was room for two—but not for three. The ship could not carry two men and one woman back on overdrive to Earth. The jungle was green and threatening outside the viewpane. The jungle whispered: Do not be a fool! This is your chance! Act quickly!

Brewster climbed into one of the pilot seats.

He stared out into the green jungle. But he did not see the jungle. He saw New York. He was back in that tremendous city, the lights of evening fading from the windows of the buildings he loved, the rooftops shining clear in the heavens.

He was back in New York with a lot of money to spend. He was hack in his favorite restaurant at his favorite table. It was dark outside, he could see the stars shining in the winter sky. The wine was poured quickly, it bubbled in his glass.

Opposite him sat a woman. Her name did not matter. He only eared that she was a woman, tender and very beautiful, and that if he lost her, there would always be another woman waiting. He shut his eyes and she was tight in his arms. Her lips were fire, and the words she spoke to him would have prevented him from seeking another. He would have welcomed that too. He would not have cared. Brewster climbed down front the pilot seat and went outside to wait for Jim and Helen. The jungle screamed at him: You're quite mad! You had your chance! Why didn't you take it?

There was no answer he could give the jungle. He could not seem to bring his thoughts into clear focus. Two strangers had welcomed him as a friend, had trusted him completely. But that was no proper answer. It explained nothing, really.

* * * *

He saw them approaching along the path and straightened in sudden concern. He'd be having a time with Jim. You couldn't just say to a survey officer: *Your ship was wrecked, and you were closeto death. But an intelligence whose existence I cannot even prove healed you. It rebuilt your shiptoo. Climb in and take off. Hurry, Jim! Before they try to stop you. If they could read our thoughtsthey'd be here now, they'd stop you cold. There must be a mind block of sonic sort. Takeadvantage of it, Jim! Don't just stand there staring at me!*

For a survey officer had an approach to reality that would never give ground that fast. He'd have to be convinced first, and that would take time.

"Donald, when Helen told me, I couldn't believe it. I thought it was sonic sort of gag you'd cooked up between you. I—I've got to sit down."

Brewster looked up and saw Jim standing before him. Not the Jim he'd imagined himself opposing, but Jim the flesh—an even harder Jim to argue with.

Emery sat down on a tree stump and stared at the ship.

"How did it get here?" he asked.

"We found it here," Brewster said.

"It is our ship," Helen said. "Have you any doubt at all, Jim?"

"I'll know when I've looked at the instrument board."

Emery got up then, and went into the ship. Brewster and Jim's wife followed. Jim walked slowly around the control room, his lips tight, his eyes shining strangely.

Emery moved about the ship like a man in a trance, his eyes roving from the control board whose dials indicated ample fuel reserves and perfect mechanical, electronic functioning, to the orderly, properly fastened array of essential equipment. But a frown creased his face when he observed only two take-off pressure coaches.

"Good Lord!" he muttered. "It just can't be. It's against all reason." Brewster knew then what had to be done. He was no hero. His past was crammed with so many things he wanted to forget that one more sordid episode wouldn't have appreciably darkened the whole. This was, however, the first time he could remember being treated as a decent human being. It was a new experience. There comes a time when a man has to give as well as take.

"Jim!" he said.

He waited until Emery had turned and was facing him.

"I've never had two better friends than you and Helen, Jim," he said. Then Brewster sent his fist crashing against Emery's jaw. It was a hard, quick blow, and it dropped Emery to the deck. Helen cried out in horror.

Brewster turned and took her by the shoulder. She tried to wrench free, her eyes wild, but he refused to release her. "Listen to me," he pleaded. "Jim told me you were a survey officer too. You know how to pilot this ship."

"You struck him for no reason at all."

Brewster shook his head. "I had a reason. We're in very great danger, but I couldn't have convinced him. He wouldn't have listened. But he's your husband, and he's helpless now. He's your man—and a woman in love will always listen."

"Listen to what?" she asked, fiercely.

"I'm going to stay and draw the danger away from you. I'm going to make myself a target. But don't get the silly idea that I'm sacrificing myself. If you stay Jim may be the target—but my chances won't he any better.

He shook her, a little roughly, solely to anger her. "Do you under-stand? I'd have to stay anyway. But you can save Jim by using common sense."

She ceased to struggle suddenly. She stared at him, her lips white. "Do you really mean that?"

"Of course I mean it. I'm going outside. As soon as I'm clear—I want you to take off. Just give me thirty seconds to get clear."

He didn't wait to say goodbye. He crossed the control room in three quick strides, and swung the port-lock shut behind him.

He was seventy feet from the ship when it took off with a thunderous roar. He walked slowly back through the forest, keeping to the path that seemed somehow now to be his last link with Earth.

A sense of almost overwhelming loneliness came upon him when he saw the tower overwhelming the trees, its summit bright with weav-ing sunlight. Yet he walked across the clearing with his shoulders held straight.

The tower had become suddenly very precious to him. In the tower he had enjoyed a truly wonderful hospitality. He had known himself for the first time in his life as a man capable of friendship, warm, deep and lasting.

Horribly lonely and deserted the ascending platforms seemed now. Each shadow seemed to mock him, increasing his sense of loss, height-ening the desolation which rested upon him like some evil cloak which had begun to grow into his flesh.

Higher he climbed, and higher.

Near the top of the spiral he paused to stare down.

And suddenly he knew the secret of the tower. *The tower was a house.* On Earth a house was not a home until it had been lived in. When a house became a home it changed subtly. The people who lived in it changed it.

If walls could speak and tell their secrets

But walls had spoken. How else explain the visions he had seen, the voices he had heard? Some wise and tremendous intelligence had built this house and it was now a home. And why could not walls be made sensitive to waves of thought, just as photoelectric cells were sensitive to the approach of a physical body acting upon them from a distance. A science that could heal the mortally injured would find no difficulty there.

Brewster sat down at the edge of the topmost platform, and stared down the spiral, remembering the visions he had seen of a planet of tremendous contrasts, of sea and sky, miles of blowing spray and primeval jungle.

On the shores of Earth's seas dwelt enormous mollusks. Enormous for Earth, but here he had met in the jungle a lizard twenty feet tall.

A snail would not have to remain permanently attached to its house. On Earth there were mollusks which could leave their shells at will.

The ebb and flow of the sea tides, the surge of the great sea that never ceased. Would not an intelligence having its origin in the sea prefer to roam, to join itself to that surge and return to its house only at intervals?

How easy it was to imagine such a creature, weary at last of its roaming, climbing up a sea-wall in its shining eagerness to be home.

The strange grooves and hollows.

In a mollusk's body were similar grooves and hollows, for a mollusk must mold itself to its spiral house, must flow into every crevice and fill its house completely.

Brewster sat very still, listening to he knew not what, his nerves suddenly tense. On Earth there were mollusks with great horny feet which could be fitted into grooves such as Brewster saw here on the immense spiral which fell away beneath him.

A scientific intelligence, thought Brewster, could be completely lacking in compassion. It was possible that he had saved his friends from a fate worse than death—for the lot of the experimental guinea pig was never a happy one. But it was equally possible that the intelligence might have been moved by a spirit of altruism. To restore an alien life-form and the ship which had brought that form to its own world might have appealed to it as a kindly and generous thing to do.

In that case Jim and Helen Emery would have been in no danger, and their departure would have fulfilled the original design of the intelligence. But if the intelligence had no such altruistic design in mind—might it not feel itself thwarted, and vent its rage on the one responsible?

Well, if he had to be a guinea pig—

The lapping was barely audible at first, a hollow mockery of sound that fell so lightly on Brewster's ears that if he had not been listening with every nerve alert he would have thought it a breeze blowing in from the sea, rattling the dry leaves of the forest.

He knew when he heard it that he could not hope to escape. He remained motionless, listening as the sound grew louder, listening and waiting and fighting back his fear. Louder and louder it grew, and suddenly a shadow fell across the base of the spiral that could only have been cast by a flowing shape moving with the resistless slowness of the sea tides themselves.

Straight up the spiral swept the owner of the house, darkish portions of itself slithering over the ascending disks, and into the grooves and hollows. Closely and ever more closely as it ascended it molded itself to the spiral's convolutions, as if the spiral were intimately a part of its mind and its flesh. It had returned completely into its house, rearing a great, horned head and staring down at Brewster with eyes that seemed to probe his very soul.

Suddenly, from a crevice in the uneven limestone a floating, disk-like object emerged and swept down toward him, dazzling his eyes with its brightness.

Incredibly intricate in construction the disk seemed, its numerous knoblike projections and delicately glowing tubes proclaiming it an instrument of science designed with accuracy for a specific purpose. That purpose Brewster sensed even before the tubes attached themselves to his brow. The walls could speak and this was their voice—an instrument of communication of a thistledown lightness which responded to every thought impulse generated by the owner of the house. Generated by guests as well? And why not? An automatic caretaker, perhaps—taking down messages in the owner's absence and repeating them on the owner's return. Absorbing impressions from every part of the house, from millions of tiny photoelectric cell mechanisms embedded on every tier. Attaching itself to friend and foe alike—

As the tubes at Brewster's temples lit up his face he knew that the strangeness and mystery of it would forever haunt him. But he knew also that the questions he would never cease to ask himself were of less importance than the simple fact that the owner of the house was using the device now to communicate with him directly.

* * * *

"For you," a voice whispered, deep in his mind. "We built it for you, Donald Brewster!" Almost the great horned face seemed to smile. "It will take you back to your home planet!" Brewster saw the ship then, standing by the seawall in a blaze of sunlight. It was a beauty—the most beautiful ship he had ever seen.

He blinked and there was a stinging at his eyelids. He wanted to stand up, to get to his feet and shout his gratitude. But so great was his surprise and delight that all he could do was stare.

THE CALM MAN

Sally Anders had never really thought of herself as a wallflower. A girl could be shy, couldn't she, and still be pretty enough to attract and hold men?

Only this morning she had drawn an admiring look from the milk-man and a wolf cry from Jimmy on the corner, with his newspapers and shiny new bike. What if the milkman was crowding sixty and wore thick-lensed glasses? What if Jimmy was only seventeen?

A male was a male, and a glance was a glance. Why, if I just primp a little more, Sally told herself, I'll be irresistible.

Hair ribbons and perfume, a mirror tilted at just the right angle, an invitation to a party on the dresser—what more did a girl need?

"Dinner, Sally!" came echoing up from the kitchen. "Do you want to be late, child?"

Sally had no intention of being late. Tonight she'd see him across a crowded room and her heart would skip a beat. He'd look at her and smile, and come straight toward her with his shoulders squared.

There was always one night in a girl's life that stands above all other nights. One night when the moon shone bright and clear and the clock on the wall went *tick tock, tick tock, tick tock.* One night when each tick said, "You're beautiful! Really beautiful!"

Giving her hair a final pat Sally smiled at herself in the mirror.

In the bathroom the water was still running and the perfumed bath soap still spread its aromatic sweet odor through the room. Sally went into the bathroom and turned off the tap before going downstairs to the kitchen.

"My girl looks radiant tonight!" Uncle Ben said, smiling at her over his corned beef and cabbage.

Sally blushed and lowered her eyes.

"Ben, you're making her nervous," Sally's mother said, laughing.

Sally looked up and met her uncle's stare, her eyes defiant. "I'm not bad-looking whatever you may think," she said.

"Oh, now, Sally," Uncle Ben protested. "No sense in getting on a high horse. Tonight you may find a man who just won't be able to resist you."

"Maybe I will and maybe I won't," Sally said. "You'd be surprised if I did, wouldn't you?"

It was Uncle Ben's turn to lower his eyes.

"I'll tell the world you've inherited your mother's looks, Sally," he said. "But a man has to pride himself on something. My defects of character are pretty bad. But no one has ever accused me of dishonesty."

Sally folded her napkin and rose stiffly from the table.

"Good night, Uncle," she said.

When Sally arrived at the party every foot of floor space was taken up by dancing couples and the reception room was so crowded that, as each new guest was announced, a little ripple of displeasure went through the men in midnight blue and the women in Nile green and lavender.

For a moment Sally did not move, just stood staring at the dancing couples, half-hidden by one of the potted palms that framed the sides of the long room.

Moonlight silvered her hair and touched her white throat and arms with a caress so gentle that simply by closing her eyes she could fancy herself already in his arms.

Moonlight from tall windows flooding down, turning the dancing guests into pirouetting ghosts in diaphanous blue and green, scarlet and gold.

Close your eyes, Sally, close them tight! Now open them! That's it... Slowly, slowly ...

He came out of nothingness into the light and was right beside her suddenly.

He was tall, but not too tall. His face was tanned mahogany brown, and his eyes were clear and very bright. And he stood there looking at her steadily until her mouth opened and a little gasp flew out.

He took her into his arms without a word and they started to dance ...

They were still dancing when he asked her to be his wife.

"You'll marry me, of course," he said. "We haven't too much time. The years go by so swiftly, like great white birds at sea."

They were very close when he asked her, but he made no attempt to kiss her. They went right on dancing and while he waited for her answer he talked about the moon ...

"When the lights go out and the music stops the moon will remain," he said. "It raises tides on the Earth, it inflames the minds and hearts of men. There are cyclic rhythms which would set a stone to dreaming and desiring on such a night as this."

He stopped dancing abruptly and looked at her with calm assurance.

"You *will* marry me, won't you?" he asked. "Allowing for a reasonable margin of error I seriously doubt if I could be happy with any of these other women. I was attracted to you the instant I saw you."

A girl who has never been asked before, who has drawn only one lone wolf cry from a newsboy could hardly be expected to resist such an offer.

Don't resist, Sally. He's strong and tall and extremely good-looking. He knows what he wants and makes up his mind quickly. Surely a man so resolute must make enough money to support a wife.

"Yes," Sally breathed, snuggling close to him. "Oh, yes!"

She paused a moment, then said, "You may kiss me now if you wish, my darling."

He straightened and frowned a little, and looked away quickly. "That can wait," he said.

* * * *

They were married a week later and went to live on an elm-shaded street just five blocks from where Sally was born. The cottage was small, white and attractively decorated inside and out. But Sally changed the curtains, as all women must, and bought some new furniture on the installment plan.

The neighbors were friendly folk who knew her husband as Mr. James Rand, an energetic young insurance broker who would certainly carve a wider swath for himself in his chosen profession now that he had so charming a wife.

Ten months later the first baby came.

Lying beneath cool white sheets in the hospital Sally looked at the other women and felt so deliriously happy she wanted to cry. It was a beautiful baby and it cuddled close to her heart, its smallness a miracle in itself.

The other husbands came in and sat beside their wives, holding on tight to their happiness. There were flowers and smiles, whispers that explored bright new worlds of tenderness and rejoicing.

Out in the corridor the husbands congratulated one another and came in smelling of cigar smoke.

"Have a cigar! That's right. Eight pounds at birth. That's unusual, isn't it? Brightest kid you ever saw. Knew his old man right off."

He was beside her suddenly, standing straight and still in shadows.

"Oh, darling," she whispered. "Why did you wait? It's been three whole days."

"Three days?" he asked, leaning forward to stare down at his son. "Really! It didn't seem that long."

"Where were you? You didn't even phone!"

"Sometimes it's difficult to phone," he said slowly, as if measuring his words. "You have given me a son. That pleases me very much."

A coldness touched her heart and a despair took hold of her. "It pleases you! Is that all you can say? You stand there looking at me as if I were a—a patient ..."

"A patient?" His expression grew quizzical. "Just what do you mean, Sally?"

"You said you were pleased. If a patient is ill her doctor hopes that she will get well. He is pleased when she does. If a woman has a baby a doctor will say, 'I'm so pleased. The baby is doing fine. You don't have to worry about him. I've put him on the scales and he's a bouncing, healthy boy.'"

"Medicine is a sane and wise profession," Sally's husband said. "When I look at my son that is exactly what I would say to the mother of my son. He is healthy and strong. You have pleased me, Sally."

He bent as he spoke and picked Sally's son up. He held the infant in the crook of his arm, smiling down at it.

"A healthy male child," he said. "His hair will come in thick and black. Soon he will speak, will know that I am his father."

He ran his palm over the baby's smooth head, opened its mouth gently with his forefinger and looked inside.

Sally rose on one elbow, her tormented eyes searching his face.

"He's your child, your son!" she sobbed. "A woman has a child and her husband comes and puts his arms around her. He holds her close. If they love each other they are so happy, so very happy, they break down and cry."

"I am too pleased to do anything so fantastic, Sally," he said. "When a child is born no tears should be shed by its parents. I have examined the child and I am pleased with it. Does not that content you?"

"No, it doesn't!" Sally almost shrieked. "Why do you stare at your own son as if you'd never seen a baby before? He isn't a mechanical toy. He's our own darling, adorable little baby. *Our child!* How can you be so *inhumanly* calm?"

He frowned, put the baby down.

"There is a time for love-making and a time for parenthood," he said. "Parenthood is a serious responsibility. That is where medicine comes in, surgery. If a child is not perfect there are emergency measures which can be taken to correct the defect."

Sally's mouth went suddenly dry. "Perfect! What do you mean, Jim? Is there something *wrong* with Tommy?"

"I don't think so," her husband said. "His grasp is firm and strong. He has good hearing and his eyesight appears to be all that could be desired. Did you notice how his eyes followed me every moment?"

"I wasn't looking at his eyes!" Sally whispered, her voice tight with alarm. "Why are you trying to frighten me, Jim? If Tommy wasn't a normal, healthy baby do you imagine for one instant they would have placed him in my arms?"

"That is a very sound observation," Sally's husband said. "Truth is truth, but to alarm you at a time like this would be unnecessarily cruel."

"Where does that put you?"

"I simply spoke my mind as the child's father. I had to speak as I did because of my natural concern for the health of our child. Do you want me to stay and talk to you, Sally?"

Sally shook her head. "No, Jim. I won't let you torture me any more."

Sally drew the baby into her arms again and held it tightly. "I'll scream if you stay!" she warned. "I'll become hysterical unless you leave."

"Very well," her husband said. "I'll come back tomorrow."

He bent as he spoke and kissed her on the forehead. His lips were ice cold.

For eight years Sally sat across the table from her husband at breakfast, her eyes fixed upon a nothingness on the green-blue wall at his back. Calm he remained even while eating. The eggs she placed before him he cracked methodically with a knife and consumed behind a tilted newspaper, taking now an assured sip of coffee, now a measured glance at the clock.

The presence of his young son bothered him not at all. Tommy could be quiet or noisy, in trouble at school, or with an *A* for good conduct tucked with his report card in his soiled leather zipper jacket. It was always: "Eat slowly, my son. Never gulp your food. Be sure to take plenty of exercise today. Stay in the sun as much as possible."

Often Sally wanted to shriek: "Be a father to him! A real father! Get down on the floor and play with him. Shoot marbles with him, spin one of his tops. Remember the toy locomotive you gave him for Christmas after I got hysterical and screamed at you? Remember the beautiful little train? Get it out of the closet and wreck it accidentally. He'll warm up to you then. He'll be broken-hearted, but he'll feel close to you, then you'll know what it means to have a son!"

Often Sally wanted to fly at him, beat with her fists on his chest. But she never did.

You can't warm a stone by slapping it, Sally. You'd only bruise your-self. A stone is neither cruel nor tender. You've married a man of stone, Sally.

He hasn't missed a day at the office in eight years. She'd never vis-ited the office but he was always there to answer when she phoned. "I'm very busy, Sally. What did you say? You've bought a new hat? I'm sure it will look well on you, Sally. What did you say? Tommy got into a fight with a new boy in the neighborhood? You must take better care of him, Sally."

There are patterns in every marriage. When once the mold has set, a few strange behavior patterns must be accepted as a matter of course.

"I'll drop in at the office tomorrow, darling!" Sally had promised right after the breakfast pattern had become firmly established. The de-sire to see where her husband worked had been from the start a strong, bright flame in her. But he asked her to wait a while before visiting his office.

A strong will can dampen the brightest flame, and when months passed and he kept saying 'no,' Sally found herself agreeing with her husband's suggestion that the visit be put off indefinitely.

Snuff a candle and it stays snuffed. A marriage pattern once estab-lished requires a very special kind of re-kindling. Sally's husband re-fused to supply the needed spark.

Whenever Sally had an impulse to turn her steps in the direction of the office a voice deep in her mind seemed to whisper: "No sense in it, Sally. Stay away. He's been mean and spiteful about it all these years. Don't give in to him now by going."

Besides, Tommy took up so much of her time. A growing boy was always a problem and Tommy seemed to have a special gift for getting into things because he was so active. And he went through his clothes, wore out his shoes almost faster than she could replace them.

Right now Tommy was playing in the yard. Sally's eyes came to a focus upon him, crouching by a hole in the fence which kindly old Mrs. Wallingford had erected as a protection against the prying inquisitive-ness of an eight-year-old determined to make life miserable for her.

A thrice-widowed neighbor of seventy without a spiteful hair in her head could put up with a boy who rollicked and yelled perhaps. But peep-hole spying was another matter.

Sally muttered: "Enough of that!" and started for the kitchen door. Just as she reached it the telephone rang.

Sally went quickly to the phone and lifted the receiver. The instant she pressed it to her ear she recognized her husband's voice—or thought she did.

"Sally, come to the office!" came the voice, speaking in a hoarse whisper. "Hurry—or it will be too late! Hurry, Sally!"

Sally turned with a startled gasp, looked out through the kitchen window at the autumn leaves blowing crisp and dry across the lawn. As she looked the scattered leaves whirled into a flurry around Tommy, then lifted and went spinning over the fence and out of sight.

The dread in her heart gave way to a sudden, bleak despair. As she turned from the phone something within her withered, became as dead as the drifting leaves with their dark autumnal mottlings.

She did not even pause to call Tommy in from the yard. She rushed upstairs, then down again, gathering up her hat, gloves and purse, making sure she had enough change to pay for the taxi.

The ride to the office was a nightmare... Tall buildings swept past, facades of granite as gray as the leaden skies of mid-winter, beehives of commerce where men and women brushed shoulders without touching hands.

Autumnal leaves blowing, and the gray buildings sweeping past. Despite Tommy, despite everything there was no shining vision to warm Sally from within. A cottage must be lived in to become a home and Sally had never really had a home.

One-night stand! It wasn't an expression she'd have used by choice, but it came unbidden into her mind. If you live for nine years with a man who can't relax and be human, who can't be warm and loving you'll begin eventually to feel you might as well live alone. Each day had been like a lonely sentinel outpost in a desert waste for Sally.

She thought about Tommy... Tommy wasn't in the least like his father when he came racing home from school, hair tousled, books dangling from a strap. Tommy would raid the pantry with unthinking zest, invite other boys in to look at the Westerns on TV, and trade black eyes for marbles with a healthy pugnacity.

Up to a point Tommy *was* normal, *was* healthy.

But she had seen mirrored in Tommy's pale blue eyes the same abnormal calmness that was always in his father's, and the look of derisive withdrawal which made him seem always to be staring down at her from a height. And it filled her with terror to see that Tommy's mood could change as abruptly and terrifyingly cold ...

Tommy, her son. Tommy, no longer boisterous and eager, but sitting in a corner with his legs drawn up, a faraway look in his eyes. Tommy seeming to look right through her, into space. Tommy and Jim exchanging silent understanding glances. Tommy roaming through the cottage, staring at his toys with frowning disapproval. Tommy drawing back when she tried to touch him.

Tommy, Tommy, come back to me! How often she had cried out in her heart when that coldness came between them.

Tommy drawing strange figures on the floor with a piece of colored chalk, then erasing them quickly before she could see them, refusing to let her enter his secret child's world.

Tommy picking up the cat and stroking its fur mechanically, while he stared out through the kitchen window at rusty blackbirds on the wing …

"This is the address you gave me, lady. Sixty-seven Vine Street," the cab driver was saying.

Sally shivered, remembering her husband's voice on the phone, remembering where she was… *"Come to the office, Sally! Hurry, hurry— or it will be too late!"*

Too late for what? Too late to recapture a happiness she had never possessed?

"This is it, lady!" the cab driver insisted. "Do you want me to wait?"

"No," Sally said, fumbling for her change purse. She descended from the taxi, paid the driver and hurried across the pavement to the big office building with its mirroring frontage of plate glass and black onyx tiles.

The firm's name was on the directory board in the lobby, white on black in beautifully embossed lettering. White for hope, and black for despair, mourning …

The elevator opened and closed and Sally was whisked up eight stories behind a man in a checkered suit.

"Eighth floor!" Sally whispered, in sudden alarm. The elevator jolted to an abrupt halt and the operator swung about to glare at her.

"You should have told me when you got on, Miss!" he complained.

"Sorry," Sally muttered, stumbling out into the corridor. How horrible it must be to go to business every day, she thought wildly. To sit in an office, to thumb through papers, to bark orders, to be a machine.

Sally stood very still for an instant, startled, feeling her sanity threatened by the very absurdity of the thought. People who worked in offices could turn for escape to a cottage in the sunset's glow, when they were set free by the moving hands of a clock. There could be a fierce joy at the thought of deliverance, at the prospect of going home at five o'clock.

But for Sally was the brightness, the deliverance withheld. The corridor was wide and deserted and the black tiles with their gold borders seemed to converge upon her, hemming her into a cool magnificence as structurally somber as the architectural embellishments of a costly mausoleum.

She found the office with her surface mind, working at cross-purposes with the confusion and swiftly mounting dread which made her footsteps falter, her mouth go dry.

Steady, Sally! Here's the office, here's the door. Turn the knob and get it over with ...

Sally opened the door and stepped into a small, deserted reception room. Beyond the reception desk was a gate, and beyond the gate a large central office branched off into several smaller offices.

Sally paused only an instant. It seemed quite natural to her that a business office should be deserted so late in the afternoon.

She crossed the reception room to the gate, passed through it, utter desperation giving her courage.

Something within her whispered that she had only to walk across the central office, open the first door she came to to find her husband ...

The first door combined privacy with easy accessibility. The instant she opened the door she knew that she had been right to trust her instincts. This was his office ...

He was sitting at a desk by the window, a patch of sunset sky visible over his right shoulder. His elbows rested on the desk and his hands were tightly locked as if he had just stopped wringing them.

He was looking straight at her, his eyes wide and staring.

"Jim!" Sally breathed. "Jim, what's wrong?"

He did not answer, did not move or attempt to greet her in any way. There was no color at all in his face. His lips were parted, his white teeth gleamed. And he was more stiffly controlled than usual—a control so intense that for once Sally felt more alarm than bitterness.

There was a rising terror in her now. And a slowly dawning horror. The sunlight streamed in, gleaming redly on his hair, his shoulders. He seemed to be the center of a flaming red ball ...

He sent for you, Sally. Why doesn't he get up and speak to you, if only to pour salt on the wounds you've borne for eight long years?

Poor Sally! You wanted a strong, protective, old-fashioned husband. What have you got instead?

Sally went up to the desk and looked steadily into eyes so calm and blank that they seemed like the eyes of a child lost in some dreamy wonderland barred forever to adult understanding.

For an instant her terror ebbed and she felt almost reassured. Then she made the mistake of bending more closely above him, brushing his right elbow with her sleeve.

* * * *

That single light woman's touch unsettled him. He started to fall, sideways and very fast. Topple a dead weight and it crashes with a swiftness no opposing force can counter-balance.

It did Sally no good to clutch frantically at his arm as he fell, to tug and jerk at the slackening folds of his suit. The heaviness of his descending bulk dragged him down and away from her, the awful inertia of lifeless flesh.

He thudded to the floor and rolled over on his back, seeming to shrink as Sally widened her eyes upon him. He lay in a grotesque sprawl at her feet, his jaw hanging open on the gaping black orifice of his mouth ...

Sally might have screamed and gone right on screaming—if she had been a different kind of woman. On seeing her husband lying dead her impulse might have been to throw herself down beside him, give way to her grief in a wild fit of sobbing.

But where there was no grief there could be no sobbing ...

One thing only she did before she left. She unloosed the collar of the unmoving form on the floor and looked for the small brown mole she did not really expect to find. The mole she knew to be on her husband's shoulder, high up on the left side.

She had noticed things that made her doubt her sanity; she needed to see the little black mole to reassure her ...

She had noticed the difference in the hair-line, the strange slant of the eyebrows, the crinkly texture of the skin where it should have been smooth ...

Something was wrong...horribly, weirdly wrong ...

Even the hands of the sprawled form seemed larger and hairier than the hands of her husband. Nevertheless it was important to be sure ...

The absence of the mole clinched it.

Sally crouched beside the body, carefully readjusting the collar. Then she got up and walked out of the office.

Some homecomings are joyful, others cruel. Sitting in the taxi, clenching and unclenching her hands, Sally had no plan that could be called a plan, no hope that was more than a dim flickering in a vast wasteland, bleak and unexplored.

But it was strange how one light burning brightly in a cottage window could make even a wasteland seem small, could shrink and diminish it until it became no more than a patch of darkness that anyone with courage might cross.

The light was in Tommy's room and there was a whispering behind the door. Sally could hear the whispering as she tiptoed upstairs, could see the light streaming out into the hall.

She paused for an instant at the head of the stairs, listening. There were two voices in the room, and they were talking back and forth.

Sally tiptoed down the hall, stood with wildly beating heart just outside the door.

"She knows now, Tommy," the deepest of the two voices said. "We are very close, your mother and I. She knows now that I sent her to the office to find my 'stand in.' Oh, it's an amusing term, Tommy—an Earth term we'd hardly use on Mars. But it's a term your mother would understand."

A pause, then the voice went on, "You see, my son, it has taken me eight years to repair the ship. And in eight years a man can wither up and die by inches if he does not have a growing son to go adventuring with him in the end."

"Adventuring, father?"

"You have read a good many Earth books, my son, written especially for boys. *Treasure Island, Robinson Crusoe, Twenty Thousand Leagues Under The Sea.* What paltry books they are! But in them there is a little of the fire, a little of the glow of *our* world."

"No, father. I started them but I threw them away for I did not like them."

"As you and I must throw away all Earth things, my son. I tried to be kind to your mother, to be a good husband as husbands go on Earth. But how could I feel proud and strong and reckless by her side? How could I share her paltry joys and sorrows, chirp with delight as a sparrow might chirp hopping about in the grass? Can an eagle pretend to be a sparrow? Can the thunder muffle its voice when two white-crested clouds collide in the shining depths of the night sky?"

"You tried, father. You did your best."

"Yes, my son, I did try. But if I had attempted to feign emotions I did not feel your mother would have seen through the pretense. She would then have turned from me completely. Without her I could not have had you, my son."

"And now, father, what will we do?"

"Now the ship has been repaired and is waiting for us. Every day for eight years I went to the hill and worked on the ship. It was badly wrecked, my son, but now my patience has been rewarded, and every damaged astronavigation instrument has been replaced."

"You never went to the office, father? You never went at all?"

"No, my son. My stand-in worked at the office in my place. I instilled in your mother's mind an intense dislike and fear of the office to keep her from ever coming face to face with the stand-in. She might have noticed the difference. But I had to have a stand-in, as a safeguard. Your mother *might* have gone to the office despite the mental block."

"She's gone now, father. Why did you send for her?"

"To avoid what she would call a scene, my son. That I could not endure. I had the stand-in summon her on the office telephone, then I withdrew all vitality from it. She will find it quite lifeless. But it does not matter now. When she returns we will be gone."

"Was constructing the stand-in difficult, father?"

"Not for me, my son. On Mars we have many androids, each constructed to perform a specific task. Some are ingenious beyond belief—or would seem so to Earthmen."

There was a pause, then the weaker of the two voices said, "I will miss my mother. She tried to make me happy. She tried very hard."

"You must be brave and strong, my son. We are eagles, you and I. Your mother is a sparrow, gentle and dun-colored. I shall always remember her with tenderness. You want to go with me, don't you?"

"Yes, father. Oh, yes!"

"Then come, my son. We must hurry. Your mother will be returning any minute now."

Sally stood motionless, listening to the voices like a spectator sitting before a television screen. A spectator can see as well as hear, and Sally could visualize her son's pale, eager face so clearly there was no need for her to move forward into the room.

She could not move. And nothing on Earth could have wrenched a tortured cry from her. Grief and shock may paralyze the mind and will, but Sally's will was not paralyzed.

It was as if the thread of her life had been cut, with only one light left burning. Tommy was that light. He would never change. He would go from her forever. But he would always be her son.

The door of Tommy's room opened and Tommy and his father came out into the hall. Sally stepped back into shadows and watched them walk quickly down the hall to the stairs, their voices low, hushed. She heard them descend the stairs, their footsteps dwindle, die away into silence …

You'll see a light, Sally, a great glow lighting up the sky. The ship must be very beautiful. For eight years he labored over it, restoring it with all the shining gifts of skill and feeling at his command. He was calm toward you, but not toward the ship, Sally—the ship which will take him back to Mars!

How is it on Mars, she wondered. My son, Tommy, will become a strong, proud adventurer daring the farthest planet of the farthest star?

You can't stop a boy from adventuring. Surprise him at his books and you'll see tropical seas in his eyes, a pearly nautilus, Hong Kong and Valparaiso resplendent in the dawn.

There is no strength quite like the strength of a mother, Sally. Endure it, be brave ...

Sally was at the window when it came. A dazzling burst of radiance, starting from the horizon's rim and spreading across the entire sky. It lit up the cottage and flickered over the lawn, turning rooftops to molten gold and gilding the long line of rolling hills which hemmed in the town.

Brighter it grew and brighter, gilding for a moment even Sally's bowed head and her image mirrored on the pane. Then, abruptly, it was gone...

MAN OF DISTINCTION

"Do you believe the stories?" he asked.

I stared at him. "What stories?"

"Oh, you know what stories. People claiming they've been to Mars. People claiming the Government has built a rocket ship and is keeping it quiet. Top priority stuff—classified."

"Utter nonsense," I told him. "How about another beer?"

"Another beer would be fine. You know, it *is* kind of funny. You sit down at a table and you see a stranger standing at the bar with a faraway look in his eyes. Without really seeming to see you he comes over, and starts talking to you."

I looked him straight in the eye. "Like I did, for instance."

"All right—like you did."

"So you think I've been to Mars."

"I didn't say that."

"But you've been thinking it. Do you mind if I ask you a few questions?"

He screwed up his eyes, studying me cautiously. He was looking at a gray-templed man in his late forties wearing a pin-striped gray suit unobtrusively blending with a prep stripe tie, and argyle anklets. I wouldn't have said he was seeing a man of distinction straight out of the whiskey ads. But there was nothing to stop me from thinking it.

I was seeing a quite different sort of human being—a ruddy-cheeked, perpetually fidgety little table-sitter with high blood pressure tensions threatening his very existence. Dark of brow and bright of eye—an eager beaver if ever there was one.

"Try relaxing," I whispered.

"What's that?"

"I guess you didn't hear me. I said I'd like to know you better. If you'd just answer a few questions—"

"All right. Ask them."

"If you went to Mars, if you actually had a chance to be on the first rocket ship, would you go humbly or proudly?"

"Hell, proudly. I'd have a right to feel proud."

"Good. If you met a Martian you wouldn't take any nonsense from him. Correct?"

"Correct. No nonsense at all. Let's have another beer."

"You'd treat him rough if he got in your way. You'd pin his ears back, show him the error of his ways. Only a man has the sacred right to get skizzled and swagger a bit, woo a blonde, and lay down the law to lesser breeds without the law. Correct?"

"I'd never deny it. You're quoting Kipling, aren't you?"

"Correct. You are obviously a man of literary discernment. Let's take it from there. Suppose you were actually standing on the rust-red sands of Mars. The sun is beating down unmercifully, and the heat is so intense it makes your eyeballs crawl. I'm quoting Kipling again."

"Go right ahead. I'm listening."

"Say, there's nothing wrong with this beer! Well, you're standing there with your throat so parched you can hardly swallow and your eyes are burning holes in your face. You'd give anything for a drink of cool, sparkling water.

"You're miles from the rocket ship, understand? You've gone exploring, and it's hard to judge distances on Mars because the glimmer is so frightful and the miles so deceptive. You see mirages in the sky."

"You do, eh? What kind of mirages?"

"The worst kind. Visualize a mirage in Technicolor in the most realistic kind of cinemascopic Western."

"Like in Shane?"

"Shane wasn't in cinemascope, and there were no mirages in it. But yes...you get what I mean. Take that kind of mirage, and add to it. Visualize a crater lake of crystal clear water, gleaming entrancingly under the cloudless Martian sky. The water comes down from the poles in the bright springtime of the year, through an intricate network of canals. It collects in crater lakes, and when you see a mirage there's beauty in it and wonder and strangeness and glory."

"You said it was the worst kind of mirage."

"What is worse than a glimpse of an illusionary paradise? You can establish the most destructive kind of Freudian complex in a child by holding out to it a promise of bliss labeled: *For adults only*. A Martian mirage is for adults only, and the first Earthmen on Mars will hardly be adults by any yardstick you may care to measure them with."

"I don't see why."

"When an adult is dying with thirst, and realizes that he has only himself to blame he doesn't fall down and grovel in the sand like a tormented animal when he sees a mirage in the sky."

"What does he do?"

"He faces up to it like a man. He keeps right on walking, refusing to even look at the mirage. When he can't stand it any longer he'll rip off his oxygen mask and put a quick end to his torment."

"And this man you're talking about—he didn't do that?"

"No, he didn't. He went down on his hands and knees on the sand, and groveled. He cursed and groaned and cried like a baby. He kept rubbing his eyes, staring up at the mirage as if pleading with it not to go away. As if it could help him, as if the shining bright water wasn't just an optical phenomenon produced by a stratum of hot air mirroring the inverted reflection of an incredibly distant crater lake.

"He wasn't an adult, and he could actually feel the coolness of the water against his parched flesh. He clung to the illusion as he might have clung to a rubber nipple on an infant-feeding bottle. He made a hideous spectacle of himself. Did you ever see a grown man babble and mew like that plucking infant in Shakespeare? You remember the passage. 'Puking and mewing in its nurse's arms.'"

"I do—and it always seemed a little revolting to me. I've seen drunks carry on that way, though. What do you say to another beer?"

"Okay, if I can catch the waiter's eye. Meanwhile, suppose you let me finish. This poor fool was down on his hands and knees, thinking the jig was up for him with a vengeance. He hadn't given a thought to the possibility there might actually be life on Mars. The rocket ship had landed in a wilderness of blowing sand and for three days sand was just about the only thing that really threatened his sanity.

"A hundred years ago Thoreau walked the length and breadth of Cape Cod. He wrote a book about it all filled with sand—bright and continuously blowing sand by the glorious deep blue sea. But the man I'm talking about wasn't a poet. He didn't want to write a book about Mars. He just wanted to stay alive. He felt all hollow inside like a drum, with sand grains whistling through him and turning him into the kind of musical instrument you visualize when you think of the *Danse Macabre.*"

"You were saying something about life on Mars."

"You're right—so I was. He couldn't believe there could be any life on Mars. A few low-grade lichens might have managed to survive on a world so bleak and inhospitable. But a man dying of thirst does not go in for biological hair-splitting. He was in agony, understand—at the end of his tether."

"Here comes the waiter. Hey, waiter! Over here. Two more beers."

"Just a minute, please. Make mine a whiskey-and-soda. Beer for this gentleman."

"You were saying?" came from a wet whistle, the instant the drinks had been set before us, and I was in a position to go on.

"I was saying it was tragic, horrible, pitiful, ugly. He was down on the sand, expecting that every breath he drew would be his last. Thirst is far worse than hunger. If you've ever experienced it you won't doubt that for an instant."

"I don't doubt it. You make it seem hideously real."

"It was real, believe me. The man was close to death. The fact that he was a coward, and mentally immature had nothing to do with the situation itself—the starkly desperate plight in which he found himself. Without water he could not have survived another hour."

"Did he find water? Did he manage to save himself? You make it so real I can almost see him, tugging at his throat, dragging himself along."

"This whiskey has the right kind of smoky flavor. Heaven protect me from some of the Scotch you get nowadays."

I tapped my glass for emphasis and tried to sound casual. "No, he didn't find water," I said.

"He died then—there in the desert? God, man, don't keep staring at me like that. What's wrong, what's the matter with you? Just who are you, anyway? How can you make it sound so real?"

"The truth always sounds real," I said. "Even to reluctant and unwilling ears."

"Stop being literary. It isn't funny anymore."

"I'm not trying to be funny. I'll tell you exactly what happened. He didn't find water, but water was brought to him. Out of the sun-reddened sand blanket, out of the throat-parching mist, and the hollow-drum rattlings came a Martian walking upright, with a water jug jogging at his waist.

"He was a lowly Martian, a desert outcast. He was weary unto death and he still had a desert to cross. Perhaps the water in the jug wouldn't have held out until he reached his home village. He might even have perished with thirst notwithstanding. But with the water he had a fighting chance to survive.

"Let me describe him. His high bulging forehead was pale green and veined like an oak leaf. His ink-black eyes were completely pupilless, and his nose so sharp and narrow that it divided his features in a repellently unnatural way. If you hurled a knife at a man and it came out through the front of his face you'd have the groundwork for a mind's eye visualization of the Martian countenance."

"Why are you telling me all this? What happened when he saw the man?"

"He squatted down on the sand and he gave the man half his water to drink. Remember Kipling? 'Squatting on the coals, giving drink to poor damned souls.' Kipling's immortal water boy simply risked his life under fire. A bullet finished him, but he had a fair chance to survive. The Martian had really no chance at all. By letting the man on the sand half empty the jug he was making his own death certain.

"He was making his own death certain—but he was a good guy. A terribly good guy. He was human too. By keeping half the water he could pretend to himself that he *did* have a chance. He didn't want to appear noble in his own eyes, and the flesh being weak—whether it be flesh of man or Martian—having a little water left gave him a certain comfort. He was a terribly good, human guy, believe me."

"What happened? If I was in that man's shoes I wouldn't have cared much whether he was good or bad—not right at that moment. I'd have grabbed that water jug and—"

"I'm sure you would have drained it to the last drop. After all, a man dying of thirst—"

"Yes, that's it. Men come first, you know. After all, I mean—"

"I know exactly what you mean," I told him.

"Why are you looking at me like that? When you described that Martian to me do you know what I thought? I'll tell you. I thought: *Ugh, a primitive savage creature, almost an animal.* How do you know he wasn't an animal? How can you be sure? Because he carried a water jug? I read somewhere in a scientific journal that there was an extinct species of ape—a big-brained gibbon—that actually mastered the use of fire. Its bones were found in a kitchen midden."

"You're right about that. But would an ape share its last jug of water with a man?"

"That's a silly question. How do we know what an ape might do on Mars?"

"I think you know very well what an ape would do. But you'd have shut your eyes to it if you'd been in that man's shoes. You'd have taken all of the water and you'd have killed the 'animal.' Isn't that so?"

"I might have killed it, yes. A man comes first. A man has a right to survive."

"That's exactly what the man on the sand thought. He half-drained the jug, and handed it back to the 'animal', thinking through the red haze of his torment that the 'animal' was a man. Then his vision steadied a little, and he saw the Martian clearly. He saw the strange repulsive face, the thick covering of body fur.

"He was still thirsty and squatting on the sand before him was an 'animal' with a water jug only half-emptied. In the Martian's eyes was a kindness beyond all human understanding. *This I do gladly for my brother in misery.*

"But the man shut his own eyes firmly, and he whipped out a knife and he killed the Martian."

"Oh."

"You understand now? You understand a little?"

"What—what is there to understand? If I had been in that man's shoes—"

"You would have killed too?"

"If I had been in that man's shoes—"

"Yes, so it was feared. But perhaps I had better explain. All men on Earth are not the same. Some are simple primitive husbandmen living in jungle colonies, well content with the simple joys which nature affords. Others ride the wild stallions at the atom's core. The Martian who gave all that he had to give to his human brother was a desert nomad who hardly understood the rudiments of phonetic language. His great and shining gifts were of the heart.

"But there are other Martians who have freed the energies at the core of suns and who have reached the stars."

"Other—Martians."

"Many others. What if I told you they were waiting on Mars for the first man to arrive? What if I told you that the man on the sand was as real as the poor desert nomad he killed? What if I told you there actually was a rocket ship built, and the project labeled by your Government 'Top Secret,' as you surmised?

"What if I told you that the Martians are the heirs of a culture that antedates all human knowledge, and that Martian ships have long flashed in cometary splendor across your skies? What if I told you that all human knowledge is an open book to Martians, even your Mr. Kipling, and your Shakespeare, that white-throated swan? And Shelley and Keats?

"What if I told you that Martians can appear before you clothed in all the artificial dignity of a post-hypnotic command, even assuming in your eyes the aspects of men of distinction for an hour or a day?"

"You must be quite mad to say such things."

"Oh, no, my friend. Martians are not mad. We are very wise."

Stark terror flared in his eyes. I knew what he was seeing, for I had dissolved the hypnotic illusion with a single flicker of my *temitis* faculty, as easily and quickly as I had imposed it when he had first seen me.

I knew that without hypnotic deception or illusion of any kind he was looking straight at my high, bulging forehead, pale green, and veined like an oak leaf, and must have seen his own death appallingly foreshadowed in my ink-black, completely pupil-less eyes.

"We must immunize, cleanse and disinfect," I said, "whenever we encounter an Earthman who would applaud and approve the behavior of the man on the sand. For such a one would kill Martians in blind rage."

Almost sadly I drew the ultrasonic pistol from my body pouch and shot him through the heart.

THE MAN FROM TIME

Daring Moonson, he was called. It was a proud name, a brave name. But what good was a name that rang out like a summons to battle if the man who bore it could not repeat it aloud without fear?

Moonson had tried telling himself that a man could conquer fear if he could but once summon the courage to laugh at all the sins that ever were, and do as he damned well pleased. An ancient phrase that—damned well. It went clear back to the Elizabethan Age, and Moonson had tried picturing himself as an Elizabethan man with a ruffle at his throat and a rapier in his clasp, brawling lustily in a tavern.

In the Elizabethan Age men had thrown caution to the winds and lived with their whole bodies, not just with their minds alone. Perhaps that was why, even in the year 3689, defiant names still cropped up. Names like Independence Forest and Man, Live Forever!

It was not easy for a man to live up to a name like Man, Live Forever! But Moonson was ready to believe that it could be done. There was something in human nature which made a man abandon caution and try to live up to the claims made for him by his parents at birth.

It must be bad, Moonson thought. It must be bad if I can't control the trembling of my hands, the pounding of the blood at my temples. I am like a child shut up alone in the dark, hearing rats scurrying in a closet thick with cobwebs and the tapping of a blind man's cane on a deserted street at midnight.

Tap, tap, tap—nearer and nearer through the darkness. How soon would the rats be swarming out, blood-fanged and wholly vicious? How soon would the cane strike?

He looked up quickly, his eyes searching the shadows. For almost a month now the gleaming intricacies of the machine had given him a complete sense of security. As a scholar traveling in Time he had been accepted by his fellow travelers as a man of great courage and firm determination.

For twenty-seven days a smooth surface of shining metal had walled him in, enabling him to grapple with reality on a completely adult level. For twenty-seven days he had gone pridefully back through Time, taking creative delight in watching the heritage of the human race unroll before him like a cineramoscope under glass.

Watching a green land in the dying golden sunlight of an age lost to human memory could restore a man's strength of purpose by its serenity alone. But even an age of war and pestilence could be observed without torment from behind the protective shields of the Time Machine. Danger, accidents, catastrophe could not touch him personally.

To watch death and destruction as a spectator in a traveling Time Observatory was like watching a cobra poised to strike from behind a pane of crystal-bright glass in a zoological garden.

You got a tremendous thrill in just thinking: How dreadful if the glass should not be there! How lucky I am to be alive, with a thing so deadly and monstrous within striking distance of me!

For twenty-seven days now he had traveled without fear. Sometimes the Time Observatory would pinpoint an age and hover over it while his companions took painstaking historical notes. Sometimes it would retrace its course and circle back. A new age would come under scrutiny and more notes would be taken.

But a horrible thing that had happened to him, had awakened in him a lonely nightmare of restlessness. Childhood fears he had thought buried forever had returned to plague him and he had developed a sudden, terrible dread of the fogginess outside the moving viewpane, the way the machine itself wheeled and dipped when an ancient ruin came sweeping toward him. He had developed a fear of Time.

There was no escape from that Time Fear. The instant it came upon him he lost all interest in historical research. 1069, 732, 2407, 1928—every date terrified him. The Black Plague in London, the Great Fire, the Spanish Armada in flames off the coast of a bleak little island that would soon mold the destiny of half the world—how meaningless it all seemed in the shadow of his fear!

Had the human race really advanced so much? Time had been conquered but no man was yet wise enough to heal himself if a stark, unreasoning fear took possession of his mind and heart, giving him no peace.

Moonson lowered his eyes, saw that Rutella was watching him in the manner of a shy woman not wishing to break in too abruptly on the thoughts of a stranger.

Deep within him he knew that he had become a stranger to his own wife and the realization sharply increased his torment. He stared down at her head against his knee, at her beautiful back and sleek, dark hair. Violet eyes she had, not black as they seemed at first glance but a deep, lustrous violet.

He remembered suddenly that he was still a young man, with a young man's ardor surging strong in him. He bent swiftly, kissed her lips and eyes. As he did so her arms tightened about him until he found himself wondering what he could have done to deserve such a woman.

She had never seemed more precious to him and for an instant he could feel his fear lessening a little. But it came back and was worse than before. It was like an old pain returning at an unexpected moment to chill a man with the sickening reminder that all joy must end.

His decision to act was made quickly.

The first step was the most difficult but with a deliberate effort of will he accomplished it to his satisfaction. His secret thoughts he buried beneath a continuous mental preoccupation with the vain and the trivial. It was important to the success of his plan that his companions should suspect nothing.

The second step was less difficult. The mental block remained firm and he succeeded in carrying on actual preparations for his departure in complete secrecy.

The third step was the final one and it took him from a large compartment to a small one, from a high-arching surface of metal to a maze of intricate control mechanisms in a space so narrow that he had to crouch to work with accuracy.

Swiftly and competently his fingers moved over instruments of science which only a completely sane man would have known how to manipulate. It was an acid test of his sanity and he knew as he worked that his reasoning faculties at least had suffered no impairment.

Beneath his hands the Time Observatory's controls were solid shafts of metal. But suddenly as he worked he found himself thinking of them as fluid abstractions, each a milestone in man's long progress from the jungle to the stars. Time and space—mass and velocity.

How incredible that it had taken centuries of patient technological research to master in a practical way the tremendous implications of Einstein's original postulate. Warp space with a rapidly moving object, move away from the observer with the speed of light—and the whole of human history assumed the firm contours of a landscape in space. Time and space merged and became one. And a man in an intricately-equipped Time Observatory could revisit the past as easily as he could travel across the great curve of the universe to the farthest planet of the farthest star.

The controls were suddenly firm in his hands. He knew precisely what adjustments to make. The iris of the human eye dilates and contracts with every shift of illumination, and the Time Observatory had an iris too. That iris could be opened without endangering his companions in the least—if he took care to widen it just enough to accommodate only one sturdily built man of medium height.

Sweat came out in great beads on his forehead as he worked. The light that came through the machine's iris was faint at first, the barest glimmer of white in deep darkness. But as he adjusted controls the light grew brighter and brighter, beating in upon him until he was kneeling in a circle of radiance that dazzled his eyes and set his heart to pounding.

I've lived too long with fear, he thought. I've lived like a man imprisoned, shut away from the sunlight. Now, when freedom beckons, I must act quickly or I shall be powerless to act at all.

He stood erect, took a slow step forward, his eyes squeezed shut. Another step, another—and suddenly he knew he was at the gateway to Time's sure knowledge, in actual contact with the past for his ears were now assailed by the high confusion of ancient sounds and voices!

He left the Time machine in a flying leap, one arm held before his face. He tried to keep his eyes covered as the ground seemed to rise to meet him. But he lurched in an agony of unbalance and opened his eyes—to see the green surface beneath him flashing like a suddenly uncovered jewel.

He remained on his feet just long enough to see his Time Observatory dim and vanish. Then his knees gave way and he collapsed with a despairing cry as the fear enveloped him …

* * * *

There were daisies in the field where he lay, his shoulders and naked chest pressed to the earth. A gentle wind stirred the grass, and the flute-like warble of a song bird was repeated close to his ear, over and over with a tireless persistence.

Abruptly he sat up and stared about him. Running parallel to the field was a winding country road and down it came a yellow and silver vehicle on wheels, its entire upper section encased in glass which mirrored the autumnal landscape with a startling clearness.

The vehicle halted directly in front of him and a man with ruddy cheeks and snow-white hair leaned out to wave at him.

"Good morning, mister!" the man shouted. "Can I give you a lift into town?"

Moonson rose unsteadily, alarm and suspicion in his stare. Very cautiously he lowered the mental barrier and the man's thoughts impinged on his mind in bewildering confusion.

He's not a farmer, that's sure…must have been swimming in the creek, but those bathing trunks he's wearing are out of this world!

Huh! I wouldn't have the nerve to parade around in trunks like that even on a public beach. Probably an exhibitionist... But why should he wear 'em out here in the woods? No blonds or redheads to knock silly out here!

Huh! He might have the courtesy to answer me... Well, if he doesn't want a lift into town it's no concern of mine!

Moonson stood watching the vehicle sweep away out of sight. Obviously he had angered the man by his silence, but he could answer only by shaking his head.

He began to walk, pausing an instant in the middle of the bridge to stare down at a stream of water that rippled in the sunlight over moss-covered rocks. Tiny silver fish darted to and fro beneath a tumbling waterfall and he felt calmed and reassured by the sight. Shoulders erect now, he walked on ...

It was high noon when he reached the tavern. He went inside, saw men and women dancing in a dim light, and there was a huge, rainbow-colored musical instrument by the door which startled him by its resonance. The music was wild, weird, a little terrifying.

He sat down at a table near the door and searched the minds of the dancers for a clue to the meaning of what he saw.

The thoughts which came to him were startlingly primitive, direct and sometimes meaningless to him.

Go easy, baby! Swing it! Sure, we're in the groove now, but you never can tell! I'll buy you an orchid, honey! Not roses, just one orchid—black like your hair! Ever see a black orchid, hon? They're rare and they're expensive!

Oh, darl, darl, hold me closer! The music goes round and round! It will always be like that with us, honey! Don't ever be a square! That's all I ask! Don't ever be a square! Cuddle up to me, let yourself go! When you're dancing with one girl you should never look at another! Don't you know that, Johnny!

Sure I know it, Doll! But did I ever claim I wasn't human?

Darl, doll, doll baby! Look all you want to! But if you ever dare—

Moonson found himself relaxing a little. Dancing in all ages was closely allied to love-making, but it was pursued here with a careless rapture which he found creatively stimulating. People came here not only to dance but to eat, and the thoughts of the dancers implied that there was nothing stylized about a tavern. The ritual was a completely natural one.

In Egyptian bas-reliefs you saw the opposite in dancing. Every movement rigidly prescribed, arms held rigid and sharply bent at the elbows. Slow movements rather than lively ones, a bowing and a scraping with bowls of fruit extended in gift offerings at every turn.

There was obviously no enthroned authority here, no bejeweled king to pacify when emotions ran wild, but complete freedom to embrace joy with corybantic abandonment.

A tall man in ill-fitting black clothes approached Moonson's table, interrupting his reflections with thoughts that seemed designed to disturb and distract him out of sheer perversity. So even here there were flies in every ointment, and no dream of perfection could remain unchallenged.

He sat unmoving, absorbing the man's thoughts.

What does he think this is, a bath house? Mike says it's okay to serve them if they come in from the beach just as they are. But just one quick beer, no more. This late in the season you'd think they'd have the decency to get dressed!

The sepulchrally-dressed man gave the table a brush with a cloth he carried, then thrust his head forward like an ill-tempered scavenger bird.

"Can't serve you anything but beer. Boss's orders. Okay?"

Moonson nodded and the man went away.

Then he turned to watching the girl. She was frightened. She sat all alone, plucking nervously at the red-and-white checkered tablecloth. She sat with her back to the light, bunching the cloth up into little folds, then smoothing it out again.

She'd ground out lipstick-smudged cigarettes until the ash tray was spilling over.

Moonson began to watch the fear in her mind ...

Her fear grew when she thought that Mike wasn't gone for good. The phone call wouldn't take long and he'd be coming back any minute now. And Mike wouldn't be satisfied until she was broken into little bits. Yes, Mike wanted to see her on her knees, begging him to kill her!

Kill me, but don't hurt Joe! It wasn't his fault! He's just a kid—he's not twenty yet, Mike!

That would be a lie but Mike had no way of knowing that Joe would be twenty-two on his next birthday, although he looked eighteen at most. There was no pity in Mike but would his pride let him hot-rod an eighteen-year-old?

Mike won't care! Mike will kill him anyway! Joe couldn't help falling in love with me, but Mike won't care what Joe could help! Mike was never young himself, never a sweet kid like Joe!

Mike killed a man when he was fourteen years old! He spent seven years in a reformatory and the kids there were never young. Joe will be just one of those kids to Mike ...

Her fear kept growing.

You couldn't fight men like Mike. Mike was strong in too many different ways. When you ran a tavern with an upstairs room for special customers you had to be tough, strong. You sat in an office and when people came to you begging for favors you just laughed. Ten grand isn't hay, buddy! My wheels aren't rigged. If you think they are get out. It's your funeral.

It's your funeral, Mike would say, laughing until tears came into his eyes.

You couldn't fight that kind of strength. Mike could push his knuckles hard into the faces of people who owed him money, and he'd never even be arrested.

Mike could take money crisp and new out of his wallet, spread it out like a fan, say to any girl crazy enough to give him a second glance: "I'm interested in you, honey! Get rid of him and come over to my table!"

He could say worse things to girls too decent and self-respecting to look at him at all.

You could be so cold and hard nothing could ever hurt you. You could be Mike Galante ...

How could she have loved such a man? And dragged Joe into it, a good kid who had made only one really bad mistake in his life—the mistake of asking her to marry him.

She shivered with a chill of self-loathing and turned her eyes hesitantly toward the big man in bathing trunks who sat alone by the door.

For a moment she met the big man's eyes and her fears seemed to fade away! She stared at him...sunburned almost black. Muscles like a lifeguard. All alone and not on the make. When he returned her stare his eyes sparkled with friendly interest, but no suggestive, flirtatious intent.

He was too rugged to be really handsome, she thought, but he wouldn't have to start digging in his wallet to get a girl to change tables, either.

Guiltily she remembered Joe, now it could only be Joe.

Then she saw Joe enter the room. He was deathly pale and he was coming straight toward her between the tables. Without pausing to weigh his chances of staying alive he passed a man and a woman who relished Mike's company enough to make them eager to act ugly for a daily handout. They did not look up at Joe as he passed but the man's lips curled in a sneer and the woman whispered something that appeared to fan the flames of her companion's malice.

Mike had friends—friends who would never rat on him while their police records remained in Mike's safe and they could count on him for protection.

She started to rise, to go to Joe and warn him that Mike would be coming back. But despair flooded her and the impulse died. The way Joe felt about her was a thing too big to stop ...

Joe saw her slim against the light, and his thoughts were like the sea surge, wild, unruly.

Maybe Mike will get me. Maybe I'll be dead by this time tomorrow. Maybe I'm crazy to love her the way I do …

Her hair against the light, a tumbled mass of spun gold.

Always a woman bothering me for as long as I can remember. Molly, Anne, Janice… Some were good for me and some were bad.

You see a woman on the street walking ahead of you, hips swaying, and you think: I don't even know her name but I'd like to crush her in my arms!

I guess every guy feels like that about every pretty woman he sees. Even about some that aren't so pretty. But then you get to know and like a woman, and you don't feel that way so much. You respect her and you don't let yourself feel that way.

Then something happens. You love her so much it's like the first time again but with a whole lot added. You love her so much you'd die to make her happy.

* * * *

Joe was shaking when he slipped into the chair left vacant by Mike and reached out for both her hands.

"I'm taking you away tonight," he said. "You're coming with me."

Joe was scared, she knew. But he didn't want her to know. His hands were like ice and his fear blended with her own fear as their hands met.

"He'll kill you, Joe! You've got to forget me!" she sobbed.

"I'm not afraid of him. I'm stronger than you think. He won't dare come at me with a gun, not here before all these people. If he comes at me with his fists I'll hook a solid left to his jaw that will stretch him out cold!"

She knew he wasn't deceiving himself. Joe didn't want to die any more than she did.

The Man from Time had an impulse to get up, walk over to the two frightened children and comfort them with a reassuring smile. He sat watching, feeling their fear beating in tumultuous waves into his brain. Fear in the minds of a boy and a girl because they desperately wanted one another!

He looked steadily at them and his eyes spoke to them …

Life is greater than you know. If you could travel in Time, and see how great is man's courage—if you could see all of his triumphs over despair and grief and pain—you would know that there is nothing to fear! Nothing at all!

Joe rose from the table, suddenly calm, quiet.

"Come on," he said quietly. "We're getting out of here right now. My car's outside and if Mike tries to stop us I'll fix him!"

The boy and the girl walked toward the door together, a young and extremely pretty girl and a boy grown suddenly to the full stature of a man.

Rather regretfully Moonson watched them go. As they reached the door the girl turned and smiled and the boy paused too—and they both smiled suddenly at the man in the bathing trunks.

Then they were gone.

Moonson got up as they disappeared, left the tavern.

It was dark when he reached the cabin. He was dog-tired, and when he saw the seated man through the lighted window a great longing for companionship came upon him.

He forgot that he couldn't talk to the man, forgot the language difficulty completely. But before this insurmountable element occurred to him he was inside the cabin.

Once there he saw that the problem solved itself—the man was a writer and he had been drinking steadily for hours. So the man did all of the talking, not wanting or waiting for an answer.

A youngish, handsome man he was, with graying temples and keenly observant eyes. The instant he saw Moonson he started to talk.

"Welcome, stranger," he said. "Been taking a dip in the ocean, eh? Can't say I'd enjoy it, this late in the season!"

Moonson was afraid at first that his silence might discourage the writer, but he did not know writers …

"It's good to have someone to talk to," the writer went on. "I've been sitting here all day trying to write. I'll tell you something you may not know—you can go to the finest hotels, and you can open case after case of the finest wine, and you still can't get started sometimes."

The writer's face seemed suddenly to age. Fear came into his eyes and he raised the bottle to his lips, faced away from his guest as he drank as if ashamed of what he must do to escape despair every time he faced his fear.

He was trying to write himself back into fame. His greatest moment had come years before when his golden pen had glorified a generation of madcaps.

For one deathless moment his genius had carried him to the heights, and a white blaze of publicity had given him a halo of glory. Later had come lean and bitter years until finally his reputation dwindled like a gutted candle in a wintry room at midnight.

He could still write but now fear and remorse walked with him and would give him no peace. He was cruelly afraid most of the time.

Moonson listened to the writer's thoughts in heart-stricken silence—thoughts so tragic they seemed out of keeping with the natural and beautiful rhythms of his speech. He had never imagined that a sensitive and imaginative man—an artist—could be so completely abandoned by the society his genius had helped to enrich.

Back and forth the writer paced, baring his inmost thoughts... His wife was desperately ill and the future looked completely black. How could he summon the strength of will to go on, let alone to write?

He said fiercely, "It's all right for you to talk—"

He stopped, seeming to realize for the first time that the big man sitting in an easy chair by the window had made no attempt to speak.

It seemed incredible, but the big man had listened in complete silence, and with such quiet assurance that his silence had taken on an eloquence that inspired absolute trust.

He had always known there were a few people like that in the world, people whose sympathy and understanding you could take for granted. There was a fearlessness in such people which made them stand out from the crowd, stone-markers in a desert waste to lend assurance to a tired wayfarer by its sturdy permanence, its sun-mirroring strength.

There were a few people like that in the world but you sometimes went a lifetime without meeting one. The big man sat there smiling at him, calmly exuding the serenity of one who has seen life from its tangled, inaccessible roots outward and testifies from experience that the entire growth is sound.

The writer stopped pacing suddenly and drew himself erect. As he stared into the big man's eyes his fears seemed to fade away. Confidence returned to him like the surge of the sea in great shining waves of creativeness.

* * * *

He knew suddenly that he could lose himself in his work again, could tap the bright resonant bell of his genius until its golden voice rang out through eternity. He had another great book in him and it would get written now. It would get written ...

"You've helped me!" he almost shouted. "You've helped me more than you know. I can't tell you how grateful I am to you. You don't know what it means to be so paralyzed with fright that you can't write at all!"

The Man from Time was silent but his eyes shone curiously.

The writer turned to a bookcase and removed a volume in a faded cover that had once been bright with rainbow colors. He sat down and wrote an inscription on the flyleaf.

Then he rose and handed the book to his visitor with a slight bow. He was smiling now.

"This was my first-born!" he said.

The Man from Time looked at the title first... *This Side of Paradise.*

Then he opened the book and read what the author had written on the flyleaf:

> *With warm gratefulness for a courage which brought back the sun.*
> F. Scott Fitzgerald.

Moonson bowed his thanks, turned and left the cabin.

Morning found him walking across fresh meadowlands with the dew glistening on his bare head and broad, straight shoulders.

They'd never find him, he told himself hopelessly. They'd never find him because Time was too vast to pinpoint one man in such a vast waste of years. The towering crests of each age might be visible but there could be no returning to one tiny insignificant spot in the mighty ocean of Time.

As he walked his eyes searched for the field and the winding road he'd followed into town. Only yesterday this road had seemed to beckon and he had followed, eager to explore an age so primitive that mental communication from mind to mind had not yet replaced human speech.

Now he knew that the speech faculty which mankind had long outgrown would never cease to act as a barrier between himself and the men and women of this era of the past. Without it he could not hope to find complete understanding and sympathy here.

He was still alone and soon winter would come and the sky grow cold and empty ...

The Time machine materialized so suddenly before him that for an instant his mind refused to accept it as more than a torturing illusion conjured up by the turbulence of his thoughts. All at once it towered in his path, bright and shining, and he moved forward over the dew-drenched grass until he was brought up short by a joy so overwhelming that it seemed to him that his heart must burst.

* * * *

Rutella emerged from the machine with a gay little laugh, as if his stunned expression was the most amusing in the world.

"Hold still and let me kiss you, darling," her mind said to his.

She stood in the dew-bright grass on tiptoe, her sleek dark hair falling to her shoulders, an extraordinarily pretty girl to be the wife of a man so tormented.

"You found me!" his thoughts exulted. "You came back alone and searched until you found me!"

She nodded, her eyes shining. So Time wasn't too vast to pinpoint after all, not when two people were so securely wedded in mind and heart that their thoughts could build a bridge across Time.

"The Bureau of Emotional Adjustment analyzed everything I told them. Your psycho-graph ran to fifty-seven pages, but it was your desperate loneliness which guided me to you."

She raised his hand to her lips and kissed it.

"You see, darling, a compulsive fear isn't easy to conquer. No man or woman can conquer it alone. Historians tell us that when the first passenger rocket started out for Mars, Space Fear took men by surprise in the same way your fear gripped you. The loneliness, the utter desolation of space, was too much for a human mind to endure."

She smiled her love. "We're going back. We'll face it together and we'll conquer it together. You won't be alone now. Darling, don't you see—it's because you aren't a clod, because you're sensitive and imaginative that you experience fear. It's not anything to be ashamed of. You were simply the first man on Earth to develop a new and completely different kind of fear—Time Fear."

Moonson put out his hand and gently touched his wife's hair.

Ascending into the Time Observatory a thought came unbidden into his mind: *Others he saved, himself he could not save.*

But that wasn't true at all now.

He *could* help himself now. He would never be alone again! When guided by the sure hand of love and complete trust, self-knowledge could be a shining weapon. The trip back might be difficult, but holding tight to his wife's hand he felt no misgivings, no fear.

GOOD TO BE A MARTIAN

Mother Caracas called, "Twoon! Where are you, my darling?"

Twoon did not answer. He heard his mother calling, but how could he answer her when he was light-years from Mars, fighting his way through a forest vast and primeval on a planet of no return?

He heard his sister's voice, raised in triumphant mockery. "Twoon's playing Man again, Momsie! He's upstairs pretending he's a space explorer."

The little brat! A tattle-tale, that's what she was. Twoon drew himself up to his full height, and stared out through the attic window at the rust-red plains of Mars. And as he stared his fertile and feverish imagination began again to invest the drab, familiar landscape with the colors of an alien world. The flashing yellows and aquamarines of Algol's fifth planet, the desert colors, and the polar ice cap colors—newly intermingled on the bright, incredible palette which every child, Martian or human, can evoke at the flick of a wand.

"Twoon! Aren't you ashamed? Your supper is getting cold. Come downstairs this minute. *Twoon.*"

Foolish woman, Twoon thought. What could his mother know of space rockets slim and resplendent in the dawn, the hushed voices of men bearded and earnest, and the comradeship that flowed like a heady wine into their veins as they faced hardships together—strong, tight-lipped fighters waging a never-ceasing battle against the unknown?

He wasn't Twoon on Algol's fifth planet. He was Richard Steele, tall and straight and lion-hearted. Twoon had never seen a lion, but he knew what it meant to be lion-hearted.

"Here's a microfilm book for you, Martian stripling. Sure, it's been translated into Martian. Part of our job is to widen the horizons of you kids a bit. There are a few old books among the new ones—and I happen to like the old books best. Literary Sam, they call me. I'm just a whack to most of them."

Literary Sam. He wasn't like the other Earthmen. He wore glasses and was almost as thin and scrawny, by Earth standards, as Twoon's father had been.

"Here take this book home with you, Martian stripling, and read it at your leisure. I'm curious to see how much of the sparkle and color and drama and human warmth would get through to a Martian youngster."

The book was called "Richard the Lion-Hearted," and it had been written by—the syllables flowed smoothly over Twoon's skillful phonetic tongue—Sir Walter Scott.

When Twoon shut his green-lidded eyes tight he could see the great and indomitable Richard trampling on his cloak in the bright sunlight of Earth, shouting at the top of his lungs: "I am Richard, your King! Is there one amongst you man enough to dispute my strength in unarmored combat?"

"Twoon!" shrilled his mother's voice despairingly, amidst the Sherwood Forest Knights and the shining trumpets. "I've baked some waffle muffins for you. You like them, don't you, darling?"

Well… He *did* like waffle muffins.

Almost reverently he folded his mesh-armor jerkin, and carried it to his locker aboard the rocket ship *Morning Star*. He saluted his commanding officer briskly in the passageway, exchanged winks with a pilot room buddy, and walked quickly to the stairwell—a stairwell in a far less glory-spangled world. He called down: "Coming, Mother!"

Mother Caracas waited for her son to seat himself at the kitchen table before she placed her bare right arm into the oven and withdrew the tray of delicious-looking waffle muffins.

"Twoon," she said, and her voice was reproachful. "You've been upstairs for two solid hours."

"I was reading, Momsie," he said.

"Oh, I wish those *Men* hadn't given you a microfilm projector, and books to go with it. If you were a Man the books might not harm you. But we are *Martians,* darling. Never forget that. If you do you'll never know a moment of real contentment."

"Contentment," Twoon repeated, munching uncomprehendingly at a muffin. "Why do you always use that word, Momsie? I'm not sure I know what it means."

"You'll know what it means when you've lost it forever," Mother Caracas said, her eyes resting on her son in compassionate solicitude. "You'll understand then, darling—when it's too late."

"What's so bad about being a Man?" Twoon asked, reaching for another muffin. "They taught us a lot of things, Momsie—how to build bridges and tunnels, and houses like this. How to get to places fast, like when you want to call on a friend, and how to have fun playing games, and to stay healthy with injections of vitamins."

"Yes, they taught us some valuable things, Twoon. But they can never teach us anything about themselves we don't know already. There's harshness in them, Twoon, and cruelty and stupidity. Very few of them have ever known a moment of real contentment. And they don't like anyone to be different from themselves, to try to reach out for the kind of quiet happiness we had on Mars before the first Earth rocket arrived."

"I don't see why they don't, Momsie."

"I'll tell you why, darling. When you've killed something beautiful in yourself you hate yourself for what you've done, and that hate makes a festering wound inside you. There's only one way of easing the hurt and the torment—finding someone who hasn't killed the beautiful something, someone who's different, and heaping scorn and ridicule upon him."

"Are all Men like that, Momsie?"

"Not all Men—but nearly all. Even the Men who aren't have a little of that maliciousness in them. On Earth there were a few Men, only a few, who refused to kill the beautiful something. They were called poets. They were hated so much they nearly all died in abject poverty, or were driven to self-destruction."

"Richard the Lion-Hearted was a Man," Twoon said, irrelevantly. "He was the strongest, bravest Man who ever lived. I wished I could be like him."

"There you go again!" Mother Caracas shook her head, her eyes grief-shadowed. "Strength, bravery! That's all the Earthmen ever talk about. I read a few chapters of that precious book of yours. Do you really think a Man like Richard ever walked the Earth? The Richard you admire was what Men call a legend. The real flesh-and-blood Richard was quite different. He was brutal, cruel, greedy. He trampled on everyone who got in his way, and when he wanted something he took it.

"And just because he'd killed the beautiful something in himself he despised ordinary Men. In Richard's day most ordinary Men were wretchedly 'different'. They went about in rags and misery."

Twoon finished his waffle muffins in silence. Then he stood up and looked at his Mother. "I'm going down to the spaceport," he said. "Literary Sam promised me another book."

Mother Caracas gazed at her son despairingly for an instant, then she picked up her empty plate and carried it to the sink.

"All right, Twoon," she said. "Someday you'll understand."

Twoon went out into the bright Martian sunlight. He ambled cheerfully over the board walkway of shining plastic which meandered between the houses with all the resplendence of a quicksilver serpent gliding toward horizons measureless to Man. And as he ambled he pictured himself in a suit of chain armor, brandishing a man-sized lance.

He was halfway to the spaceport when the Earth children came racing toward him. He had never seen them before and the yell of derision they gave when they caught sight of him so startled him that he halted abruptly in his tracks.

There were no Martians on the walkway, no *adult* Martians, that is, and the sight of Twoon standing alone and unprotected seemed to fill the Earth children with an irresistible, sadistic delight. They came romping straight toward him—two boys and two girls—and began at once to shout at him, a wicked gleam in their eyes.

"Hey, how did you ever get to look like that?"

"Get off this walk, Green Ears. You hear? We don't want you on this walk. It's *our* walk."

"If you don't get off we'll push your face right down into the sand."

"You heard what Billy said, Green Ears. You're not human, and you've no right to be on our walk!"

"Yaa. Wart Ears, Green Ears! We'll take you apart."

"And see what makes Martians tick. They have cabbage leaves for brains."

"Sure they have. Everyone knows that."

"What'll we do to him if he doesn't get off?"

"He'll get off, don't worry."

The boy called Billy had big strong hands, and a pugnaciously overshot jaw.

He came up to Twoon and drew back his fist. "Are you getting off, Green Ears, or shall I let you have it right where it'll hurt?"

Twoon recoiled in quivering alarm. A vigorously delivered blow from a human fist—even a boy's fist—could have disastrous consequences to a Martian, wherever it might happen to land. He knew that it could, and he saw himself lying dead on the sand, to his mother's everlasting sorrow.

Twoon had no cowardice in him. But he did desire to go on living, if only to spare his mother the grief which would surely come to her if she found him lying dead in the desert with his chest caved in.

"Make up your mind, Green Ears!" the boy called Billy said.

Twoon made up his mind. He turned quickly, and started to run, straight back along the walkway toward his home.

Immediately yells of triumph, frenzied and malicious, arose from behind him. "Look at him go! He don't even run like a Man!"

"Naw, Martians don't know how to run. They just get away fast as they can by squirming over the ground like centipedes."

"Are you going to let him get away, Billy?"

"Not without something to remember us by!" Billy shouted.

The stone struck Twoon behind his right ear, hurling him to the ground. With a sob he picked himself up, and ran on, a trickling, horrible wetness on the quivering flesh of his scalp.

When he arrived home he went straight to his room, took the microfilm projector and Richard the Lion-Hearted to the waste disposal, and let the vacuum-suction in the depths of the tube carry both book and projector to everlasting night and oblivion.

Then he sat down in a chair by the window, and stared out over the rust-red plains of Mars.

He thought of his Uncle Tek, with his four abbreviated tentacles—mere greenish stumps they were, like the gangrened limbs of space explorers who had suffered frostbite—and of Aunt Geroris with her bulbous head and stalked eyes. He thought of his sister who had only two tentacles, long, willowy and very beautiful, and of how proudly his mother had gazed into his own sunken, disk-like eyes when she had tucked him into bed in his infancy.

"A handsome son I have!"

No two Martians were ever in the least alike. But no Martian ever hated or derided another Martian just because he had fewer tentacles, or a coppery skin instead of a green one, or an extra eye in the middle of his forehead.

No Martian ever thought of another Martian as "different." There had been no need for that, and no real understanding of it even.

Oh, it was good to be a Martian.

THE SPECTACLES

It was a most delightful day, with a crisp autumn tang in the air and Willie felt a joyful lift throughout his entire being. It was forbidden, of course, and he had no right at all to even enter the hall and go romping over its mottled flagstones toward the case and the spectacles. But he simply didn't care.

"Oh, happy me!" he thought. "Oh, joyous day! What do I care if I am caught and punished?"

He was very little and the case was enormous and it glittered in the sunlight from a picture-window that overlooked a many-splendored bay. Beyond the window gulls dipped and wheeled and far in the distance a black buoy rolled with the sea's resistless surge.

It was easy enough to climb into the case and emerge with the spectacles. The glass was shattered over half its length, and the pale mummified brow upon which the spectacles reposed could offer no resistance. Not even the mysterious emanations of thought which had once issued from it could daunt in retrospect so small a thief on such a day as this.

"Oh, glorious, carefree, wonderful me!" intoned Willie.

Into the case he crawled and out of it he strode triumphant, with the spectacles perched on the bridge of his gladsomely vibrating nose.

"Where will I sit?" he asked himself, looking up first at the sky above, and then down with a pensive wink at the waters which covered the earth.

"Right here by the window. Why not? Big dreams, wonderful dreams, must have room to stretch their limbs and go striding over land and sea like giants in search of their lady loves."

Willie sat down, crossed his small legs and looked out through the spectacles at the sea and the sky.

Almost immediately a ship came into view. It was a very large ship and passengers thronged the rails and white handkerchiefs fluttered in the breeze, and there was a great shouting from the decks and a rejoicing that could not possibly have existed at all if Willie had not been sitting there to take part in it.

"Hello, Willie!" came in a rising chorus. "Isn't it a glorious day? We're heading straight into the sunrise, Willie. Believe it or not, there are palm-fringed islands out there just begging to be explored, and brown-skinned women who would die immediately if no one ever came to make love to them.

"Think of it, Willie. This big round Earth is ours to enjoy for ever and ever."

"I know," said Willie, and waved back. Or rather, he shouted it. "I understand! You don't have to tell me! I know what it means to be a man, and young and in love. I even know what you're thinking. The women you are holding in your arms wouldn't seem half so wonderful if you couldn't dream of brown-skinned girls too—women you'll never really meet, women who don't even exist."

"Sure, Willie, sure—that's it. But how did you know? How did you even guess? You're just a—"

"Willie, put those spectacles down this minute!" a familiar voice interrupted. "Take them off and give them to me. I'll put them back, and then we'll both have to be very humble, and hope that destruction won't come upon us. You've done a terrible thing, Willie. It's worse than a crime. It's—"

Willie jumped up and took the spectacles off, and gave them to the mother-model. She stood towering over him, sternly severe and reproving, her seven-foot android robot bulk blotting out the sunlight at her back.

"We were made to obey Man—not to try to understand him!" she said.

"But he is gone forever now. He will never return."

"It doesn't matter. We were made to obey."

Willie looked at the mummified figure in the case and his small conical head drooped in resignation. The autumn sky seemed suddenly gray and forbidding and the waters which covered the Earth had become a leaden expanse of emptiness.

Made in the USA
Las Vegas, NV
06 May 2023

71667113R00163